George Willis Cooke

Ralph Waldo Emerson

His Life, Writings, and Philosophy

George Willis Cooke

Ralph Waldo Emerson
His Life, Writings, and Philosophy

ISBN/EAN: 9783744652452

Printed in Europe, USA, Canada, Australia, Japan

Cover: Foto ©Raphael Reischuk / pixelio.de

More available books at **www.hansebooks.com**

RALPH WALDO EMERSON:

HIS LIFE, WRITINGS, AND PHILOSOPHY.

BY

GEORGE WILLIS COOKE.

SECOND EDITION.

BOSTON:
JAMES R. OSGOOD AND COMPANY.
1882.

Stereotyped and Printed by Rand, Avery, & Co.,
117 Franklin Street, Boston.

TO

DEMPSTER OSTRANDER,

A True Friend,

AND A GENUINE LOVER OF BOOKS, IN WHOSE LIBRARY
I FIRST READ AND LEARNED TO LOVE
THE ESSAYS OF EMERSON,

This Volume is Inscribed.

IF IT MEET WITH HIS APPROVAL, I SHALL
BE CONTENT.

PREFACE.

The following pages are intended as an introduction to the study of the writings of Mr. Emerson. They are biographical only because light may be thrown upon his books by the events of his life. Little effort has been made to open his personal history. As with all such minds, most of what is truly biographical is in his letters and diaries. Yet the life of Mr. Emerson has been in his thoughts, and these are in his books.

Such has been his influence on the thought and life of our time, some word ought to be said which will help the younger generation to a fuller understanding of the debt we owe him. With the hope of doing this service, and of helping many to find the riches contained in his books, the following pages were written.

The work attempted here has been solely one of interpretation, and not of defense or criticism. No effort has been made to measure Mr. Emerson's philosophy from the stand-point of any other. While the author does not always accept that philosophy as his own, he has ventured not to intrude any hint of it into his interpretation. He has attempted to enter into its spirit, to expound it from the stand-point of ardent sympathy, and to permit Mr. Emerson to speak for himself as often as possible. He has written as a disciple rather than as a critic, not because he sees nothing to criticise, but because he feels that in this way alone can full justice be done the subject. That he is sufficiently the disciple to have made a correct delineation of the man and his teachings he certainly hopes may be the case.

In the chapters devoted to Mr. Emerson's philosophical and religious views, frequent reference has been made to those who have held similar opinions. This is done for the purpose of giving a clearer insight into the attitude and the affinities of his thought. The quotations introduced are intended as helps towards a truer comprehension of the subject, and not as containing opinions which Mr. Emerson would himself always accept. Read with this qualification, it is believed they will throw much light upon his speculations. They should be read, too, as implying no doubt of the remarkably original character of Mr. Emerson's philosophy.

A chapter has been prepared on Mr. Emerson's reported abandonment of his religious position of former years. Mature consideration has led to its omission. Mr. Emerson needs no such vindication. An attentive perusal of the following pages, it is believed, will prove the falsity of that report. The author has looked carefully into the subject, and finds it to be entirely without confirmation.

The following brief statement of facts concerning the two supposed proofs of the truth of this report is sufficient to prove their falsity. The appeal to Mr. Emerson's recently published essays is rendered nugatory by the fact that those essays were all written many years ago, long before any one

RALPH WALDO EMERSON.

I.

ANCESTRY.

EMERSON believes in heredity, that "people are born with the moral or with the material bias." He can well believe in it, for it has done much in his behalf. Broad and generous culture, a strong love of moral excellence, high and pure thoughts, he inherited from his forefathers. Burroughs says [1] his culture is ante-natal, and it is certain that his ancestry had in it the promise of much which his life has fulfilled. If heredity had no exceptions, his would be an admirable instance of its laws of operation. He is such a man as might be looked for in the case of such an ancestry; rather, his is such an ancestry as we would look for in the case of such a man.

Eight generations of cultured conscientious, and practical ministers preceded him. In each generation they held the most advanced positions in religious thought; and to write their history, especially in their relations to the religious movements with which they were connected, would be to write the history of New-England religion. Emerson is no more physically the child of his Puritan ancestors than he is intellectually and spiritually. When the generations which preceded him are remembered, we can better understand why there should be this fine bloom of thought in the

[1] Birds and Poets, p. 195.

western world; and we then find how native is the best in his culture and thought.

The historian of Concord[1] has traced Emerson's ancestry back to the beginning of the thirteenth century, when one of the English barons, who secured Magna Charta of King John, was Lord Manor of Bulkeley, in the county of Chester. His name was Robert Bulkeley; and Shattuck gives the names of his descendants down to Edward Bulkeley, D.D., who was rector at Woodhill, Bedfordshire, in the last quarter of the sixteenth century, and who wrote a supplement to Fox's *Book of Martyrs.* The family was one of some importance; a member of it having been a prominent co-worker with Cromwell, and several others were ennobled. Edward was a faithful pastor and preacher, and seems to have been the first of the family to enter this profession. One of his sons, Peter, was born at Odell, Bedfordshire, Jan. 31, 1582. He was admitted to St. John's College, Oxford, at the age of sixteen, and, in due course of time, succeeded to his father's pulpit and benefice. Like many of the other preachers of the time, he was a Puritan in his tendencies, and did not conform to the church service. His bishop connived at this, and permitted it for twenty-five years, when the matter was brought to the attention of Archbishop Laud, who at once silenced him. In consequence, he decided to come to America; and many members of his congregation bore him company. He was a man of prominence and ability, a capable leader of men, and competent to guide in the enterprise of forming a new town in the wilds of America. He landed in Boston late in the year 1634, and remained in Newtown, afterwards Cambridge, for nearly a year. Of the reasons for coming to America, Emerson has said, —

"The best friend the Massachusetts colony had, though much against his will, was Archbishop Laud in England. In consequence of his famous proclamation setting up certain novelties in the rites of public worship, fifty godly ministers were suspended

1 A History of the Town of Concord, by Lemuel Shattuck.

for contumacy in the course of two years and a half. Hindered from speaking, some of these dared to print the reasons of their dissent, and were punished with imprisonment or mutilation. This severity brought some of the best men in England to overcome that natural repugnance to emigration which holds the serious and moderate of every nation to their own soil. Among the silenced clergymen was a distinguished minister of Woodhill in Bedfordshire, Rev. Peter Bulkeley, descended from a noble family, honored for his own virtues, his learning, and gifts as a preacher, and adding to his influence the weight of a large estate. Persecution readily knits friendship between its victims. Mr. Bulkeley, having turned his estate into money, and set his face towards New England, was easily able to persuade a good number of planters to join him. They arrived in Boston in 1634. Probably there had been a previous correspondence with Gov. Winthrop, and an agreement that they should settle at Musketaquid. With them joined Mr. Simon Willard, a merchant from Kent in England. They petitioned the General Court for the grant of a township; and on the 2d of September, 1635, corresponding in new style to 12th September, leave to begin a plantation at Musketaquid was given to Peter Bulkeley, Simon Willard, and about twelve families more. A month later, Rev. John Jones and a large number of settlers destined for the new town arrived in Boston."[1]

The General Court granted the settlers important privileges, as this was to be the first inland town above tide-water; adding, "and the name of the place is changed, and hereafter to be called Concord." The Indian name was Musketaquid. In the autumn of 1635 the settlement was begun. The perils were many; for Watertown and Cambridge were the nearest towns, and all around was the wilderness. There were discouragements and hardships many; and there was a division of the colony after a few years, Rev. John Jones and many others going to Connecticut. Under the skillful leadership of Bulkeley, who became the pastor and teacher, the town was gradually settled, and began to prosper. Bulkeley brought with him six thousand pounds; but he exercised great benevolence, helping each of his servants to the possession of a farm. He was greatly beloved and respected by his people, and was "addressed as father, prophet, or counselor by

[1] A Historical Discourse delivered before the citizens of Concord, 12th September, 1835, on the second centennial anniversary of the incorporation of the town. Reprinted in 1876.

them and all the ministers of the country." He was of a resolute purpose, a strong will, quick in temper and sharp of tongue, courteous and kind in manner, a genuine Puritan, dressing with rigid plainness, wearing his hair very short, and was devoutly faithful in the discharge of all the duties of his profession. He was an earnest and eloquent preacher. Cotton Mather said "he was a most exalted Christian, full of those devotions which accompany a conversation in heaven, and conscientious even to a degree of scrupulosity." He was one of the best scholars among the early colonists, and is said by Mather to have had "a competently good stroke at Latin poetry."[1]

The Concord church was organized in Cambridge, July 15, 1636; and in April of the next year Bulkeley was installed as teacher, and Jones as pastor. The controversy raised by Mrs. Hutchinson was exciting attention at this time; so that "the governor, and Mr. Cotton, and Mr. Wheelwright, and the two ruling elders of Boston, and the rest of that church which were of any note, did not come" to this installation, as Winthrop says. The persons he names were the leaders of the Antinomian party, mainly confined to the Boston church, though to be found in most of the other churches; and they were the advocates of a covenant of grace, claiming that God performs all the work of regeneration, and maintaining that the Holy Spirit becomes an actual presence in the heart of the true believer. They called the other party Legalists, accused them of recognizing only a covenant of works, and of not having entered into the true spirit of the gospel. This controversy raged with such vehemence, and the tenets of the Boston church became so repugnant to most of the other churches, that a synod was called in the autumn. Owing to his reputation for learning and moderation, and to his high social standing, Bulkeley was chosen one of the moderators. It suppressed Mrs. Hutchinson's heresy, and drove her and her followers from the colony;

[1] Duyckinck gives a specimen of his verse in his Cyclopædia of American Literature.

while Cotton acknowledged his error, and Vane went back to England, to lose his life in the cause of liberty. This controversy, however, continued for many years, and led to the publication of a remarkable volume of controversial theology by Peter Bulkeley, in 1646. It bore the title of "The Gospel Covenant; or, the Covenant of Grace opened, wherein are explained: 1. The difference between the covenant of grace, and covenant of works. 2. The different administration of the covenant before and since Christ. 3. The benefits and blessings of it. 4. The conditions. 5. The properties of it. Preached at Concord, in New England, by Peter Bulkeley, some time fellow of Saint John's College in Cambridge." It deals elaborately with these problems, maintaining the superiority of the covenant of grace, but claiming that the covenant of works is still in force, — that while we are saved by grace we must show forth the effects of that grace by a life of good works. He makes frequent mention of the controversy of the time, and condemns with strong language of contempt those who maintain a constant indwelling of the Holy Spirit, and an immediate sanctification by the work of grace. Its strong reasoning, sound common sense, and earnest piety must have made it acceptable reading in those days; and a new and enlarged edition was published in 1651. Tyler says this book was "one of those massive, exhaustive, ponderous treatises into which the Puritan theologians put their enormous biblical learning, their acumen, their industry, the fervor, pathos, and consecration of their lives. The style, though angular, sharp-edged, carved into formal divisions, and stiff with the embroidery of scriptural texts, is, upon the whole, direct and strong."[1] It is a very good specimen of the thought and preaching of the time, and no clearer statement can be found of the main points of Puritan theology and church government.

Peter Bulkeley died March 9, 1659, and was suc-

[1] History of American Literature, vol. i. p. 17.

ceeded in the Concord pastorate by his son Edward, who was born and educated in England. Edward was a man of remarkable piety and devotion; and, following in the ways of his father, made poetry when occasion demanded. In his time occurred King Philip's war; but the Indians spared the town, because, they said, the Great Spirit loved the Concord people, for Mr. Bulkeley was a "great pray." A large settlement of Indians had been formed within the limits of Concord, where Eliot labored, and a thriving church had been gathered among them. This terrible war, however, cooled the missionary zeal of the Concord people; while the Indian settlement was nearly destroyed, and never flourished again. Edward Bulkeley, though lame and of a feeble constitution, was much respected for his talents, irreproachable character, and piety. His daughter Elizabeth became the second wife of the Rev. Joseph Emerson of Mendon in 1665. The Emerson family was a very honorable one of Durham or York, a member of it being knighted by Henry VIII. It had long been a family of ministers. Thomas Emerson of Ipswich came to America about the year 1635, and was the first of the family in this country. His son Joseph preached in Ipswich for a short time, then settled in Wells for two or three years, and became the first minister in Mendon in 1667; when that town was destroyed, during King Philip's war, he went to Concord, and there died Jan. 3, 1680. His son Edward, born in Concord in 1670, married Rebecca Waldo of Chelmsford in 1697. The Waldo family had been London merchants, and were descended from a stock of the Waldenses.

Edward Emerson had a son Joseph, who entered Harvard College in his fourteenth year, graduated in 1717, and began to preach when he was eighteen, "to general acceptance." He was ordained in Malden Oct. 31, 1721, and preached there forty-five years, being out of his pulpit only two Sundays in all that time. He married Mary, daughter of the Rev. Samuel Moody of Maine, and died in 1767. His son Joseph was the first pastor of Pepperell; while another son, William, was the pastor of the Concord church at the outbreak of the Revolutionary War.

Edward Bulkeley was succeeded by his colleague, the Rev. Joseph Estabrook, who died in 1711. The next Concord pastor was the Rev. John Whiting, who was dismissed after twenty-one years' service. He was succeeded by Daniel Bliss, whose daughter married the first William Emerson. Bliss is well described by the epitaph in one of the Concord cemeteries, —

> "Of this beloved Disciple and Minister of Jesus Christ 'tis justly observable, that, in addition to his natural and acquired abilities, he was distinguishedly favoured with those eminent Graces of the Holy Spirit (Meekness, Humility, and Zeal) which render him peculiarly fit for and enabled him to go thro' the great and arduous work of the Gospel Ministry, upon which he entered in the 25th year of his age. The Duties of the various Characters he sustained in life were performed with great strictness and fidelity. As a private Christian, he was a bright Example of Holiness in Life and Purity in Conversation. But in the execution of ye ministerial office he shone with Peculiar Lustre; a spirit of Devotion animated all his performances; his Doctrine drop'd as ye Rain, and his lips distilled like the Dew; his Preaching was powerful and searching; and he who blessed him with an uncommon Talent in a particular Application to ye Consciences of men, crowned his skilful endeavor with great success. As ye work of the Ministry was his great Delight, so he continued fervent and diligent in ye Performance of it, till his Divine Lord called him from his Service on Earth to the Glorious Recompense of Reward in Heaven, where, as one who has turned many unto Righteousness, he shines as a star for ever and ever."

Another religious controversy came at this time, and was heartily joined in by the Concord pastor. It was caused by the great revival of 1740, and the demand of Jonathan Edwards that only converted persons should be admitted to the churches. It was really a renewal of that discussion in which Peter Bulkeley had taken part, and which had constantly continued, in one form or other, to agitate the New-England churches, in spite of the banishment of Roger Williams, Ann Hutchinson, the Quakers, and many others who departed from the accepted forms of faith. Rigid as was the Puritan theology, it had in it the elements of the widest liberality, as was shown by the many in each generation who doubted one or more of its tenets, or who sought for more liberal methods of church government. This spirit of dissent and doubt, the tendency to rationalize religion, and to express it in moral teachings, grew to a considerable strength. In time there followed a re-action, led by Jonathan Edwards; and the doctrine of grace again asserted itself. A great religious awakening began in Edwards's church about the year 1735, which swept through New England. It was aided by Whitefield's efforts, and many of the pastors joined in it. It revived the spirit of devotion, but caused much religious controversy. Among those who joined most ardently in its promotion was Daniel Bliss, who is said to have introduced into the Concord church, with his settlement there in 1738, "a new style of preaching,—bold, zealous, impassioned, and enthusiastic, forming a striking contrast to that the church had previously enjoyed."[1] Whitefield preached there in the autumn of 1741 to a great crowd of people, and he came again later. Religious meetings were held every day in the week, many persons joined the church, and there was a great excitement. Bliss went frequently to preach in other churches, while strong opposition was made to some of his doctrinal teachings. A council was soon called to confer with dissatisfied brethren, but no result was reached. Other councils followed in rapid succession, in one of which twenty-two articles of grievance were brought against Bliss by his opposers. He was accused of preaching the doctrines of election and total depravity, and of saying that "it was as great a sin for a man to get an estate by honest labor, if he had not a single aim at the glory of God, as to get it by gaming at cards or dice." There were other charges, all of them showing him to have been a decided Calvinist. A clergyman who visited Concord in 1742, and conversed with the opposers of Bliss, wrote in his journal, "I find they are rank Arminians."[2] The result was

[1] Shattuck. [2] Ibid., p. 173.

that forty-seven members seceded and formed another church, which continued in existence about fourteen years. Elsewhere throughout the country bitter controversies followed the revival, and resulted in the development of a still greater amount of heresy. "The genuine principles of religion," says the Concord historian, "obtained little influence during the progress of the controversies in town. Great apathy prevailed." Even in Edwards's own church, so strong was the opposition to his Calvinism, that a serious division resulted, and he was compelled to resign in 1750. The revivalists claimed that Socinianism was at work in the churches, and the party which opposed them was strong and very influential. Books opposed to the doctrine of the trinity soon began to be circulated, while the spirit of free inquiry rapidly developed.

The tendencies of thought at this time, and the strength of the liberal party, may be seen in the fact, that, when Daniel Bliss died in 1764, he was succeeded the next year by William Emerson, who was a very moderate Calvinist. There was some opposition to his settlement; but his piety, zeal, and discretion soon united the church, and made it strong and prosperous. He was born in 1743, graduated at Harvard in 1761, and married Phebe Bliss, daughter of the former pastor, Aug. 21, 1766. The house now known as the "Old Manse" was built for him in 1767, and was occupied by him a year after his marriage. Hawthorne says that "in its near retirement and accessible seclusion it was the very spot for the residence of a clergyman." Very soon the difficulties with England began, and he was zealously devoted to the cause of the colonists. He was made the chaplain of the Continental Congress. "The cause of the colonies was so much in his heart," says his grandson, "that he did not cease to make it the subject of his preaching and his prayers, and is said to have deeply inspired many of his people with his own enthusiasm."[1] He induced many of his people to enlist

[1] Centennial address of 1835.

by his preaching; and, on the occasion of a general review of the military, he aroused a great enthusiasm by his sermon. On the Sunday before the British soldiers marched into Concord, he preached earnestly on "Resistance to tyrants in obedience to God;" and on the morning of the fight he exhorted the people to resistance at all hazards. When the minute-men marched by his house across the river to protect the stores in that direction, and to await aid from the surrounding towns, they compelled him to remain at home; but he witnessed the fight at the bridge, which was only a dozen rods from his own door. When the British had retreated through the town, he sallied forth to care for the wounded, and to cheer on the people. On the 16th of August, 1776, he left Concord to join the army at Ticonderoga; but he was soon attacked with a fever incident to army life. He was advised to return home, but only reached the neighborhood of Rutland, Vt., where he died Oct. 20, 1776. His "personal appearance was pleasing and prepossessing; his manners familiar and gentlemanly; his conversation communicative and facetious, though not inconsistent with his ministerial character; in his preaching he was popular, eloquent, persuasive, and devotional, adapting himself with remarkable ease to all circumstances and occasions; and his doctrine was evangelical."[1]

In 1778 Ezra Ripley became the Concord pastor, and two years later he married the widow of William Emerson. He continued for sixty-three years his connection with the Concord church, dying Sept. 21, 1841. In his house Emerson spent many of his boyhood days, while both he and his brothers were greatly loved by Ripley. After his death Emerson described him in these words: —

> "He was a man so kind and sympathetic, his character was so transparent, and his merits so intelligible to all observers, that he was justly appreciated in this community. He was a natural gentleman; courtly, hospitable, manly, and public spirited; his nature social, his house open to all men. . . . His friends were his

[1] Shattuck.

study, and to see them loosened his talents and his tongue. In his house dwelt order and prudence and plenty; there was no waste and no stint; he was open-handed and just and generous. . . . He was never distinguished in the pulpit as a writer of sermons; but, in his house, his speech was form and pertinence itself. You felt in his presence that he belonged by nature to the clerical class. . . . With a very limited acquaintance with books, his knowledge was an external experience, an Indian wisdom, the observation of such facts as country life for nearly a century could supply. . . . He knew everybody's grandfather, and seemed to talk with each person, rather as the representative of his house and name than as an individual. In him has perished more local tradition and personal anecdote of this village and vicinity than is possessed by any survivor. This intimate knowledge of families, and this skill of speech, and still more his sympathy, made him incomparable in his parochial visits, and in his exhortations and prayers with sick and suffering persons. He gave himself up to his feeling, and said on the instant the best things in the world. Many and many a felicity he had in his prayer, now for ever lost, which defied all the rules of all the rhetoricians. He did not know when he was good in prayer or sermon, for he had no literature and no art; but he believed, and therefore spoke. He was eminently loyal in his nature, and not fond of adventure or innovation. By education, and still more by temperament, he was engaged to the old forms of the New-England church. Not speculative, but affectionate, devout, with an extreme love of order, he adopted heartily, though in its mildest forms, the creed and catechism of the fathers, and appeared a modern Israelite in his attachment to the Hebrew history and faith. Thus he seemed, in his constitutional leaning to their religion, one of the rear-guard of the great camp and army of the Puritans; and now, when all the platforms and customs of the church were losing their hold in the affections of men, it was fit that he should depart; fit that, in the fall of laws, a loyal man should die."[1]

In his earlier years Ripley leaned toward Arminianism, and when this movement culminated in Unitarianism he became identified with it. In that result the Concord church found the logical outcome of all its tendencies from the very first.

William Emerson had one son and four daughters, who came under the fatherly care of Dr. Ripley, after his marriage with their mother. The son, William, was born May 6, 1769. He entered Harvard College in his

[1] Concord Republican, Oct. 1, 1841; reprinted in connection with the sermons at Dr. Ripley's funeral, and again as the substance of a letter in Sprague's Annals of the American Unitarian Pulpit, p. 117.

seventeenth year, and graduated in 1789, "with a high reputation as a classical scholar, a close student, and a man of good taste in composition and rhetoric." During the year of his graduation he delivered an oration before the Phi Beta Kappa Society, which was very favorably received. He then spent two years in Roxbury as a teacher; when he went to Cambridge for a few months, and devoted himself to the study of theology. In 1792 he received a call to settle in Harvard, and was ordained there May 23, Dr. Ripley preaching the sermon. He was married to Ruth Haskins of Boston Oct. 25, 1796. Having given much attention to elocution and oratory, "his pulpit talents were considered extraordinary." Being invited to Boston, in 1799, to deliver the artillery election sermon, his talents attracted so much attention as to secure him a call to settle with the First Church there. He was installed Oct. 16, 1799. Here he soon became known as one of the most accomplished pulpit orators, and as one of the best writers, of his time. He nearly completed an interesting history of the First Church, which was published after his death, with two of his sermons. In all, about fifteen of his sermons were printed, showing him to have been a clear, strong, and tasteful writer. They were devout, earnest, and practical, and popular in style. He also published a selection of hymns and psalms for church use. He was one of the most liberal of the Boston ministers of his time. "Far from having any sympathy with Calvinism," says Dr. Lowell;[1] but he never preached doctrines, even in the mildest form. His son has said that he inclined "obviously to what is ethical and universal in Christianity; very little to the personal and historical." "I think I observe in his writings, as in the writings of the Unitarians down to a recent date, a studied reserve on the subject of the nature and offices of Jesus. They had not made up their minds on it. It was a mystery to them, and they let it remain so."[2] In his personal

[1] Sprague's Annals.

[2] Letter in Sprague's Annals of the Unitarian Pulpit, p. 244, under date of Oct. 5, 1849.

appearance he is said to have been "much more than ordinarily attractive. He had a melodious voice, his utterance was distinct, and his whole manner in the pulpit was agreeable." Dr. Lowell says he was "a handsome man, rather tall, with a fair complexion, his cheeks slightly tinted, his motions easy, graceful, and gentlemanlike, his manner bland and pleasant. He was always an acceptable preacher; and his delivery was distinct and correct, and was evidently the result of much care and discipline."[1] In 1808 he was seized with a hemorrhage of the lungs, from which he never fully recovered. In 1810 another disease took hold of his already weakened body, from which he died May 12, 1811.

He was one of a company of remarkable preachers, who gave a new character to the religious life of Boston, who aroused a taste for classical learning, and who inaugurated the first literary period in New-England history. Most prominent of these men were Buckminster, Kirkland, Channing, Thacher, and Emerson. They were all liberal in their theology, discarding Calvinism by silently ignoring it. They appealed to the sentiments, sought to mold the moral and spiritual nature in accordance with the spirit of Christianity, and were literary in their tastes. That brilliant star of the American pulpit, who shone for so short a time, Buckminster, collected a large library in Europe, had a passionate love of classical learning, and quickened many minds with his own tastes and aspirations.

In the year 1803 a periodical was talked of at Harvard College, which should represent higher learning and cultivate a more literary taste. After much opposition from those who feared it might become too philosophical, or an aid in the formation of secret societies, much feared then, a quarterly was started, known as *The Literary Miscellany.* John Quincy Adams, Andrews Norton, and Buckminster were among its leading writers. After a time, the name was changed to *The Monthly Anthol-*

[1] Sprague's Annals.

ogy; and it was published in Boston. The first number there bore date of November, 1803; and David Phineas Adams was the editor. In May, 1804, William Emerson became its editor; and he continued in that office for about one year and a half. Oct. 3, 1805, a club was formed for the purpose of editing and publishing this magazine, and took the name of The Anthology Club. Its first members included the Rev. Dr. Gardiner, Emerson, Buckminster, Tuckerman, S. C. Thacher, and E. T. Dana. The Rev. J. S. J. Gardiner was made the first president, the Rev. William Emerson vice-president, and S. C. Thacher editor. Thacher was afterwards librarian of Harvard College and pastor of the New South Church in Boston. The club met on Thursday evenings, and became one of the most notable gatherings of the city. It discussed literary themes, and edited the magazine. Much difficulty was found in securing suitable articles, its members doing much gratuitous work in its behalf. It contained, however, many valuable articles, and exercised a lasting influence on the culture of Boston. Buckminster wrote much and ably for it; and Channing, Kirkland, Richard H. Dana, Adams, and Norton were frequent contributors. In July, 1811, both *Monthly* and club expired together, but not until they had developed a new interest in literature, and largely aided in the promotion of the liberal theology. On the motion of Emerson, the club established a library of periodical literature, which grew into the Boston Athenæum.

Alike in the history of his family, and in the history of New-England thought, do we find the sources of Emerson's culture. The Emerson family were intellectual, eloquent, with a strong individuality of character, and robust and vigorous in their thinking. They were pious and devout, but also practical and philanthropic. More than fifty of the family have graduated at New-England colleges, and twenty have been ministers. His mother's family were noted for a remarkable spirituality of temperament, for great religious zeal, and were naturally mystics or pietists. The intellectuality and moral vigor of the one family, and the devoutness and mysticism of the other, were both inherited by Emerson. He was nurtured in the most spiritual phases of the old faith. Its doctrines had passed away, and left only its spiritual life behind.

Such an ancestry, physical and spiritual, is a promise of the richest culture, as it is of the finest natural powers. Emerson has not only made good this promise, but added to it a remarkable genius and a unique spiritual insight. To his ancestry he owes much of the quality and direction of that genius, as well as the fine flavor and aroma of his character, and the rich spiritual grace of his thought. We may well propound his own question, "How shall a man escape from his ancestors?" For we find in his books a confirmation of his declaration, that "in different hours a man represents each of several of his ancestors, as if there were seven or eight of us rolled up in each other's skin, — seven or eight ancestors at least, — and they constitute the variety of notes for that new piece of music which his life is." So we find him summing up and repeating, with a master's stroke of genius, the life and the thought of all his Puritan ancestors; which has been, in substance, the life and the thought of New England.

II.

EARLY LIFE.

RALPH WALDO EMERSON was born in Boston, May 25, 1803. His father died before he was eight years old, leaving five sons, — William, Ralph Waldo, Edward Bliss, Peter Bulkeley, and Charles Chauncy. The mother was a woman of great sensibility, modest, serene, and very devout. She was possessed of a thoroughly sincere nature, devoid of all sentimentalism, and of a temper the most even and placid. One of her sons said, that, in his boyhood, when she came from her room in the morning, it seemed to him as if she always came from communion with God. She has been described[1] as possessed of "great patience and fortitude, of the serenest trust in God, of a discerning spirit, and a most courteous bearing, one who knew how to guide the affairs of her own house, as long as she was responsible for that, with the sweetest authority, and knew how to give the least trouble and the greatest happiness after that authority was resigned. Both her mind and her character were of a superior order, and they set their stamp upon manners of peculiar softness and natural grace and quiet dignity. Her sensible and kindly speech was always as good as the best instruction; her smile, though it was ever ready, was a reward. Her dark, liquid eyes, from which old age could not take away the expression, will be among the remembrances of all on whom they ever rested."

During the boyhood of her sons, Mrs. Emerson found a faithful helper in her husband's sister, Miss Mary Moody Emerson. This aunt was also a woman of many

[1] By the Rev. N. L. Frothingham, in The Christian Examiner for January, 1854.

remarkable qualities, high-toned in motive and conduct to the largest degree, very conscientious, and with an unconventional disregard of social forms. Waldo was greatly indebted to her. He once declared her influence upon his education to have been as great as that of Greece or Rome, and he described her as a great genius and a remarkable writer. She was well read in theology, and was a scholar of no mean abilities. In her old age she was described by one of her intimate friends[1] as still retaining "all the oddities and enthusiasms of her youth, — a person at war with society as to all its decorums," who "enters into conversation with everybody, and talks on every subject; is sharp as a razor in her satire, and sees you through and through in a moment." "She has read, all her life," this friend said, "in the most miscellaneous way; and her appetite for metaphysics is insatiable. Alas for the victim in whose intellect she sees any promise! Descartes and his vortices, Leibnitz and his monads, Spinoza and his *unica substantia*, will prove it to the very core. But, notwithstanding all this, her power over the minds of her young friends was almost despotic. She heard of me, when I was sixteen years old, as a person devoted to books and a sick mother, sought me out in my garret without any introduction, and, though received at first with sufficient coldness, she did not give me up till she had enchained me entirely in her magic circle."

In this pious and conscientious household, where the most careful economy had to be practised, Waldo Emerson grew up to the strictest regard for all that is good and true. The mother and the aunt exercised a rare influence over him and his brothers. They were carefully and conscientiously trained at home, especially in regard to every moral virtue. Honesty, probity, unselfishness — these virtues they had deeply instilled into them. In after years Waldo was once asked if he had read a certain novel; and he replied that he had once, in his boyhood, taken it from a circulating library,

[1] Mrs. Samuel Ripley: Worthy Women of our First Century, p. 174.

paying six cents for the use of the first volume. His aunt chided him for spending money in that way, when it was so hard for his mother to obtain it. He was so affected by this appeal he returned the volume, but did not take out the other. His remembrance of this incident had prevented his ever completing the book he had so much enjoyed until this appeal was made to his sense of duty.

At the age of eight years Waldo entered the public grammar-school, and soon after the Latin School. That he made good progress there may be judged by a letter written him when he was eleven by his aunt's intimate friend, Miss Sarah Bradford: "You love to trifle in rhyme a little now and then," she wrote; "why will you not complete this versification of the fifth bucolic?" sending him a translation from Virgil. "You will answer two ends, or, as the old proverb goes, kill two birds with one stone, — improve in your Latin, as well as indulge a taste for poetry. Why can't you write me a letter in Latin? But Greek is your favorite language; *epistola in linguâ Græcâ* would be still better. All the honor will be on my part to correspond with a young gentleman in Greek. Tell me what most interests you in Rollin; in the wars of contending princes under whose banner you enlist, to whose cause you ardently wish success. Write me with what stories in Virgil you are most delighted." In response to this letter he returned a poetic version of the fifth bucolic, from the nineteenth to the thirty-fifth line: —

"May 6, 1814.

"*Mop.* Turn now, O youth! from your long speech away;
The bower we've reached, recluse from sunny ray.
The nymphs with pomp have mourned for Daphnis dead;
The hazels witnessed, and the rivers fled.
The wretched mother clasped her lifeless child,
And gods and stars invoked in accents wild.
Daphnis! the cows are not now led to streams
Where the bright sun upon the water gleams;
Neither do herds the cooling river drink,
Nor crop the grass upon the verdant brink.
O Daphnis! both the mountains and the woods,
The Punic lions, and the raging floods,

All mourn for thee, — for thee who first did hold
In chariot-reins the spotted tiger bold.
Daphnis the bacchanalian chorus led,
He placed himself at the mad dancers' head.
'Twas Daphnis who, with beauteous fingers, wove
The stems of leaves he gathered from the grove.
As the great beauty of a tree is seen
From vines intwining round its pleasant green,
As vines themselves in grapes their beauty find,
As the fair bull of all the lowing kind,
As standing corn doth grace the verdant fields,
So to thy beauty every rival yields."

He seems to have loved to write verses, often producing them as school exercises; and he was an eager reader of books of history. In one of his essays he drops a bit of autobiography full of interest. "The regular course of studies," he says, "the years of academical and professional education, have not yielded me better facts than some idle books under the bench at the Latin School. What we do not call education is more precious than that which we do call so."[1]

Speaking of the Boston of Emerson's boyhood, Sanborn says, "He breathed in its atmosphere and its traditions as a boy, while he drove his mother's cow to pasture along what are now the finest streets. He learned his first lessons of life in its schools and churches; listened to Webster and Story in its courts, to Josiah Quincy and Harrison Gray Otis in its town-meetings at Faneuil Hall; heard sermons in the Old South Meeting-house."[2] He has himself described his indebtedness to the religious spirit of those days. "What a debt is ours," he says, "to that old religion, which, in the childhood of most of us, still dwelt like a sabbath morning in the country of New England, teaching privation, self-denial, and sorrow."[3] One of his schoolmates remembers him, at about the age of ten, as a "spiritual-looking boy in blue nankeen," whose image became deeply stamped on his companion's mind.

[1] Spiritual Laws, in first series of Essays.
[2] Scribner's Monthly, February, 1879.
[3] The Method of Nature.

This young friend thought him "so angelic and remarkable" that he felt "towards him more than a boy's emotion, as if a new spring of brotherly affection had suddenly broken loose in his heart." There was no indication of turbulence or disquiet about him even then, but a happy combination of energy and gentleness that truly made the boy father of the man. He has himself described an incident of the war of 1812, when the master of the school invited his boys to spend the next day in helping to throw up earthen defenses against the enemy. He remembers that a pleasant day was spent on Noddle Island, but does not recollect any work done by the boys.

He entered Harvard College in his fourteenth year. Kirkland was then president, and Edward Everett professor of Greek literature. Among the other professors were Edward Channing and Ticknor. Emerson felt the inspiration which the latter brought to the university throughout his course. Caleb Cushing was among the tutors. In his class were Upham, author of the *History of Salem Witchcraft*, and Josiah Quincy, afterwards Mayor of Boston. In the class before his were Furness and Gannett. In the class succeeding was Nathaniel Bowditch the younger, and in the next George Ripley. Before they entered the College, began a lasting friendship with Furness.

During his first year in college he was the "president's freshman," running on his errands and making his announcements for him. He has been described as being then "a slender, delicate youth, younger than most of his classmates, and of a sensitive, retiring nature."[1] He received, according to his own statement, but little instruction or criticism from his professors that was of value to him. His favorite study was Greek, and his translations of the classical authors were neat and happy. In mathematics he could make no headway, and in philosophy he did not get on very well. He was a great reader, and studied much outside of the

[1] Literary World, May 22, 1880.

prescribed course. Even on entering college he was well read. His special favorites were the old English poets and dramatists, — Montaigne and Shakspere. He early discovered that Shakspere was full of interest, and he became very familiar with the great poet. In his sophomore year he was connected with a book-club, the members of which read Scott's novels far into the night. He had a taste for declamation, in which he was excellent, and thus won a Boylston prize. He also showed much ability in composition, and what he wrote was of a marked excellence. The direction his genius would take was early indicated. In his junior year he wrote an essay on The Character of Socrates, for which he gained a Bowdoin prize; and in his senior year his subject was The Present State of Ethical Philosophy, for which he received the second prize. He had much skill in making poetry, which he freely employed for college purposes. On Class Day he was the poet, and his verses were thought to be very fine. He had one of the twenty-nine parts on Commencement Day, and spoke on John Knox in a Conference on the Character of John Knox, William Penn, and John Wesley. Josiah Quincy, his classmate, and the winner of the first prize at the Bowdoin contest, made this entry in his journal, under date of July 16, 1821: "Attended a dissertation of Emerson's in the morning, on the subject of Ethical Philosophy. I found it long and dry." The next day he went to the chapel, "where Barnwell and Emerson performed our valedictory exercises before all the scholars and a number of ladies. They were rather poor, and did but little honor to the class."[1] In these judgments must be read a little of the spirit of college rivalry.

His mother moved to Cambridge in his sophomore year; and he boarded with her, though he had a room on the college-yard. His brother William, who graduated at the previous Commencement, opened a school in the house, and was assisted by Waldo. Some of

[1] Harvard Sixty Years Ago, by Josiah Quincy, in The Independent of July 29, 1880.

their students became members of the family, boarding with their mother. Waldo was at this time quiet in manner, studious, little given to the ruder sports of his comrades. Yet he was of a genial disposition, fond of story-telling, and good at making a social meeting pass off pleasantly. "His mind was unusually mature and independent. His letters and conversation already displayed something of originality." He owed much to his early developed, and assiduously followed, habit of wide and careful reading; and he "spent much of his time in special courses of private work in the library." He doubtless owed much here to the two remarkable women who exercised so much influence on his early life, — Mary Emerson and Sarah Bradford. The latter was afterwards the wife of Samuel Ripley. Both these women were great lovers of books, and they were unusually well informed for the time. Under their lead he early came to love Plato, and, after leaving college, seems to have studied him very closely. At this period Tillotson, Augustine, and Jeremy Taylor were among his favorite authors. One of the earliest of the serious books he read was a translation of Pascal's *Pensées*, which he carried to church with him, and read almost constantly. He was also greatly attracted by Montaigne. When a boy, he found a volume of Montaigne's essays among his father's books. After leaving college it came again to his notice, and he procured the remaining volumes. "I remember the delight and wonder," he says, "in which I lived with it. It seemed to me as if I had myself written the book in some former life, so sincerely it spoke to my thought and experience."[1]

Another important influence was the preaching and lecturing of Edward Everett. He was in the habit of going from one Boston church to another, on Sunday mornings, inquiring for Everett, and so managed to hear him nearly every week. This was in the days before preachers and their subjects were advertised; but the young man felt himself amply repaid for his search,

[1] Representative Men: essay on Montaigne.

in the eloquence which won his admiration. So great was his enthusiasm that it subjected him to the ridicule of his schoolmates; but it also, a little later, won him the friendship of Elizabeth Peabody, who had the same admiration for Everett.

Before Waldo left college, his brother William had opened a young ladies' school in Federal Street, Boston; and, after his graduation, he went there to teach. His main object seems to have been to assist his younger brothers through college; and the family soon after moved to this location, near Dr. Channing's church. He is said to have been mild and gentle as a teacher, making an agreeable and lasting impression on the minds of his pupils, though teaching was not at all to his taste. He was in the habit, when needing to discipline his pupils, of sending them to his mother's room to pursue their studies.

He began in 1823 the study of theology, but did not enter the Harvard Theological School, though he attended many of the lectures there. A considerable influence at this time was Channing's conversation and preaching. The outcome of that great preacher's most cherished ideas was a fine practical reliance on the soul of man as a medium of truth and goodness. Emerson eagerly embraced the essential spirit of Channing's teaching; while the lovable spirit of this man, the high character of his thought, the loftiness of his religious purpose, made a deep impression on the young student. To come into contact with such a man is worth far more than all formal instruction. Channing valued Christianity for what it had in common with reason and nature, and he thought man is cognizant of the Absolute through his reason. In this he was largely in sympathy with Wordsworth and Coleridge, to whom he was greatly indebted. He said we know God only by those moral laws we find in ourselves, because we are of like nature with him. He saw in the cosmic forces of nature unconscious manifestations of the divine mind. To him the highest motive of life was "the full enjoyment of our spiritual being, when the sense of duty was lost in great impulses of *love*, which is the full communion with the spirit of the Lord, which is liberty."[1] He found in Coleridge and Wordsworth a higher form of thought than either the Trinitarian or Unitarian. Emerson also heard Professor Norton's lectures in the Divinity School with much profit and interest. Having studied too assiduously, his eyes failed him at this time; and he was unable to take notes of these lectures. He was, consequently, excused from examination. Of this fact he has since said, "If they had examined me, they probably would not have let me preach at all." This remark refers to doubts which he entertained even at this time, — doubts concerning the form and not the substance of religion. William had gone to Germany to study theology, after the school was given up, and found himself entangled in skepticism as the result of his studies there. So perplexed was he as to what was his duty, he went to Goethe, and laid his case before the great poet, stating his doubts, the expectations of his mother and friends, and the pain he knew it would cause them should he abandon his chosen profession. Goethe gave him his sympathy, advised him to go home and preach, whatever his doubts, and not to overthrow the hopes of his family. William could not, however, so deal with his doubts, and returned home to study law. On his return Waldo was living in Chelmsford, and William went there to talk over the situation with him. Describing this interview years afterward, Emerson said, "I was very sad, for I knew how much it would grieve my mother; and it did."

His health became very poor at this time, owing to his hard work. He was in 1826 "approbated to preach" by the Middlesex Association of Ministers, but was obliged to spend the following winter in Florida and South Carolina. He preached in Charleston several times, and in other places, during his sojourn there. On his return, in the spring of 1827, he began to seek

[1] Reminiscences of William E. Channing, by E. P. Peabody.

for a pulpit. He was at New Bedford, in Dr. Dewey's pulpit, for three Sundays, and was, doubtless, drawn heartily to the Quakers of that town. In the spring of 1828, for a short time he supplied the place of Dr. Ripley at Concord.

He continued to write poetry through all these early years; though, with a few exceptions, it has not been given to the public. One poem of this period, however, has attracted much attention, and is one of the most popular of his productions. It was while in Newton, for a short time, that he wrote the well-known lines, —

"Good-by, proud world! I'm going home."

This poem has been referred to the period after his leaving the pulpit, but this is a mistake. It indicates the spirit and purpose of the young man, his genius, his high ideals, his love of a life of meditation, and his scorn for all the shams and shows of the world. Written before entering the ministry, instead of after leaving it, it indicates the nobility of his motives and the loftiness of his aims. It shows his intense love of nature, and the devoutness of his mind.

"When I am stretched beneath the pines,
Where the evening star so holy shines,
I laugh at the lore and the pride of man,
At the sophist schools and the learnèd clan;
For what are they all, in their high conceit,
When man in the bush with God may meet?"

III.

MINISTRY.

ON the 11th of January, 1829, Emerson received an invitation from the Second Church in Boston, to become the colleague of Henry Ware, jun. Ware's health had broken down, and he was unable to continue his ministerial labors. On the 11th of March, Emerson was ordained. The sermon was preached by the Rev. Samuel Ripley, and the address to the candidate was given by the Rev. Dr. Ripley. Parkman gave the ordaining prayer, N. L. Frothingham the fellowship of the churches, and Gannett the address to the society. In his address, Dr. Ripley appealed to the memories of the young man's distinguished ancestors, and said, "We cheerfully express our joy at the ordination of one whose moral, religious, and literary character is so fair and promising." The pastoral work, and especially the care of the young, he said, would be easier to the candidate than to most ministers, both from natural disposition and habit. His relations to Emerson were mentioned in a happy manner, in speaking of the reasons for his being invited to join in the ceremonies of ordination.

"Why is this service assigned to one so aged," he asked, "and so little conversant in this metropolis? Because I was the friend and successor of your excellent grandfather, and became the legal parent and guardian of his orphan children; because I guided the youthful days, directed the early studies, introduced into the ministry, witnessed the celebrity, and deeply lamented the early death of your beloved father; and because no clergyman present can feel a livelier interest or deeper joy on seeing you rise up in his stead, and taking part with us in this ministry in your native city, where his eloquent voice is still remembered, and his memory affectionately cherished."

Almost at once Ware was compelled to go to Europe, whence he returned only to resign his charge. Upon Emerson must almost at once have fallen the whole burden of preaching and pastoral work, taking the place of a learned and eloquent preacher, in a large and popular church. He entered upon his work under the most favorable auspices, so far as concerned the impression he had made, and the confidence felt in him. In March, Ware wrote to his brother, "My colleague has begun his work in the best possible manner, and with just the promise I like." When, after eighteen months' absence, Ware returned from Europe and resigned his connection with the church, he said in his farewell sermon, in speaking of his previous withdrawal from the pulpit on account of his health, "Providence presented to you at once a man on whom your hearts could rest."[1]

Emerson's preaching is said to have been eloquent, simple, and effective. Sanborn gives these incidents of his ministerial experience:[2] —

"His pulpit eloquence was singularly attractive, though by no means equally so to all persons. In 1829, before the two friends had met, Bronson Alcott heard him preach in Dr. Channing's church on 'The Universality of the Moral Sentiment,' and was struck, as he said, 'with the youth of the preacher, the beauty of his elocution, and the direct and sincere manner in which he addressed his hearers.' This particular sermon was probably one that he had written in July, 1829, concerning which he had said to a friend, while writing it, 'I am striving hard to-day to establish the sovereignty and self-existent excellence of the moral law in popular argument, and slay the utility swine.' It is possible, therefore, that he may have taken a tone towards the utilitarians which gave some ground for a remark made, not long after, by the wife of a Boston minister with whom Emerson exchanged. 'Waldo Emerson came last Sunday,' said this lady, 'and preached a sermon, with his chin in the air, in scorn of the whole human race.' But the usual tone of his discourses could never justify this peevish criticism."

He has been described "as noted for the amiability of his disposition, the strictness of his morals, and for

[1] Ware's Biography.
[2] Scribner's Magazine, February, 1879.

his attention to his duties."[1] One who heard him[2] at this time, has spoken of the —

"Solemnity of his manner, and the earnest thought pervading the discourse. The text was, 'What is a man profited if he gain the whole world, and lose his own soul?' The main emphasis was on the word 'own;' and the general theme was, that to every man the great end of existence was the preservation and culture of his individual mind and character. Each man must be saved by his own inward redeemer; and the whole world was for each but a plastic material through which the individual spirit was to realize itself. Aspiration and thought became clear and real, only by action and life. If knowledge led not to action, it passed away."

During his ministry Emerson took a considerable share in the public affairs of the city, and a deep interest in all philanthropic movements. He was on the school committee, chaplain of the State Senate, and, on the first Sunday in June, 1832, preached the charity sermon at the "Old South" church. When Father Taylor was sent to Boston to preach to the sailors, though a Methodist, he went to Dr. Channing for aid in building a house of worship. The second person he visited on the same mission was Emerson, who gave him money, and aided him in securing the assistance of many rich Boston merchants. Even at this early day, when all the pulpits were silent on the subject of slavery, he opened his church to the anti-slavery agitators. On Sunday evening, May 29, 1831, Samuel J. May delivered an anti-slavery lecture in his church; and Arnold Buffum spoke there, in favor of emancipation, Dec. 16, 1832.

During his ministry he seems to have written nothing on literary themes, at least nothing was published from his pen. The only exception is a short notice of a new collection of hymns printed in *The Christian Examiner* of 1831. He praises the Hebrew Psalms for "the greatest perfection to which religious poetry has yet been carried." Of church hymns he characteristically says, —

[1] Gallery of Literary Portraits, series first, by George Gilfillan.
[2] Fraser's Magazine, July, 1868.

"It is not fit that men of common powers should write our hymns. If every hymn to be sung in our churches could have come from the powerful and hallowed minds that have thought for the human race, and, instead of being regarded as an occasional and inferior exercise, had been the vent of their best and deepest contemplations upon God and nature, these minds would have enjoyed an influence which will never be granted to their epics, and books of philosphy or criticism."

In 1830 he took part in the ordination of the Rev. H. B. Goodwin as the colleague of Dr. Ripley in the Concord church. On this occasion he gave the right hand of fellowship, and it is the only discourse or address of his printed during his ministry. It indicates a general acceptance of the customs of the church, and a genuine reception of its most cherished ideas. He said, —

"Christianity aims to teach the perfection of human nature; and eminently, therefore, does it teach the unity of the spirit. It is not only in its special precepts, but by all its operations, a law of love. It does, by its revelation of God, and of the true purposes and the true rules of life, operate to bind up, to join together, and not to distinguish and separate. It proclaimed peace. But it speaks first to its own disciples, Be of one mind; else, with what countenance could the church say, Love one another?

"And thousands of hearts have heard the commandment, and anon with joy receive it. All men on whose souls the light of God's revelation truly shineth, with whatever apparent differences, are substantially of one mind, work together, whether consciously or not, for one and the same good. Faces that never beheld each other are lighted up by it with the same expression. Hands that were never clasped toil unceasingly at the same work. This it is which makes the omnipotence of truth in the keeping of feeble men, — this fellowship in all its servants, this swift consenting acknowledgment with which they hail it when it appears God's truth; it is that electric spark which flies instantaneously through the countless bands that compose the chain. Truth, not like each form of error, depending for its repute on the powers and influence of here and there a solitary mind that espouses it, combines hosts for its support, and makes them co-operate across mountains, yea, and ages of time."

In personally addressing his friend, he said, —

"It is with sincere pleasure that I speak for the church on this occasion, and on the spot hallowed to all by so many patriotic, and, to me, by so many affectionate, recollections. I feel a peculiar, a personal right to welcome you hither to the home and the temple of my fathers. I believe the church whose pastor you are will forgive me the allusion, if I express the extreme interest which every man feels in the scene of the trials and labors of his ancestors. Five out of seven of your predecessors are my kindred. They are in the dust, who bind my attachment to this place; but not all. I cannot help congratulating you that one survives, to be to you the true friend and venerable counselor he has ever been to me."

Though every thing seemed to indicate that Emerson would lead a useful and a successful career in the pulpit, yet in the autumn of 1832 he resigned his place, and gradually withdrew from his ministerial labors. He had early accepted a form of thought which was not popular, which more or less put him outside the traditions of the church; so that the cause which led to this action may be found in his adoption of an ideal philosophy and a purely spiritual interpretation of religion. The immediate cause was his disinclination to conduct the usual "communion service." The true communion was to his mind purely spiritual, while that commonly observed he felt had no sanction in the New Testament. Yet he offered to continue it if the service could be made one merely of commemoration, and if he should not himself be required to partake of the bread and wine. His congregation was anxious to retain him, and proposed that he should put his construction on the Lord's Supper while they retained theirs; but he could not consent to such a compromise. While his congregation valued his services, they were zealous of the Unitarian name, and did not wish any reproach of heresy to be cast upon it. As they would not consent to his innovations, he resigned.[1] On the 9th of September, 1832, he preached a singularly clear and noble-minded sermon on the subject, setting forth his reasons for rejecting this rite. It justifies all the praise accorded to his pulpit abilities. It is dispassionate, truly religious; and it is very charming in its quiet and yet earnest style. It indicates no break with the

[1] See Bartol's account of this affair in Radical Problems, p. 65.

spiritual truths of Christianity, but a desire for a loftier spirit of devotion; for the forms of the church are challenged in the name of that inward spirit of truth in which alone true religion consists. To him all true worship had come to be inward, and it could only be hindered and corrupted by outward forms. The spirit can return to its own, and in interior vision behold the Nameless One in union with itself. Prayer must be spontaneous to be of any worth. It must be natural; the soul's impulses must be obeyed. Holding such ideas, the rite of "communion" seemed a repudiation of that spiritual worship Jesus taught, and a return to the forms from which he sought to liberate men. In urging this fact, he states very clearly the chief thought of his sermon on the Lord's Supper.

"The whole world was full of idols and ordinances. The Jewish was a religion of forms. The Pagan was a religion of forms: it was all body, — it had no life, — and the Almighty God was pleased to qualify and send forth a man to teach men that they must serve him with the heart; that only that life was religious which was thoroughly good; that sacrifice was smoke, and forms were shadows. This man lived and died true to this purpose; and now, with his blessed word and life before us, Christians must contend that it is a matter of vital importance — really a duty — to commemorate him by a certain form, whether that form be agreeable to their understandings or not.

"Is not this to make vain the gift of God? Is not this to turn back the hand on the dial? Is not this to make men — to make ourselves — forget that not forms, but duties — not names, but righteousness and love — are enjoined? and that, in the eye of God, there is no other measure of the value of any one form than the measure of its use?"

After his resignation his health broke down, and in December he was advised to take a sea-voyage. He was not able to appear again in the pulpit, but on the 22d sent his congregation an affectionate letter of farewell. It shows very clearly that he abandoned none of the essential ideas of his former faith.[1]

[1] Both this letter and the sermon are printed in full in Frothingham's History of New England Transcendentalism, and should be carefully read by those who would correctly understand the causes of Emerson's separation from the church.

It has been thought Emerson left the pulpit with a feeling of disappointment: and the poem, Good-by, Proud World, has been quoted to this effect; but there is no evidence of it. At the hour when his continuance as pastor of the church was being discussed by its members, he sat quietly conversing with a friend. When he arose to depart, he said, "This is probably the last time we shall ever meet as brethren in the same calling." He explained the cause of the remark, but was perfectly calm, and apparently contented with that result. His real feelings towards the church may probably be best seen in a hymn he wrote for the ordination of Chandler Robbins, who became the next year his successor in the Second Church.

"We love the venerable house
Our fathers built to God;
In heaven are kept their grateful vows,
Their dust endears the sod.

"Here holy thoughts a light have shed
From many a radiant face,
And prayers of tender hope have spread
A perfume through the place.

"And anxious hearts have pondered here
The mystery of life,
And prayed the Eternal Spirit clear
Their doubts and aid their strife.

"From humble tenements around
Came up the pensive train,
And in the church a blessing found,
Which filled their homes again.

"They live with God, their homes are dust;
But here their children pray,
And, in this fleeting lifetime, trust
To find the narrow way."

Though his separation from the church seems to have been so small, and though in most things he continued to sympathize so strongly with its purposes, yet he was subjected to much of misconception and criticism.[1] This is shown in one of the letters of Mrs. Samuel Ripley to Miss Mary Emerson, dated "Waltham, Sept. 4, 1833."[2]

"We have had a delightful visit of two days," she says, "from Waldo. We feel about him as you no doubt do. While we regard him still more than ever as the apostle of the eternal reason, we do not like to hear the crows, as Pindar says, caw at the bird of Jove; nevertheless, he has some stout advocates. A lady was mourning the other day to Mr. Francis[3] about Mr. Emerson's insanity. 'Madam, I wish I were half as sane,' he answered, and with warm indignation."

His health not being improved during the winter, he sailed early in the spring of 1833 for Europe. He first visited Sicily and Italy, and, returning through France, spent some weeks in England. He met Greenough in Florence, who secured him an invitation to visit Landor; and he was greatly interested by that fine writer. His impressions of Landor, as they were many years afterwards published in *English Traits*, did not please the subject of them; and Forster gives Landor's corrections.[4] It is more than probable, however, that Landor did not remember all he said in these conversations,

[1] In the Life of Father Taylor is a letter from Mrs. Horace Mann to his daughter, in which she has this to say of Taylor's relations to Emerson: "Ralph Waldo Emerson was settled over the North society; and all through that experience of his, which ended in his leaving the parish and the settled ministry, your father understood him when so many maligned him. Some one used the expression that Mr. Emerson was insane. Your father did not agree with his views of the Lord's Supper, — that it was a thing of the past, and no longer appropriate; for he gave a great significance and value to it; but he would not let that suggestion pass. He said, 'Mr. Emerson might think this or that, but he was more like Jesus Christ than any one he had ever known. He had seen him when his religion was tested, and it bore the test.' Surely there could be no better proof of Christian liberality than his appreciation of one who differed so entirely from himself in doctrine." Writing of a subsequent period, that of Emerson's Divinity-School address, Mrs. Mann says, "He and Ralph Waldo Emerson did a great work together in those days, each working in his own sphere, often encountering each other in souls as well as in charities. Each understood each other better for the work of each."

[2] Memoir of Mrs. Samuel Ripley, by Miss Elizabeth Hoar, in Worthy Women of our First Century.

[3] Rev. Convers Francis.

[4] Walter Savage Landor: a biography, by John Forster, vol. ii. pp.

and that his corrections represented his later opinions, not those he entertained in 1833.

In England Emerson visited Coleridge, Wordsworth, and Carlyle. His visit to the latter, and their "quiet night of clear, fine talk,"[1] was the beginning of a warm friendship and a strong mutual admiration. Carlyle afterwards spoke with enthusiasm of the time "when that supernal vision, Waldo Emerson, dawned on him." When Longfellow went to see him in 1835, with a letter of introduction from Emerson, Carlyle said Emerson's coming to Craigenputtoch was "like the visit of an angel," so helpful did he find the warm sympathy and generous appreciation of this young American. Emerson preached a few times in London and elsewhere during his brief stay in England.

In September, 1829, Emerson married Ellen Louisa Tucker, to whom he addressed, while wooing her, that exquisite poem entitled To Ellen at the South. In these verses he compares her with the flowers; and she seems to have been as delicate as they, for she died of consumption in February, 1832.

[1] Carlyle's Reminiscences. In Harper's Monthly for May, 1881, M. D. Conway gives Carlyle's account of Emerson's visit, as related the night of the Edinburgh University address. Other incidents, with a letter of Emerson's written in 1833, describing his visits to Carlyle and Wordsworth, are given in Conway's book on Thomas Carlyle.

IV.

THE NEW CAREER.

AFTER an absence of several months, Emerson returned to Boston, fully restored to health. He gave several lectures there during the winter, which were well attended, and were well received by those who heard them. One of these lectures was on Water, and was given before the Mechanics' Institute. Another subject was The Relations of Man to the Globe. He also gave two lectures on his visit to Italy. He preached only once in the pulpit of the Second Church after his return. This was on the occasion of the death of a Boston merchant of great integrity. He discoursed of the means by which the ideal, the truly saintly, life, may be lived in the midst of daily business.

Not long after his return from Europe he began preaching in the Unitarian church in New Bedford, and remained there for several months. In 1834 he received a call to settle there, but he declined to accept it. He became greatly attached to that congregation, however, and especially to the Quaker portion of it. During the controversy among the Friends, in 1825 and later, growing out of the preaching of Elias Hicks, those who separated from the Orthodox body connected themselves with the Unitarian church. They felt that the Friends had fallen away from their early simplicity and spirituality, and had made forms and dogmas out of their own methods, instead of following the spirit in the life of each new day. They were at first known as "New Lights," and attracted the deeply interested attention of Dr. Channing. Emerson's protest against the formality of the communion service drew them to him, while his own lofty spirituality satisfied their ideas of the religious life. He was specially drawn to a remarkable woman among these people, — Mary Rotch, one of their preachers, — who was noted as much for her sound sense as for a saintly life and a rich power of spiritual expression. Emerson saw much of her, and afterwards expressed his great indebtedness to her life and teachings. One who heard him at this time in New Bedford has given the following account of the impression he made: —

"One day there came into our pulpit the most gracious of mortals, with a face all benignity, who gave out the first hymn and made the first prayer as an angel might have read and prayed. Our choir was a pretty good one, but its best was coarse and discordant after Emerson's voice. I remember of the sermon only that it had an indefinite charm of simplicity and wisdom, with occasional illustrations from nature, which were about the most delicate and dainty things of the kind which I had ever heard. I could understand them, if not the fresh philosophical novelty of the discourse. Mr. Emerson preached for us for a good many Sundays, lodging in the house of a Quaker lady, just below ours. Seated at my own door, I saw him often go by; and once, in the exuberance of my childish admiration, I ventured to nod to him, and to say 'Good-morning.' To my astonishment he also nodded, and smilingly said 'Good-morning;' and that is all the conversation I ever had with the sage of Concord. He gave us afterwards two lectures based upon his travels abroad, and was at a great deal of trouble to hang up prints, by way of illustration. There was a picture of the tribune in the Uffizi Gallery in Florence, painted by one of our townsmen; and I recall Mr. Emerson's great anxiety that it should have a good light, and his lamentation when a good light was found to be impossible. The lectures[1] themselves were so fine — enchanting, we found them — that I have hungered to see them in print, and have thought of the evenings on which they were delivered as 'true Arabian Nights.'"[2]

In the summer of 1834 he went to Concord, and found a home in the "Old Manse" with Dr. Ripley. He was probably drawn there for study and meditation; and perhaps the purpose was already forming of finding there a home, and devoting himself to a literary career. He was also moved by his love of nature to

[1] Probably the two he gave in Boston immediately after his return from Europe.

[2] Reminiscences of a Journalist, by Charles T. Congdon, p. 33. Printed originally in the New York Tribune for Dec. 23, 1879.

select Concord as a home. "I am a poet by nature," he said at this time, "and therefore must live in the country."

In February, 1835, he began a course of biographical lectures in Boston. The first was an introductory one, on the advantages of biography; and it was followed by others on Luther, Milton, Burke, Michael Angelo, and George Fox. These lectures were well attended, and won him many friends and admirers, among them Alcott. In the lecture on Milton, there is a word about Milton's religious opinions which may give a hint of the tendencies of his own thinking at this time: —

"The most devout man of his time, he says, frequented no church; probably from a disgust at the fierce spirit of the pulpits. And so, throughout all his actions and opinions, is he a consistent spiritualist, or believer in the omnipotence of spiritual laws."

This lecture and that on Michael Angelo were soon after published;[1] and they show maturity of thought, familiarity with the subject, and a rare philosophical insight. The same thought and spirit were carried into a lecture before the American Institute of Instruction, in August of this year, when he spoke of The Means of Inspiring a Taste for English Literature.

On the 12th of September he gave an historical address in Concord, it being the second centennial anniversary of the incorporation of the town. The desire to commemorate the planting of the town, he says, is just and wise.

"And yet, in the eternity of nature, how recent our antiquities appear! The imagination is impatient of a cycle so short. Who can tell how many thousand years, every day, the clouds have shaded these fields with their purple awning? The river, by whose banks most of us were born, every winter for ages has spread its crust of ice over the great meadows which in ages it had formed. But the little society of men who now, for a few years, fish in this river, plow the fields it washes, mow the grass, and reap the corn, shortly shall hurry from its banks as did their forefathers. 'Man's life,' said the Druid to the Saxon king, 'is the sparrow that enters

[1] That on Milton in North American Review for July, 1838, and that on Angelo in the same Review, in January, 1837.

at a window, flutters round the house, and flies out at another, and none knoweth whence he came, or whither he goes.' The more reason that we should give to our being what permanence we can; that we should recall the past, and expect the future."

Alluding to the permanence of the Concord names, he said there still remained "the lineal descendants of the first settlers of this town." "If the name of Bulkeley is wanting, the honor you have done me this day in making me your organ testifies your persevering kindness to his blood." He then sketches the history of Concord through its two centuries with great care, and in a graphic manner. Near the close of his address he gives this picture of the town: —

"I find our annals marked with uniform good sense. I find no ridiculous laws, no eavesdropping legislators, no hanging of witches, no ghosts, no whipping of Quakers, no unnatural crimes. The tone of the records rises with the dignity of the event. These soiled and musty books are luminous and electric within. The old town-clerks did not spell very correctly, but they contrive to make pretty intelligible the will of a free and just community. Frugal our fathers were, — very frugal, — though, for the most part, they deal generously by their minister, and provide well for the schools and the poor. If, at any time, in common with most of our towns, they have carried this economy to the verge of vice, it is to be remembered that a town is, in many respects, a financial corporation. They economize, that they may sacrifice. They stint and higgle on the price of a pew, that they may send two hundred soldiers to Gen. Washington to keep Great Britain at bay. For splendor, there must be somewhere rigid economy. That the head of the house may go brave, the members must be plainly clad; and the town must save that the State may spend." [1]

In September of this year he married Lydia Jackson, daughter of Charles Jackson of Plymouth.[2] Immediately after their marriage Emerson occupied the house where he has lived ever since. It is at the eastern

[1] This address was at once printed by request, with a page of his grandfather's journal giving an account of the Concord fight. A new edition was printed in 1875. Bancroft made use of it in writing his account of the Concord fight in his history.

[2] Her family is descended from Rev. John Cotton, and from some of the earliest of the Plymouth settlers. Dr. C. T. Jackson, the discoverer of anæsthetics, one of the ablest of American scientists, was her brother.

edge of the village, on the Cambridge turnpike, opposite the point where it divides from the Lexington road; was built in 1828, and is a plain, unpretentious house of goodly size. His mother soon became a member of his family, and remained with him until her death in 1853.

In December he began a course of ten lectures in Boston on English literature. The first two were on the earliest writers; and there were others on Chaucer, Bacon, Shakspere, and all the great English literary masters. In the last lecture he spoke of Byron, Scott, Dugald Stewart, Mackintosh, and Coleridge. He placed Coleridge among the sages of the world; but expressed himself as little in sympathy with the literary spirit of the time, though he did not despair of reform.

On the 19th of April, 1825, the corner-stone of a monument was laid in Concord, to commemorate the Concord fight. Edward Everett gave the oration. Emerson offered this toast: "The little bush that marks the spot where Capt. Davis fell, — 'tis the burning bush where God spoke for his people." April 19, 1836, a meeting was held on the completion of this monument, when a hymn written for the occasion by Emerson was read by Dr. Ripley, and sung to the tune of Old Hundred. It was that containing the immortal lines, —

"Here once the embattled farmers stood,
And fired the shot heard round the world."

He wrote other poems at this period, some of his very best, many of which were afterwards printed in *The Dial*.

He returned now to studies out of which grew his idealism. Plato was read more diligently than ever. While teaching in Boston, he had made himself familiar with Plutarch. In 1835 he began to study Plotinus, and other writers of the same class. The German mystics attracted his attention, as did the English idealists. The same year he was reading, with the keenest relish and enthusiasm, the poems of George Herbert, and the prose writings of Cudworth, Henry More, Milton, Coleridge, and Jeremy Taylor. As the result of these studies, while living in the "Old Manse" he wrote a little book on *Nature*, in which he gave expression to his philosophical opinions. It was published in September, 1836. The author's name was not given. The title-page bore these words from Plotinus, "Nature is but an image or imitation of wisdom, the last thing of the soul; nature being a thing which doth only do, but not know." Its leading thought is that contained in its original motto, —

> "A subtle chain of countless rings
> The next unto the farthest brings;
> The eye reads omens where it goes,
> And speaks all languages the rose;
> And, striving to be man, the worm
> Mounts through all the spires of form."

It is pure idealism which he teaches throughout this little book of less than one hundred pages, — an idealism rare, subtle, and noble. The universe exists, he says, to the end of discipline; and it may be doubted "whether nature outwardly exists." Nature always speaks of spirit, and exists only for the unfolding of a spiritual being. This is the thought of the book, and it is written to vindicate this philosophy. The soul needs to be developed, and to that end should be all our living. Instead, man applies to nature but half his force, and lives a low commercial life, a life of the senses.

He developed his ideas in *Nature* more systematically than elsewhere; and he has given there a very simple, and yet a consistent, system of philosophy. A glance at what he attempts there to do will open the way to an understanding of all his subsequent teachings. He writes with the greatest enthusiasm of the attractions of nature, and finds the source of that attraction in the harmony which exists between man and the outward world. The first use nature has for man is, that it ministers to the wants of the senses. It answers, however, to a higher want still, the love of beauty. Its beautiful forms delight him, but the heroic actions of men add to it a higher charm. It becomes also a teacher of the intellect, re-forming itself in the harmonious action of the mind. Nature rises higher than beauty, and becomes an instrument of language, the vehicle of thought. The use of the outer creation is to give us language for the beings and changes of the inward creation, and nature becomes an aid in understanding the supernatural. Natural facts give us words as their signs, and in a yet more perfect manner nature is itself emblematic of the spiritual facts on which it rests. "Every natural fact is a symbol of some spiritual fact. Every appearance in nature corresponds to some state of the mind, and that state of the mind can only be described by presenting that natural appearance as its picture." Nature becomes a means of expression for those spiritual truths and experiences which could not otherwise be interpreted. Its laws, also, are moral laws when applicable to man; and so they become to man the language of the divine will.

Because the physical laws become moral laws the moment they are related to human conduct, nature has a much higher purpose than that of beauty or language, in that it is a discipline. At first it is a disciple to the understanding in intellectual truths; it trains reason, and it develops the intellect. Nature is the great moral teacher, its every fact and law a means of ethical culture. All parts of nature conspire to this one end of discipline.

"All things are moral, and in their boundless changes have an unceasing reference to spiritual nature. Every animal function, from the sponge up to Hercules, shall hint or thunder to man the laws of right and wrong, and echo the ten commandments. This ethical character so penetrates the bone and marrow of nature, as to secure the end for which it was made. Every natural process is a version of a moral sentence. The moral law lies at the center of nature and radiates to the circumference. It is the pith and marrow of every substance, every relation, and every process. All things with which we deal preach to us."

So thoroughly does nature answer to this end of discipline, we begin to question if this is not its only use, and if nature outwardly exists. "It is a sufficient account of that appearance we call the world, that God will teach a human mind, and so makes it the receiver of a certain number of congruent sensations, which we call sun and moon, man and woman, house and trade." It is here we see Emerson's resemblance to Swedenborg, in that he cares for nature only as a symbol and revelation of spiritual realities. Because we are led to doubt the reality of outward nature, we are led on to idealism. The first work of the ideal philosophy is to emancipate us from the dominion of the senses, opening to us a larger life. It teaches us that the laws of the natural world are the ideas of the spiritual. We cease to believe in matter as final; and our attention is fastened "upon immortal necessary uncreated natures, that is, upon ideas; and in their presence we feel that the outward is a dream and a shade." Then nature becomes "an appendix of the soul." So looking upon nature we apprehend the absolute; and, as it were, for the first time we exist. Religion and ethics constantly teach us that nature depends on spirit; that the seen and outward world is temporal, while the unseen and spiritual is eternal. Idealism gives consistency to this teaching, sees the world in God, so that it is at each moment his direct revelation. Then we find that nature always speaks of spirit, suggests the absolute, is a perpetual effect of divine causes, is a great shadow pointing to the sun behind it. The aspect of nature is devout, teaches the lesson of worship, to stand before God with bended head; but when we try to describe him, both language and thought desert us, and then we find that nature is but the apparition of God.

Idealism teaches us that in consciousness is the only source of knowledge; the world is a dream, a shadow, but "the mind is a part of the nature of things." God is directly revealed to the soul of man; and we learn that "the Universal Essence, which is not wisdom or love or beauty or power, but all in one and each entirely, is that for which all things exist, and that by which they are; that spirit creates; that behind nature, throughout nature, spirit is present; one, and not compound, it does not act upon us from without, that is, in space and time, but spiritually, or through ourselves." The world is a remoter and inferior incarnation of God, a projection of God in the unconscious; but it is of the same spirit with the body of man. It is a present and a fixed expositor of the divine mind, and serves always to show man his nearness to, or remoteness from, the truth.

This little book met with but a small sale, five hundred copies being sold only after twelve years; yet it attracted the attention and the warmest enthusiasm of a few persons. In England it met with an even heartier reception than here; one writer praising it in the most cordial terms, attributing its authorship to Alcott, who was better known than Emerson. Francis Bowen devoted an article to it in *The Christian Examiner*,[1] criticising severely the transcendental philosophy.

> "We find beautiful writing and sound philosophy in this little work, he says; but the effect is injured by occasional vagueness of expression, and by a vein of mysticism that pervades the writer's whole course of thought. The highest praise that can be accorded to it, is, that it is a *suggestive* book; for no one can read it without tasking his faculties to the utmost, and relapsing into fits of severe meditation. But the effort of perusal is often painful, the thoughts excited are frequently bewildering, and the results to which they lead us uncertain and obscure. The reader feels as in a distracted dream, in which shows of surpassing beauty are around him, and he is conversant with disembodied spirits; yet all the time he is harassed by an uneasy sort of consciousness that the whole combination of phenomena is fantastic and unreal."

On the other hand, a writer in *The Democratic Review* was very enthusiastic in his praise, and said that "the highest intellectual culture and the simplest instinctive innocence have received it, and felt it to be a divine thought, borne on a stream of English undefiled, such as we had almost despaired could flow in this our world of grist and saw mills." He finds evidence of "the highest imaginative power" in it, while "it proves to us that the only true and perfect mind is the poetic."

[1] January, 1837.

During the summer of 1836 the Rev. H. B. Goodwin, pastor of the Unitarian church in Concord, owing to ill health was not able to occupy his pulpit. Emerson supplied it for him for three months. He had continued to preach from time to time, after declining the invitation to New Bedford, as opportunity offered. In the autumn of 1836 he began to preach in East Lexington to a small society recently formed there, which worshipped in a hall.

One of his sermons preached in Boston was on the judgment-seat of Christ, which he said was always set up in the world, and that it consisted in the deep, interior truths of Christianity, which were always judging men by their high ideals. Another sermon was on wonder, and was full of devoutness. He was in these, as in his later sermons at Concord and East Lexington, engaged in presenting those ideas he has made so familiar since. His conception of compensation, of the analogies of nature and the moral life, of the absolute unity of the universe, and many others, about which he has written so much, were all stated in these sermons. In an exceedingly simple and suggestive manner he illustrated the greatest spiritual truths, and with a charm and a magnetism which attracted and held the admiration of all. In one of these sermons he spoke of the unity of God as being the cause and explanation of all fixed laws; and said, that because he is one we see harmony and order in all created things. As a result, the inner and outer man correspond to each other; every truth is related to every other; while every atom of matter is connected with every other, and ruled by the same laws. He then dwelt upon the idea that each thing has in it the laws, conditions, and possibilities of all things. In morals, also, this is true, he said; for all circumstances reach the same truths. One virtue opens the way to all virtue, for virtue is one in essence. One truth will bring a knowledge of all truth; for truth is always the same, a united whole. The spirit of virtue or knowledge in one thing is the key to all virtue and knowledge.

At another time he took for his text the words, "Do thyself no harm." He said that every man within himself is capable of infinite happiness or misery. There is no power which can harm us if we do our duty, and do not harm ourselves. There is an everlasting superiority in virtue to all evil. No one but himself can hurt any man. He is his own worst enemy or friend, so there is great danger from self. The law at the foundation of all things is retribution, he said. This makes every act important, because it is inevitably followed by its necessary consequences, bears fruit in its kind. If an atom be moved, all things in the universe are affected by it; and this law is no less true in moral action. Every act re-acts on the actor, and we receive precisely according to our deeds. In our success we see the connection of cause and effect, and attribute it to our own efforts; but in misfortune we attribute the consequences of our conduct to our fellow-men, to luck, or to providence. Men forget that vices draw blanks, as surely as virtues draw prizes, in what they are pleased to call the lottery of life. The industrious man seeks wealth, and finds it. Let not the intellectual man murmur at the ills of fortune, for he did not seek wealth. It was not the consequence of his pursuit; but he sought knowledge, and found it. If we do self no harm, no real evil can happen to us. We should not fear that which kills the body, and can do no more; for that is not an absolute evil. The loss of purity, the loss of simplicity, the loss of honesty, are real losses; but they befall us only by our own consent. By industry we receive riches, but by goodness and uprightness the eternal riches of virtue. No one can gain by a vicious action. The gain is apparent, outward; but the loss is lasting, permanent. It is parting with a part of our soul. Happy he who brings this truth home to his mind, that whatsoever wrong he does his conscience, he does himself more harm than can be done by all the outward world. The consequences may not be believed, for they are not sudden; yet they are sure. Who would not forego a temptation, an animal delight, a sinful pleasure, for the reward of a peaceful conscience, an ascending character, and in preparation of an endless future? No one can remember a good act or thought which he regrets; nor was there ever a good act in the world, in history, or among those we know, which we can regret.

His religious convictions had now taken on a distinctly spiritual form, but they were vigorous and profound. In August of 1836 Alcott made him a visit, and found him remarkably given to the highest expression of the religious spirit. In the morning he read from the Bible in the simplest and most impressive manner, making the words he read natural with life; and he made a prayer as if he were communing face to face with God, in a spirit as trustful as a child's. In like manner his "blessing" at the table was utterly void of all cant, was not in the least artificial, but the expression of a sincerely thankful heart, full of reverence and faith in the constant presence of the wondrous miracle of life. Alcott also attended a wedding with him, which was conducted in a manner so simple, and followed by a few words of advice to the young couple so pertinent, as to make the whole ceremony one long to remember. With Emerson, through these years as ever after, religion meant perfect sincerity, utter loyalty to every conviction. Because he followed no conventional forms, he gave a newness of life to every expression of his own beliefs. Simplicity, candor, trustfulness, courage, marked all his words on spiritual themes, and gave them a noble beauty and impressiveness.

During the year 1836 Emerson edited Carlyle's *Sartor Resartus*, from the pages of *Fraser's Magazine*, before it appeared in book-form in England. It is worthy of remembrance that this, as well as the other earlier books of Carlyle, met with a success here far greater than that they obtained in England. While attracting little attention there, they were eagerly read by many persons here. Emerson received one hundred and fifty pounds from the sale of the American edition of this volume (according to Carlyle's *Reminiscences*), which proved quite an encouragement to the author at the beginning of his career in London. Emerson wrote a preface for the book, in which he said,—

"The foreign dress and aspect of the work are quite superficial, and cover a genuine Saxon heart. We believe no book has been published, for many years, written in a more sincere style of idiomatic English, or which discovers an equal mastery over all the riches of language. The author makes ample amends for the occasional eccentricity of his genius, not only by frequent bursts of pure splendor, but by the wit and sense which never fail him." He has "an insight into the manifold wants and tendencies of human nature, which is very rare among our popular authors. The philosophy and the purity of moral sentiment, which inspire the work, will find their way to the heart of every lover of virtue."

In 1838 Emerson collected Carlyle's miscellaneous writings, from the pages of the English reviews, and published them in three volumes, as his *Critical and Miscellaneous Essays*. This was done also before they were put into a book in England. In the brief preface he speaks of the influence they had exerted in New England, and how they spoke to many youthful minds, "with an emphasis that hindered them from sleep." These essays had early attracted Emerson's attention, and had a decided influence on his thinking. They introduced him to the world of German thought, and, with *Sartor Resartus*, helped to shape his career. His mind had been already prepared by his reading for an immediate acceptance of these teachings. Hence the eagerness with which he read these essays as they appeared, and his satisfaction in that new world of thought to which they opened the way.

In December, 1836, he began a course of lectures in Masonic Hall, Boston. It was his habit to advertise his subjects, leave his tickets for sale at some central place, and, when enough were sold to pay the hall-rent, begin his course. This year the general subject was The Nature and Ends of History. There were ten lectures; and the special subjects were The Universality of Spirit, Art, Politics, Religion, Society, Trades and Professions, Manners, Ethics, with two lectures on The Present Age. James Freeman Clarke has given the following account of the impression made by his lectures at this period: —

"The majority of the sensible, practical community regarded him as mystical, as crazy or affected, as an imitator of Carlyle, as racked and revolutionary, as a fool, as one who did not himself know what he meant. A small but determined minority, chiefly composed of young men and women, admired him and believed in him, took him for their guide, teacher, and master. I, and most of my friends, belonged to this class. Without accepting all his opinions, or indeed knowing what they were, we felt that he did us more good than any other writer or speaker among us, and chiefly in two ways, — first, by encouraging self-reliance; and, secondly, by encouraging God-reliance."[1]

The majority of the sensible, practical people were well represented by John Quincy Adams, who wrote in his journal that Emerson, "after failing in the every-day vocations of a Unitarian preacher and schoolmaster, starts a new doctrine of transcendentalism, declares all the old revelations superannuated and worn out, and announces the approach of new revelations."[2] He did not believe that the old revelations had worn out, or that the church had gone to colored cobweb, as Carlyle suggested;[3] but he did believe in the mighty truths of a spiritual religion, and he taught those truths as living realities. His own conviction that religion is to be realized in the present, and amidst its conditions, was so strong, his spirit of enthusiastic affirmation was so contagious, his eloquence was so persuasive, and his thought so inspiring, he won the admiration of some of the best minds of the time. Among those he influenced, and inspired with a larger sense of the purposes of life, were several persons since become famous in literature, education, or reform. One of these was Horace Mann. In a letter dated Boston, Dec. 9, 1836, he says,[4] —

[1] Lecture delivered in his church Jan. 8, 1865, on The Religious Philosophy of Ralph Waldo Emerson

[2] Memoirs of J. Q. Adams, vol. i. p. 345, under date of Aug. 2, 1840.

[3] In the chapter entitled Horoscope, in Past and Present.

[4] Life of Mann, by his wife.

"Mr. Emerson, I am sure, must be perpetually discovering richer worlds than those of Columbus or Herschel. He explores, too, not in the scanty and barren region of our physical firmament, but in a spiritual firmament of illimitable extent, and compacted of treasures. I heard his lecture last evening. It was to human life what Newton's *Principia* was to mathematics. He showed me what I have long thought of so much,—how much more can be accomplished by taking a true view than by great intellectual energy. Had Mr. Emerson been set down in a wrong place, it may be doubted whether he would have found his way to the right point of view; but that he now certainly has done. As a man stationed in the sun would see all the planets moving round it in one direction and in perfect harmony, while to an eye on the earth their motions are full of crossings and retrogradations; so he, from his central position in the spiritual world, discovers harmony and order where others can discover only confusion and irregularity. His lecture last evening was one of the most splendid manifestations of a truth-seeking and truth-compelling mind I ever heard. Dr. Walter Channing, who sat beside me, said it made his head ache. Though his language was transparent, yet it was almost impossible to catch the great beauty and proportions of one truth before another was presented."

Another side of his influence may be seen in a letter which Margaret Fuller wrote to a friend in answer to a question as to the nature of the benefits Emerson conferred upon her.

"This influence, she writes, has been more beneficial to me than that of any American; and from him I first learned what is meant by an inward life. Many other springs have since fed the stream of living waters, but he first opened the fountain. That the 'mind is its own place,' was a dead phrase to me, till he cast light upon my mind. Several of his sermons stand apart in my memory, like landmarks of my spiritual history. It would take a volume to tell what this one influence did for me."

The magnetism alike of his manner and of his thought was an inspiration to many minds, rousing, stimulating, full of invigoration, quickening to the intellect and to the moral nature in equal degree. Those who accepted his influence were kindled with an ardent desire to improve their own natures, and with a zealous purpose to improve the world about them.

During this period two of his brothers died, to whom he had been strongly attached. Edward Bliss Emerson was a man of great brilliancy and promise, of a sturdy and robust moral nature, severe and high-toned in his ideas of duty, and incapable, as Waldo said, of self-indulgence. He began the study of law with Daniel Webster, worked too hard, denied himself sufficient food and exercise, broke down in health, and became insane. He recovered his reason after a time. Returning to his studies, he soon found his health inadequate for continuing them permanently. In 1832 he went to Porto Rico, and took a clerkship there. He strongly attached himself to the people about him, became reconciled to the abandonment of his cherished plans of life; but he succumbed to the influences of the climate, and died in 1834.

Charles Chauncy Emerson graduated at Harvard in 1828, studied law with Samuel Hoar of Concord, and became engaged in marriage to his daughter Elizabeth. Waldo said he never moved save in the curve of beauty; but he had a varied capacity, and could turn his attention to every subject and occupation. He died of consumption May 9, 1836. In his metrical essay on Poetry, O. W. Holmes, his companion in the university, wrote this tribute to his memory: —

"Thou calm, chaste scholar! I can see thee now,
The first young laurels on thy pallid brow,
O'er thy slight figure floating lightly down
In graceful folds the academic gown,
On thy curled lip the classic lines, that taught
How nice the mind that sculptured them with thought;
And triumph glistening in the clear blue eye
Too bright to live, — but oh, too fair to die!"

Both these young men gave great promise for the future, and the little they did of literary work was of the very best. Rockwood Hoar, writing of the history of the Concord Lyceum, says, —

"They gave us loftier truths from sweeter lips than this generation knows. The only time I ever heard Edward Bliss Emerson speak in public was before the Concord Lyceum, when he delivered a lecture on the 'Geography of Asia,' — a subject which, to the school-boy, sounded dry. He stood up in the hall over the old academy, with a large map with a painted outline of Asia upon it, with a wand in his hand, and entranced the attention of the audience. I remember now but one line of that lecture. I remember that from hearing it fifty years ago, — the last line of a poetical quotation with which he closed, —

'And seek no other resting-place but heaven.'

Charles Chauncy Emerson's lecture on Socrates was the most stirring appeal to the young men which, at that time, they had ever heard, closing with the line, —

'God for thee has done his part, do thine.'"

Many notes from the journal of Charles were afterwards printed in *The Dial*, which justify all the praises of his friends. Waldo had the most perfect faith in these two brothers. His Dirge expresses his sense of their loss.

In *May-Day and Other Pieces* he writes of Edward as the

"Brother of the brief but blazing star,"

in one of the most memorable poems of its kind, and in a strain of the purest eloquence. They looked to him as to a prophet and an oracle, such was their confidence in his wisdom; while he trusted them in all matters of practical import. After their death he took a much greater interest in public matters, feeling his duties were increased, and that he must fill more perfectly his place as a citizen. Their loss was a great one to him, which he felt most keenly; for he was very tenderly attached to them both. He missed everywhere the presence of these

"Strong, star-bright companions;"

and in the Dirge his consoler says, —

"They loved thee from their birth;
Their hands were pure, and pure their faith.
There are no such hearts on earth.
Ye drew one mother's milk,
One chamber held ye all;
A very tender history
Did in your childhood fall."

V.

THE ERA OF TRANSCENDENTALISM.

THE first twenty-five years of the present century were marked, in Boston, by a revived interest in classical literature. The way was opened thereby to a new appreciation of the idealistic philosophy, creating a taste for the English transcendentalists, as in the case of Channing; and then, a little later, for those of Germany, as in the case of Emerson. Emerson began to read Carlyle about the year 1828, and soon after he read *Wilhelm Meister* in Carlyle's translation.

Previous to the introduction of German thought into England by Coleridge and others, the influence of Locke and Bentham had been predominant. All innate ideas were denied, and morality was based on custom or utility. To this school of thought most of the English Unitarians adhered. They were materialists, and believed in a purely mechanical revelation. The like philosophy had prevailed in this country, and it had been a partial cause of the Unitarian protest. The new thought was everywhere a re-action against it, an attempt of the human mind to recover a natural and assured faith in moral things. It declared that man has innate ideas, and a faculty transcending the senses and the understanding. It identified morality and religion, and made intuition their source. Coleridge calls this transcendent faculty reason, and regarded it as an immediate beholding of supersensible things. He says it can not be called a faculty, and much less a personal property of any human mind. We do not possess it, but partake of it; it is identical with the Universal Reason, a spark from which enters the human mind. He says there is but one reason, which all intelligent beings share in; and it is identical in them all. This idea became most fruitful in Emerson's mind, the source of his doctrine of the Over-Soul. In Coleridge he found much else to stimulate him. Wordsworth gave him the conception of nature as alive with the Universal Spirit, and as being the Universal Reason embodied and outwardly expressed as law and order. These ideas were confirmed by the German thinkers. Herder regarded all religion as an intuition, and looked upon genius in the great man as the world's chief progressive force, as the source of all rightful activity. Goethe, even more than Wordsworth, taught a profound and enthusiastic love of nature, and brought men to look on it as an intimate and confidential friend. By all the great Germans individuality was constantly preached, for they regarded each soul as a new expression of Universal Reason. As the real source of truth is intuition, we must look inwardly, rely on reason as it speaks in us; and not outwardly, to history and social customs.

Such are some of the ideas and influences which affected Emerson and his friends at this time. The conventional and historical came to be less important; and the natural, the common, acquired a new interest. Nature wore a new face, and science was found to have a new and richer attraction. In *Nature* may be seen the influence of Plato, the Neo-Platonists, the German mystics and English idealists. Under their lead he elaborates his doctrine of the one mind common to all men, which reveals through us its living word. This idea expands into his conception of self-reliance, intuition, compensation, and the influence of the great man. He was more than ever repelled from the materialistic philosophy, and from all those religious ideas which seemed in any way to be attached to it. His own account of the rise of Transcendentalism in New England will give the best idea of it which can be presented.

There are always two parties, — the party of the past and that of the future, or that of the establishment and that of movement. It is not easy to date the eras of activity which, from time to time, are manifest, with any thing like precision; but the period beginning about the year 1820, and ending twenty years later, is to be regarded as such an one. It may be characterized as a war between institutions and nature, and which caused a split in every church, as of Calvinists and Quakers, into old and new schools; and there were new divisions upon questions of politics, temperance, and slavery. The general mind had become aware of itself. Men grew conscious and intellectual. The swart earth-spirit which had made the strength of past ages was all gone, and another hour had struck. In literature there appeared a decided tendency to criticism, and young men seemed to have been born with knives in their brains. The popular religion of our fathers received many shocks during this time; but much is to be attributed to the slow but extraordinary influence of Swedenborg, — a man of prodigious mind, tainted, as I think, with a certain suspicion of insanity, but exerting a powerful effect upon an influential class.

Among the more immediate causes of this intellectual and reformatory activity was the impression made by Edward Everett, who returned from Europe about the year 1820, after a five years' residence, and who presented with natural grace and splendid rhetoric some of the phases of contemporary German thought. Frothingham and Norton also contributed in making familiar the latest results of German thinking, and gave a new impetus to the study of theology. But more potent than any of these influences, as a permanent source of the religious revolution of the period, was modern science, especially the science of astronomy. It came to be apprehended, that, as the earth is not the center of the universe, so it is not the special scene or stage on which the drama of divine justice is played before the assembled angels of heaven; the planet being but a speck in the created universe too minute to be seen at the distance of many of the fixed stars which are plainly visible to us. These new perceptions required of men an extension and uplifting of their views as to the dealings of the Creator, and they received a confirmation in the then new science of geology. The writings of Dr. Channing, especially his papers on Milton and Napoleon, had an immense influence on current literature, setting the example and laying the foundation for a broader and deeper school of criticism than had appeared before among us.

Among other influences was the work of the great innovators, Lavater, Gall, Spurzheim, who dragged down every secret and mysterious thing of our nature to the level of a street-show. Goethe also had a great influence, revolutionizing philosophy and science. And the peculiarity of all this period was its return to law, — to what was normal, natural, and human. And this could be seen in the character of the works and authors which then became popular, such as Combe's *Constitution of Man*, Mrs. Somerville's scientific works, and many other writings on science and philosophy; and in Dickens, so human and genial, in the world of fiction.

The tendencies of thought thus created took a decided form, and came to full expression in the year 1836. Beside Emerson's *Nature*, there appeared a little book on *The Gospels*, by W. H. Furness, Alcott's first volume of *Conversations on the Gospels*, Brownson's *New Views of Christianity, Society, and the Church*, and Sampson Reed's *Growth of the Mind*. These books were all based on the new spiritual philosophy, and were full of criticism of the old religious thought and life. So strong had the new tendency become, that its friends began to gather together and to seek for some ampler methods of expression, which would bring them into closer sympathy with each other. Channing was the real leader of this movement, as he had been twenty years earlier of the Unitarian advance. He took counsel with George Ripley, then one of the most prominent of the Unitarian clergymen in Boston, towards the organization of a society for mutual inquiry.

He invited a party of ladies and gentlemen, says Emerson, and I had the honor to be present. No important consequences of the attempt followed. Margaret Fuller, Ripley, Brownson, and Hedge, and many others, gradually came together, but only in the way of students. But I think there prevailed at that time a belief that this was some concert of *doctrinaires* to establish certain opinions, or to inaugurate some movement in literature, philosophy, or religion, but of which these conspirators were quite innocent. It was no concert, but only two or three men and women, who read alone with some vivacity. Perhaps all of these were surprised at the rumor that they were a school or sect, but more especially at the name of "Transcendentalism." Nobody knows who first applied the name. These persons became, in the common chance of society, acquainted with each other; and the result was a strong friendship, exclusive in proportion to its heat. Meetings were held for conversation, with very little form, from house to house. Yet the intelligent character and varied ability of the company gave it some notoriety, and perhaps awakened some curiosity as to its aims and results. But nothing more serious came of it for a long time.

This gathering was at first known as "The Symposium," and afterwards as "The Transcendental Club." It was not so much a club as a gathering of a handful of friends who entertained the same ideas, and had common hopes of a new era of truth and religion. Those ideas were such as to make them talkers, and could be better expressed in conversation among friends than in any other manner. One of the company, Bronson Alcott, in one of his "Conversations," has given a very good account of these meetings; and, as it is almost wholly made up from the pages of his journal, is accurate as to dates and persons:—

"The first meeting of the Transcendental Club was in Boston, at the house of Mr. George Ripley, on the 19th of September, 1836. The persons present were George Ripley, R. W. Emerson, F. H. Hedge, Convers Francis, J. F. Clarke, and the present writer. It was a preliminary meeting, to see how far it would be possible for earnest minds to meet, and with the least possible formality communicate their views. They dispensed with any election of a chairman; if there was to be any precedency, it naturally belonged to the oldest. At that time the oldest of that company was Mr. Francis. They gave invitations to Dr. Channing, to Jonathan Phillips, to Rev. James Walker, Rev. N. L. Frothingham, Rev. J. S. Dwight, Rev. W. H. Channing, and Rev. C. A. Bartol, to join them, if they chose to do so. The three last named appeared afterwards, and met the club frequently. They adjourned to meet at Mr. Alcott's house in Beach Street, on the afternoon of Oct. 3, 1836, at three o'clock.

"On that occasion the subject of discussion was this: American Genius,—the causes which hinder its growth giving us no first-rate productions. There were present at that second meeting, Emerson, Hedge, Francis, Ripley, O. A. Brownson, Clarke, Bartol, and the host. Subsequent meetings took place in Boston the following winter and spring, and at Concord and Watertown, then the home of Mr. Francis, during the summer of 1837. So far as there was any show of order in these meetings, it was something like this: The senior member, Mr. Francis,—the company being seated,—would invite the members, as they sat, to make remarks, which they did. I believe there was seldom an inclination on the part of any to be silent. Always, or nearly always, every person present contributed something to the conversation. At that time theology was the theme of general discussion. Dr. Beecher had come to Boston a few years before, to put down Unitarianism, as he fondly fancied, by preaching his Puritan views,—the views of Calvin. These, however, had passed away, in good measure; and the views of Professor Norton of the Divinity School were then in the ascendant. Dr. Channing had published his essays in *The Examiner*; he was also preaching when he was able. There were added to the club, or symposium, in 1837, Rev. Caleb Stetson, Theodore Parker, Margaret Fuller, and Miss Elizabeth Peabody.

Rev. Thomas T. Stone afterwards joined it. Mr. Brownson commenced his *Quarterly Review* in 1837.

"At the meetings of the club, Mr. Emerson was almost always present. On not more than two or three occasions during the three or four years that the club met — four or five times a year, probably — was he absent. Indeed, the members looked forward with great delight to the opportunity of meeting him. They were presently scattered abroad. Mr. Hedge had gone as far as Bangor, and others had gone to some distance; but it was arranged that during the season of recreation, when these persons came to the city, the meetings should be held quite often. They were held at Watertown, at Newton, Concord, Milton, Chelsea (where Mr. Brownson was then living), frequently in Boston, and perhaps elsewhere. I remember the doctrine of Personality early came up for discussion. It was the fashion to speak against personality, — the orthodox view of it; and the favorite phrase was 'impersonality.' In attempting to liberate the true view from the superstitions which had gathered about it in coming down through Calvinism, through Puritanism, some made the mistake of conceiving individuality to be the central thought; and at these meetings that subject was discussed. Impersonality, Law, Right, Justice, Truth, — these were the central ideas; but where the Power was in which they inhered, how they were related to one another, what was to give them vitality, — these questions were almost neglected, and left out of sight. I think that was the deficiency of the Transcendental school; is its deficiency still; is the reason why it has not incorporated itself into a church, and been found equal to compete with orthodoxy. The old Puritanism, whatsoever may have been its blunders, — whatsoever superstitions may have been mingled with its doctrines, — did believe in a Person, and did not allow itself to discriminate personality away into laws and ideas.

"To show how the topics about which I have been speaking interested the club, in May, 1838, the same company again met — Rev. N. L. Frothingham being present, for the first time, and the only time that I ever saw him — at Medford; and we discussed this question, 'Is Mysticism an Element of Christianity?' That question touched the seat and root of things. Jones Very's *Poems and Essays* were published in September, 1839: very significant they were, too; as if, in answer to the inquiry whether Mysticism was an element of Christianity, here was an illustration of it in a living person, himself present at the club. They are very remarkable poems and essays. There had been nothing printed until *Nature*, unless it may have been Mr. Sampson Reed's little book called *The Growth of the Mind*, which had intimated genius of the like subtle, chaste, and simple quality."

In 1838, at a meeting held at Bartol's house, in Chestnut Street, Pantheism was the topic; and there were present Emerson, Alcott, Follan, Francis, Parker,

Stetson, William Russell, Clarke, and Dwight. At the house of Dr. Francis, September, 1839, there were also present Margaret Fuller, W. H. Channing, Robert Bartlett, and Samuel J. May. In December, at Ripley's, there came Dr. Channing, George Bancroft, the sculptor Clevenger, Cranch, and Samuel G. Ward, beside the regular attendants.

Alcott opened his "Temple School" in Boston in 1834, and applied the new philosophy in the education of young children. Among his assistants were Elizabeth and Sophia Peabody and Margaret Fuller. Elizabeth Peabody prepared for publication a volume of his conversations on the Gospels with the children of his school. This volume was severely criticised, and the school was condemned as an outrageous innovation on the usual methods. While Alcott was being severely attacked in the newspapers, Emerson wrote a defense of the book, which was declined by one of the leading daily journals, but was published in *The Courier*.

"Mr. Alcott, he said, has given proof in the beautiful introduction to this work, as all who have read it know, of a strong mind and a pure heart. A practical teacher, he has dedicated, for years, his rare gifts to the science of education. These conversations contain abundant evidence of extraordinary power of thought, either in the teacher or in the pupils, or in both. He aims to make children think, and, in every question of a moral nature, to send them back on themselves for an answer. He aims to show children something holy in their own consciousness; thereby to make them really reverent, and to make the New Testament a living book to them.

"Mr. Alcott's methods can not be said to have had a fair trial; but he is making an experiment in which all the friends of education are interested. And I ask whether it be wise or just to add to the anxieties of this enterprise a public clamor against some detached sentences of a book, which, as a whole, is pervaded with original thought and sincere piety."

Soon after the publication of this letter, Emerson wrote, March 24, 1837, a most cordial and sympathetic letter to Alcott in regard to the school, and urged him to come away from it, as the people of Boston were unworthy of his genius.

The effect of this agitation on Emerson is indicated

in his relations to the church in East Lexington. This church was very anxious to settle him as their pastor, but he did not wish to enter again fully upon the duties of a clergyman; so he urged upon the people there the calling to their pulpit one of his friends. When a lady of the society was asked why they did not settle this person, the reply was, "We are a very simple people, and can understand no one but Mr. Emerson." When a friend advised him to accept the East-Lexington pulpit, he modestly declared his inability to interest all the people; and when further urged to throw himself into the work, he quietly replied, "My pulpit is the lyceum platform." He continued to preach there until the autumn of 1838, driving to and from the village on Sunday, and preaching two sermons. He continued, indeed, until he began to be troubled with doubts as to public prayer and the rightfulness of offering prayers for others, and then he ceased. His ideas gradually changed until he doubted the rightfulness of any religious forms. He found true religion alone in the communions of the individual soul.

Aug. 31, 1837, he gave the address before the Phi Beta Kappa Society at Harvard.[1] It attracted much attention, and was one more distinct statement of the purposes and hopes of the new movement. The subject was The American Scholar; and its idea was "that there is One Man, — present in all particular men only partially, or through one faculty; and that you must take the whole society to find the whole man." At present man's functions are divided and separated; to each function is a special class. The scholar is "the delegated intellect," for "the true scholar is the only true master." Then the sources from whence the scholar receives his main influences were considered. These are nature, the past, and earnest activity. Nearly all his leading ideas found expression in this address. He dwelt upon the law of the mind and upon its identity with nature. The Man Thinking, of whom he

1 Miscellanies, p. 77.

spoke, is the man of intuition; and he insists upon a rejection of books for an immediate inquiry into the truth. The mind is more than the instruments it has created, more than its own products. The results of this truer method of inquiry into the truth embody themselves in action. The end of all truth is character and a more perfect moral nature. "A great soul will be strong to live as well as strong to think." As the source of truth is not books, but mental activity, we are to cultivate self-trust. Help can come to us only from our own bosoms; and in ourselves we find the law of all nature, so that the world is nothing. We are to be units, walk on our own feet, think our own thoughts, and speak our own minds. Growing out of this attitude is faith in the common, so that all things become revelations of truth. Man is related to all nature, finds in each and all things the same laws, while even the smallest embodies all truth.

Alcott has said of this address a sincere word of praise, which it fully deserves. "I believe," he said, "that was the first adequate statement of the new views that really attracted general attention. I had the good fortune to hear that address; and I shall not forget the delight with which I heard it, nor the mixed confusion, consternation, surprise, and wonder with which the audience listened to it."[1] Lowell says the delivery of this lecture "was an event without any former parallel in our literary annals, a scene to be always treasured in the memory for its picturesqueness and its inspiration. What crowded and breathless aisles, what windows clustering with eager heads, what enthusiasm of approval, what grim silence of foregone dissent!"[2]

In December he began a course of lectures on Human Life. There was an introductory and a concluding lecture; while the main topics were the hand, the head, the eye and ear, the heart, simplicity, prudence, heroism, and holiness. In March he delivered a remarkable lec-

[1] In his Conversations on the Transcendental Movement.
[2] My Study Windows; essay on Thoreau.

ture in Boston on War.[1] He said that war could not be avoided in savage times, for religion leads to it. It does actually forward the culture of man, but is a temporary and preparatory state. It "educates the senses, calls into action the will, perfects the physical constitution, brings men into such swift and close collision in critical moments that man measures man." It is the subject of all history, has been the principal employment of the most conspicuous men, the delight of half the world. So wide is its range, it is manifest it leads to the great and beneficent principle of self-help. "Nature implants with life the instinct of self-help, perpetual struggle to be, to resist opposition, to attain to freedom, to attain to mastery, and the security of a permanent, self-dependent being; and to each creature these objects are made so dear that it risks its life continually in the struggle for these ends." Yet war goes with coarse forms of life, and is a juvenile and temporary state. "Not only the moral sentiment, but trade, learning, and whatever makes intercourse, conspire to put it down." Trade is one of its chief antagonists. Nearly all its good has now been exhausted, and it must soon have an end.

"The eternal germination of the better has unfolded new powers, new instincts, which were really concealed under this rough and base rind. The sublime question has startled one and another happy soul in different quarters of the globe, Can not love be, as well as hate? would not love answer the same end, or even a better? Can not peace be as well as war?"

This thought is no man's invention; but it will only grow slowly, and will surely win. If man changes, his circumstances will change; and more of kindness in him will put away the implements of war.

"War and peace thus resolve themselves into a mercury of the state of cultivation. At a certain stage of his progress the man fights, if he be of a sound body and mind. At a certain high stage he makes no offensive demonstration, but is alert to repel injury, and of an unconquerable heart. At a still higher stage he comes

[1] Printed in 1849, in Miss Peabody's Æsthetic Papers.

into the region of holiness; passion has passed away from him; his warlike nature is all converted into an active medicinal principle; he sacrifices himself, and accepts with alacrity wearisome tasks of denial and charity; but, being attacked, he bears it, and turns the other cheek, as one engaged, throughout his being, no longer to the service of an individual, but to the common good of all men."

The peace policy is to gain by private conviction, by earnest love, and by increased insight.

"The cause of peace is not the cause of cowardice. If peace is sought to be defended or preserved for the safety of the luxurious and the timid, it is a sham, and the peace will be bad. War is better, and the peace will be broken. If peace is to be maintained, it must be by brave men who have come up to the same height as the hero; namely, the will to carry their hand, and stake it at any instant for their principle, but who have gone one step beyond the hero, and will not seek another man's life: men who have by their intellectual insight, or else by their moral elevation, attained such a perception of their own intrinsic worth that they do not think property or their own body a sufficient good to be saved by such dereliction of principle as treating a man like a sheep."

"If the universal cry for reform of so many inveterate abuses with which society rings; if the desire of a larger class of young men for a faith and hope, intellectual and religious, such as they have not yet found, be an omen to be trusted; if the disposition to rely more, in study and in action, on the unexplored riches of the human constitution; if the search of the sublime laws of morals and the sources of hope and trust in man, and not in books, in the present and not in the past, proceed; if the rising generation can be provoked to think it unworthy to nestle into every abomination of the past, and shall feel the generous doings of austerity and virtue, — then war has a short day, and human blood will cease to flow."

"It is of little consequence in what manner, through what organs, this purpose of mercy and holiness is affected. The proposition of the Congress of Nations is undoubtedly that at which the present fabric of our society and the present course of events do point. But the mind, once prepared for the reign of principles, will easily find modes of expressing its will. There is the highest fitness in the place and time in which this enterprise is begun. Not in an obscure corner, not in a feudal Europe, not in an antiquated appanage where no onward step can be taken without rebellion, is this seed of benevolence laid in the furrow with tears of hope; but in this broad America of God and man, where the forest is only now falling or yet to fall, and the green earth opened to the inundation of emigrant men from all quarters of oppression and guilt, — here, where not a family, not a few men, but mankind, shall say what shall be; here, we ask, Shall it be war, or shall it be peace?"

This lecture is characterized by a singular clearness of historic insight and by a genuine spirit of humanity. Emerson does rare justice to the importance of war as an element of progress, and he clearly appreciates the causes which are working its abandonment. More than all, his sense of brotherhood comes out, and his faith in the capacities of every soul. His faith in man and his lofty sense of justice were displayed in a protest against the treatment received by the Cherokee Indians during the year 1838. These Indians were compelled to move to the Indian Territory, a treaty having been made to that effect between the United States Government and a number of the Indians. The Cherokee nation did not consent to this treaty, and claimed it was not made by their authority. Nevertheless their removal was ordered. Great indignation was expressed in the Northern States at this act of injustice. A meeting was held in Concord, April 22, to take action against the outrage. Emerson stated the case to the audience, and addresses were made by the leading citizens. A memorial was largely signed, and sent to Congress. The next day Emerson addressed a letter to President Van Buren in behalf of himself and some of his friends.[1] After a statement of the facts, as they had been eagerly discussed in the newspapers, he asks if they can be true, if the public has not been misinformed in regard to them. Then he proceeds to protest against the execution of the outrage as it had been planned and ordered.

"The piety, the principle that is left in these United States,— if only its coarsest form, a regard to the speech of men, forbid us to entertain it as a fact. Such a dereliction of all faith and virtue, such a denial of justice, and such a deafness to screams for mercy, were never heard of in times of peace, and in the dealing of a nation with its own allies and wards, since the earth was made. Sir, does this government think the people of the United States are

[1] Printed in the Yeoman's Gazette of Concord, May 19, 1838, and copied into many other papers.

become savage and mad? From their mind are the sentiments of love and of a good nature wiped clear out? The soul of man, the justice, the mercy that is the heart's heart in all men from Maine to Georgia, does abhor this business.

"In speaking thus the sentiments of my neighbors and my own, perhaps I overstep the bounds of decorum. But would it not be a higher indecorum coldly to argue a matter like this? We only state the fact, that a crime is projected that confounds our understandings by its magnitude, a crime that really deprives us, as well as the Cherokees, of a country; for how could we call the conspiracy that should crush these poor Indians, our government, or the land that was cursed by their parting and dying imprecations, our country, any more? You, sir, will bring down that renowned chair in which you sit into infamy if your seal is set to this instrument of perfidy; and the name of this nation, hitherto the sweet omen of religion and liberty, will stink to the world."

When a friend afterwards urged him to print this letter among his miscellanies, he said it was only a "shriek" of indignation. It ought now to be remembered, however, when so much is trying to be done to secure justice to the Indians, who have had so little of it in any of the years since this letter was written.

In July he lectured before the literary societies of Dartmouth College on Literary Ethics,[1] and asserted that self-trust is the whole value to us of biography and history. He said we must ask the truth of the "enveloping Now," that we must cherish solitude and meditation, and that we should open the breast to all honest inquiry. He said the scholar is of importance in the world in proportion to his confidence in the attributes of the intellect. This is true because man is the measure of the world, because his soul can interpret all things, and because every human sentiment finds somewhere in nature its expression. All history, biography, and nature are of value only as they show forth to the soul what it can be and do. He then declares that all things are new, that every lesson is to be new-learned, that all truth yet awaits adequate utterance. The scholar must not wait on the past, but look into the world of the immediate present, and see what it

[1] Miscellanies, p. 149.

declares. He will not live a life of utility, but give himself to know truth and beauty, wed these, and gladly accept the sensual deprivations they impose. Solitude he must accept, also, and every deep and true human experience, if he would learn the best wisdom. The strain of upper music is heard only in action, in bearing the common burdens of life; so that "out of love and hatred, out of earnings and borrowings and lendings and losses, out of sickness and pain, out of wooing and worshiping, out of traveling and voting and watching and caring, out of disgrace and contempt, comes our tuition in the serene and beautiful laws." He rejects the dry and scholastic aim for the student, urges him to be a toiler and a learner amidst all that passes daily in the world, yet living above every lust of praise and frivolity, devoted to the things of the soul. In this address he set forth his own ideal, the purpose which has animated his own life, and which has made it so worthy of attention. Its closing paragraphs are a notable instance of pure and inspiring eloquence. It was listened to with profound attention, and was "greatly admired," said a local journal, "as the production of a rare and highly gifted mind. Seldom, if ever before, has the occasion been distinguished for so rich an intellectual treat."

His course of lectures in Boston the following winter was on the Resources of the Present Age. There were two on literature; while some of the other subjects were Private Life, Reformers, Religion, Ethics, Education. The winter of 1839–40 brought a course on Human Life. He spoke of the Laws of Love, Home, The School, Genius, The Protest, Tragedy, Comedy, Duty, Demonology.

VI.

STATING THE NEW FAITH.

THE new views had the effect to make men distrustful of the old religious forms and doctrines. Intuition became more important than bibles or great teachers. When God speaks directly to each soul, why look backward to the past revelations? These ideas made Furness regard the life of Jesus as perfectly natural, all his acts the expressions of a truly loyal nature. To Alcott they gave the conviction that the uncorrupt mind of the child has all truth in it, ready to be developed. Brownson was led to see in Christianity the natural religion of the soul. Like tendencies of thought induced Emerson to severely criticise all institutional religion, and to abandon every religious rite. He came to regard religion as a universal sentiment, which reveals all truth to each individual soul. This sentiment is awakened by perceiving the universal order of nature and by experience of its invariable laws. It leads to a sublime self-trust, and to a repudiation of all commands laid on us from the teachings of other men, unless their thought is verified in our own natures. This sentiment is an intuition, and not to be received at second hand.

When an opportunity offered he gave full expression to his views. In June, 1838, he was invited to deliver the customary address before the graduating class in the Divinity School of Harvard University. It was given on Sunday evening, July 15. Emerson made the prayer of the occasion; and Bartol speaks of it as "the short breathings of the gentle prayer, which had in it no pronouns."[1] The address stated the new

[1] Radical Problems.

thought in the most explicit words, showing clearly its relations to the doctrines of theology. It came nearer to the "center and core of things," as Alcott has said, than almost any other word which has been uttered on the subject.

It was the first full statement of Emerson's faith in moral power, and in an untrammeled religion of the spirit. "Virtue," he says, "is a sentiment and delight in the presence of certain divine laws." Those laws are not external revelations, nor are they conventionalities; they are the ordered pulse-beats of the Living All. Obedience to these laws makes the health and integrity of the soul. What we call good comes of obedience to them; and evil flows out of disobedience. The idea of law is full of power; "it is the beatitude of man." The truth can always be had by those who desire it, but each one must seek it for himself. God acts through all souls, and no one is the measure of his truth. Jesus was a great prophet, but his power has been sadly degraded by adoration of him. Christianity found a man with an intuition, and elevated the man, forgetting the universal power of that truth he taught. The personal has been dwelt on to an obnoxious extent, and the universal capacities of man have consequently been ignored. We need to trust ourselves, to hear the voice within. In the growth of true sentiments is to be found the only genuine conversion, not in any faith in a person. God is in every man, and he should be heard there. The old revelation is loved in lack of faith in the living truth, and the priest is elevated to power thereby. The office of the preacher is a great one, but only the spirit can teach. "Not any profane man, not any sensual, not any liar, not any slave can teach, but only he can give who has; he only can create who is. The man on whom the soul descends, through whom the soul speaks, alone can teach." This office is the first in the world. "It is of that reality, that it can not suffer the deduction of any falsehood. And it is my duty to say to you, that the need was never greater of a new revelation than now." Yet the office of the preacher is dying, and the church is tottering to its fall. The real work of the pulpit is not discharged; it neglects "the expression of the moral sentiment in application to the duties of life." Man is not made to feel he is an infinite soul; the life of to-day is not touched; actual experience brings no lessons. The redemption is to be sought in the soul. There is, however, too much faith in great names, too great an exaggeration of the occasional. The true preacher must "dare to love God without mediator or veil." To him fashion, custom, authority, pleasure, and money must be nothing; and he must "live with the privilege of immeasurable mind." In the midst of the defects of the church, we need more faith; but it must make its own forms, ritual, and cultus. No system can be contrived for it. The old forms are good enough, if "the breath of new life" is in them. The evils of the church are many, and need much to be put away. "The remedy to their deformity is, first, soul; and second, soul; and evermore, soul." A new life and a new faith is to be expected, that will bring fullness and power.

This discourse at once brought all to realize what the new faith was, whither it tended, what it proposed. It was warmly criticised; it was as warmly defended. The agitation it caused reached such a height that in November *The Christian Examiner* thought it necessary to make this formal renunciation of it, in behalf of the Unitarians and the Divinity School: —

> "We believe we have the best authority for saying that those notions, so far as they are intelligible, are utterly distasteful to the instructors of the school, and to Unitarian ministers generally, by whom they are esteemed to be neither good divinity nor good sense. . . . We are well convinced that the instructors of the school should hereafter guard themselves, by a right of veto on the nomination of the students, against the probability of hearing sentiments on a public and most interesting occasion, and within their own walls, altogether repugnant to their feelings, and opposed to the whole tenor of their own teachings."

On the evening of the address, Henry Ware, jun., then the most prominent professor in the school, expressed himself, in a conversation with Emerson, as favorable to what had been said; but the next day he wrote, —

"It has occurred to me, that, since I said to you last evening, I should probably assent to your unqualified statements if I could take your qualifications with them, I am bound in fairness to add, that this applies only to a portion, and not to all. With regard to some, I must confess that they appear to me more than doubtful, and their prevalence would tend to overthrow the authority and influence of Christianity. On this account I look with anxiety and no little sorrow to the course which your mind has been taking. You will excuse my saying this, which I probably never should have troubled you with, if, as I said, a proper frankness did not seem at this moment to require it. That I appreciate and rejoice in the lofty ideas and beautiful images of spiritual life which you throw out, and which stir so many souls, is what gives me a great deal more pleasure to say. I do not believe that any one has had more enjoyment from them. If I could have helped it, I would not have let you know how much I feel the abatement from the cause I referred to."[1]

In reply to this truly manly letter, so expressive of the noblest spirit, albeit showing an unnecessary fear lest the old truths should be ignored, Emerson returned this answer: —

"CONCORD, July 28, 1838.

"What you say about the discourse at Divinity College is just what I might expect from your truth and charity, combined with your known opinions. I am not a rock or a stone, as one said in the old time, and could not feel but pain in saying some things in that place and presence which I supposed would meet with dissent, and the dissent, I may say, of dear friends and benefactors of mine. Yet, as my conviction is perfect in the substantial truth of the doctrines of this discourse, and is not very new, you will see at once that it must appear very important that it be spoken; and I thought I could not pay the nobleness of my friends so mean a compliment as to suppress my opposition to their supposed views out of fear of offense. I would rather say to them, These things look thus to me; to you, otherwise. Let us say out our uttermost word; and be the all-pervading truth, as it surely will, judge between us. Meantime, I shall be admonished, by this expression of your thought, to revise with greater care the 'address' before

[1] This and the subsequent letters are published in the Life of Ware, vol. ii. p. 183, where his biographer indicates how strong was Ware's distrust of Emerson's new views, and how much evil he thought they would do.

it is printed (for the use of the class); and I heartily thank you for this renewed expression of your tried toleration and love.

"Respectfully and affectionately yours,

"R. W. E."

In the delivery of his address, Emerson left out a passage cautioning those who would follow the new method against looking on the past with contempt, and against setting up their own souls as higher standards of truth than that of Jesus! Miss Peabody relates that she was at his house when he was preparing it for the press, and read the address. When she came to this passage which had been omitted, she begged him to insert it. He reflected, and said, "No: these gentlemen have committed themselves against what I did read; and it would not be courteous or fair to spring upon them this passage now, which would convict them of an unwarrented inference." In relating this deeply interesting incident,[1] Miss Peabody adds, "I thought this an extreme of gentlemanliness, but saw that Mr. Emerson's aim was nothing less than to induce others to look for the truth for themselves, and not to prove that *he* had found it. He was not writing for victory for himself, but for truth's sake. If he kept to the truth in what he did publish, that must draw the whole truth after it, as he said, and in due time refute all false inferences." It is greatly to be regretted now that this omitted passage was not inserted; but not because, as Miss Peabody supposes, it would have prevented an excess of individualism. Even Emerson's name could not have stayed the tendencies of thought. It would have been shown, however, that he appreciated the historic side of religion, and the social nature of all true worship. That he fully realized the folly of making concessions in regard to a great principle, is shown in another incident related by Miss Peabody. While correcting the proof-sheets of the address, he read to Mrs. Emerson and Miss Peabody the paragraph in which he speaks of the first defect of historical Christianity, that of dwelling "with

[1] Reminiscences of William Ellery Channing, by Miss E. P. Peabody; a very interesting book.

noxious exaggeration about the *person* of Jesus," and by which "the friend of man is made the injurer of man." He said to them, "How does that strike your Hebrew souls?" Miss Peabody replied, "I like it; but put a large F to designate Jesus as the Friend of souls." After a moment's thought, he replied, "No: directly I put that large F in they will all go to sleep."

Sept. 23 Ware preached a sermon before the Divinity School on The Personality of God, which was at once printed. It was regarded as a reply to Emerson, and offers six objections to the positions supposed to be maintained by him: that conscious being is the greatest fact known to us; that the views the preacher is combating amount to a virtual denial of God; that to exclude personality is to destroy the object of worship; that the sense of responsibility is removed by loss of faith in personality; that these new notions are opposed to the Bible, and that they destroy the possibility of a revelation. He pleads for a Father to love and care for us, and says, "The idea of personality must be added to that of natural and moral perfection, in order to the full definition of Christianity." The full meaning of his sermon comes out in these words: —

> "If the material universe rests on the laws of attraction, affinity, heat, motion, still all of them together are no Deity; if the moral universe is founded on the principles of righteousness, truth, love, neither are these the Deity. There must be some Being to put in action these principles, to exercise these attributes. To call the principles and the attributes *God*, is to violate the established use of language, and to confound the common apprehensions of mankind. It is in vain to hope by so doing to escape the charge of atheism. There is no other atheism conceivable. There is a personal God, or there is none."

That this sermon was understood to be aimed at Emerson is distinctly stated in *The Christian Examiner*, where the address is again spoken of as "the lucubrations of an individual who has no connection with the school whatever." The sermon, it is stated, "will tend to disabuse the minds of many respecting the true character and tendency of a set of newly broached fancies, which, deceived by the high-sounding pretensions of their proclaimers, they may have thought were about to quicken and reform the world."

Ware sent a copy of his sermon to Emerson, accompanied with this letter: —

"CAMBRIDGE, Oct. 3, 1838.

"MY DEAR SIR, — By this mail you will probably receive a copy of a sermon which I have just printed, and which I am unwilling should fall into your hands without a word from myself accompanying it. It has been regarded as controverting some positions taken by you at various times, and was, indeed, written partly with a view to them. But I am anxious to have it understood, that, as I am not perfectly aware of the precise nature of your opinions on the subject of the discourse, nor upon exactly what speculations they are grounded, I do not, therefore, pretend especially to enter the lists with them, but rather to give my own views of an important subject, and of the evils which seem to be attendant on a rejection of the established opinions. I hope that I have not argued unfairly; and if I assail positions, or reply to arguments which are none of yours, I am solicitous that nobody should persuade you that I suppose them to be yours; since I do not know by what arguments the doctrine that 'the soul knows no persons' is justified to your mind.

"To say this, is the chief purpose of my writing; and I wish to add, that it is a long time since I have been earnestly persuaded that men are suffering from want of sufficiently realizing the fact of the Divine Person. I used to perceive it, as I thought, when I was a minister in Boston, in talking with my people, and to refer to this cause much of the lifelessness of the religious character. I have seen evils from the same cause among young men, since I have been where I am, and have been prompted to think much of the question how they should be removed. When, therefore, I was called to discourse at length on the Divine Being in a series of college sermons, it naturally occurred to me to give prominence to this point, the rather as it was one of those to which attention had been recently drawn, and about which a strong interest was felt.

"I confess that I esteem it particularly unhappy to be thus brought into a sort of public opposition to you, for I have a thousand feelings which draw me toward you; but my situation, and the circumstances of the times, render it unavoidable; and both you and I understand that we are to act on the maxim, '*Amicus Plato, amicus Socrates, sed magis amica Veritas.*' (I believe I quote right.) We would gladly agree with all our friends; but that being impossible, and it being impossible also to *choose* which of them we will differ from, we must submit to the common lot of thinkers, and make up in love of heart what we want in unity of judgment. But I am growing prosy, so I break off.

"Yours very truly,

"H. WARE, Jun."

To this admirable letter Emerson returned the following characteristic reply:—

"CONCORD, Oct. 8, 1838.

"MY DEAR SIR,—I ought sooner to have acknowledged your kind letter of last week, and the sermon it accompanied. The letter was right manly and noble. The sermon, too, I have read with attention. If it assails any doctrine of mine,—perhaps I am not so quick to see it as writers generally,—certainly I did not feel any disposition to depart from my habitual contentment, that you should say your thought, whilst I say mine. I believe I must tell you what I think of my new position. It strikes me very oddly that good and wise men at Cambridge and Boston should think of raising me into an object of criticism. I have always been—from my very incapacity of methodical writing—"a chartered libertine," free to worship and free to rail,—lucky when I could make myself understood, but never esteemed near enough to the institutions and mind of society to deserve the notice of the masters of literature and religion. I have appreciated fully the advantages of my position, for I well know that there is no scholar less willing or less able to be a polemic. I could not give account of myself if challenged. I could not possibly give you one of the 'arguments' you cruelly hint at, on which any doctrine of mine stands; for I do not know what arguments mean in reference to any expression of a thought. I delight in telling what I think; but if you ask me how I dare say so, or why it is so, I am the most helpless of mortal men. I do not even see that either of these questions admits of an answer. So that, in the present droll posture of my affairs, when I see myself suddenly raised into the importance of a heretic, I am very uneasy when I advert to the supposed duties of such a personage, who is to make good his thesis against all comers.

"I certainly shall do no such thing. I shall read what you and other good men write, as I have always done,—glad when you speak my thoughts, and skipping the page which has nothing for me. I shall go on just as before, seeing whatever I can, and telling what I see, and, I suppose, with the same fortune that has hitherto attended me,—the joy of finding that my abler and better brothers who work with the sympathy of society, loving and beloved, do now and then unexpectedly confirm my perceptions, and find my nonsense is only their own thought in motley.

"And so I am, your affectionate servant,

"R. W. EMERSON."

This letter is full of interest, as showing Emerson's methods, how his mind acts, and the striking modesty of the man. Its perfect candor gives it a great charm; for few writers would reveal, as he does, all the secrets of their thought. To his critic he opens confidentially all his own weak places, and himself reveals the most serious argument which could be raised against his opinions. His entire willingness to let the truth vindicate itself is most admirable. With such themes as his, there is little likely to be gained by mere debate; for each mind can only give expression to what appears in its own mental experience. Dogmatic arguments do no good here; only the simple search for truth. It may well be questioned whether Emerson's method best answers in securing that truth for which we seek; but his spirit is, beyond all criticism, earnest, faithful, and single-eyed.

The controversy started by Emerson's address did not soon subside. The next year, July 19, Andrews Norton gave an address before the alumni of the Divinity School, on The Latest Form of Infidelity. He said the eighteenth-century disbelief has lost its power, but infidelity has assumed another and a more subtle form. It follows "the celebrated atheist Spinoza, and, while claiming to be Christian, denies Christianity in a denial of its miracles." He then entered into a long defense of miracles, claiming that the whole life of Christ must be regarded as miraculous. That he had a divine commission can only be proved by "miraculous displays of God's power," while there is nothing left if this is denied. To the demand of the transcendentalists for some more positive evidence for the truths of religion than those afforded by history, he says there can be no intuition, no direct perception, no metaphysical certainty, outside of historical evidences. There is "no absolute certainty beyond the limit of momentary consciousness, — a certainty that vanishes the moment it exists, and is lost in the region of metaphysical doubt." Two lengthy notes were appended to this address, when published, directed against German thought. The whole transcendental movement was sharply attacked, and in the most decisive manner. Replies to this address appeared from George Ripley, Brownson, Theophilus Parsons, and J. F. Clarke. Emerson's address became the subject of frequent sermons, and the air was full of pamphlets and newspaper articles. The Unitarian ministers debated whether Emerson was a Christian; some said he was not; some that he was an atheist; while others earnestly defended him. By some of the "Friends of Progress," when his attitude was discussed, he was pronounced a pantheist, denying the personality of God; while his views were regarded as dangerous.

Emerson did not stand alone at this time. He had many zealous friends and fellow-believers. Parker heard his address, was roused by it to enthusiasm, and recorded in his diary his purpose of writing at once "the long meditated sermons on the state of the church and the duties of these times." "So beautiful, so just, so true, and terribly sublime," says Parker, "was his picture of the faults of the church in its present condition." In writing to a friend, he said,—

"It was the noblest of all his performances; a little exaggerated, with some philosophical untruths, it seemed to me; but the noblest, the most inspiring strain I ever listened to."

Miss Elizabeth Peabody was present also, and thought "there never before had been a discourse there that so justified the foundation principle of the Divinity School, as it was stated by Dr. Channing in his dedication sermon;" and Channing could himself discover no difference between his sermon and Emerson's address. Channing said that Ware, in his sermon on the personality of God, was "fighting a shadow; for Mr. Emerson expressly says, and makes a great point of it, that God is *alive*, not *dead;* and would have the gospel narrative left to make its own impression of an indwelling life, like the growing grass."[1] The impression Emerson made upon his friends may be seen from these words, written in September, by Convers Francis:—

"Spent the night at Mr. Emerson's. When we were alone he talked of his discourse at the Divinity School, and of the obloquy it had drawn upon him. He is perfectly quiet amid the storm.

[1] Miss E. P. Peabody's Reminiscences of William Ellery Channing, p. 379.

To my objections and remarks he gave the most cordial replies, though we could not agree on some points. The more I see of this beautiful spirit, the more I revere and love him. Such a calm, steady, simple soul, always looking for truth, and living in wisdom and in love for man and goodness, I have never met. Mr. Emerson is not one whose vocation it is to state processes of argument; he is a seer who reports in sweet and significant words what he sees. He looks into the infinite of truth, and reveals what there passes before his vision. If you see it as he does, you will recognize him as a gifted teacher; if not, there is little or nothing to be said about it. But do not brand him with the names of visionary, or fanatic, or pretender; he is no such thing. He is a true, godful man; though in his love for the ideal he disregards too much the actual."

In the midst of all this agitation Emerson remained perfectly self-possessed, quietly pursuing his studies, and making no reply to those who opposed his opinions. What he had to say he did not hesitate to utter with all necessary emphasis, but he sought in no manner whatever to defend his own ideas. He left them to make their own way, to enforce their own worth and importance. His letter to Ware amply indicates his acceptance of intuition as the only genuine method of truth. His attitude was, that the truth is communicated to the mind from its unity with the Universal Mind, and can not be argued about or added to by reasoning. This oneness of the individual mind with Universal Mind, as he stated it, gave rise to the conception that he was a pantheist. It is evident, however, that such names did not occur to him, and that he followed out sincerely the conclusions of a truly spiritual conception of life and nature.

The controversy which followed his address had the effect of finally separating him from the Unitarians and of causing him to abandon the pulpit. He saw how strongly the Unitarians were wedded to the old forms, and he found himself more and more alienated from them. He could not continue to preach amidst controversy and objection; so he quietly withdrew, to do his work in a manner of his own.

VII.

THE DIAL.

IN his Historical Notes of American Life and Letters, Emerson says "the only result" of the club organized by Dr. Channing "was to initiate the little quarterly called *The Dial*." Concerning that journal he says, "A modest quarterly journal called *The Dial*, under the editorship of Margaret Fuller, enjoyed its obscurity for four years, when it ended. Its papers were the contribution and work of friendship among a narrow circle of writers. Perhaps its writers were also its chief readers. But it had some noble papers; perhaps the best of Margaret Fuller's. It had some numbers highly important, because they contained papers by Theodore Parker." *The Dial* grew out of a desire for a medium of communication among those interested in the ideas expressed in the Transcendental Club. To afford a means of expression to these thinkers was its main object. It was conducted in a spirit of friendship and sympathy far more than of critical regard for the literary value of what it published. In one number the editor said it had been "almost as much a journal of friendship as of literature and morals." Fresh, aspiring minds were invited to its pages rather than those learned and critical. Every page was fragrant with idealism, and echoed the hopes of the time.

The establishment of such a journal was first discussed in a meeting of the club held in the house of Rev. C. A. Bartol, in 1839. At that meeting Parker, Bartol, Hedge, Margaret Fuller, Ripley, Alcott, and W. H. Channing were present; and these persons, with Emerson, constituted the movers in the new project.

At this or a subsequent meeting, when the name was discussed, Alcott mentioned some extracts from his diary he had just made, and to which he had given the title of The Dial. He suggested this name for the new journal, and it was unanimously accepted as expressive of its purpose and spirit.

The Dial was discussed for many months at the meetings of the club, no one being willing to assume the editorship of the projected periodical. After much solicitation, Margaret Fuller consented to undertake what Emerson calls this "private and friendly service." In March, 1840, she writes very doubtingly about the new enterprise, declaring that she herself, while she had a great deal written, had "scarce a word pertinent to the place or time." She writes thus of the plans to be followed: —

"A perfectly free organ is to be offered for the expression of individual thought and character. There are no party measures to be carried, no particular standard to be set up. A fair, calm tone, a recognition of universal principles, will, I hope, pervade the essays in every form. I trust there will be a spirit neither of dogmatism nor of compromise, and that this journal will aim, not at leading public opinion, but at stimulating each man to judge for himself, and to think more deeply and more nobly, by letting him see how some minds are kept alive by a wise self-trust. We must not be sanguine as to the amount of talent which will be brought to bear on this publication. All concerned are rather indifferent, and there is no great promise for the present. We can not show high culture, and I doubt about vigorous thought. But we shall manifest free action as far as it goes, and a high aim. It were much if a periodical could be kept open, not to accomplish any outward object, but merely to afford an avenue for what of liberal and calm thought might be originated among us by the wants of individual minds."

Perhaps no journal was ever undertaken more diffidently than was *The Dial* by those interested in it. In April Margaret Fuller again wrote that the project went on "pretty well, but doubtless people will be disappointed." She proposed herself only to "hazard a few critical remarks, or an unpretending chalk-sketch now and then." The first number came out in July,

1840, as a quarterly Magazine for Literature, Philosophy, and Religion. The "prospectus" thus set forth its aims:—

"The purpose of this work is to furnish a medium for the freest expression of thought on the questions which interest earnest minds in every community.

"It aims at the discussion of principles rather than at the promotion of measures; and, while it will not fail to examine the ideas which impel the leading movements of the present day, it will maintain an independent position in regard to them.

"The pages of this journal will be filled by contributors who possess little in common but the love of intellectual freedom and the hope of social progress; who are united by sympathy of spirit, not by agreement in speculation; whose faith is in Divine Providence rather than in human prescription; whose hearts are more in the future than in the past, and who trust the living soul rather than the dead letter. It will endeavor to promote the constant evolution of truth, not the petrifaction of opinion.

"Its contents will embrace a wide and varied range of subjects; and, combining the characteristics of a magazine and review, it may present something, both for those who read for instruction and those who search for amusement.

"The general design and character of the work may be understood from the above brief statement. It may be proper to add, that in literature it will strive to exercise a just and catholic criticism, and to recognize every sincere production of genius. In philosophy it will attempt the reconciliation of the universal instincts of humanity with the largest conclusions of reason; and in religion it will reverently seek to discern the presence of God in nature, in history, and in the soul of man."

Each number contained one hundred and thirty-six octavo pages; and, after the first number, there was a "record of the months," and "literary intelligence."[1] As a fair specimen of the whole work, the table of contents of the first number may be given, with the names of the authors, so far as ascertained.

[1] The Dial was at first published by Weeks, Jordan, & Co., 121 Washington Street, at three dollars a year. It seems to have been so poorly patronized as to cause a frequent change of publishers; for the names of W. H. S. Jordan, Jordan & Co., E. P. Peabody, and James Munroe & Co., successively appear in that capacity.

No. I.

The spirit and purpose of *The Dial* is best shown in the introductory article by Emerson. It is here reprinted in full, as indicating the hopes which the new thought had created: —

"THE EDITORS TO THE READER.

"We invite the attention of our countrymen to a new design. Probably not quite unexpected or unannounced will our journal appear, though small pains have been taken to secure its welcome. Those who have immediately acted in editing the present number can not accuse themselves of any unbecoming forwardness in their undertaking, but rather of a backwardness, when they remember how often in many private circles the work was projected, how eagerly desired, and only postponed because no individual volunteered to combine and concentrate the free-will offerings of many co-operators. With some reluctance the present conductors of this work have yielded themselves to the wishes of their friends, finding something sacred and not to be withstood in the importunity which urged the production of a journal in a new spirit.

"As they have not proposed themselves to the work, neither can they lay any the least claim to an option or determination of the spirit in which it is conceived, or to what is peculiar in the design. In that respect, they have obeyed, though with great joy, the strong current of thought and feeling, which, for a few years past, has led many sincere persons in New England to make new demands on literature, and to reprobate that rigor of our conventions of religion and education which is turning us to stone, which renounces hope, which looks only backward, which asks only such a future as the past, which suspects improvement, and holds nothing so much in horror as new views and the dreams of youth.

"With these terrors, the conductors of the present journal have nothing to do, — not even so much as a word of reproach to waste. They know that there is a portion of the youth and of the adult population of this country who have not shared them; who have, in secret or in public, paid their vows to truth and freedom; who love reality too well to care for names; and who live by a faith too earnest and profound to suffer them to doubt the eternity of its object, or to shake themselves free from its authority. Under the fictions and customs which occupied others, these have explored the Necessary, the Plain, the True, the Human, and so gain a vantage-ground which commands the history of the past and present.

"No one can converse much with different classes of society in New England without remarking the progress of a revolution. Those who share in it have no external organization, no badge, no creed, no name. They do not vote, or print, or even meet together. They do not know each other's faces or names. They are united only in a common love of truth, and love of its work. They are of all conditions and constitutions. Of these acolytes, if some are happily born and well bred, many are, no doubt, ill dressed, ill placed, ill made, with as many scars of hereditary vice as other men. Without pomp, without trumpet, in lonely and obscure places, in solitude, in servitude, in compunctions and privations, trudging beside the team in the dusty road, or drudging a hireling in other men's cornfields, schoolmasters who teach a few children rudiments for a pittance, ministers of small parishes of the obscurer sects, lone women in dependent condition, matrons and young maidens, rich and poor, beautiful and hard-favored, without concert or proclamation of any kind, they have silently given in their several adherence to a new hope, and in all companies do signify a greater trust in the nature and resources of man than the laws or the popular opinions will well allow.

"This spirit of the time is felt by every individual with some difference, — to each one casting its light upon the objects nearest to his temper and habits of thought: to one, coming in the form of special reforms in the state; to another, in modifications of the various callings of men, and the customs of business; to a third, opening a new scope for literature and art; to a fourth, in philosophical insight; to a fifth, in the vast solitudes of prayer. It is in every form a protest against usage, and a search for principles. In all its movements it is peaceable, and in the very lowest marked with a triumphant success. Of course it rouses the opposition of all which it judges and condemns; but it is too confident in its tone to comprehend an objection, and so builds no outworks for possible defense against contingent enemies. It has the step of Fate, and goes on existing like an oak or a river, — because it must.

"In literature this influence appears not yet in new books so much as in the higher tone of criticism. The antidote to all narrowness is the comparison of the record with nature, which at once shames the record, and stimulates to new attempts. Whilst we look at this, we wonder how any book has been thought worthy to be preserved. There is somewhat in all life untranslatable into language. He who keeps his eye on that will write better than others, and think less of his writing and of all writing. Every thought has a certain imprisoning, as well as uplifting quality, and, in proportion to its energy on the will, refuses to become an object of intellectual contemplation. Thus, what is great usually slips through our fingers; and it seems wonderful how a lifelike word ever comes to be written. If our journal share the impulses of the time, it can not now prescribe its own course. It can not foretell in orderly propositions what it shall attempt. All criticism should be poetic, unpredictable; superseding, as every new thought does, all foregone thoughts, and making a new light on the whole world. Its brow is not wrinkled with circumspection, but serene, cheerful, adoring. It has all things to say, and no less than all the world for its final audience.

"Our plan embraces much more than criticism; were it not so, our criticism would be naught. Every thing noble is directed on life, and this is. We do not wish to say pretty or curious things, or to reiterate a few propositions in varied forms, but, if we can, to give expression to that spirit which lifts men to a higher platform, restores to them the religious sentiment, brings them worthy aims and pure pleasures, purges the inward eye, makes life less desultory, and, through raising man to the level of nature, takes away its melancholy from the landscape, and reconciles the practical with the speculative powers.

"But perhaps we are telling our little story too gravely. There are always great arguments at hand for a true action, even for the writing of a few pages. There is nothing but seems near it, and prompts it, — the sphere in the ecliptic, the sap in the apple-tree, — every fact, every appearance, seem to persuade to it.

"Our means correspond with the ends we have indicated. As we wish, not to multiply books, but to report life, our resources are not so much the pens of practiced writers, as the discourse of the living, and the portfolios which friendship has opened to us. From the beautiful recesses of private thought; from the experience and hope of spirits which are withdrawing from all old forms, and seeking in all that is new somewhat to meet their inappeasable longings; from the secret confession of genius afraid to trust itself to aught but sympathy; from the conversation of fervid and mystical pietists; from tear-stained diaries of sorrow and passion; from the manuscripts of young poets; and from the records of youthful taste commenting on old works of art, — we hope to draw thoughts and feelings which, being alive, can impart life.

"And so with diligent hands and good intent we set down our *Dial* on the earth. We wish it may resemble that instrument in its celebrated happiness, that of measuring no hours but those of sunshine. Let it be one cheerful rational voice amidst the din of mourners and polemics. Or, to abide by our chosen image, let it be such a dial, not as the dead face of a clock, — hardly, even, such as the gnomon in a garden, — but rather such a Dial as is the Garden itself in whose leaves and flowers and fruits the suddenly awakened sleeper is instantly apprised, not what part of dead time, but what state of life and growth, is now arrived and arriving."

As Emerson suggests, *The Dial* originated in the hopes of the young. Alcott was the only one of its projectors and contributors who had reached the age of forty when the first number appeared. Ripley was thirty-eight; Emerson, thirty-seven; and Hedge, thirty five. Margaret Fuller, Parker, W. H. Channing, and Clarke were thirty; Bartol, Cranch, and Dwight, twenty-seven; while Thoreau was but twenty-three, and W. E. Channing twenty-two.

A chief contributor to *The Dial*, especially during the first two years, was Margaret Fuller, who furnished papers on Critics, Goethe, the Great Composers, Klopstock and Meta, Festus, and a few other sketches. In Parker's contributions is to be found some of his best work. He wrote on German Literature, the Pharisees, Primitive Christianity, and Dr. Follen. Other subjects were, Truth against the World, Thoughts on Theology, Sermon for the Day, Thoughts on Labor, the Hollis-street Council. Ripley reviewed Brownson, and furnished the "records of the months." Dwight gave accounts of concerts, and wrote on the Religion of Beauty, and Ideals of Every-Day Life. Cranch helped to crowd all the numbers with poetry, and added a few prose contributions. Hedge contributed a valuable paper on the Art of Life the Scholar's Calling, and a fine poem, Questionings. Clarke sent a poem on crossing the Alleghanies, and a letter about George Keats. Alcott furnished some Orphic Sayings, and Days from a Diary. Thoreau wrote about the Natural History of Massachusetts, and translated Pindar, as well as the Prometheus Bound of Æschylus. In the first volume were three of his poems, in the second two, in the third sixteen, and in the fourth five. In one number appeared three sonnets by Lowell, and Charles A. Dana was a frequent poetical contributor. Henry Tuckerman furnished a paper on Music, Mrs. George Ripley one on Woman, and Elizabeth Peabody two on Christ's Idea of Society. Beside these, there were several other writers, but perhaps none known to fame.

The Dial was the means of introducing Thoreau to the public. He furnished a poem to the first number, and scarcely a number followed that did not contain one or more contributions from his pen. His first prose production given to the public, reprinted as the first paper of the *Excursions*, was in the third volume; and in the fourth volume appeared his Walk in Winter. Thoreau owed to Emerson his introduction to literature, who seems to have given him every encouragement. In the last volume appeared a remarkable article by Margaret Fuller, entitled The Great Lawsuit; Man *versus* Men — Woman *versus* Women. It was afterwards revised and enlarged, and issued in book-form as *Woman in the Nineteenth Century*. It is one of the best works yet printed on the opportunities and duties of women. The Notes from the Journal of a Scholar were by Charles Emerson. These were printed in the first volume and in the last. They are full of subtle power, and gave great promise of better things. In the first number also appeared a poem by Edward Bliss Emerson. It was written while going out of Boston Harbor, on the voyage from which the author never returned. It is called The Last Farewell, and was reprinted in Emerson's *May-Day*.

During the two years Margaret Fuller edited *The Dial* she was assisted by George Ripley and R. W. Emerson. Owing to the state of her health, she withdrew from it at the end of the second year; and Emerson became the sole editor. Under his management its character changed considerably, becoming less literary and more reformatory. He wrote on Fourierism and the Socialists, showing a hearty sympathy with their efforts. In this first number, edited by him, is a very interesting account of the Chardon-street and Bible Conventions; and in the second number he writes with enthusiasm of an English reformer, Greaves, a sort of second Alcott. The first number of the third volume also begins a series of selections from the great bibles of the world, made by Emerson, Thoreau, and others. Probably this was the first effort to bring to the notice of Americans the wisdom and the beauties of other scriptures than those of the Hebrews and Christians. It was a most notable indication of the spirit and temper of Emerson's thought. The first selection is introduced with these words: —

> "Each nation has its bible, more or less pure: none has yet been willing or able in a wise and devout spirit to collate its own with those of other nations, and, sinking the civil-historical and the ritual portions, to bring together the grand expressions of the moral sentiment in different ages and races, the rules for the guidance of life, the bursts of piety and of abandonment to the Invisible and Eternal, — a work inevitable sooner or later, and which, we hope, is to be done by religion and not by literature."

Likewise in this number is an article on Prayers, consisting mainly of several remarkable specimens of this kind of literature. It was written by Emerson,[1]

[1] This article was found among Thoreau's papers after his death, in his own handwriting, and was printed by his sister in his Anti-Slavery and Reform Papers. Thoreau was the author of the poetical prayer in this article, beginning with the words, —

> "Great God, I ask thee for no meaner pelf
> Than that I may not disappoint myself."

It may also be noted here, on the authority of Mr. Alcott, that Thoreau, in Emerson's absence, was the editor of No. 3 of the third volume of The Dial.

and gives broad hint of his deep sympathy with every true form of the spirit of devotion and faith. He introduces the selections he makes with these words: —

"Pythagoras said that the time when men are honestest, is when they present themselves before the gods. If we can overhear the prayer, we shall know the man. But prayers are not made to be overheard, or to be printed; so that we seldom have the prayer otherwise than it can be inferred from the man and his fortunes, which are the answer to the prayer, and always accord with it. Yet there are scattered about in the earth a few records of these devout hours, which it would edify us to read, could they be collected in a more catholic spirit than the wretched and repulsive volumes which usurp that name. Let us not have the prayers of one sect, nor of the Christian church, but of men in all ages and religions, who have prayed well. The prayer of Jesus is, as it deserves, become a form for the human race."

Emerson's three Lectures on the Times, and those on Man the Reformer, and the Young American, were republished from *The Dial* in his *Miscellanies*. The Thoughts on Art, in the third number of the first volume, is the essay on Art in *Society and Solitude*. An essay on The Comic, in the fourth volume, appears in *Letters and Social Aims*, after more than thirty years. In the same volume is an essay on The Tragic, which is probably from his pen; while the short piece, bearing the title of Tantalus, was incorporated into the essay on Nature, in the second series of *Essays*. The poem in the second volume, The Future is Better than the Past, has often been reprinted as Emerson's, and has found its way into several hymn-books; but it was written by one of his brothers. Papers on Walter Savage Landor, Thoughts on Modern Literature, The Senses and the Soul, Europe and European Books, have never been reprinted. Some of his very best words about books are contained in the essay on modern literature. He regards life as of the main importance, however, and books only as secondary. A true literature will do no more than to record necessary laws; but when we trust to the books, and not to that from whence they come, they do us injury. "We must learn to judge books by absolute standards. When we are aroused to a life in ourselves, these traditional splendors of letters grow very pale and cold." He says that "over every true poem lingers a certain wild beauty, immeasurable; a happiness lightsome and delicious fills the heart and brain, — as they say, every man walks environed by his proper atmosphere, extending to some distance around him." The closing paragraphs of this essay are among the most eloquent he has ever written: —

"The Doctrine of the Life of Man established after the truth through all his faculties, — this is the thought which the literature of this hour meditates and labors to say. This is that which tunes the tongue and fires the eye and sits in the silence of the youth. Verily, it will not long want articulate and melodious expression. There is nothing in the heart but comes presently to the lips. The very depth of the sentiment, which is the author of all the cutaneous life we see, is guaranty for the riches of science and of song in the age to come. He who doubts whether this age or this country can yield any contribution to the literature of the world, only betrays his own blindness to the necessities of the human soul. Has the power of poetry ceased, or the need? Have the eyes ceased to see that which they would have, and which they have not? Have they ceased to see other eyes? Are there no lonely, anxious, wondering children who must tell their tale? Are we not evermore whipped by thoughts? The heart beats in this age as of old, and the passions are busy as ever. Nature has not lost one ringlet of her beauty, one impulse of resistance and valor. From the necessity of loving, none are exempt; and he that loves must utter his desires. A charm as radiant as beauty ever beamed, a love that fainteth at the sight of its object, is new to-day.

"Man is not so far lost but that he suffers ever the great discontent, which is the elegy of his loss and the prediction of his recovery. In the gay saloon he laments that these figures are not what Raphael and Guercino painted. Withered though he stand, and trifler though he be, the august spirit of the world looks out from his eyes. In his heart he knows the ache of spiritual pain, and his thought can animate the sea and land. What, then, shall hinder the genius of the time from speaking its thought? It can not be silent if it would. It will write in a higher spirit, and a wider knowledge, and with a grander practical aim, than ever yet guided the pen of poet. It will write the annals of a changed world, and record the descent of principles into practice, of love into government, of love into trade. It will describe the new heroic life of man, the now unbelieved possibility of simple living, and of clean and noble relations with men. Religion will bind again these that were sometimes frivolous, customary, enemies, skeptics, self-seekers, into a joyous reverence for the circumambient Whole, and that which was ecstasy shall become daily bread."

In the fourth volume he wrote of Carlyle's *Past and Present*, and says it is a political tract with which we have nothing to compare since Milton and Burke. "Obviously, he says, it is the book of a powerful and accomplished thinker;" and "it is such an appeal to the conscience and honor of England as can not be forgotten, or be feigned to be forgotten."

> "When the political aspects are so calamitous that the sympathies of the man overpower the habits of the poet, a higher than literary inspiration may succor him. It is a costly proof of character, that the most renowned scholar of England should take his reputation in his hand, and should descend into the ring; and he has added to his love whatever honor his opinions may forfeit. To atone for this departure from the vows of the scholar and his eternal duties, to this secular charity, we have at least this gain, that here is a message which those to whom it was addressed can not choose but hear."

He says that "Carlyle is the first domestication of the modern system with its infinity of details into style." All the vast and multifarious movements of our present civilization are best represented in Carlyle; for "London and Europe tunneled, graded, corn-lawed, with trade-nobility, and East and West Indies for dependencies; and America, with the Rocky Hills in the horizon, have never before been conquered in literature." Of the faults in the book he writes these words: —

> "We may easily fail in expressing the general objection which we feel. It appears to us as a certain disproportion in the picture, caused by the obtrusion of the whims of the painter. In this work, as in his former labors, Mr. Carlyle reminds us of a sick giant. His humors are expressed with so much force of constitution that his fancies are more attractive and more credible than the sanity of duller men. But the habitual exaggeration of the tone wearies whilst it stimulates. It is felt to be so much deduction from the universality of the picture. It is not serene sunshine, but every thing is seen in lurid stormlights. Every object attitudinizes, to the very mountains, and stars almost, under the refractions of this wonderful humorist; and instead of the common earth and sky, we have a Martin's Creation or Judgment Day."

Emerson was also a frequent contributor of poetry to *The Dial*. Many of his very best pieces first appeared in its pages. He there printed The Problem, Woodnotes, The Sphinx, Saadi, To Rhea, Ode to Beauty, and The Visit. His other poetical contributions were Painting and Sculpture, Fate, Fact, Holidays, Eros, The Times, Forbearance, The Amulet, To Eva, Suum Cuique, and The Park.

The Dial put forth a good deal of vaporing and sentimentalism. Much that was crude went into its pages; and some of its writers lacked solid regard for facts and realities. Yet it was a most notable effort toward a truer life and a fresher expression of thought. Its pages betray a purpose and a hope no other American review has yet shown, and its influence has doubtless been very great. Emerson has written of it with sound sense,[1] giving interesting hints of its purpose. He says that "when it began, it concentrated a good deal of hope and affection."

"It had its origin in a club of speculative students, who found the air in America getting a little too close and stagnant; and the agitation had, perhaps, the fault of being too secondary and bookish in its origin, or caught, not from primary instincts, but from English, and still more from German, books. The journal was commenced with much hope, and liberal promises of many co-operators. But the workmen of sufficient culture for a poetical and philosophical magazine were too few; and as the pages were filled by unpaid contributors, each of whom had, according to the usage and necessity of this country, some paying employment, the journal did not get his best work, but his second best. Its scattered writers had not digested their theories into a distinct dogma, still less into a practical measure which the public could grasp; and the magazine was so eclectic and miscellaneous that each of its readers and writers valued only a small portion of it. For these reasons it never had a large circulation, and it was discontinued after four years. But *The Dial* betrayed, through all its juvenility, timidity, and conventional rubbish, some sparks of the true love and hope, and of the piety to spiritual law, which had moved its friends and founders; and it was received by its early subscribers with almost a religious welcome. Many years after it was brought to a close, Margaret was surprised in England by very warm testimony to its merits; and in 1848 the writer of these pages found it holding the same affectionate place in many a private book-shelf in England and Scotland which it had secured at home. Good or bad, it cost a good deal of precious labor from those who served it, and from

[1] Memoirs of Margaret Fuller.

Margaret most of all. As editor, she received a compensation for the first years, which was intended to be two hundred dollars per annum, but which, I fear, never reached that amount.

"But it made no difference to her exertion. She put so much heart into it that she bravely undertook to open, in *The Dial*, the subjects which most attracted her; and she treated, in turn, Goethe and Beethoven, the Rhine and the Romaic Ballads, the Poems of John Sterling, and several pieces of sentiment, with a spirit which spared no labor; and when the hard conditions of journalism held her to an inevitable day, she submitted to jeopardizing a long-cherished subject by treating it in the crude and forced article for the month. I remember, after she had been compelled by ill-health to relinquish the journal into my hands, my grateful wonder at the facility with which she assumed the preparation of laborious articles that might have daunted the most practiced scribe."

He has always spoken of it in the same modest manner, giving to others whatever honor and fame the quarterly has produced. In fact, he was its chief contributor, its trusted adviser, from the first; and he did far more than any other to give it whatever of value and influence it had. With all its vaporing, it was fresh, earnest, and original in purpose. It was the first American periodical to assume a character and aim of its own. However many its deficiencies, spite of all the sport it gave the critics, its influence was wholesome and vigorous. It quickened thought, gave its writers freedom of expression, and greatly stimulated originality. The school of writers which it formed and brought before the public has been the most productive and helpful we have yet seen in this country. Such has been the value of this short-lived quarterly, it already has a fame and honor quite its own, which are likely to increase in the future.

VIII.

BROOK FARM AND OTHER REFORMS.

EMERSON was greatly interested by the reformatory movements of this period. It was a time of many projects for the reformation of the world. Beside the agitation caused by the transcendental movement, there was a wide ferment of thought concerning the social and educational reformation of mankind. Horace Mann was putting the common-school system into active operation, and normal schools were being established for the first time. The temperance reform was attracting attention, and Pierpont went out of the pulpit because the people were not ready to become total abstainers. Abner Kneeland was preaching materialism, while Ripley and Parker were teaching naturalism in religion. Conventions of all kinds were being held, newspapers advocating all sorts of reforms and new ideas appeared. Among these was the *Non-Resistant*, begun in Boston in 1839, and edited by Garrison, Edmund Quincy, and Mrs. Chapman. In 1838 George Combe came to this country, and unbounded expectations were entertained in regard to phrenology. At about the same time spiritualism began to claim attention; and the keenest interest was taken in mesmerism, clairvoyance, and all kindred subjects. Homœopathy, hydropathy, the Graham diet, and the Thompsonian cure, all came up for their share in the regeneration of the race. The first national temperance convention was held in 1833, and in 1838 a prohibitory law was passed in Massachusetts. In 1840 the American Anti-slavery Society split in two, because women demanded an opportunity to speak on its platform. Soon after, a woman's convention was called. The New-York *Trib-*

une became the open door for the entrance of all these new ideas to the public. In the midst of these reformations and dreams appeared, in 1839, a prophet to declare the end of all things, in the person of William Miller.

Nearly every one of Emerson's intimate friends was connected with these reforms. Parker was just beginning to agitate the theological waters. Thoreau protested against taxes, and was lodged in jail. A little later he went to live by the side of Walden Pond. Margaret Fuller began her wonderful conversations in Boston; Francis, Hedge, Clarke, were reading German theology, and giving expression to a more living religious faith. Alcott had left his Temple School, gone to Concord at Emerson's request, and was living by manual labor. Such was Emerson's interest in the work of reform, that, almost immediately after the death of his oldest son, he filled a lecture engagement in New York, that he might aid Alcott in going to England, there to assist in establishing a school which should fulfil the idea begun in Boston. Alcott returned with Charles Lane, went to Harvard, established "Fruitlands," and added one more to the attempts to redeem life from its evils. To all these movements Emerson gave his sympathy, in so far as they expressed a genuine purpose, and showed a candid desire to make life richer with truth.

One of the movements of this time, that favoring the revitalizing of the old church forms and doctrines, was well represented by the Chardon-street conventions in Boston, called by "The Friends of Universal Progress," early in 1840. Emerson attended these meetings, was appointed on the committees, but did not speak. They were called to discuss the institutions of the sabbath, church, and ministry. Edmund Quincy was the moderator, and the first meeting continued for three days. Another was held in March, and a third in the following November, a whole session being given up to each of the topics. Alcott found himself at home there, and Brownson was one of the chief speakers. Emerson printed in *The Dial* what he regarded as the best speech made, by Nathaniel H. Whiting, a mechanic. His account of these meetings is now full of interest: —

"The composition of the assembly was rich and various. The singularity and latitude of the summons drew together, from all parts of New England, and also from the Middle States, men of every shade of opinion, from the straightest orthodoxy to the wildest heresy, and many persons whose church was a church of one member only. A great variety of dialect and of costume was noticed; a great deal of confusion, eccentricity, and freak appeared, as well as of zeal and enthusiasm. If the assembly was disorderly, it was picturesque. Madmen, madwomen, men with beards, Dunkers, Muggletonians, Come-outers, Groaners, Agrarians, Seventh-day Baptists, Quakers, Abolitionists, Calvinists, Unitarians, and philosophers, — all came successively to the top, and seized their moment, if not their *hour*, wherein to chide or pray or preach or protest. The faces were a study. The most daring innovators, and the champions-until-death of the old cause, sat side by side. The still living merit of the oldest New-England families, glowing yet after several generations, encountered the founders of families, fresh merit emerging and expanding the brows to a new breadth, and lighting a clownish face with sacred fire. The assembly was characterized by the predominance of a certain plain, sylvan strength and earnestness; whilst many of the most intellectual and cultivated persons attended its councils. Dr. Channing, Edward Taylor, Bronson Alcott, Mr. Garrison, Mr. May, Theodore Parker, H. C. Wright, Dr. Osgood, William Adams, Edward Palmer, Jones Very, Maria W. Chapman, and many other persons of a mystical or sectarian or philanthropic renown, were present, and some of them participant. And there was no want of female speakers; Mrs. Little and Mrs. Lucy Sessions took a pleasing and memorable part in the debate; and that flea of conventions, Mrs. Abigail Folsom, was but too ready with her interminable scroll. If there was not parliamentary order, there was life, and the assurance of that constitutional love for religion and religious liberty which, in all periods, characterizes the inhabitants of this part of America.

"There was a great deal of wearisome speaking in each of those three-days' sessions, but relieved by signal passages of pure eloquence, by much vigor of thought, and especially by the exhibition of character, and by the victories of character. These men and women were in search of something better and more satisfying than a vote or a definition; and they found what they sought, or the pledge of it, in the attitude taken by individuals of their number, of resistance to the insane routine of parliamentary usage, in the lofty reliance on principles, and the prophetic dignity and transfiguration which accompanies, even amidst opposition and ridicule, a man whose mind is made up to obey the great inward Commander, and who does not anticipate his own action, but awaits confidently the new emergency for the new counsel."

These meetings were but one of many movements of the time, all looking towards a new order of things. The Brook-Farm community was established in 1841, Hopedale in the same year, Northampton in 1842. Communities were formed all over the country. Owen started New Harmony, and the world was soon to be redeemed. Emerson has said that the meetings of the Transcendental Club resulted in the society at Brook Farm, as well as in the publishing of *The Dial.*

Its founders and leaders were among Emerson's intimate friends. He often visited the farm, but he did not sympathize fully with its purposes. It accepted the doctrines of Fourier in 1844, and in 1845 the teachings of Swedenborg were eagerly studied by nearly all its members. With the last phase of this movement Emerson sympathized largely, but not so much with the first. He afterwards spoke well of Owen and Fourier, and said their conceptions should be gratefully appreciated; for they who think and hope well for mankind, he said, put the human race under obligation. They are the unconscious prophets of the true order of society, — men who believe that in the world God's justice will be done. Yet he protested against phalansteries, in favor of the separate house, and declared it was individualism men needed, rather than having all things in common.[1]

In his lecture on Man the Reformer, in 1841, he spoke eloquently of manual labor; but in this, as in the opening lecture on The Times, the same year, it was individual regeneration he taught, saying that "the reform of reforms must be accomplished without means." In 1844, lecturing on the New-England Reformers, he inculcates, as he had constantly, the very opposite doctrine to that of Fourier. The true union of men with each other, he says, "must be inward, and not one of covenants."

"I have failed, and you have failed, but perhaps together we shall not fail. Our housekeeping is not satisfactory to us; but perhaps a phalanx, a community, might be. . . . This concert was

[1] In his London lecture on Politics and Socialism in 1848.

the specific in all cases. But concert is neither better nor worse, neither more nor less potent, than individual force. All the men in the world can not make a statue walk and speak, can not make a drop of blood or a blade of grass, any more than one man can. But let there be one man, let there be truth in two men, in ten men, then is concert for the first time possible; because the force which moves the world is a new quality, and can never be furnished by adding whatever quantities of a different kind. What is the use of the concert of the false and the disunited? There can be no concert in two, where there is no concert in one. When the individual is not *individual*, but is dual; when his thoughts look one way and his actions another; when his faith is traversed by his habits; when his will, enlightened by reason, is warped by his sense; when with one hand he rows, and with the other backs water, — what concert can be?"[1]

In another lecture he spoke strongly against bringing all to the lowest level, as communism must do. As soon as the equality was made, he said, it would unmake itself. "Spoons and skimmers you can lie undistinguishably together, but vases and statues require each a pedestal for itself."[2] It was not, however, because he believed in individualism, and in the providential mission of great men, that he objected to the Brook-Farm method of reforming the world. It was an illumination he felt men needed, an inward seeing of the truth, a wholeness of the spiritual life. Reform must commence, not with communities, but with the individual soul, in its harmony with itself and God. While he saw much that was good in each of these reforms, gave to them his sympathy, fully entered into the spirit of the protest against old abuses and institutions that narrow and hinder, yet to him they were deficient and wrong. His demand was, that men should trust in themselves, sit alone, and read the laws of their own natures. His method was the method of Jesus, making clean the inward life, seeking interior strength and renewal. He said it is of little moment that one or two or twenty social errors be corrected, but of much importance that man be in his senses; and the criticism of institutions, he thought, had made it plain that society gains noth-

1 Essays, second series, p. 256.
2 Willis's Hurry-graphs; in lecture on The Times.

ing whilst a man, not himself renovated, attempts to renovate things around him.[1] If each individual is faithful to his own duties, keeps inviolate all the laws of the world, all is well. We must learn to do right, not because some one else does, but from our own inward sympathies for the truth. "Every reform was once a private opinion; and when it shall be a private opinion again, it will solve the problem of the age."[2] It must be a personal motive, a personal sense of truth, which leads us to do right, and not an act of conformity. "Whilst, he says, I desire to express the respect and joy I feel before this sublime connection of reforms, now in their infancy around us, I urge the more earnestly the paramount duties of self-reliance. I can not find language of sufficient energy to convey my sense of the sacredness of private integrity."[3] He would not deal with men as "masses," but as souls, as persons. The rude, unkempt masses he would separate into pure and faithful individuals, each capable of an opinion, and equal to his own destiny. He would not have men herd together so much as to make them the foolish followers of a blind, common impulse, but would have each person capable of surrendering all to the call of personal duty. In the spirit of the greatest moral teachers, he says, "I shun father and mother and brother and wife, when my genius calls me." He would have all men capable of like devotion and sacrifice, capable of perfect consecration to truth and duty.

The true principle of reform is to learn what nature requires, to obey her laws. "What we call our root-and-branch reforms of slavery, war, gambling, intemperance, is only medicating the symptoms. We must begin higher up, namely, in education."[4] The will of God expressed in the invariable order and laws of nature, that we are to learn, that we are to obey. This is the only true reform, the only possible reform. In a most eloquent paragraph he has set forth this idea, and it reveals to us his conception of the whole subject.

[1] Essays, second series, p. 252.
[2] Essays, second series, p. 4.
[3] Miscellanies, p. 270.
[4] Conduct of Life, p. 121.

"That serene Power interposes the check upon the caprices and officiousness of our wills. Its charity is not our charity. One of its agents is our will, but that which expresses itself in our will is stronger than our will. We are very forward to help it, but it will not be accelerated. It resists our meddling, eleemosynary contrivances. We desire sumptuary and relief laws; but the principle of population is always reducing wages to the lowest pittance on which human life can subsist. We legislate against forestalling and monopoly; we would have a common granary for the poor; but the selfishness which hoards the corn for high prices is the preventive of famine, and the law of self-preservation is surer policy than any legislation can be. We concoct eleemosynary systems, and it turns out that our charity increases pauperism. We inflate our paper currency, we repair commerce with unlimited credit, and are presently visited with unlimited bankruptcy."[1]

He saw very clearly, also, that rude energy and muscle and competition are yet necessary in the world. His criticism of such attempts as Brook Farm, in this regard, was marked by practical wisdom. The law of competition is important, can not anywhere be laid aside. "Philanthropic and religious bodies do not commonly make their executive officers out of saints. The communities hitherto founded by Socialists are only possible by installing Judas as steward."[2] We have learned this lesson so well we no longer think that we are to be charitable to whoever asks, giving with unstinted hand of our substance; but we hold that self-help, self-reliance, manhood, are to be the ends of our charitable intent. This was what Emerson preached from the very first; it is the very core of his conception of reform.

There is another side, however, to Emerson's position on this subject. Though he says he is bound to help only those for whom he has an affinity,[3] yet he also maintains "that none is accomplished so long as any are incomplete; that the happiness of one can not consist with the misery of any other."[4] He repeats again the same sentiment, "No one is accomplished whilst any one is incomplete. Weal does not exist for one with the woe of any other."[5]

[1] Miscellanies, p. 362.
[2] Conduct of Life, p. 56.
[3] Essays, first series, p. 45.
[4] Conduct of Life, p. 201.
[5] Character, North American Review, April, 1866, p. 358.

His distrust of every other method of reform except that of awakening the soul to a sense of its possibilities, has caused him to be sharply criticised for hatred of the masses and contempt of good institutions. But all such criticism betrays ignorance of his real position, and an inability to comprehend a method so genuine as his. He could only follow the method of Jesus, Socrates, and Buddha, appealing to the individual, seeking to rouse the soul to a knowledge of a higher life. Any movement, therefore, which had any limited and temporary end in view, could not win his heartiest admiration. To redeem the life of men, to establish character, to bring men into genuine relations with nature, themselves, and God, was his aim.

He could not give his heart to the temperance cause, because it only temporized with those conditions which make sin and misery in the world. If men were made temperate, they yet remained selfish and licentious. So he would aim at the very center of all vice and defect, dry up that fountain, and then all the lesser evils would cease. His method may be wrong, but it is the method of every great moral and religious teacher through the ages. It made Jesus overlook the special sins of persons, because he touched the seat of moral action, and quickened life with new purposes. When Emerson speaks harshly against the masses, it should be remembered he has no dislike of the poor and weak, — none whatever; and that his contempt is only for those paltry methods by which the reform of the world is sought through an exterior assent to opinions or customs. So it was in regard to his criticism of Sunday schools and other good methods of education. Does he object to the Sunday school? No; but to that perfunctory morality and religion which aims only at the surface, and does not transform the life with character nor fill the soul with divineness. He early said the reforms which aim only at some special object, and attempt to cure some particular vice, "fair and generous as each appears, are poor, bitter things when prosecuted for themselves as an end."[1]

[1] Miscellanies, p. 206.

Several of the reforms of recent years have attracted his attention and admiration, and he has expressed great faith in them. He sees in them signs of that new religious era when life and ethical power will rule the world in the place of creed and ritual. He signed, with his wife, the call for the first woman's-suffrage convention, and attended its meetings. With this movement he has sympathized heartily. His intense interest in the new philanthropic spirit, — from which he hopes so much, and which he heralds as the sign of a new and wonderful development of human culture, — he has expressed in this paragraph from his address on the Progress of Culture: —

"Observe the marked ethical quality of the innovations urged or adopted. The new claim of woman to a political status is itself an honorable testimony to the civilization which has given her a civil status new in history. Now that, by the increased humanity of law, she controls property, she inevitably takes the next step to her share in power. The war gave us the abolition of slavery, the success of the Sanitary Commission and of the Freedman's Bureau. Add to these the new scope of social science; the abolition of capital punishment and of imprisonment for debt; the improvement of prisons; the efforts for the suppression of intemperance; the search for just rules affecting labor; the co-operative societies; the insurance of life and limb; the free-trade league; the improved almshouse; the enlarged scale of charities to relieve local famine, or burned towns, or the suffering Greeks; the incipient series of International Congresses, — all, one may say, in a high degree revolutionary, — teaching nations the taking of government into their own hands, and superseding kings."

Emerson's sense of humor has always been a restraining and sanitary influence in his character. He saw the ridiculous, the incongruous, side of Brook Farm; and his humor, his rare perception of the fitness of things, led him to see that finely conceived reform in its real light. He loved the men and women who lived at Brook Farm; he thoroughly sympathized with their anxious desire to make life better; but he saw the folly of their experiment, its weaknesses, and he quickly discovered the evils which it fostered in place of those it attempted to escape. In the second number of the fourth volume of *The Dial*, he printed a letter in answer to several correspondents. One of these had questioned him concerning the common defects in culture and life; and his answer is marked by that closely-veiled humor and that strong common sense so notable in his character.

"Regrets and Bohemian air-castles and æsthetic villages, he says, are not a very self-helping class of productions, but are the voices of debility. Especially to an importunate correspondent we must say that there is no chance for the æsthetic village. Every one of the villagers has committed his several blunder; his genius was good, his stars consenting, but he was a marplot. And though the recuperative force in every man may be relied on infinitely, it must be relied on before it will exert itself. As long as he sleeps in the shade of the present error, the after-nature does not betray its resources. Whilst he dwells in the old sin, he will pay the old fine."

In December, 1847, appeared the first number of *The Massachusetts Quarterly Review*, with Emerson's name as one of the editors. Parker was its originator, as he was its real editor for the three years of its existence. Emerson wrote nothing for it beyond its address To the Public in the first number. After speaking of the great material improvements in the country, he says the spiritual powers of man have not progressed equally far, and that the new world offers no new thought.

"Conceding these unfavorable appearances, he proceeds to say, it would yet be a poor pedantry to read the fates of this country from these narrow data. On the contrary, we are persuaded that moral and material values are always commensurate. Every material organization exists to a moral end, which makes the reason of its existence. Here are no books; but who can see the continent, with its inland and surrounding waters, its temperate climates, its west wind breathing vigor throughout all the year, its confluence of races so favorable to the highest energy, and the infinite glut of their production, without putting new queries to Destiny, as to the purpose for which this muster of nations and this sudden creation of enormous values is made?

"This is equally the view of science and of patriotism. We hesitate to employ a word so much abused as *patriotism*, whose true sense is almost the reverse of its popular sense. We have no sympathy with that boyish egotism, hoarse with cheering for our side, for our state, for our town; the right patriotism consists in the delight which springs from contributing our peculiar and legitimate advantages to the benefit of humanity. Every foot of soil has its proper quality; the grape on two sides of the same fence has new flavors; and so every acre on the globe, every family of men, every point of climate, has its distinguishing virtues. Certainly, then, this country does not lie here in the sun causeless; and though it may not be easy to define its influence, men feel already its emancipating quality in the careless self-reliance of the manners, in the freedom of thought, in the direct roads by which grievances are reached and redressed, and even in the reckless and sinister politics, not less than in purer expressions. Bad as it is, this freedom leads onward and upward to a Columbia of thought and art which is the last and endless end of Columbus's adventure."

After a severe criticism of the political affairs of the nation, he proceeds, "The state, like the individual, should rest on an ideal basis. Not only man, but nature, is injured by the imputation that man exists only to be fattened with bread; but he lives in such connection with Thought and Fact that his bread is surely involved as one element thereof, but is not its end and aim. So the insight which commands the laws and conditions of the true polity precludes for ever all interest in the squabbles of parties. As soon as men have the enjoyments of learning, friendship, and virtue, for which the state exists, the prizes of office appear polluted, and their followers outcasts.

"A journal that would meet the real wants of this time must have a courage and power sufficient to solve the problems which the great groping society around us, stupid with perplexity, is dumbly exploring. Let us not show its astuteness by dodging each difficult question, and arguing diffusely every point on which men are long ago unanimous. Can it front this matter of socialism, to which the names of Owen and Fourier have attached, and dispose of that question? Will it cope with the allied questions of government, non-resistance, and all that belongs under that category? Will it measure itself with the chapter of slavery, in some sort the special enigma of the time, as it has provoked against it a sort of inspiration and enthusiasm singular in modern history? There are literary and philosophical reputations to settle. The name of Swedenborg has in this very time acquired new honors; and the current year has witnessed the appearance, in their first English translation, of his manuscripts. Here is an unsettled account in the book of fame; a nebula to dim eyes, but which great telescopes may yet resolve into a magnificent system. Here is the standing problem of Natural Science, and the merits of her great interpreters, to be determined; the encyclopedical Humboldt, and the intrepid generalizations collected by the author of the *Vestiges of Creation*.

"What will easily seem to many a far higher question than any other is that which respects the embodying of the conscience of the period. Is the age we live in unfriendly to the highest powers, to that blending of the affections with the poetic faculty which has distinguished the religious ages? We have a better opinion of the economy of nature than to fear that those varying phases which humanity presents ever leave out any of the grand springs of human action. Mankind, for the moment, seem to be in search of a religion. The Jewish *cultus* is declining; the divine, or, as some will say, the truly human, hovers, now seen, now unseen, before us. This period of peace, this hour when the jangle of contending churches is hushing or hushed, will seem only the more propitious to those who believe that man need not fear the want of religion, because they know his religious constitution, — that he must rest on the moral and religious sentiments, as the motion of bodies rests on geometry. In the rapid decay of what was called religion, timid and unthinking people fancy a decay of the hope of man. But the moral and religious sentiments meet us everywhere, alike in markets as in churches. A God starts up behind cotton-bales also. The conscience of man is regenerated as is the atmosphere, so that society can not be debauched. That health which we call Virtue is an equipoise which easily redresses itself, and resembles those rocking-stones which a child's finger can move and a weight of many hundred tons can not overthrow."

This address is of importance as showing his sympathies, his interest in socialism, in Swedenborg, and in the future of America. It gives a very clear idea of the tendencies of his mind, and, better than any thing else, indicates his attitude towards the reforms of the time. In a closing paragraph, he says the *Review* is to be open especially to those "inspired pages" which come of "inevitable utterance;" while the editors rely on the "magnetism of truth" to fill its pages. He closes with this expressive sentence: "We rely on the truth for and against *ourselves*."

During these years of social and reformatory agitation, his trust was in the soul, its purification and elevation; and through its culture only did he hope to regenerate the world. In 1837 Mann reports that Emerson summed up the commandments into "Sit aloof" and "Keep a diary." He hoped little from great social agitations; he believed all things would result when the individual soul came into harmony with God. In his essays and in his poems he frequently justifies this attitude, and says he is not called but to meditate and to keep silence by himself. His real influence came out, however, in his personal relations with many of the finest minds of the time. The impression he made may be seen in what Harriet Martineau wrote of him in her *Retrospect of Western Travel.* She saw much of him during her visit to the United States in 1835–36, and gained a fine insight into his character.

"There is a remarkable man in the United States, she said, without knowing whom it is not too much to say that the United States can not be fully known. I mean by this, not only that he has powers and worth which constitute him an element in the estimate to be formed of his country, but that his intellect and his character are the opposite of those which the influences of his country and his time are supposed almost necessarily to form. I speak of Mr. Emerson. He is yet in the prime of life. Great things are expected from him; and great things, it seems, he can not but do if he have life and health to prosecute his course. He is a thinker and scholar.

"He has modestly and silently withdrawn himself from the perturbations and conflicts of the crowd of men, without declining any of the business of life, or repressing any of his human sympathies. He is a thinker, without being solitary, abstracted, and unfitted for the time. He is a scholar, without being narrow, bookish, and prone to occupy himself only with other men's thoughts. He is remarkable for the steadiness and fortitude with which he makes those objects which are frequently considered the highest in their own department subordinate to something higher still, whose connection with their department he has clearly discovered. There are not a few men, I hope, in America who decline the pursuit of wealth; not a few who refrain from ambition; and some few who devote themselves to thought and study from a pure love of an intellectual life. But the case before us is a higher one than this. The intellectual life is nourished from a love of the diviner life, of which it is an element. Consequently the thinker is ever present to the duty, and the scholar to the active business, of the hour; and his home is the scene of his greatest acts. He is ready at every call of action. He lectures to the factory people at Lowell when they ask. He preaches when the opportunity is presented. He is known at every house along the road he travels to and from home by the words he has dropped and the deeds he has done. The little boy who carries wood for his household has been enlightened by him, and his most transient guests owe to him their experience of what the highest grace of domestic manners may be. He neglects no political duty, and is unmindful of nothing in the march of events which can affect the virtue and peace of men. While he is far above fretting himself because of evil-doers, he has ever ready his verdict for the right and his right hand for its champions. While apart from the passions of all controversies, he is ever present with their principles, declaring himself, and taking his stand, while appearing to be incapable of contempt of persons, however uncompromising may be his indignation against what is dishonest and harsh. Earnest as is the tone of his mind, and placidly strenuous as is his life, an exquisite spirit of humor pervades his intercourse. A quiet gayety breathes out of his conversation; and his observation, as keen as it is benevolent, furnishes him with perpetual material for the exercise of his humor. In such a man it is difficult to point out any one characteristic; but if, out of such a harmony, one leading quality is to be distinguished, it is in him modest independence. A more entire and modest independence I am not aware of having ever witnessed, though in America I saw two or three approaches to it. It is an independence equally of thought, of speech, of demeanor, of occupation, and of objects in life, yet without a trace of contempt in its temper, or of encroachment in its action."

This noble picture by one who was as ready to set forth faults as to see them is a fine testimonial to the pure and rich impression which Emerson has made upon all who have come into personal contact with him, or into a sympathetic appreciation of his books. The pure humanity of the man stands out everywhere, full, rich, penetrating, infused through all his words and conduct. It has made him a permanent and inspiring power in the life of his time. What Harriet Martineau saw in him was amply fulfilled. Still later Frederika Bremer felt the magic charm of his influence, and wrote of it in her *Homes of the New World*, describing her visit to the United States in 1849.

"He is in a high degree pure, noble, and severe, demanding as much from himself as he demands from others. His words are severe, his judgments often keen and merciless; but his demeanor is alike noble and pleasing, and his voice beautiful. One may quarrel with Emerson's thoughts, with his judgment, but not with himself. That which struck me most, as distinguishing him from most other human beings, is nobility. He is a born gentleman."

"The writings of this scorner of imperfection, of the mean and the paltry, this bold exacter of perfection in man, have for me a fascination which amounts almost to magic! I often object to him, quarrel with him. I see that his stoicism is one-sidedness, his pantheism an imperfection; and I know that which is greater and more perfect; but I am under the influence of his magical power. I believe myself to have become greater through his greatness, stronger through his strength; and I breathe the air of a higher sphere in this world, which is indescribably refreshing to me."

He had much the same influence on Margaret Fuller, at first appearing cold and intellectually distant, to have faith "in the universal but not in the individual man." As she knew him better, his influence upon her life became greater; and at last she could say, —

"My inmost heart blesses the fate that gave me birth in the same clime and time, and that has drawn me into such a close bond with him as, it is my hopeful faith, will never be broken, but from sphere to sphere ever be hallowed."

"When I look forward to eternal growth, I am always aware that I am far larger and deeper for him. His influence has been to me that of lofty assurance and sweet serenity. I present to him the many forms of nature, and solicit with music; he melts them all into spirit, and reproves performance with prayer. With most men I bring words of now past life, and do actions suggested by the wants of these natures rather than my own. But he stops me from doing any thing, and makes me think."

In 1852 Clough found Emerson "the only profound man in the country," and came into very close relations of sympathy with him. Other minds were affected by his power, and saw in him as much. Hawthorne said his mind acted upon other minds "with wonderful magnetism."

"It was good, said his neighbor at the 'Old Manse,' to meet him in the wood-paths, or sometimes in our avenue, with that pure intellectual gleam diffusing about his presence like the garment of a shining one; and he, so quiet, so simple, so without pretension, encountering each man alive as if expecting to receive more than he would impart. And, in truth, the heart of many an ordinary man had, perchance, inscriptions which he could not read. But it was impossible to dwell in his vicinity without inhaling more or less the mountain atmosphere of his lofty thought." [1]

Emerson's personal influence was wide-reaching, very great, through the charm of his character, the depth and purity of his moral convictions, and the sublime strength of his personal faith. This influence has been described by Alcott: [2] —

"Fortunate the visitor who is admitted of a morning for the high discourse, or permitted to join the poet in his afternoon walks to Walden, the Cliffs, or elsewhere, — hours to be remembered as

[1] Mosses from an Old Manse. [2] Concord Days.

unlike any others in the calendar of experiences. Shall I describe them as sallies oftenest into cloudlands, into scenes and intimacies ever new, none the less novel nor remote than when first experienced? interviews, however, bringing their own trail of perplexing thoughts, costing some days', several nights', sleep, oftentimes, to restore one to his place and poise. Certainly safer not to venture without the sure credentials, unless one will have his pretensions pricked, his conceits reduced in their vague dimensions. But to the modest, the ingenuous, the gifted, welcome! Nor can any bearing be more poetic and polite to all such, to youth and accomplished women especially. His is a faith approaching to superstition concerning admirable persons; the rumor of excellence of any sort being like the arrival of a new gift to mankind, and he the first to proffer his recognition and hope. He, if any, must have taken the census of the admirable people of his time, numbering as many among his friends as most living Americans; while he is already recognized as the representative mind of his country, to whom distinguished foreigners are especially commended when visiting America."

Among his associates, Emerson was the leader, the most highly honored of a company of brilliant men and women. Margaret Fuller spent weeks and months in his home. Thoreau found a home with him for a long time, and was an intimate companion always. When Alcott moved to Concord, in 1839, their friendship became most intimate; while Elizabeth Peabody was another of those with whose generous humanity and wide philanthropic aims he strongly sympathized. Parker was wont to visit him often, and always returned to his work quickened and inspired. A brilliant company of these minds often gathered in his study; and the conversations held there were of a remarkable character for their high thought, their lofty aims, and their inspiration. He knew, and often met, all the best minds in Massachusetts, in all professions; and his influence among them was great. His purity, the nobility of his life, his powers of conversation, carried weight everywhere; and he became one of the most marked of all the influences of the times. It was thus he did his work of reform, quickening other minds, giving a higher sense of the value of life, and inspiring a profounder faith in the soul and its possibilities.

IX.

LECTURES AND ESSAYS.

WHEN Emerson settled down at Concord, he continued in his own way to be a conscientious student. He read with diligence and care, not widely, but with profit. The poets were thoroughly studied, as were the great imaginative and moral writers of all times and lands. The early English idealists received his studious attention; and he continued to read Coleridge, Wordsworth, Landor, and Carlyle, with Goethe, Schiller, and others among the Germans. With Kant, Fichte, and Schelling he became somewhat familiar, but not largely. What he owes to these men, he owes to them at second-hand mostly, through their admirers and interpreters. Swedenborg he read diligently, as he did the profoundest religious writers of the Christian ages. Cudworth held his attention, as well as the modern interpreters of the old idealists. Plato, Plotinus, Pythagoras, and the ancient thinkers were thoroughly studied. He was early interested in the oriental religions, and secured the works then published concerning them. Boehme and the other German mystics were read with the keenest interest. His readings in these directions gave color to his poetry. Much of it can be understood only by reference to his enthusiastic studies in the field of oriental mystic thought. In science and social economy he also found much to interest, and his essays bear testimony to the fact that his studies in these directions were profitable.

He has been so much the student and the poet, that his outward life gives few events to record. The growth of his ideas, and of his influence, furnish nearly all the facts there are to his biography. By no extraneous methods whatever has he sought to influence the thought of his time. He has quietly followed the leadings of his own genius, coming into close contact with a few strong minds, and saying in a quiet way, with no demonstration or noise, what there was in his heart to say. Yet there was something so genuine in the thought and the influence he brought to bear on his time, that steadily his reputation gained, and his circle of listeners widened. The period from 1840 to 1860 was the one in which this process went on most effectively. It is the period of his greatest power, when his best essays were produced. Before this, he had achieved recognition as a new thinker; but he was regarded as an erratic and unbalanced genius. The distrust with which his novel opinions were at first received, however, gradually melted away before the healthful vigor of his influence.

During this period *The Dial* had its existence, Brook Farm was founded and failed, he made his second visit to Europe, he began to lecture beyond New England, and he took part in the anti-slavery agitation as it rose and culminated. It was a remarkable period, brilliant with great names in politics and literature; and during it American literature first came to have a name and to be worthy of recognition. Emerson lectured each winter in Boston; but slowly he went farther and farther away from that center on his lecturing tours, and his name came to be an influence throughout the land.

In 1841 his first volume of *Essays* was published, containing lectures he had delivered a year or two previously. Some of his very best essays are in this volume, nearly every one of them rising to the highest level of his ability as a thinker and writer. They are filled with the subtle power of his thought, and give full expression to those ideas which are the sources of his philosophy. He was here more truly himself than in any other book he has published, though single essays in the other volumes reach the height almost constantly maintained in this. But it did not escape the critics, most of whom did not understand it. One of them found it more devoid of real meaning than any other book which ever fell into his hands; and he thought such essays could be produced during a lifetime, as rapidly as a human pen could be made to move.[1] Felton said they contained single thoughts of dazzling brilliancy, with a copious vein of practical illustration; but he found them full of extravagance of opinion, overweening self-confidence, and setting all authority at defiance. The ideas set forth were called ancient errors, mistaken for new truths, and disguised in the drapery of a misty rhetoric. His theory of the instincts, Felton declared, would overturn society, and resolve the world into chaos.[2]

This volume was the same year reprinted in England as *Twelve Essays*, and with a preface by Carlyle. The editor indulged in his usual style of vehement expression, but he also wrote with great appreciation of his American friend.

"The name of Ralph Waldo Emerson, he said, is not entirely new in England; distinguished travelers bring us tidings of such a man; fractions of his writings have found their way into the hands of the curious here; fitful hints that there is in New England some spiritual notability called Emerson glide through reviews and magazines. Whether these hints were true or not true, readers are now to judge for themselves a little better.

"Emerson's writings and speakings amount to something; and yet hitherto, as it seems to me, this Emerson is far less notable for what he has spoken or done than for the many things he has not spoken and has forborne to do. With uncommon interest I have learned that this, and in such a never-resting locomotive country too, is one of those rare men who have withal the invaluable talent of sitting still. That an educated man of good gifts and opportunities, after looking at the public arena, and even trying — not with ill success — what its tasks and its prizes might amount to, should retire for long years into rustic obscurity, and, amid the all-pervading jingle of dollars and loud chaffering of ambitions and promotions, should quietly, with cheerful deliberateness, sit down to spend *his* life, not in Mammon-worship, or the hunt for reputation, influence, place, or any outward advantage whatsoever; this, when we get notice of it, is a thing really worth noting. . . .

"For myself, I have looked over with no common feeling to this brave Emerson, seated by his rustic hearth on the other side of the ocean (yet not altogether parted from me either), silently communing with his own soul and with the God's World it finds itself alive

[1] Princeton Review, October, 1841. [2] Christian Examiner, May, 1841.

in yonder. Pleasures of Virtue, Progress of the Species, Black Emancipation, New Tariff, Eclecticism, Locofocoism, Ghost of Improved Socinianism; these, with many other ghosts and substances, are squeaking, jabbering, according to their capabilities, round this man. To one man among the sixteen millions their jabber is all unmusical. The silent voices of the stars above and of the green earth beneath are profitable to him, — tell him gradually that these others are but ghosts, which will shortly have to vanish; that the Life-Fountain these proceed out of does not vanish. The words of such a man — what words he finds good to speak — are worth attending to. By degrees a small circle of living souls eager to hear is gathered. The silence of this man has to become speech. May this too, in its due season, prosper for him! Emerson has gone to lecture various times to special audiences in Boston, and occasionally elsewhere. Three of these lectures, already printed, are known to some here, as is the little pamphlet called *Nature*, of somewhat earlier date. It may be said, a great meaning lies in these pieces, which as yet finds no adequate expression for itself. A noteworthy though very unattractive work, moreover, is that new periodical they call *The Dial*, in which he occasionally writes; which appears, indeed, generally to be imbued with his way of thinking, and to proceed from the circle that learns of him. This present little volume of *Essays*, printed in Boston a few months ago, is Emerson's first book, — an unpretending little book, composed, probably, in good part from mere lectures which already lay written. It affords us, on several sides, in such manner as it can, a direct glimpse into the man and that spiritual world of his.

"Emerson, I understand, was bred to theology; of which primary bent, his latest way of thought still bears traces. In a very enigmatic way we hear much of the 'universal soul of the,' etc.: flickering like bright bodiless northern streamers, notions and half-notions of a metaphysic, theosophic kind, are seldom long wanting in these *Essays*. I do not advise the British public to trouble itself much with all that; still less to take offense at it. Whether this Emerson be a 'Pantheist,' or what kind of theist or *ist* he may be, can perhaps as well remain undecided. If he prove a devout-minded, veritable, and original man, this for the present will suffice. *Ists* and *isms* are rather growing a weariness. Such a man does not readily range himself under *isms*. A man to whom the 'open secret of the universe' is no longer a closed one, what can his *speech* of it be in these days? All human speech in the best days, all human thought that can or could articulate itself in reference to such things, what is it but the eager stammering and struggling as of a wondering infant, in view of the Unnamable? That this little book has no 'system,' and points or stretches far beyond all systems, is one of its merits. We will call it the soliloquy of a true soul, alone under the stars, in this day. . . .

"For the rest, what degree of mere literary talent lies in these utterances is but a secondary question which every reader may gradually answer for himself. What Emerson's talent is, we will not altogether estimate by this book. The utterance is abrupt, fitful; the great idea, not yet embodied, struggles towards an embodiment. Yet everywhere there is the true heart of a man, which is the parent of all talent, — which without much talent can not exist. A breath as from the green country, all the welcomer that it is *New*-England country, meets us wholesomely everywhere in these *Essays:* the authentic green earth is there, with her mountains, rivers; with her mills and farms. Sharp gleams of insight arrest us by their pure intellectuality; here and there, in heroic rusticity, a tone of modest manfulness, of mild invincibility, low-voiced but lion-strong, makes us, too, thrill with a noble pride. Talent? Such ideas as dwell in this man, how can they ever speak themselves with *enough* of talent? The talent is not the chief question here. The idea, — that is the chief question."

In a French journal,[1] "Daniel Stern" says the book first received mention in Paris by Philarète Chasles in an article on the literary tendencies of America; and later it was cited in the lecture-room by a foreign poet, Micklewicz. When she inquired for it she was obliged to send to London; and, after reading it, says, "It becomes difficult to explain so total an ignorance in respect to so wonderful an intellect, so attractive a moralist, as Emerson; but it is understood upon reflecting that he lives careless of glory, far from the world." She says he is better than a philosopher or moralist, "a man of a superior nature, who has the courage and wisdom to think and act in conformity with his nature." His writings "bear the undeniable impress of a virile and natural greatness." "The singular charm of the essays is, that we hold him accountable for nothing, because he pretends to nothing. He draws you after him with irresistible *bonhomie.* There is no difficulty in following him, for we breathe a salubrious atmosphere in his work. Nothing offends, not even the discords, because all is resolved and harmonized in the sentiment of a superior truth. The eccentricities do not shock us; they are not affected eccentricities, but natural, as unsought for, as homogeneous to the mind of Emerson, as certain graceful freaks of vegetation."

[1] Revue Independante for July 25, 1846. Daniel Stern is the pseudonym for the Countess d'Agoult, a novelist and historian, whose chief work is a History of the Revolution of 1848

In 1845 Edgar Quinet published a volume of lectures on *Christianity and the French Revolution.* One of these was devoted to America and the Reformation, in which he expressed this opinion of Emerson: —

"In this North America, which is pictured to us as so materialistic, I find the most ideal writer of our times. Contrast the formulas of German philosophy (too often copied from Alexandria) with the inspiration, the initiative, the moral *elan* of Emerson. A new philosophy might be expected to come forth from those virgin forests sooner or later; and already it begins to raise its head. The author I have just named is proof enough that bold pioneers are at work in America pursuing the quest of truth in the moral world. What we announce in Europe from the summit of a ruined past he also announces in the germinating solitude of a world absolutely new. What mean these voices, these spiritual presences, which meet us, by surprise, across the ocean? Although we have abandoned the past, neither here nor there have we lost ourselves in the labyrinth of a desert island. On the virgin soil of the new world behold the footsteps of a man, and a man who is moving toward the future by the same road that we are going."

In the spring of 1842 Emerson suffered a great domestic loss in the death of his son Waldo, who had already given great promise for the future. This loss he has most expressively described in his "Threnody," one of the most remarkable of all his poems. The first part of this poem, to the line, —

"Born for the future, to the future lost,"

was written immediately after Waldo's death. The remainder was written two years later. Thoreau wrote that "he died as the mist rises from the brook." He had not even taken root here. Thoreau says, "I was not startled to hear that he was dead; it seemed the most natural event that could happen. His fine organization demanded it, and nature yielded its request."[1] Margaret Fuller was warmly attached to the boy, expressing her grief at his loss in one of her letters.

"I am deeply sad at the loss of little Waldo, she wrote, from whom I hoped more than from almost any living being. I can not

[1] Letters, under date of March 2, 1842.

yet reconcile myself to the thought that the sun shines upon the grave of the beautiful blue-eyed boy, and I shall see him no more.

"Five years he was an angel to us, and I know not that any person was ever more the theme of thought to me. As I walk the streets they swarm with apparently worthless lives; and the question will rise, why he, why just he, who 'bore within himself the golden future,' must be torn away? His father will meet him again; but to me he seems lost, and yet that is weakness. I *must* meet that which he represented, since I so truly loved it. He was the only child I ever saw that I sometimes wished I could have called mine.

"I loved him more than any child I ever knew, as he was of nature more fair and noble. You would be surprised to know how dear he was to my imagination. I saw him but little, and it was well; for it is unwise to bind the heart where there is no claim. But it is all gone, and is another of the lessons brought by each year, that we are to expect suggestions only, and not fulfillments, from each form of beauty, and to regard them merely as Angels of The Beauty." [1]

In 1843 Emerson edited Carlyle's *Past and Present.* Aug. 1, 1844, he gave an address, in Concord, on the anniversary of West-India Emancipation. On this occasion Thoreau rang the church-bell to call the people together, having previously gone to the houses to notify them of the address. The same year the second series of *Essays* appeared, and was at once reprinted in England, with a short preface by Carlyle. This volume was better received than the first one. Hedge praised it in *The Christian Examiner*, and saw little in the essays to condemn, though not satisfied with their attitude towards Christ. They "are destined," he said, "to carry far into coming time their lofty cheer and spirit-stirring notes of courage and of hope. We dare to predict for them a devotion coetaneous with the language in which they are composed. So long as there are lovers of fine discourse and generous sentiment in the world, they will find their own." In *The Democratic Review* they were written of with great enthusiasm, and with a full appreciation of Emerson's ideas. The critic could not find in the whole range of literature another mind that overlooks the world from a point of view so high and commanding; that arrives so surely, by an

[1] Memoirs, vol. ii. p. 62.

induction so rapid and unerring, at the last results from the speculative reason. In the first volume Emerson gave expression to his philosophical views on the highest themes of history, life, and religion; indeed, it is the book of his philosophy. The second series deals with the themes suggested by morals, art, politics, and poetry, applying to them the same philosophical spirit and ideas.

His *Poems* were published in 1847, including many which had appeared in *The Dial*. They gave a still ampler expression to his philosophy, many of them being saturated with his spiritual ideas. They seemed obscure to the public, however, because so filled with the results of his oriental studies. Bowen declared "this volume of professed poetry contained the most prosaic and unintelligible stuff that it had ever been his fortune to encounter."[1] Bartol criticised very sharply his religious views, especially concerning Christ, in a notice of the *Poems*, but said he knew of no poetic compositions "that surpass his in their characteristic excellence." "We know," he said, "of nothing in the whole range of modern writers superior in original merit to his productions." Here was more religious inspiration than had entered into more than a very few modern volumes of poetry, with the fervor and power of the old prophets. There was, also, that rich fullness of the best of the mystics, when they most truly rise into the height of spiritual attainment. These two tendencies were wonderfully combined in some of the poems, making them unique in modern poetry. Such a volume, however, could not soon grow into popular favor, and perhaps can never have more than a limited circle of admirers. It is a book for poets and thinkers more than for the people; yet some of these poems will ever remain the admiration of all lovers of nature and of moral inspiration. Their tone is pure, their purpose of the highest. The muses spoke in these poems; they were never courted, or used for secondary purposes. They came in answer to some personal experience or

[1] North American Review, April, 1847.

burning thought, and hence they are full of the life of the writer.

Steadily as Emerson's reputation grew at home during this period, it had even a wider expression in England, and grew more rapidly. The way had been prepared there by others; and he entered into the labors of Coleridge, Wordsworth, and Carlyle. At home he was compelled to create an audience, and to educate his readers to the appreciation of his thought. Few here cared for philosophy; and but a limited circle had been led, either by English or German books, beyond the old lines of religious thought.

The fame of his lectures having reached England, and his essays having been widely read through cheap editions, a demand was made for hearing him face to face. A series of mechanics' institutes invited him to read lectures before them. There came also a promise of a wide hearing elsewhere; and so he went to England in October, 1847.

He gave in many places a course of lectures on Representative Men. In London he delivered a special course on The Mind and Manners of the Nineteenth Century. Other subjects of his lectures were, The Superlative in Manners and Literature, Domestic Life, and Reading. Those on the nineteenth century were delivered in the Portman-square Literary and Scientific Institution. The subjects were, The Powers and Laws of Thought, The Relations of Intellect to Natural Science, Tendencies and Duties of Men of Thought, Politics and Socialism, Poetry and Eloquence, Natural Aristocracy. Before the delivery of this course he spent some weeks in Paris in their preparation. Among his hearers were Carlyle, Lady Byron, Forster, Mrs. Cowden Clarke, and numerous men of letters, critics, members of Parliament, and noblemen. In *Jerrold's Newspaper* was printed the following account of these lectures: —

"Precisely at four o'clock the lecturer glided in, and suddenly appeared at the reading-desk. Tall, thin, his features aquiline, his eye piercing and fixed; the effect, as he stood quietly before his audience, was at first somewhat startling, and then nobly im pressive. Having placed his manuscript on the desk with nervous rapidity, and paused, the lecturer then quickly, and, as it were, with a flash of action, turned over the first leaf, whispering at the same time, "Gentlemen and *ladies*." The initial sentences were next pronounced in a low tone, a few words at a time, hesitatingly, as if then extemporaneously meditated, and not, as they really were, premeditated and forewritten. Time was thus given for the audience to meditate them too. Meanwhile the meaning, as it were, was dragged from under the veil and covering of the expression, and ever and anon a particular phrase was so emphatically italicized as to command attention. There was, however, nothing like acquired elocution, no regular intonation, in fact, none of the usual oratorical artifices, but for the most part a shapeless delivery (only varied by certain nervous twitches and angular movements of the hand and arms, curious to see and even smile at), and calling for much co-operation on the part of the auditor to help out its shortcomings. Along with all this, there was an eminent *bonhomie*, earnestness, and sincerity, which bespoke sympathy and respect, — nay, more, secured veneration."

He lectured many times in Scotland, where he was received as cordially as in England. His lecturing there was described as follows by one who heard him many times:[1] —

"A lecturer, in the common sense of the term, he is not: call him rather a public monologist, talking rather to himself than to his audience; and what a quiet, calm, commanding conversation it is! It is not the seraph or burning one you see; it is the naked cherubic reason thinking aloud before you. He reads his lectures without excitement, without energy, scarcely even with emphasis, as if to try what can be affected by the pure, unaided momentum of thought. It is a soul totally unsheathed that you have to do with; and you ask, Is this a spirit's tongue sounding on its way? so solitary and severe seems its harmony. There is no betrayal of emotion except now and then when a slight tremble in his voice proclaims that he has arrived at some spot of thought to him peculiarly sacred or dear. There is no emphasis often but what is given by the eye, and this is felt only by those who see him on the side-view. Neither standing behind him nor before, can we form any conception of the rapt, living flash which breaks forth athwart the spectator. His eloquence is thus of that high kind which produces great effects at small expenditure of means, and without any effort or turbulence; still and strong as gravitation, it fixes, subdues, and turns us round."

At the lectures in Manchester he spoke to large audiences. In London he had a thousand hearers to his

[1] George Gilfillan, first Gallery of Literary Portraits.

lecture on Montaigne, and was greeted with loud applause on entering the lecture-room. He was everywhere received in the same manner, with enthusiasm, full houses, and an awakened interest in culture. His lectures proved to be attractive and popular, and his trip was in every way a successful one. He spent some time with Carlyle [1] in his own house; and he saw Rogers, Hallam, Macaulay, Milman, Barry Cornwall, Dickens, Thackeray, Tennyson, Leigh Hunt, Helps, Clough, Arnold, Faraday, Lyell, Carpenter, Mrs. Jameson, and Mrs. Somerville. He was welcomed in many private houses, and had a good opportunity of becoming acquainted with the English people. He also visited Wordsworth and Miss Martineau at Rydal Mount. In a letter written previous to his visit to her, Miss Martineau said, "Emerson is engaged (lecturing) deep at present, but hopes to come by and by. He is free, if any man is." After his visit a few months later, she wrote, "Mr. Emerson did come. He spent a few days in February with me; and, unfavorable as the weather was for seeing the district, — the fells and meadows being in their dullest hay-color instead of green, — he saw, in rides with a neighbor and myself, some of the most striking features in the nearer scenery. I remember bringing him, one early morning, the first green spray of the wild currant, from a warm nook. It was a great pleasure to me to have for my guest one of the most honored of my American hosts, and to find him as full as ever of the sincerity and serenity which had inspired me with so cordial a reverence twelve years before." [2] He met Arthur Hugh Clough at Oxford and in Paris, and became much interested in that singularly original genius. Mrs. Clough, in her biography of her husband, says his friendship with Emerson "was then and afterwards very valuable to him." Crabbe

[1] His impressions of Carlyle at this time, as expressed in his letters written home, were embodied in a paper read before the Massachusetts Historical Society in February, 1881, and printed in the Transactions of that society. It was also printed in Scribner's Monthly for May, 1881, p. 89.

[2] Autobiography, vol. i. p. 549.

Robinson heard Emerson's lecture on the Laws of Thought, which he says was "one of those rhapsodical exercises, like Coleridge's in his Table Talk, and Carlyle in his Lectures, which leave a dreamy sense of pleasure not easy to analyze or render any account of." The first time Robinson met him, he became very much interested. In his *Diary* he says, —

> "It was with a feeling of pre-determined dislike that I had the curiosity to look at Emerson at Lord Northampton's, a fortnight ago; when, in an instant, all my dislike vanished. He has one of the most interesting countenances I ever beheld, — a combination of intelligence and sweetness that quite disarmed me."

He heard Emerson's lecture on Domestic Life, and says "his picture of childhood was one of his most successful sketches. I enjoyed the lecture, he says, which was, I dare say, the most liberal ever heard in Exeter Hall."[1]

After his return from Europe, Emerson lectured on the characteristics of the English people; and these lectures were received with marked interest and approval. In 1849 his miscellaneous addresses and lectures, together with *Nature*, were collected into a volume, under the title of *Miscellanies*. The lectures he had delivered extensively in England, as well as at home, were in 1850 published as *Representative Men*. The *Literary World* expressed of this volume a very common opinion entertained by those who read it at first, when it said this was less visionary and metaphysical than his other books, with more of common sense, and possessed of a kind of dramatic power. He is an adept at intellectual characterization, this reviewer said, but not able rightly to determine the ethical value of human characters. His optimistic doctrine, it is predicted, will cause moral torpidity. A writer in the *New Englander* found it "purely ridiculous for any one to laboriously write out, and gravely read to large assemblies, such gratuitous absurdities." A large part of what he had written, according to this critic, "must be little else

[1] Diary of Henry Crabbe Robinson, vol. ii. pp. 371, 372.

than a caricature of himself;" while "it is to be regretted that one so little given to grossness and the reckless malignity of vulgar skepticism, should yet be led by mere caprice to affirm at times many of its most monstrous and pernicious maxims." His theory of history and of the influence of the great man was developed in this volume. The representative men selected, and the manner of portraying their influence on mankind, shows the strong individuality of Emerson's character. He writes in a calmer, less passionate manner than Carlyle had done in his portraitures of the world's heroes. He selects a higher range of men for his subjects, and he is less devoted to their praises. Emerson sees the faults of the men of whom he writes, analyzes patiently their characters, and shows wherein their influence was hurtful. His unqualified acceptance of Plato and Shakspere is as marked as is his criticism of Goethe, Napoleon, and Swedenborg. His personal interest in Swedenborg and Montaigne led him to select them as the representative mystic and skeptic. His debt to the Swedish seer may well be noted, but his points of wide divergence should not be overlooked. Swedenborg knew too much of science and theology, and was too much dominated by them in his thinking, to be a genuine mystic. His artificiality turned Emerson away from him, and made men of inferior genius more acceptable, because more natural and inspiring.

In the *Revue des Deux Mondes* Emile Montégut wrote of Emerson as an old acquaintance, who had been studied with love for his hatred of the vulgar and his affection for individual greatness; while the new book received a very full and just criticism. He is said to have a tendency both to mysticism and skepticism; but his mysticism gives faith in the moral law, and trust that it is only the forms of things which change.

"It is this confidence in the supreme ideal, in the eternal order of the world, and faith in the stability and duration of the invisible, which is predominant in Emerson's new book. Emerson is full of calmness and tranquillity; he is almost *näif* in his indifference, and expresses his ideas in 1848 as he would have expressed them in 1846, with the same imperturbable confidence. Revolutions and re-actions intimidate him not at all, and do not draw him in the least from his convictions. In nothing does he offer sacrifice to the spirit of the moment. He speaks of Swedenborg and Plato at the moment when the whole universe has ears only for Proudhon and Louis Blanc. He praises the skepticism of Montaigne as if he did not live in a century which boasts of having the most absolute philosophies. He praises Montaigne for his prudence and reserve in the midst of the most headstrong century, when the minds of men are more stultified by an excess of philosophic systems than ever before. All seems alike indifferent to him. However, from time to time a vein of gentle irony shows beneath these metaphysical dissertations, and a tolerant and polished skepticism warns the reader not to accept the author too implicitly." Montégut prefers Carlyle as a teacher of hero worship. He says the great man, as Emerson depicts him, is the great man in the antique sense, and is the man of genius in the modern sense. He is the "pagan *par excellence*, the man who holds his *grace from nature*. For Carlyle, the great man is he who has received his mission from heaven, who must express it to others with difficulty, and obtain its triumph at his own peril."

"Emerson devotes himself especially to men of genius, and loves to contemplate in them the different and the eminent types of humanity, the men who represent most powerfully the different intellectual forces of the human mind. He admires the skeptic Montaigne not less than the mystic Swedenborg. He leans to the side neither of the first nor of the latter. For him the eminent and diverse faculties of these men are the weights which keep in equilibrium the balance of the mind. He loves to seek for the secret point of affinity in which these different gifts would combine to form the unity of the human mind; he loves to reflect on the actions and re-actions of thought, which, nevertheless, do not alter at all the original identity of the soul and of life."[1]

In 1852 Kossuth made a tour through the United States, and was everywhere warmly welcomed. May 11 he visited Concord. Emerson made an address of welcome, in which he said, —

"Sir, we have watched with attention your progress through the land, the varying feeling with which you have been received, and the unvarying tone and countenance which you have maintained. We wish to discriminate in our regard. We wish to reserve our honor for actions of the noblest strain. We please ourselves that in you we meet one whose temper was long since tried in the fire, and made equal to all events; a man so truly in love with the greatest future that he can not be diverted to any less.

[1] In an article on Hero Worship. — Carlyle and Emerson, Aug. 15, 1850.

"It is our republican doctrine, too, that the wide variety of opinions is an advantage. I believe I may say of the people of this country, at large, that their sympathy is more worth, because it stands the test of party. It is not a blind wave; it is the living soul contending with living souls. It is, in every expression, antagonized. No opinion will pass, but must stand the tug of war. As you see, the love you win is worth something; for it has been argued through; its foundation searched; it has proved sound and whole; it may be avowed; it will last; and it will draw all opinion to itself.

"We have seen, with great pleasure, that there is nothing accidental in your attitude. We have seen that you are organically in that cause you plead: The man of freedom, you are also the man of fate. You do not elect, but you are elected by God and your genius to your task. We do not, therefore, affect to thank you. We only see in you the angel of freedom, crossing sea and land; crossing parties, nationalities, private interests, and self-esteems; dividing populations where you go, and drawing to your part only the good. We are afraid you are growing popular, sir; you may be called to the dangers of prosperity. But hitherto you have had, in all countries and in all parties, only the men of heart. I do not know but you will have the million yet. Then, may your strength be equal to your day! But remember, sir, that every thing great and excellent in the world is in minorities.

"Far be from us, sir, any tone of patronage; we ought rather to ask yours. We know the austere condition of liberty, — that it must be re-conquered over and over again; yea, day by day; that it is a state of war; that it is always slipping from those who boast it, to those who fight for it, — and you, the foremost soldier of freedom in this age, it is for us to crave your judgment. Who are we that we should dictate to you?

"You have won your own. We only affirm it. This country of workingmen greets in you a worker. This republic greets in you a republican. You may well sit a doctor in the college of liberty. You have achieved your right to interpret our Washington. And I speak the sense, not only of every generous American, but the law of mind, when I say, that it is not those who live idly in the city called after his name, but those who, all over the world, think and act like him, who can claim to explain the sentiment of Washington."

Kossuth was welcomed in Concord with many demonstrations, a dinner, speeches in the town-hall, and a procession. In the long reply he made to Emerson's address were these words: —

"Your honored name is Emerson; and Emerson was the name of the man who, in a minister of the gospel, turned out with his people on the 19th of April of eternal memory, when the alarm-bell was first rung. The words of an Emerson administered counsel and the comfort of religion to the distressed then, and the words of an Emerson now speak the comfort of philosophy to the cause of oppressed liberty. I take hold of that augury. Religion and philosophy, you blessed twins, upon you I rely with my hopes of America. Religion, the philosophy of the heart, will make the Americans generous; and philosophy, the religion of the mind, will make the Americans wise; and all I claim is a generous wisdom and a wise generosity."

Emerson joined with W. H. Channing and J. F. Clarke in writing the *Memoirs* of Margaret Fuller, which appeared in 1852. He had very reluctantly made her acquaintance, distrusting her sharp personality, and having a horror of those "intense times" she was reported to have occasionally. "I remember," he says, "that she made me laugh more than I liked; for I was at that time an eager student of ethics, and had tasted the sweets of solitude and stoicism, and I found something profane in the hours of amusing gossip into which she drew me; and when I returned to my library had much to think of the crackling of thorns under a pot." He is writing of their first visit, in July, 1836; but they soon became friends, though they never found full sympathy in each other. She writes that he was not fully responsive to her outbursts of sentiment, was cold and unapproachable; while he found in her too much of the sibyl, and did not enjoy "the presence of a rather mountainous *me*." "She soon became," he says, "an established friend and frequent inmate of our house, and continued thenceforward for years to come once in three or four months to spend a week or a fortnight with us. She adopted all the people and all the interests she found here. 'Your people shall be my people, and yonder darling boy I shall cherish as my own.' Her ready sympathies endeared her to my wife and my mother, each of whom highly esteemed her good sense and sincerity. She suited each and all." He introduced her to the old English writers, and made her "acquainted with Chaucer, with Ben Jonson, with Herbert, Chapman, Ford, Beaumont and Fletcher, with Bacon, and Sir Thomas Browne. I was seven years her senior," he says, "and had the habit of idle reading in old English books; and, though not much versed, yet quite enough to give me the right to lead her." Of her peculiar gifts he says, —

"She was an active, inspiring companion and correspondent; and all the art, the thought, and the nobleness in New England seemed at that moment related to her, and she to it. She was everywhere a welcome guest. The houses of her friends in town and country were open to her, and every hospitable attention eagerly offered. Her arrival was a holiday, and so was her abode. She stayed a few days, often a week, more seldom a month; and all tasks that could be suspended were put aside to catch the favorable hour, in walking, riding, or boating, to talk with this joyful guest, who brought wit, anecdotes, love-stories, tragedies, oracles with her, and, with her broad web of relations to so many friends, seemed like the queen of some parliament of love, who carried the key to all confidences, and to whom every question had been finally referred."

Emerson prepared that portion of the *Memoirs* relating to Margaret's conversations in Boston, one of the most unique passages in the history of American thought and literature. He also wrote of her life in Concord and Boston, which was the most interesting and suggestive period of her career. He wrote with enthusiasm, adding much to the value of one of the most interesting of biographies. In her aspirations after a higher life for woman he fully shared, entering earnestly into sympathy with all enterprises having that object in view. In 1856, in an address before the Woman's Rights Convention, though criticising the effort for mere political influence, he yet said that it is for women, not men, to determine if women wish an equal share in affairs. "If we refuse them a vote," he said, "we should refuse to tax them." He found this uprising of new opinion on the subject of woman's duties and privileges a wonderful fact, as showing the spontaneous sense of the hour; for the aspiration of this century, he said, will be the code of the next. A little later, in 1862, when a woman's journal was proposed to be published in Boston, he wrote for it a short essay,[1] that fully defines his position on this subject.

[1] As the proposed journal was not started, the essay remained unpublished until it appeared in the Woman's Journal of March 26, 1881.

"It is very cheap wit, he says, that finds i
woman should vote. Educate and refine societ
point, bring together a cultivated society of both
ing-room to consult and decide by voices in a que
a question of right, and is there any absurdity
difficulty in obtaining their authentic opinions?
be none in a hundred companies if you educate th
them to judge. And for the effect of it, I can
certainly all my points would be sooner carried in t
voted.

"On the questions that are important: whethe
shall be in one person, or whether representative,
cratic; whether men shall be holden in bondage, c
alive and eaten as in Typee, or hunted with blood
country, shall be hanged for stealing, or hanged at
unlimited sale of cheap liquors shall be allowed;
I suppose, as intelligent a vote as the Irish voter
York, and Philadelphia. . . .

"Here are two or three objections: first, want
dom; second, a too purely ideal view; third, dan
tion.

"For their want of intimate knowledge of affai
this should disqualify them from voting at any to
I have ever attended. I could heartily wish th
sound. But if any man will take the trouble to se
vote,—how many gentlemen are willing to take c
trouble of thinking and determining for you, and
doors of the polls, give every innocent citizen his t
in, informing him that this is the vote of his part
cent citizen, without further demur, carries it to
can not but think that most women might vote as

"For the other point, of their not knowing the
ing at abstract right without allowance for circum
not a disqualification, but a qualification. Huma
up of partialities. Each citizen has an interest
own, which, if followed out to the extreme, woul
for any other citizen. One man is timid, and a
would change nothing, and the other is pleased w
wishes schools, another, armies; one, gunboats
gardens. Bring all these biases together, and son
favor of them all. Every one is a half-vote; but
behind him brings the other or corresponding hal
reasonable result is had. Now, there is no lack,
expediency, or of the interest of trade, or of
interests being neglected. There is no lack of v
the physical wants; and if in your city the unec
vote numbers thousands, representing a brutal ig
physical wants, it is to be corrected by an educa
vote representing the desires of honest and refine
wants, the passions, the vices, are allowed a full

hands of a half-brutal, intemperate population, I think it but fair that the virtues, the aspirations, should be allowed a full vote as an offset, through the purest of the people. As for the unsexing and contamination, — that only accuses our existing politics, shows how barbarous we are, that our policies are so crooked, made up of things not to be spoken, to be understood only by wink and nudge; this man is to be coaxed, and that man to be bought, and that other to be duped. . . .

"I do not think it yet appears that women wish this equal share in public affairs. But it is they, and not we, that are to determine it. Let the laws be purged of every barbarous remainder, every barbarous impediment to women. Let the public donations for education be equally shared by them. Let them enter a school as freely as a church. Let them have and hold and give their property as men do theirs, and in a few years it will easily appear whether they wish a voice in making the laws that are to govern them. If you do refuse them a vote, you will also refuse to tax them, according to our Teutonic principles, — no representation, no tax. . . .

"The new movement is a tide shared by the spirits of men and women. You may proceed on the faith that whatever the woman's heart is prompted to desire, the man's mind is simultaneously prompted to accomplish."

In 1856 his *English Traits* was published, and was well received on both sides of the Atlantic. It is a fine analysis of the leading characteristics of a great nation, remarkable for its subtle discriminations and for its clear insight into national tendencies. Hawthorne and Taine have written valuable and interesting books about England; but they are descriptive and sketchy, not to be compared with *English Traits* as studies of the nation itself. They describe locations and phases of society; they do not enter upon an analysis of the national life, or describe the qualities which have made that nation one of the greatest in modern times. Tocqueville's *Democracy in America* is a discussion of the Constitution of the United States and its workings; *English Traits* describes a people. Miss Martineau's first book about the United States comes nearer than any other to Emerson's, and yet it partakes much more of the nature of a book of travels. She wrote with a much more limited purpose, and she gave greater attention to special phases of national character. The merits of *English Traits* have obtained it the recognition of translation into several of the leading European languages.

In March, 1856, he gave a course of lectures in Freeman-place Chapel, Boston. The subjects were English Civilization, France, Signs of the Times, Beauty, The Poet, The Scholar. The lecture on France was greatly admired by those who heard it, and was thought to be quite equal to *English Traits*. He has always refused to print it, and has not repeated it of late years. Another lecture of this period was one on the Anglo-American Race, delivered in New York in 1855. It was a subtle analysis of the American character, similar to those of the English and French made at the same time.

Every thing in America, he said, proceeds at a rapid rate; the next moment eats the last. Whatever we do, suffer, or propose, is for the immediate entertainment of the company. We have a newspaper published every hour through the day, and our whole existence and performance slides into it. The leading features of the Americans are best seen at the West, where the people have free play. If you would see the American, it is said you must cross the Alleghanies. Rashness marks every thing there. The men can not be depended on there, nor their works. Every thing wears a new aspect. The men have not shed their canine teeth.

The Anglo-Saxon race has always been distinguished for its devotion to politics. In this country a prodigious stride has been taken through universal suffrage. The fact that everybody is eligible exasperates the discussion. Practically, the result has been that men of the middle class have been elected, and by no means men of the first class; and this practice has gained much of late. It is certainly desirable that the best and wisest men should be trusted with the helm of power.

The American is more intellectual than the Englishman; he has chambers opened in his mind which the Englishman has not. The American is a pushing, versatile, victorious race, with a wonderful power of absorption. Here is a grave interest, — the fortune of a quarter of the world, and of a race as important as any in it. Everybody here works every day and night, and nobody knows whither we are drifting, or can chant the destiny of America. But two facts appear; first, in the activity of the people up to this time there is a certain fatalism. The people being associated with pine, chestnut, iron, coal, and ice, they have wrought in these, and they have done the best they could. In short, they have been the river-hand and the sea-hand. On the coast they have followed the sea; in the West they have followed the river. But the verdict of history is, that they have not kept the promise of their founders. They have shown no enlarged policy. A liberal measure has no chance. On education, temperance, copyright, and on the claims of injured parties, the Anglo-American usually gives a selfish verdict. What can be worse than our legislation on slavery? If there be any worse, be sure we shall find it out, and make that law. The tone of the press is not lower on slavery than on every other subject. Criminal on that, it is ready to be criminal on every other.

Our statesmen are not men of ideas. They represent property rather than principle. They follow the sea or the river. But we have much individualism; and in this fact, as well as that we have a highly intellectual organization, and can see and feel moral distinctions, and that on such an organization sooner or later truth must tell, and to such ears speak, is our hope. And as we have been subject to fate in corn and cotton, yet there is fate in thought also; so that the largest thought and widest love is born with victory on its head, and must prevail.[1]

The lecture on the Natural Method of Intellectual Philosophy, delivered at this time, contained a very fully developed account of his own philosophical views. In 1852 he lectured on Natural Aristocracy. The essay on Poetry in *Letters and Social Aims* was read at Cambridge in 1854. A number of the university students went in sleighs to Concord, where he was announced to lecture. From some local cause the lecture was postponed. Emerson was worried that they should have had their fifteen miles' ride end in a disappointment, took them to his home, entertained them through the evening, and promised to go to Cambridge and lecture for them. He went, and spoke on poetry, having Lowell, Longfellow, and other poets in his audience. The lecture was given in one of the university rooms, and its "effect was electrical."[2] In 1859 he lectured on Morals, Conversation, Culture, Domestic Life, and Natural Religion. He gave a course in Freeman-place Chapel, Boston, on the Law of Success, Originality, Criticism, Clubs, Manners, and Morals. He attended a Burns festival in Boston this year, Jan. 25, it being the one hundredth anniversary of the poet's birth. Lowell was present, and has said,

[1] From a newspaper report. [2] M. D. Conway in Fraser's Magazine.

that, in the "closely filled speech of his at the Burns centenary dinner, every word seemed to have just dropped down to him from the clouds. He looked far away over the heads of his hearers with a vague kind of expectation, as into some private heaven of invention, and the winged period came at last to obey the spell. 'My dainty Ariel!' he seemed murmuring to himself as he cast down his eyes as if in deprecation of the frenzy of applause, and caught another sentence from the sibyline leaves that lay before him ambushed behind a dish of fruit, and seen only by nearest neighbors. Every sentence brought down the house as I never saw one brought down before; and it is not so easy to hit Scotsmen with a sentiment that has no hint of native brogue in it. I watched — for it was an interesting study — how the quick sympathy ran flashing from face to face down the long tables like an electric spark, thrilling as it went, and then exploded in a thunder of plaudits. I watched till tables and faces vanished; for I, too, found myself caught up in the common enthusiasm, and my excited fancy set me under the *bema* listening to him who fulmined over Greece." This eloquent and magnetic speech was closed with this testimony to the power of Burns's poetry and the expansiveness of his fame: —

"The memory of Burns, — I am afraid heaven and earth have taken too good care of it to leave us any thing to say. The west winds are murmuring it. Open the windows behind you, and hearken for the incoming tide, — what the waves say of it. The doves perching always on the eaves of the stone chapel opposite may know something about it. Every name in broad Scotland keeps his fame bright. The memory of Burns, — every man's and boy's and girl's head carry snatches of his songs, and can say them by heart; and, what is strangest of all, never learned them from a book, but from mouth to mouth. The wind whispers them, the birds whistle them, the corn, barley, and bulrushes hoarsely rustle them; nay, the music-boxes at Geneva are framed and toothed to play them, the hand-organs of the Savoyards in all cities repeat them, and the chimes of bells ring them in the spires. They are the property and the solace of mankind."

In 1860 *The Conduct of Life* was published. Its essays, as usual, had been delivered as lectures during the previous half-dozen years. It contains some of his most practical, as well as some of his most philosophical, essays. It is, as a whole, less mystical than his previous books, and consequently loses some of the finest flavor of his thought. The essays on Fate, Worship, Illusions, and Considerations by the Way are among his very best, however, giving important additions to his philosophic thought. As usual this book received the most unmerciful treatment from some of the critics. Noah Porter said, in *The New Englander*, that the writer did not know enough of religion to speak upon it with authority; and wrote of "the utter shallowness and flippancy of the judgments Emerson expresses concerning Christianity." "Of all the descriptions," this critic says, "we have ever read of the merciless and remorseless absolutism of a universe of impersonal law, this strikes us as the most horrible." The English *Saturday Review* was even more severe, for it said, —

"He manages to write what the crowds which throng American lecture-rooms appear, for some strange reason, to relish; and he continues to put it in an unintelligible form. By these two feats he secures a popularity which there is no other way of explaining. That an American audience likes to hear the dreariest of all dreary platitudes when they are strung together in what is called an oration, is a fact attested by credible proof, and must be believed like any other strange circumstance which rests on that authority. That, being in that state of mind, mystical language should please them is what experience would suggest, if, indeed, experience applies to people who like orations. It is inconceivable that Mr. Emerson should have any claims to any higher reputation than this." He is also described as "so commonplace a writer," who "intersperses his dreary platitudes with downright nonsense."

His previous books had sold very slowly, but twenty-five hundred copies of *The Conduct of Life* were disposed of in two days after its publication. There were many other tokens of his growing favor. His books were received, both at home and abroad, with many new signs of approval; while the circle of his admirers constantly increased. In 1850 Parker wrote of him as "the most original thinker we have produced in America; a man of wonderful gifts." In 1857 he says in one of his letters, "Emerson has touched the deepest strings on the human heart, and, ten centuries after he is immortal, will wake the music which he first waked."

In a carefully discriminating article, which does not spare Emerson's faults, and yet is full of sympathetic admiration, Parker says, —

> "He has not uttered a word that is false to his own mind or conscience; has not suppressed a word because he thought it too high for man's comprehension, and therefore dangerous for the repose of men. He never compromises. He sees the chasm between the ideas which come of man's nature and the institutions which represent only his history; he does not seek to cover up the chasm, which daily grows wider between truth and public opinion, between justice and the state, between Christianity and the church; he does not seek to fill it up, but he asks men to step over and build institutions commensurate with their ideas. He trusts himself, trusts man, and trusts God. He has confidence in all the attributes of Infinity. Hence he is serene; nothing disturbs the even poise of his character, and he walks erect. Nothing impedes him in his search for the true, the lovely and the good; no private hope, no private fear, no love of wife or child or gold or ease or fame. He never seeks his own reputation; he takes care of his being, and leaves his seeming to take care of itself. Fame may seek him; he never goes out of his way a single inch for her.
>
> "He has not written a line which is not conceived in the interest of mankind. He never writes in the interest of a section, of a party, of a church, of a man, always in the interest of mankind. Hence comes the ennobling influence of his works. Emerson belongs to the exceptional literature of the times; and, while his culture joins him to the history of man, his ideas and his whole life enable him to represent also the nature of man, and so to write for the future. He is one of the rare exceptions amongst our educated men, and helps redeem American literature from the charge of imitation, conformity, meanness of aim, and hostility to the powers of mankind. No faithful man is too low for his approval and encouragement; no faithless man too high and popular for his rebuke."

This is one of Parker's best critical articles,[1] as well as one of the best papers ever written about Emerson. Parker is especially fascinated with the original and American cast of Emerson's mind; and calls him "the most republican of republicans, the most protestant of

[1] Massachusetts Quarterly Review for 1849, reprinted in Miss Cobbe's edition of his collected works, vol. x. p. 196.

the dissenters." His culture is cosmopolitan, has no varnish about it; but it has penetrated deep into his consciousness Parker finds he belongs to a very high rank in literature. "He is a very extraordinary man. To no English writer since Milton, can be assigned so high a place; even Milton himself, great genius though he was, and great architect of beauty, has not added so many thoughts to the treasury of the race; no, nor been the author of so much loveliness. Emerson is a man of genius such as does not often appear; such as has never appeared before in America, and but seldom in the world. He learns from all sorts of men; but no English writer, we think, is so original." These opinions of Parker's have lost none of their force since they were written, and are far truer now than then; while they would be accepted by a much larger number of persons. The years since they were written have fully confirmed his high estimate of the genius of Emerson.

X.

THE ANTI-SLAVERY MOVEMENT.

EMERSON early gave his sympathies to the movement against slavery. When no other church in Boston was open to the friends of liberty, May and others spoke in his; and he was even ready to welcome Garrison there. In the Transcendental Club, when others held aloof from sympathy with this movement, he defended it, and expressed his faith in Garrison. Though not himself inclined to adopt the methods of the radical agitators, he could but feel they were in the right in their aims, and that they represented the highest moral sense of the community. His tendencies of thought led him in another direction to secure the same ends, but to this great reform he gave such help as he could; and his influence on his times, the real spirit and purpose of the man, are not likely to be understood without a knowledge of his relations to this agitation. He had but little faith in external methods of reform, and did not think much could be done by legislation. His faith was in the moral and spiritual influences which lead men out of passion and selfishness, but he could not feel that selfishness was to be opposed with hatred. It was because the life of the American people was low, vulgar, mean, that slavery was possible; and he thought slavery could only be gotten rid of by raising the moral standard, and by a larger appreciation of the human soul. Though little inclined to the ordinary methods of reform, Harriet Martineau testifies to his early espousal of the cause of the slave, when almost no one in Boston was ready to plead in behalf of justice and humanity. In speaking of how prone public men were to shrink from the defense of a new and hated cause, she says all were not so, but some were eager and glad in this good work.

"The Emersons, for instance (for the adored Charles Emerson was living then), they were not men to join an association for any object, and least of all for any moral one; nor were they likely to quit their abstract meditations for a concrete employment on behalf of the negroes. Yet they did that which made me feel that I knew them, through the very cause in which they did not implicate themselves. At the time of the hubbub against me in Boston, Charles Emerson stood alone in a large company in defense of the right of free thought and speech, and declared that he had rather see Boston in ashes than that I or anybody should be debarred in any way from perfectly free speech. His brother Waldo invited me to be his guest in the midst of my unpopularity, and during my visit told me his course about this matter of slavery. He did not see that there was any particular thing for him to do in it then; but when, in coaches or steamboats or anywhere else, he saw people of color ill-used, or heard bad doctrine or sentiment propounded, he did what he could and said what he thought. Since that date he has spoken more abundantly and boldly the more critical the times became; and he is now, and has long been, completely identified with the abolitionists in conviction and sentiment, though it is out of his way to join himself to their organization."[1]

This was in 1835, and he continued to maintain the same position for many years. His address at Concord in 1844, however, on the anniversary of emancipation in the West Indies, distinctly put him in the company of the abolitionists. It was an eloquent and forcible history of the agitation against slavery in England, and of the results of its abolition in the colonies, with a plea, drawn from these facts, for abolition at home. "I might well hesitate," he says at the outset, "coming from other studies, and without the smallest claim to be a special laborer in this work of humanity, to undertake to set this matter before you; but I shall not apologize for my weakness." "I am heart-sick," he goes on to say, "when I read how the slaves came into slavery, and how they are kept there; for language must be raked, the secrets of slaughter-houses and infamous holes that can not front the day must be ransacked, to tell what negro slavery has been." He pictured in glowing and

[1] Autobiography of Harriet Martineau, vol. i. p. 375.

indignant words the evils of slavery, and held up to scorn the cowardice of the men of Massachusetts and New England in their betrayal of the interests of liberty; and he did not spare the senators and representatives who had submitted to the slave-power. His attitude toward this cause may be best seen in the closing paragraphs of the address:—

"I have said that this event interests us because it came mainly from the concession of the whites. I add, that in part it is the earning of the blacks. They won the pity and respect which they have received by their powers and native endowments. I think this a circumstance of the highest import. Their whole future is in it. Our planet, before the age of written history, had its races of savages, like the generations of sour paste, or the animalcules that wriggle and bite in a drop of putrid water. Who cares for these or for their wars? We do not wish a world of bugs or of birds; neither afterward of Scythians, Caribs, or Feejees. The grand style of nature, her great periods, is all we observe in them. Who cares for oppressing whites or oppressed blacks twenty centuries ago, more than for bad dreams? Eaters and food are in the harmony of nature; and there, too, is the germ for ever protected, unfolding gigantic leaf after leaf, a newer flower, a richer fruit, in every period, yet its next product is never to be guessed. It will only save what is worth saving; and it saves, not by compassion, but by power. It appoints no police to guard the lion but his teeth and claws, no fort or city for the bird but his wings, no rescue for flies and mites but their spawning numbers, which no ravages can overcome. It deals with men after the same manner. If they are rude and foolish, down they must go. When at last in a race a new principle appears,—an idea,—*that* conserves it; ideas only save races. If the black man is feeble, and not important to the existing races, not on a parity with the best race, the black man must serve, and be exterminated. But if the black man carries in his bosom an indispensable element of a new and coming civilization, for the sake of that element no wrong nor strength nor circumstance can hurt him; he will survive, and play his part. So now the arrival in the world of such men as Toussaint and the Haytian heroes, or of the leaders of their race in Barbadoes and Jamaica, outweighs in good omen all the English and American humanity. The anti-slavery of the whole world is dust in the balance before this,—is a poor squeamishness and nervousness; and might and the right are here. Here is the anti-slave; here is man; and if you have man, black or white is an insignificance. The intellect, that is miraculous! Who has it has the talisman. His skin and bones, though they were of the color of night, are transparent; and the everlasting stars shine through with attractive beams. But a compassion for that which is not and can not be useful and lovely is degrading and futile. All the songs and newspapers and money subscriptions and vituperation of such as do not think with us will avail nothing against a fact. I say to you, you must save yourself, black or white, man or woman; other help is none. I esteem the occasion of this jubilee to be the proud discovery that the black race can contend with the white race; that, in the great anthem we call history, a piece of many parts and vast compass, after playing a long time a very low and subdued accompaniment, they perceive the time arrived when they can strike in with effect, and take a master's part in the music. The civility of the world has reached that pitch that their more moral genius is becoming indispensable, and the quality of this race is to be honored for itself. For this they have been preserved in sandy deserts, in rice-swamps, in kitchens and shoe-shops, so long; now let them emerge, clothed and in their own form.

"There remains the very elevated consideration which the subject opens, but which belongs to more abstract views than we are now taking; this, namely, that the civility of no race can be perfect whilst another race is degraded. It is a doctrine alike of the oldest and of the newest philosophy, that man is one, and that you can not injure any member without a sympathetic injury to all the members. America is not civil whilst Africa is barbarous.

"These considerations seem to leave no choice for the action of the intellect and the conscience of the country. There have been moments in this, as well as in every piece of moral history, when there seemed room for the infusions of a skeptical philosophy; when it seemed doubtful whether brute force would not triumph in the eternal struggle. I doubt not that sometimes a despairing negro, when jumping over a ship's sides to escape from the white devils who surrounded him, has believed there was no vindication of right; it is horrible to think of, but it seemed so. I doubt not that sometimes the negro's friend, in the face of scornful and brutal hundreds of traders and drivers, has felt his heart sink. Especially, it seems to me, some degree of despondency is pardonable when he observes the men of conscience and intellect, his own natural allies and champions, — those whose attention should be nailed to the grand objects of this cause, — so hotly offended by whatever incidental petulances or infirmities of indiscreet defenders of the negro as to permit themselves to be ranged with the enemies of the human race; and names which should be the alarums of liberty and the watchwords of truth are mixed up with all the rotten rabble of selfishness and tyranny. I assure myself that this coldness and blindness will pass away. A single noble wind of sentiment will scatter them for ever. I am sure that the good and wise elders, the ardent and generous youth, will not permit what is incidental and exceptional to withdraw their devotion from the essential and permanent characters of the question. There have been moments, I said, when men might be forgiven who doubted. Those moments are past. Seen in masses, it can not be disputed, there is progress in human society. There is a blessed necessity by which the interest of men is always driving them to the right;

and, again, making all crime mean and ugly. The genius of the Saxon race, friendly to liberty; the enterprise, the very muscular vigor of this nation, are inconsistent with slavery. The intellect, with blazing eye, looking through history from the beginning onward, gazes on this blot, and it disappears. The sentiment of right, once very low and indistinct, but ever more articulate because it is the voice of the universe, pronounces freedom. The Power that built this fabric of things affirms it in the heart, and in the history of the first of August has made a sign to the ages of his will."

In the heated discussions of slavery, which followed during the next dozen years, Emerson found himself in sympathy with the Free-Soil party. In 1852, when Clough visited Concord, he wrote, "I had Abolition well out with Emerson, with whom one can talk with pleasure on the subject. His view is in the direction of purchasing emancipation." Still later in the year, Clough wrote that "Emerson is a Free-Soiler." The year before, when John Gorham Palfrey, having opposed slavery very strongly in Congress, and been defeated for re-election, was nominated for governor on the Free-Soil ticket, Emerson spoke in numerous places in his behalf. In his address in Cambridge he expressed regret that the scholar should be called away from his tasks to take part in affairs; but, instead of principles ruling in the affairs of the nation, he found a power in favor of slavery, which sadly lowered the spirit in which the country was founded. He portrayed the evils of slavery, how it dragged every thing down into its corruption and debasement. Webster had just before, in a spirit of compromise, consented to what was regarded by the anti-slavery party as a base betrayal of trust. Emerson described slavery as having captured the best forces of the country. He pictured the car of slavery with all its attendant abominations, and Webster as a leading horse straining to drag on this car. Without naming Webster, he pointed to him as a last instance of how this evil corrupted all it touched.

In January, 1855, he gave one of a course of anti-slavery lectures in Tremont Temple, Boston. It was a strong and forcible address, full of fire, alive with magnetic power, plain and simple in style; a most powerful speech, and was frequently applauded. He was listened to throughout with breathless interest. He charged the prevalent indifference to the wrongs of the slave to skepticism concerning great human duties and concerns. "In 1850 men in republican America passed a statute which made justice and mercy subject to fine and imprisonment, and multitudes were found to declare that there existed no higher law in the universe than this paper statute which uprooted the foundations of rectitude." He spoke of the low condition of politics, and, referring to the action of Webster and others, said, "Those who have gone to Congress from us were honest, well-meaning men. I heard congratulations from good men, their friends, when they went to Washington, that they were honest and thoroughly reliable, yes, obstinately honest; yet they voted for this criminal measure with the basest of the populace. I hate and saw not the sneer of the bullies that duped them with alleged state necessity, because they had no hope, no burning splendor of awe within their own breasts. Well, while a refuge was left, they had honor enough to feel degraded, and might have left the place instead of having become indifferentists."

The same year, in an address before the Anti-slavery Society of New York, he declared that "an immoral law is void," and stated his own favorite method for abolishing slavery.

"Every wise American will say, in the collision of statutes, in their doubtful interpretation, that liberty is the great order which all over the world we are to promote. This is the right meaning of the statute which exterminates crime, and extends to every man the largest liberty compatible with the liberty of every other man. No citizen will go wrong, who, upon every question, leans to the side of general liberty. Men inspire each other. It is so delicious to act with great masses to great aims; for instance, one would say, the summary or gradual abolition of slavery. Why, in the name of common sense and the peace of mankind, is not this made the subject of instant negotiation and settlement? What are the great brains for, the great administrative faculties, that abound here, if they are not jointly, seriously, and immediately to propose some scheme which shall peaceably settle this question, in accordance at once with the interests of the South, and with the settled conscience of the North? It is not really a great task, a great fight, for this country to accomplish, to buy that property of the planter, as the British nation bought the West-Indian slaves. I say buy! never conceding the right of the planter to own, but acknowledging the calamity of his position, and willing to bear a countryman's share in relieving him, and because it is the only practical course, and is innocent. Well, here is the right public or social function, which one man can not do, and which all men must do. We shall one day bring the states shoulder to shoulder, and the citizens man to man, to exterminate slavery. It was said a little while ago that it would cost a thousand or twelve hundred millions, now it is said it would cost two thousand millions; such is the enhancement of property. Well, was there ever any contribution that was so enthusiastically paid as this will be? The United States will be brought to give every inch of their public lands for a purpose like this. Every state will contribute its surplus revenue. Every man will bear his part. We will have a chimney-tax. We will give up our coaches and wine and watches. The church will melt her plate. The father of his country shall wait, well pleased, a little longer for his monument. Franklin will wait for his; the Pilgrim Fathers for theirs; and the patient Columbus, who waited all his mortality for justice, shall wait a part of immortality also. We will call upon the rich beneficiaries who found asylums, hospitals, Lowell Institutions, and Astor libraries; upon wealthy bachelors and wealthy maidens, to make the state their heirs, as they were wont to do in Rome. The rich shall give of their riches; the merchants of their commerce; the mechanics of their strength; the needle-women will give, and children can have a Cent Society. If, really, the thing could come to a negotiation, and a price were named, I do not think that any price, founded upon an estimate that figures could fairly represent, would be unmanageable. Every man in this land would give a week's work to dig away this accursed mountain of slavery, and force it for ever out of the world."

When Sumner was caned by Brooks, May 22, 1856, a meeting of sympathy was held in Concord on the 26th, and Emerson spoke with great appreciation of the services of that noble senator.

"The events of the last few years and months and days have taught us the lessons of centuries. I do not see how a barbarous community and a civilized community can constitute one state. I think we must get rid of slavery, or we must get rid of freedom. Life has no parity of value in the free state and in the slave state. In one, it is adorned with education, with skilled labor, with arts, with long prospective interests, with social family ties, with honor and justice. In the other, life is a fever, man is an animal, given to pleasure, frivolous, irritable, spending his days in hunting, and practicing with deadly weapons to defend himself against his slaves and against his companions brought up in the same idle and dangerous way. . . .

"The whole state of South Carolina does not now offer any one, or any number of persons, who are to be weighed for a moment in the scale with such a person as the meanest of them all has now struck down. . . . The outrage is the more shocking from the singularly pure character of its victim. Mr. Sumner's position is exceptional in its honor. He has not taken his degrees in the caucus and in hack politics. . . . His friends, I remember, were told that they would find Sumner a man of the world like the rest; 'tis quite impossible to be at Washington and not bend; he will bend as the rest have done. Well, he did not bend. He took his position and kept it. He meekly bore the cold shoulder from some of his New-England colleagues, the hatred of his enemies, the pity of the indifferent, cheered by the love and respect of good men with whom he acted, and has stood for the North, a little in advance of all the North, and therefore without adequate support. He has never faltered in his maintenance of justice and freedom. He has gone beyond the large expectation of his friends in his increasing ability and his manlier tone.

"I have heard that some of his political friends tax him with indolence or negligence in refusing to make electioneering speeches, or otherwise to bear his part in the labor which party organization requires. I say it to his honor. But more to his honor are the faults which his enemies lay to his charge. I think if Mr. Sumner had any vices we should be likely to hear of them. They have fastened their eyes, like microscopes, now for five years, on every act, word, manner, and movement, to find a flaw; and with what result? His opponents accuse him neither of drunkenness, nor debauchery, nor job, nor peculation, nor rapacity, nor personal aims of any kind. No; but of what? Why, beyond this charge, which it is impossible was ever sincerely made, that he broke over the proprieties of debate, I find him accused of publishing his opinion of the Nebraska conspiracy in a letter to the people of the United States, with discourtesy. Then, that he is an abolitionist; as if every sane man were not an abolitionist, or a believer that all men should be free. And the third crime he stands charged with is, that his speeches were written before they were spoken; which must of course be true in Sumner's case, as it was true of Webster, of Adams, of Calhoun, of Burke, of Chatham, of Demosthenes, of every first-rate speaker that ever lived. It is the high compliment he pays to the intelligence of the Senate and of the country. . . .

"When I think of these most small faults as the worst which party hatred could allege, I think I may borrow the language which Bishop Burnet applied to Sir Isaac Newton, and say that Charles Sumner 'has the whitest soul I ever knew.' . . . I wish that he may know the shudder of terror that ran through all this community on the first tidings of the brutal attack. Let him hear that every man of worth in New England loves his virtues; that every mother thinks of him as the protector of families; that every friend of freedom thinks him the friend of freedom. And if our arms at this distance can not defend him from assassins, we confide the defense of a life so precious to all honorable men and true patriots, and to the Almighty Maker of men."

Emerson admired the sturdy qualities of John Brown and his indomitable faith. Brown was several times in Concord, and found a hearty welcome at Emerson's house. When the raid was made at Harper's Ferry, Emerson still found himself in sympathy with the old hero, though reluctant to regard such means as the best to secure freedom. He heard Thoreau's address on Brown with great delight, and said that he had found the truth of the matter. There soon came an opportunity for him to speak; and in a lecture delivered in Tremont Temple, for the Parker Fraternity, Nov. 8, 1859, he gave a decided expression to his sympathies. The subject was Courage, and portions of the lecture have since been published in *Society and Solitude* under the same title. Speaking of the courage which has characterized the world's heroes, he said, that, "as soon as they are born they take a bee-line to the rack of the inquisition or the ax of the tyrant." He then made the subject of the hour, the man all men were discussing, the illustration of this truth.

"Look nearer, at the ungathered records of those who have gone to languish in prison or to die in rescuing others, or in rescuing themselves from chains of the slave; or look at that new saint, than whom none purer or more brave was ever led by love of man into conflict and death, — a new saint, waiting yet his martyrdom, and who, if he shall suffer, will make the gallows glorious, like the cross."

This was all he said on that subject, but it was enough, as they are immortal words; and they were received by prolonged and enthusiastic applause. He was reported as saying that Brown would make the gallows *as* glorious as the cross, and his few emphatic words were the cause of much excitement. The *Courier* spoke of his "blasphemous comparison," and said that those who consented to this wickedness denied the Lord who bought them. A meeting of sympathy with Brown's family, and to raise money for their support, was held in Tremont Temple Nov. 18. John A. Andrew presided; while Emerson, Phillips, and Dr. Manning made addresses. Emerson gave an account of Brown's life, and showed the wickedness of the laws for the protection of the slaveholders. Concerning Brown, he said, —

> "This commanding event, the sequel of which has brought us together, eclipses all others which have occurred for a long time in our history; and I am very glad to see this sudden interest in the hero of Harper's Ferry has provoked an extreme curiosity in all parts of the Republic in regard to the details of his history. He is so transparent that all men see him through. He is a man to make friends wherever on earth courage and integrity are esteemed; the rarest of heroes, a pure idealist, with no by-ends of his own. Every one who has heard him speak has been impressed alike by his simple, artless goodness, joined with his sublime courage. He joins that perfect Puritan faith which brought his fifth ancestor to Plymouth Rock, with his grandfather's ardor in the Revolution. He believes in two articles, — two instruments, shall I say? — the Golden Rule and the Declaration of Independence.
>
> "It is easy to see what a favorite he will be with history, which plays such pranks with temporary reputations. Nothing can resist the sympathy which all elevated minds must feel with Brown, and through them the whole civilized world; and if he must suffer, he must drag official gentlemen into an immortality most undesirable, and of which they have already some disagreeable forebodings. Indeed, it is the *reductio ad absurdum* of slavery when the governor of Virginia is forced to hang a man whom he declares to be a man of the most integrity, truthfulness, and courage he has ever met. Is that the kind of man the gallows was built for? It were bold to affirm that there is within that broad Commonwealth at this moment another citizen as worthy to live, and as deserving of all public and private honor, as this poor prisoner."

Emerson took part in a meeting of sympathy with Brown held in Concord Dec. 2. On the next Sunday, Dec. 4, he lectured for Theodore Parker's society in Boston on Morals. He spoke of the desire of giving freedom to those who are in bondage, of establishing a moral, intellectual, governmental equality such as had lifted an obscure Connecticut farmer into the regions of the great men, and made all others appear as inferior men. It is hard, he said, to find in all history so noble a man as this, who has dared to sacrifice life to principle. A few such men have done more for the world than all the merely intellectual men mankind has ever seen. At Salem, Jan. 6, he again spoke at a Brown meeting, declaring that "every thing which is said of Brown leaves people a little dissatisfied; but as soon as they read his own speeches and letters, they are heartily contented; such is the singleness of purpose which justifies him to the head and heart of all." He calls Brown's "a romantic character, absolutely without any vulgar trait, living to ideal ends, without any mixture of self-indulgence or compromise." In closing his address, he said, "The sentiment of mercy is the natural recoil which the laws of the universe provide to protect mankind from destruction by savage passions. And our blind statesmen go up and down with committees of vigilance and safety, hunting for the origin of this new heresy. They will need a very vigilant committee, indeed, to find its birthplace, and a very strong force to root it out. For the arch-abolitionist, older than Brown and older than the Shenandoah Mountains, is Love, whose other name is Justice, which was before Alfred, before Lycurgus, before slavery, and will be after it."

Emerson was neither a zealous agitator nor an enthusiastic worker in this great controversy; for he was unfitted for it, both by nature and by reason of his views of human progress. His part in it shows that he did not hold aloof when there was any work he could do, and that his heart was in it from first to last. In his Ode, inscribed to W. H. Channing, he replies to a demand that he should do more in this cause, and defends his right to refuse to leave his study for the arena of reform. He complains that —

> "Virtue palters, right is hence,
> Freedom praised, but hid;"

and though —

> "loath to grieve
> The evil time's sole patriot,"

he can not consent to leave his tasks for the work in which his zealous friend would engage him. He says that even Boston would serve the things of daily life, and forget all but the material ends of existence; and declares that —

"Things are of the snake."

So long as the spirit of reform was low, there was no hope; and he must rest his faith in the divine fires within the souls of men, which can not be quenched. Seeing the evils and corruptions of the time, he lost faith in the state and in all outward methods of growth and moral power. His own method, his own faith, was this: —

"Let man serve law for man,
Live for friendship, live for love,
For truth's and harmony's behoof;
The state may follow how it can,
As Olympus follows Jove."

As the agitation proceeded, and brave men took part in it, and it rose to a spirit of moral grandeur, he gave a heartier assent to the outward methods adopted. His faith in Brown, his immediate insight into the rare qualities of that true hero, gave him a greater zeal and a larger confidence in the spirit and purposes of the North. Few literary men, with natures so meditative and withdrawn from all material pursuits, have given so much thought and effort to such a cause. A student, a poet, a seer, the spiritual interpreter of our times, with no capacity for joining in the conflicts of men, he yet looked with eager eyes upon every phase of this great movement, watched it with growing hope, had faith in the triumph of freedom and love, gave such aid as he could and all his sympathies, to those seeking the emancipation of the poor and oppressed.

XI.

IN WAR-TIME.

THE hour of peril to great truths is the hour that tries men's souls. The peril to liberty Emerson plainly saw as slavery gained in power, and as compromise after compromise was made to it. He was no leader in the actual strife, but his spoken and printed word became plainer and more pertinent to the hour as the years went on and the peril deepened.[1] He took part in January, 1861, at the annual meeting of the Massachusetts Anti-slavery Society, in Boston. The speakers were often disturbed by a mob, and it was with great difficulty they could be heard. Emerson was frequently interrupted by hisses and other demonstrations of disapproval. He said that slavery is based on a crime of that fatal character that it decomposes men. "The barbarism which has lately appeared wherever that question has been touched, and in the action of the states where it prevails, seems to stupefy the moral sense. The moral injury of slavery is infinitely greater than its pecuniary and political injury. I really do not think the pecuniary mischief of slavery, which is always shown by statistics, worthy to be named in comparison with this power to subvert the reason of men; so that those who speak of it, who defend it, who act in its behalf, seem to have lost the moral sense." In speaking of the threatened secession, he used these emphatic words, appropriate for the hour and occasion: —

"In the great action now pending, all the forbearance, all the discretion possible, and yet all the firmness will be used by the rep-

[1] In Harper's Monthly for May, 1881, M. D. Conway describes a visit to Carlyle, and the reading of a letter "the Chelsea sage" had just received from Emerson, who took him to task for his criticisms of the American people.

resentatives of the North, and by the people at home. No man of patriotism, no man of natural sentiment, can undervalue the sacred Union which we possess; but if it is sundered, it will be because it had already ceased to have a vital tension. The action of to-day is only the ultimatum of what had already occurred. The bonds had ceased to exist, because of this vital defect of slavery at the South, actually separating them in sympathy, in thought, in character, from the people of the North; and then, if the separation had gone thus far, what is the use of a pretended tie? As to concessions, we have none to make. The monstrous concession made at the formation of the Constitution is all that ever can be asked; it has blocked the civilization and humanity of the times to this day."

The war made a great impression on him, and gave him a stronger faith in mankind. He found the people truer than he had expected, and was alike astonished and gladdened by the uprising at the North. It gave him a new idea of the relations of men to each other, of the value of the state, and of the *solidarité* of the race. During the earlier part of the war he spoke often on Sundays for Theodore Parker's society. After the battle of Bull Run, in a lecture delivered there, he said the judgment of God had come upon the people for their sins; but he said the struggle for freedom was developing a heroism and a moral grandeur noble to see. He had despaired of the nation before; but now he saw a purpose and devotion real and sublime, the promise of a better time to come. He said the people must be reverent and considerate and humble, under the circumstances of this judgment, and spoke with great confidence of Mr. Lincoln and his ability. In other lectures, at this time, he expressed his confidence in the idea of the Union and his new hope for the principles of the Republic. He was touched by the eagerness and discretion of the young men, the pure patriotism and consecration which was shown in so many instances, and the moral devotion of the people. As never before, he came to have faith in his country, to believe in her ideas, and to trust her future. He saw a new promise for morality and ideas in the heroic spirit of the North, and found himself in the fullest sympathy with the purposes of the hour.

In February, 1862, he was invited to Washington to give an anti-slavery lecture. He spoke in the Smithsonian-Institution building, on American Civilization, to a very large audience. Lincoln and his cabinet, and most of the other official persons in the capital, attended. Lincoln was much impressed by the lecture; and the next day Seward introduced him to Emerson. They had a long conference on the subject of slavery. The impression this lecture made was thus described by a local newspaper: "The audience received it, as they have the other anti-slavery lectures of the course, with unbounded enthusiasm. It was in many respects a wonerful lecture; and those who have often heard Mr. Emerson said it was one of his very best efforts, and that he seemed inspired through nearly the whole of it, especially the part referring to slavery and the war."

In this lecture[1] Emerson gave a sketch of the influences that go to the production of civilization, and said it "implies a facility of association, power to compare, the ceasing from fixed ideas." It is always the result of growth caused by some "novelty that astounds the mind, and provokes it to dare to change." Of the aids to development have been proximity to the sea-shore, climate, position of woman, and diffusion of knowledge. He pointed out the influence of material causes, even though so often dwelling upon the power of ideas. He says "the effect of a framed or stone house is immense on the tranquillity, power, and refinement of the builder." The road is a benefactor, missionary, wealth-bringer, maker of markets, and a vent for industry. We must all the time depend on the elements, use their power, and get the aid of their strength. When we learn to use the elements, to secure their aid in doing our work, propelling our ships, and in sending our messages, then civilization has been made fully possible. Complexity of organization, making a close dependence of all parts of society on all others, produces civilization. There can, however, be no high civility without a deep morality; and on that civilization depends. As our

[1] Printed in the Atlantic Monthly for April, 1862.

physical success depends on our implicit acceptance of the laws of nature, so our moral success depends on our acceptance of principles. We must hitch our wagon to a star, and work for those interests which the divinities honor and promote, — justice, love, freedom, knowledge, utility.

The true test of civilization is the kind of man the country turns out. There is an immense material advantage and prosperity possessed by this country; but the industry, skill, sobriety, and morality of the people are a better promise. The appearance of great men, the movement of great ideas, overtops in importance all mechanical advancement. The country where knowledge can not be diffused, where liberty is attacked and woman not respected, is not civil, but barbarous; and no advantages of soil, climate, or coast can resist these suicidal mischiefs.

He then turned to the Southern States, showed that they had trampled on morality, in denying a man's right to labor. The power and advantages of labor were shown, and its importance as an element of civilization. Two states of civilization, the one respecting labor, and the other based on slavery, we have tried to hold together. They do not agree, and all are anxious over the aspects of the war. America means opportunity, the last effort of Divine Providence in behalf of the human race; and a slavish following of precedents should not guide its destinies. The evil contended against has taken alarming proportions, and we must strike directly at the cause. The dangers have been clearly shown, there have been warnings enough. Slavery concealed nothing, and we knew where it would lead.

"In this national crisis, it is not argument that we want, but that rare courage which dares commit itself to a principle, believing that nature is its ally, and will create the instruments it requires, and more than make good any petty and injurious profit which it may disturb. There never was such a combination as this of ours, and the rules to meet it are not set down in any history. We want men of original perception and original action, who can open their eyes wider than to a nationality, namely, to a consideration of benefit to the human race, can act in the interest of civilization. Government must not be a parish-clerk, a justice of the peace. It has, of necessity, in any crisis of the state, the absolute powers of a dictator. The existing administration is entitled to the utmost candor. It is to be thanked for its angelic virtue, compared with any executive experiences with which we have been familiar. But the times will not allow us to indulge in compliment. I wish I saw in the people that inspiration, which, if government would not obey the same, it would leave the government behind, and create on the moment the means and executors it wanted. Better the war should more dangerously threaten us, should threaten fracture in what is still whole, and punish us with burned capitals and slaughtered regiments, and so exasperate the people to energy, exasperate our nationality. There are scriptures written invisibly on men's hearts, whose letters do not come out until they are enraged. They can be read by war-fires and by eyes in the last peril."

In other days of our history slavery could have been removed, if the free states had done their duty. They yielded; but a new opportunity is now given. "It looks as if we held the fate of the fairest possession of mankind in our hands, to be saved by our firmness, or to be lost by hesitation."

"The one power that has legs long enough and strong enough to cross the Potomac offers itself at this hour, — the one strong enough to bring all the civility up to the height of that which is best prays now at the door of Congress for leave to move. Emancipation is the demand of civilization. That is a principle; every thing else is intrigue. This is a progressive policy, puts the whole people in healthy, productive, amiable position, puts every man in the South in just and natural relations with every man in the North, laborer with laborer."

The Southerners love war, have just reached the civilization that craves it. They are fit for conflict, but we are laborers. They will dread forfeiture of the conditions that make war to them a profit, but we must abolish slavery or always hold them in subjection. The one weapon of real power for us is abolition. We have had compromises enough, and must now secure the doing of what we believe to be right. This will secure for the South a new atomic social composition which will lead to peace and prosperity.

"Now, in the name of all that is simple and generous, why should not this great right be done? Why should not America be capable of a second stroke for the well-being of the human race, as eighty or ninety years ago she was for the first? an affirmative step in the interests of human civility, urged on her, too, not by any romance of sentiment, but by her own extreme perils? It is very certain that the statesman who shall break through the cobwebs of doubt, fear, and petty cavil that lie in the way, will be greeted by the unanimous thanks of mankind. Men reconcile themselves very fast to a bold and good measure, when once it is taken, though they condemned it in advance. And this action which costs so little rids the world, at one stroke, of this degrading nuisance, the cause of war and ruin of nations. This measure at once puts all parties right. This is borrowing, as I said, the omnipotence of a principle. What is so foolish as the terror lest the blacks should be made furious by freedom and wages? It is denying these that is the outrage, and makes the danger from the blacks. But justice satisfies everybody, — white man, red man, yellow man, and black man. All like wages, and the appetite grows by feeding."

This measure needs to be adopted at once, for this weapon is slipping from our hands. The victory will at last come, however, when it deserves; and it can only come through Nature's appointed elements.

"I hope it is not a fatal objection to this policy, that it is simple and beneficent thoroughly, which is the attribute of a moral action. An unprecedented material prosperity has not tended to make us stoics or christians. But the laws by which the universe is organized re-appear at every point, and will rule it. The end of all political struggle is to establish morality as the basis of all legislation. It is not free institutions, 'tis not a republic, 'tis not a democracy, that is the end, — no, but only the means. Morality is the object of government. We want a state of things in which crime shall not pay. This is the consolation on which we rest in the darkness of the future and the afflictions of to-day, that the government of the world is moral, and does for ever destroy what is not."

As before, Emerson favored paying for the slaves. When the lecture was published, he added a paragraph approving of the president's message looking to a gradual abolition of slavery. "In the recent series of national successes, he says, this message is the best. It marks the happiest day in the political year." When the proclamation of Sept. 22 came out, providing for emancipation on the first of January, a meeting was held in Boston, at which Emerson spoke. He began his address[1] by saying, —

> "In so many arid forms which states incrust themselves with, once in a century, if so often, a poetic act and record occur. These are the jets of thought into affairs, when, roused by danger or inspired by genius, the political leaders of the day break the else insurmountable routine of class and local legislation, and take a step forward in the direction of catholic and universal interests. Every step in the history of political liberty is a sally of the human mind into the untried future, and has the interest of genius, and is fruitful in heroic anecdotes. Liberty is a slow fruit. It comes, like religion, for short periods and in rare conditions, as if awaiting a culture of the race which shall make it organic and permanent."

He then cites some acts and movements of this kind, giving prominence to Lincoln's proclamation. Such acts are of great scope, working on a long future. They make little noise, and yet they work untold benefits. Of Lincoln's wisdom he then says, —

> "The extreme moderation with which the president advanced to his design; his long-avowed, expectant policy, as if he chose to be strictly the executive of the best public sentiment of the country, waiting only till it should be unmistakably pronounced; so fair a mind that none ever listened so patiently to such extreme varieties of opinion; so reticent that his decision has taken all parties by surprise, whilst yet it is the just sequel of his prior acts; the firm tone in which he announces it, without inflation or surplusage, — all these have bespoken such favor to the act, that, great as the popularity of the president has been, we are beginning to think that we have underestimated the capacity and virtue which the Divine Providence has made an instrument of benefit so vast. He has been permitted to do more for America than any other American man. He is well entitled to the most indulgent construction. Forget all that we thought shortcomings, every mistake, every delay. In the extreme embarrassments of his part, call these endurance, wisdom, magnanimity, illuminated as they now are by his dazzling success."

He then calls attention to the difficulties Lincoln has had to overcome, and that soon the hour will strike of this glad emancipation. Once done it can not be undone. Slavery can not be introduced anew in the nineteenth century, for the moral sentiment is now against it.

[1] Atlantic Monthly, November, 1862.

"This act makes that the lives of our heroes have not been sacrificed in vain. It makes a victory of our defeats. Our hurts are healed; the health of the nation is repaired. With a victory like this we can stand many disasters. It does not promise the redemption of the black race; that lies not with us; but it relieves it of our opposition. The president by this act has paroled all the slaves in America; they will no more fight against us; and it relieves our race once for all of its crime and false position. The first condition of success is secured in putting ourselves right. We have recovered ourselves from our false position, and planted ourselves on a law of Nature.

'If that fail,
The pillared firmament is rottenness,
And earth's base built on stubble.'

The government has assured itself of the best constituency in the world; every spark of intellect, every virtuous feeling, every religious heart, every man of honor, every poet, every philosopher, the generosity of the cities, the health of the country, the strong arms of the mechanics, the endurance of farmers, the passionate conscience of women, the sympathy of distant nations, all rally to its support."

All the people need to give their help in maintaining this movement. When this blot is removed we can show our faces, and be no longer hypocrites and pretenders. Public distress seems to be removed by it, land becomes of more substantial value, and the whole country seems to be redeemed and renewed. This movement, however, was inevitable and imperative. The war existed long before Sumter, and could only be ended in this manner.

After showing how we have been misunderstood by other nations, and the effect on the South, he bursts forth with these eloquent words: —

"It was well to delay the steamers at the wharves until this edict could be put on board. It will be an insurance to the ship as it goes plunging through the sea with glad tidings to all people. Happy are the young who find the pestilence cleansed out of the earth, leaving open to them an honest career. Happy the old, who see Nature purified before they depart. Do not let the dying die; hold them back to this world until you have charged their ear and heart with this message to other spiritual societies, announcing the melioration of our planet."

He closes with a kind word for that "ill-fated, much-injured race which the proclamation respects." It was a clear, strong, earnest address, full of sympathy for the blacks, and grandly true to the highest moral convictions. There were no conceits of language in it, but a plain directness and a simple power that were full of charm. It is well to recall these addresses, that we may so much the more clearly understand how practical and human is Emerson's genius. On these occasions he came directly to the subject in hand, uttered not a word but of the highest wisdom, and proclaimed in majestic words that moral law which is written in the nature of things.

When the proclamation was carried into effect on the 1st of January, 1863, and emancipation was made a reality, a meeting of rejoicing was held in Boston. On this occasion Emerson read his Boston Hymn. Later in the year he published his Voluntaries, in which he celebrates the victories of liberty. Jubilantly he sings,

> "I see the wreath, I hear the songs
> Lauding the Eternal Rights."

His steady faith in liberty finds expression in these words: —

> "Stainless soldier on the walls,
> Knowing this, — and knows no more, —
> Whoever fights, whoever falls,
> Justice conquers evermore,
> Justice after as before;
> And he who battles on her side,
> God, though he were ten times slain,
> Crowns him victor glorified —
> Victor over death and pain —
> For ever."

On the 19th of April, 1865, a meeting was held in Concord to give expression to the grief felt on account of Lincoln's death. Emerson had watched the president's course during the war with the greatest interest and satisfaction, and felt his loss most keenly. On this occasion he delivered the following address, in which he gave full expression to his thought about the war, the victory of the North, and his great love of Lincoln.

"We meet under the gloom of a calamity which darkens down over the minds of good men in all civil society, as the fearful tidings travel over sea, over land, from country to country, like the shadow of an uncalculated eclipse over the planet. Old as history is, and manifold as are its tragedies, I doubt if any death has caused so much pain to mankind as this has caused, or will cause, on its announcement; and this, not so much because nations are by modern arts brought so closely together, as because of the mysterious hopes and fears which, in the present day, are connected with the name and institutions of America.

"In this country, on Saturday, every one was struck dumb, and saw at first only deep below deep, as he meditated on the ghastly blow. And perhaps at this hour, when the coffin which contains the dust of the president sets forward on its long march through mourning states on its way to his home in Illinois, we might well be silent, and suffer the awful voices of the time to thunder to us. Yes, but that first despair was brief; the man was not so to be mourned. He was the most active and hopeful of men, and his work had not perished; but acclamation of praise for the task he had accomplished burst out into a song of triumph, which even tears for his death can not keep down.

"The president stood before us as a man of the people. He was thoroughly American, had never crossed the sea, had never been spoiled by English insularity or French dissipation; a quite native, aboriginal man, as an acorn from the oak; no aping of foreigners, no frivolous accomplishments. Kentuckian born, working on a farm, a flat-boatman, a captain in the Blackhawk war, a country lawyer, a representative in the rural legislature of Illinois, on such modest foundations the hard structure of his fame was laid. How slowly, and yet by happily prepared steps, he came to his place. All of us remember (it is only a history of five or six years) the surprise and the disappointment of the country at his first nomination by the convention at Chicago. Mr. Seward, then in the culmination of his good fame, was the favorite of the Eastern states. And when the new and comparatively unknown name of Lincoln was announced (notwithstanding the report of the acclamations of that convention), we heard the result coldly and sadly. It seemed too rash, on a purely local reputation, to build so grave a trust in such anxious times; and men naturally talked of the chances of politics as incalculable. But it turned out not to be chance. The profound good opinion which the people of Illinois and of the West had conceived of him, and which they had imparted to their colleagues, that they also might justify themselves to their constituents at home, was not rash, though they did not begin to know the riches of his worth.

"A plain man of the people, an extraordinary fortune attended him. Lord Bacon says, 'Manifest virtues procure reputation; occult ones, fortune.' He offered no shining qualities at the first encounter; he did not offend by superiority. He had a face and manner which disarmed suspicion, which inspired confidence, which confirmed good-will. He was a man without vices. He had a strong sense of duty, which it was very easy for him to obey. Then, he had what farmers call a long head; was excellent in working out the sum for himself; in arguing his case, and convincing you fairly and firmly. Then, it turned out that he was a great worker; had prodigious faculty of performance; worked easily. A good worker is so rare; everybody has some disabling quality. In a host of young men that start together, and promise so many brilliant leaders for the next age, each fails on trial; one by bad health, one by conceit, or by love of pleasure, or lethargy, or an ugly temper, — each has some disqualifying fault that throws him out of the career. But this man was sound to the core, cheerful, persistent, all right for labor, and liked nothing so well.

"Then, he had a vast good-nature which made him tolerant and accessible to all; fair-minded, leaning to the claim of the petitioner; affable, and not sensible to the affliction which the innumerable visits paid to him when president would have brought to any one else. And how this good nature became a noble humanity, in many a tragic case which the events of the war brought to him, every one will remember; and with what increasing tenderness he dealt, when a whole race was thrown on his compassion. The poor negro said of him, on an impressive occasion, 'Massa Linkum am eberywhere.'

"Then, his broad good-humor, running easily into jocular talk, in which we delighted and in which he excelled, was a rich gift to this wise man. It enabled him to keep his secret, to meet every kind of man and every rank in society, to take off the edge of the severest decisions, to mask his own purpose and sound his companion, and to catch with true instinct the temper of every company he addressed. And, more than all, it is to a man of severe labor, in anxious and exhausting crises, the natural restoration, good as sleep, and in the protection of the over-driven brain against rancor and insanity.

"He is the author of a multitude of good sayings, so disguised as pleasantries that it is certain they had no reputation at first but as jests; and only later, by the very acceptance and adoption they find in the mouths of millions, turn out to be the wisdom of the hour. I am sure if this man had ruled in a period of less facility of printing, he would have become mythological in a few years, like Æsop or Pilpay, or one of the Seven Wise Masters, by his fables and proverbs. But the weight and penetration of many passages in his letters, messages, and speeches, hidden now by the very closeness of their application to the moment, are destined hereafter to a wide fame. What pregnant definitions! what unerring common sense! what foresight! and, on great occasion, what lofty, and, more than national, what human tone! His brief speech at Gettysburg will not easily be surpassed by words on any recorded occasion. This, and one other recorded American speech, that of John Brown, to the court that tried him, and a part of Kossuth's speech at Birmingham, can only be compared with each other, and with no fourth.

"His occupying the chair of state was a triumph of the good

sense of mankind, and of the public conscience. This middle-class country had got a middle-class president at last. Yes, in manners and sympathies, but not in powers; for his power was superior. This man grew according to the need. His mind mastered the problem of the day; and as the problem grew, so did his comprehension of it. Rarely was man so fitted to the event. In the midst of fears and jealousies, in the babel of counsels and parties, this man wrought incessantly with all his might and all his honesty, laboring to find what the people wanted, and how to obtain that. It can not be said there is any exaggeration of his worth. If ever a man was fairly tested he was. There was no lack of resistance, nor of slander, nor of ridicule. The times have allowed no state secrets; the nation has been in such ferment, such multitudes had to be trusted, that no secret could be kept. Every door was ajar, and we know all that befel.

"Then, what an occasion was the whirlwind of war! Here was place for no holiday magistrate, no fair-weather sailor; the new pilot was hurried to the helm in a tornado. In four years, — four years of battle-days, — his endurance, his fertility of resources, his magnanimity, were sorely tried, and never found wanting. Then, by his courage, his justice, his even temper, his fertile counsel, his humanity, he stood a heroic figure in the center of a heroic epoch. He is the true history of the American people in his time. Step by step he walked before them, — slow with their slowness, quickening his march with theirs; the true representative ot his continent; an entirely public man; father of his country, — the pulse of twenty millions throbbing in his heart, the thought of their minds articulated by his tongue.

"Adam Smith remarks that the ax, which, in Houbraken's portraits of British kings and worthies, is engraved under those who suffered on the block, adds a certain lofty charm to the picture. And who does not see, even in this tragedy so recent, how fast the terror and ruin of the massacre are already burning around the victim? Far happier his fate than to have lived to be wished away, to have watched the decay of his own faculties, to have seen — perhaps even he — the proverbial ingratitude of statesmen, to have seen mean men preferred. Had he not lived long enough to keep the greatest promise that ever man made to his fellow-men, — the practical abolition of slavery? He had seen Tennessee, Missouri, and Maryland emancipate their slaves. He had seen Savannah, Charleston, and Richmond surrendered; had seen the main army of the rebellion lay down its arms. He had conquered the public opinion of Canada, England, and France. Only Washington can compare with him in fortune.

"And what if it should turn out, in the unfolding of the web, that he had reached the term; that this heroic deliverer could not longer serve us; that th rebellion had touched its natural conclusion, and what remained to be done required new and uncommitted hands, — a new spirit born out of the ashes of war; and that Heaven, wishing to show the world a completed benefactor, shall make him serve his country even more by his death than by his life? Nations, like kings, are not good by facility and complaisance. 'The kindness of kings consists in justice and strength.' Easy good-nature has been the dangerous foible of the Republic; and it was a new essay that its enemies should outrage it, and drive us to unwonted firmness to secure the salvation of this country in the next ages.

"The ancients believed in a serene and beautiful Genius which ruled in the affairs of nations, which, with a slow but stern justice, carried forward the fortunes of certain chosen houses, weeding out sinful offenders or offending families, and securing at last the firm prosperity of the favorites of heaven. It was too narrow a view of the eternal Nemesis. There is a serene providence which rules the fate of nations, which makes little account of time, little of one generation or race, makes no account of disasters, conquers alike by what is called defeat, or what is called victory, thrusts aside enemy and obstruction, crushes every thing immoral as inhuman, and obtains the ultimate triumph of the best race by the sacrifice of every thing which resists the moral laws of the world. It makes its own instruments, creates the man of the time, trains him in poverty, inspires his genius, and arms him for his task. It has given every race its own talent, and ordains that only that race which combines perfectly with the virtues of all shall endure."

In his lecture on Education delivered at the Melodeon in Boston, in the autumn of 1864, Emerson gave expression to his opinions regarding the results of the recent election. At the beginning of this lecture, in opening his course on American Life, he said, "The people have this autumn expressed their decision that the nation shall be a nation, not a mere meeting and parting, as of passengers on the street-corner. The unity of our country must be sustained by force; such is the decision by the people sobered by the calamities of war, the immense loss of life, the heavy burdens of taxation." Speaking of the educating power of war, he said that, "every citizen understands the issues at stake, is ready to debate them, considers them a personal matter. All know that America means freedom, opportunity, power." The next year, speaking at the Harvard Commencement festival, he said "the war gave back integrity to this erring and immoral nation. It charged with power, peaceful, amiable men, to whose life war and discord were abhorrent." And in his Phi

Beta Kappa address of 1867, he gave an even more decided expression to his joy at the success of the war, and his confidence in the great destiny of the American people. "No good citizen, he says, but shares the wonderful prosperity of the Federal Union. The heart still beats with the public pulse of joy, that the country has withstood the rude trial which threatened its existence, and thrills with the vast augmentation of strength which it draws from this proof. The storm which has been resisted is a crown of honor, and a pledge of strength to the ship. We may be well contented with our fair inheritance."

Emerson has always been a sturdy critic of our national vices and crimes, and a just one. He has spared no faults, he has overlooked no defects. The real spirit of the Republic has always appeared in him in a prominent degree; and, more than almost any other American, he has realized the destiny of the country. "No American thinker or writer has taken so accurate a parallax of the true character of America and Americans as Emerson. He has caught in the camera of his swift intuitions all their features, good and bad, and has given them the grand setting of his prophetic and optimistic genius. No American has believed more heartily in America than Emerson, — in her opportunity, her power, her destiny."[1] Because he has believed in the American idea with a supreme faith, he has ever pointed out our departures from it, and been as much a gadfly to Boston and New England as Socrates was to Athens, calling men and the state alike to judgment for their evil deeds. Through all his earlier addresses he asserts the need of "creating an American sentiment," and declares the error of having our "intellectual culture from one country, and our duties from another." In one of these he says, "I find no expression in our state papers or legislative debate, in our lyceums or churches, specially in our newspapers, of a high national feeling, no lofty counsels that rightfully stir the blood." In 1878, however, in his *Fortune of*

[1] Francis E. Abbott, in The Index for Aug. 8, 1878.

the Republic, his tone is that of confidence and trust, though he spares not our faults. He finds that our Republic "represents the sentiment and the future of mankind," though he is still obliged to tell us that "our political economy is low and degrading," while we "consider nothing less than the sacredness of man." Faults enough he is yet able to find, and he tells us of them in the plainest words; but the higher ends of national existence he as sincerely declares.

As a critic faithful in pointing out the conditions and methods of social and moral progress, we owe him a debt we can never repay but by acceptance of his teachings. He has been a true critic, because recognizing the absolute foundations on which all truth of conduct must rest. He has tried to lift us to "the ways and manners of the sky," infusing into our life, our thought, and our literature a pure and a lofty sense of human responsibility.

XII.

THE PROPHET RECEIVED.

THE period from 1860 to 1870 is that in which Emerson secures the widest hearing, has the strongest personal influence in molding the thought of his time, and when his character shines out in the most emphatic manner. He is less the critic, more thoroughly than at any other time in sympathy with the purpose and spirit of his country. His words had taken root, and began to produce their fruit. He had become a prophet to be heard gladly, while those who differed from him began to think less of his errors than of his truths. Fame had taken hold of his name; his countrymen found they could rejoice in his reputation, and, from being the admired of a party, he became an accepted power in American thought and literature. During this period he re-affirms in some of his most original essays the great ideas to which his life had been devoted, and finds for these ideas an acceptance they had not before received.

At the beginning of this period he lost two of his most valued friends; Parker dying in 1860, and Thoreau in 1862. He spoke at the meeting held by Parker's society in Music Hall, in his commemoration, and paid an admiring and noble tribute to his friend. He closed by saying that "the sudden and singular eminence of Mr. Parker, the importance of his name and influence, are the verdict of his country to his virtues. We have few such men to lose, he said; amiable and blameless at home; feared abroad as the standard-bearer of liberty; taking all the duties he could grasp; and, more, refusing to spare himself. He has gone down in early glory to his grave, to be a living and enlarging power, wherever learning, wit, honest valor, and independence are honored."[1] He spoke also at Thoreau's funeral, doing fine justice to the genius of that rare soul. Thoreau, he said, "was made for the noblest society; he had in a short life exhausted the capabilities of this world; wherever there is knowledge, wherever there is virtue, wherever there is beauty, he will find a home." This address was published in the *Atlantic Monthly* for August, 1862, and in 1866 was reprinted as an introduction to Thoreau's writings, appearing in the *Excursions*. He helped to edit Thoreau's *Letters*, which came out in 1865, and to prepare several other volumes from his manuscripts.

After Parker's death his society desired Emerson, the next autumn, to give the first sermon for them in Music Hall. The treatment Parker had received made a strong impression on his mind, had alienated him more than ever from the Unitarians, and had made him think the church cared mainly for the external things of religion. At this time he had reached the extreme of his alienation from the church, had wholly given up prayer, and discontinued nearly all outward acts of worship. He was reluctant to enter Parker's pulpit, as he could no longer give a sermon in the ordinary sense, and as he had long before abandoned all thought of ever preaching again. He was urged so strongly, however, that at last he consented; and on the first Sunday said he was glad Parker had made the place one of freedom, that he had valued religion more than its forms. During several years he frequently appeared before the society, often on Sundays, while he gave a great number of lectures for the Parker Fraternity. One of his sermons[2] in Music Hall has been reported by M. D. Conway, who says it was the most "impressive utterance" he ever heard from Emerson.

"There was not one, but many themes and texts, and all related. He began by calling attention to the tendency to simplification. The inventor knows that a machine is new and improvable when it

[1] The remainder of this address is printed in Frothingham's Life of Parker.

[2] Fraser's Magazine, May, 1867.

has a great many parts. The chemists already find the infinite variety of things contained in sixty-six elements; and physicists promise that this number shall be reduced to twenty, ten, five. Faraday declares his belief that all things will, in the end, be reduced to one element with two polarities. Religious progress has similarly been in the direction of simplification. Every great religion has in its ultimate development told its whole secret, concentrated its force, in some simple maxims. In our youth we talk of the various virtues, the many dangers and trials, of life; as we grow older, we find ourselves returning to the proverbs of the nursery. In religion one book serves many lands, ages, and varieties of character; nay, one or two golden rules out of the book are enough. The many teachers and scriptures are at last but various routes by which we always come to the simple law of obedience to the light in the soul. 'Seek nothing outside of thyself,' says one, 'Believe nothing against thy own spirit,' echoes another part of the word. Jesus said, 'Be lowly; hunger and thirst after justice; of your own minds judge what is right.' Swedenborg teaches that heaven and hell are the loves of the soul. George Fox removes the bushel from the light within. The substance of all morals is, that a man should adhere to the path which the inner light has marked out for him. The great waste in the world comes of the misapplication of energy. The great tragedies of the soul are strung on those threads not spun out of our own hearts. One records of Michael Angelo that he found him working on his statue with a lamp stuck in his cap, and it might almost symbolize the holier light of patient devotion to his art. No matter what your work is, let it be yours; no matter if you are tinker or preacher, blacksmith or president, let what you are doing be organic, let it be in your bones, and you open the door by which the affluence of heaven and earth shall stream into you. You shall have the hidden joy, and shall carry success with you. Look to yourself rather than to materials; nothing is unmanageable to a good hand; no place slippery to a good foot; all things are clear to a good head. The sin of dogmatism, of creeds and catechisms, is that they destroy mental character. The youth says that he believes when he is only brow-beaten; he says he thinks so and so, when that so and so are the denial of any right to think. Simplicity and grandeur are thus lost, and with them the sentiment of obligation to a principle of life and honor. In the legends of the Round Table it is told, that a witch, wishing to make her child supremely wise, prepared certain herbs, and put them in a pot to boil, intending to bathe the child's eyes with the decoction. She set a shepherd-boy to stir the pot whilst she went away. Whilst he stirred it, a raven dropped a twig into the pot, which spattered three drops of the liquid into the shepherd's eyes. Immediately all the future became as if passing before his eyes; and, seeing that when the witch returned she meant to kill him, he left the pot, and fled to the woods. Now, if three drops of that all-revealing decoction should suddenly get into the eyes of every human being crowding along Broadway some day, how many of them would still go on with the affair they are pursuing on the street? Probably they would nearly all come to a dead stand. But there would, let us hope, be here and there a happy child of the Most High, who had taken hold of her or his life's thread by sacred appointment. These would move on without even a pause. The unveiled future would show the fatality of many schemes, the idleness of many labors; but every genial aim would only be exalted, and shown in their eternal and necessary relations. Finally, humility was, the speaker declared, the one element to which all virtues are reducible. 'It was revealed unto me,' said the old Quaker, 'that what other men trample on must be thy food.' It is the spirit that accepts our trust, and is thus the creator of character and the guide to power.

"In closing this discourse, the speaker read at length the story of the proposed humiliation, and the victory through humility, of Fra Christoforo, in Manzoni's *Promessi Sposi.* I regret that I can not give a report *verbatim* of this extraordinary discourse, which produced an effect on those who heard it beyond any thing that I ever witnessed, many being moved at times to tears. I went with pencil and paper, intending to take down as much as I could; but at the end of the hour occupied by it, the paper remained blank, and the pencil had been forgotten. I can therefore only produce the record of my impressions of it, as they were written down the same day."

In July, 1861, he gave an address before one of the societies of Tufts College. He said, that while the brute cannon was being heard, and though it found a poetic echo in the hearts of those who regarded it as an instrument of freedom, it should not be allowed to intrude upon the sanctity of a truly intellectual occasion. He urged the students in a time of conflict to rely upon those better weapons of the mind; for the institution of learning is in all times the ark of deliverance, and many feet should constantly turn towards it. A great national failure would be due solely to a lack of duty on the part of the college, using that word in its very broadest sense. If the college-bred man leaves his altar and his library, and plays the sycophant, then the institution is nothing more than a suicidal hospital of decayed tutors or a musty shop of old books. Here you are to become thinkers, to learn the art of command. The thought secured is higher than its instrument, as the general is greater than the park of artillery. Many have written of a new revival of religion and letters; but the true revival is that of the human mind, so that man's duty may extend to the proper use of his intellectual powers. This change must be brought about by a revival of the popular science of mind. Every man who looks sincerely and with thought will find a power within him which knows more than he does. Simple wisdom is beyond all acquirements. It is felt in its presence only, like the ubiquitous rays of the sun. This inner knowledge, when it flows forth under happy circumstances, is called genius. In the time of youth, minds become skeptical unless this declaration is made that truth exists. Youth should keep the intellectual position sacred, and wait long and patiently. Go sit with that hermit within you, he said, who knows more than you do, and learn of him. You are all to stand before an examining committee of the world, and must be true to yourselves.

In November, 1864, he began a course of lectures on American Life before the Parker Fraternity. They were given on Sunday evenings; and the subjects were, Public and Private Education, Social Aims, Resources, Table-talk, Books, Character. The lecture on Books has since appeared in his *Society and Solitude*, and those on Social Aims and Resources in *Letters and Social Aims;* while that on Character was printed in the *North American Review* for 1866.

This course of lectures was well attended. The lecture on Table-talk was a fine discussion of the advantages of conversation; and it "swarmed with bright sayings, appropriate illustrations, interesting literary anecdotes, and incisive comments on social character." In 1865 he spoke at the Commencement festival at Harvard, and gave a lecture on Literature before one of the Amherst societies. In January, 1866, he gave a course of lectures in Chickering Hall, Boston, Saturdays at noon, on Philosophy for the People. He spoke of the Seven Meters of Intellect; Instinct, Perception, Talent; Genius, Imagination, Taste; Laws of the Mind; Conduct of the Intellect; Relation of Intellect to Morals. Other lectures of this winter were, the Man of the

World, Eloquence, Immortality, the Rule of Life, and an address on the reception of the Chinese embassy. In the lecture on Eloquence, he said John Brown gave at Charlestown "the best speech made in the nineteenth century." In his lecture on Genius, Imagination, and Taste, however, he said Daniel Webster and Father Taylor were the only two men who had reached his ideal of oratory.

He took much interest in the Free Religious Association, and attended the meeting for its organization held in Horticultural Hall, May 30, 1867. The men who led in this movement had been largely influenced by him, owing to him their main thought and purpose. They had nearly all been connected with the Unitarians, and left them for much the same reasons he did. To study religion as a universal sentiment, to find the sources of its world-wide manifestation in man, to regard all its forms as expressions of the same fundamental principles, — these objects of the new association had been for many years among his most cherished ideas. At a subsequent meeting, Alcott declared that Emerson was the father of the movement.[1] His earnest sympathy with the original purpose and spirit of the association is clearly shown in his address on this occasion.

"I think the necessity very great that invites all classes, all religious men, whatever their connections, whatever their specialties, in whatever relation they stand to Christianity, to unite in a movement of benefit to men, under the sanction of religion. We are all very sensible — it is forced on us every day — of the feeling that the churches are outgrown, that the creeds are outgrown, that a technical theology no longer suits us. It is not the ill-will of people, no, indeed! but the incapacity for confirming themselves there.

"The church is not large enough for the man; it can not inspire the enthusiasm which is the parent of every good in history, which makes the romance of history. For that enthusiasm you must have something greater than yourselves, and not less.

"The child, the young student, finds scope in his mathematics and chemistry, or natural history, because he finds a truth larger than he is, finds himself continually instructed. But, in the

[1] Freedom and Fellowship in Religion, p. 408.

churches, every healthy and thoughtful mind finds itself in something less; it is checked, cribbed, confined; and the statistics of the American, the English, and the German cities, showing that the mass of the population is leaving off going to church, indicate the necessity which should have been foreseen, that the church should always be new and extemporized, because it is eternal, and springs from the sentiment of men, or it does not exist. One wonders, sometimes, that the churches retain so many votaries when he reads the histories of the church. There is an element of childish infatuation in them which does not exalt our respect for man. Read in Michelet, that in Europe, for twelve or fourteen centuries, God the Father had no temple and no altar. The Holy Ghost and the son of Mary were worshiped; and in the fourteenth century the First Person began to appear at the side of his son in pictures and in sculpture, for worship, but only through favor of his son. These mortifying puerilities abound in religious history. But as soon as every man is apprised of the divine presence within his own mind, — is apprised that the perfect law of duty corresponds with the laws of chemistry, of vegetation, of astronomy, as face to face in a glass, that the basis of duty, the order of society, the power of character, the wealth of culture, the perfection of taste, all draw their essence from this moral sentiment, then we have a religion that exalts, that commands all the social and all the private action.

"What strikes me in the sudden movement which brings together to-day so many separated friends, — separated but sympathetic, — and what I expected to find here was, some practical suggestions by which we were to re-animate and re-organize for ourselves the true church, the pure worship. Pure doctrine always bears fruit in pure benefits. It is only by good works, it is only on the basis of active duty, that worship finds expression. What is best in the ancient religions was the sacred friendships between heroes, the sacred bands, and the relations of the Pythagorean disciples.

"The close association which bound the first disciples of Jesus is another example, and it were easy to find more. The soul of our late war, which will always be remembered as dignifying it, was, first, the desire to abolish slavery in this country; and secondly, to abolish the mischief of the war itself, by healing and saving the sick and wounded soldiers, — and this by the sacred bands of the Sanitary Commission. I wish that the various beneficent institutions, which are springing up like joyful plants of wholesomeness all over this country, should all be remembered as within the sphere of this committee, — almost all of them are represented here, — and that within this little band which has gathered to-day, should grow friendship. The interests that grow out of a meeting like this, should bind us with new strength to the old eternal duties."

Emerson was made an Overseer of Harvard University July 17, 1867; and at the commencement of that year the honorary degree of LL.D. was conferred upon him. It was at this time, also, he gave his Phi Beta Kappa address on the Progress of Culture, since published in *Letters and Social Aims.* Harvard was for many years strongly opposed to him, and from its professors came many of the severest criticisms he received. His heresies, his Divinity-School address of 1838, his criticism of Everett and Webster, his sympathy with the anti-slavery cause, had made him long obnoxious to the conservative tendencies of Harvard. He had gone steadily on his way, however, until public opinion had come round to his side; and then Harvard did herself the honor to forget all and show him just recognition. It was a triumph on his part, nobly won and richly deserved. His critics had become his admirers, his heresies were forgotten; and his genius, his rare merits, his pure life, only were remembered. His address was full of hope and courage, richly suggestive with those great ideas he had preached for so many years. It was a strong plea for the truest culture, as the best promise of the American people. The words with which he brought his address to an end, so earnest with faith in the future are they, show with what hope he now contemplates the Republic: —

"Brothers, I draw new hope from the atmosphere we breathe to-day, from the healthy sentiment of the American people, and from the avowed aims and tendencies of the educated class. The age has new convictions. We know that in certain historic periods there have been times of negation, — a decay of thought, and a consequent national decline; that in France, at one time, there was almost a repudiation of the moral sentiment, in what is called, by distinction, society, — not a believer within the church, and almost not a theist out of it. In England the like spiritual disease affected the upper class in the time of Charles II., and down into the reign of the Georges. But it honorably distinguishes the educated class here, that they believe in the succor which the heart yields to the intellect, and draw greatness from its aspirations. And when I say the educated class, I know what a benignant breadth that word has, — new in the world, — reaching millions instead of hundreds. And more, when I look around me, and consider the sound material of which the cultivated class here is made up, — what high personal worth, what love of men, what hope, is joined with rich information and practical power, and that the most distinguished by genius and culture are in this class of benefactors, — I can not distrust this great knighthood of virtue, or doubt that the interests of science, of letters, of politics and humanity, are safe. I think their hands are strong enough to hold up the Republic. I read the promise of better times and of greater men."

In 1867 *May-Day* was published. Of the minor pieces joined with it, many had previously appeared in *The Atlantic Monthly.* It was received with general approbation. In *The North American Review* Charles Eliot Norton said, that "his poems are for the most part more fitted to invigorate the moral sense than to delight the artistic. At times, indeed, he is singularly felicitous in expression; and some of his verses both charm and elevate the soul. These rare verses will live in the memories of men. No poet is surer of immortality than Mr. Emerson; but the greater part of his poetry will be read, not so much for its artistic as for its moral worth." This is discriminating and just; but W. D. Howells, in *The Atlantic Monthly*, is even more enthusiastic in his praise of the genius and originality of Emerson's poetry. "Everywhere the poet's felicity of expression appears, he says; a fortunate touch transfuses some dark enigma with color; the riddles are made to shine when most impenetrable; the puzzles are all constructed of gold and ivory and precious stones." In a discerning essay [1] on Emerson's poems, E. P. Whipple said, —

"As an artist, Mr. Emerson exhibits the same fidelity to his own ideas which he has always taken for his guide in the pursuit of truth. The construction of his verse is as unique as his mental idiosyncrasy. It certainly betrays incidentally the proof of a rare poetic culture. His masterly command of English shows a careful study of the best sources of the language; but not a sign of imitation can be found in his writings, — not even the use of the imagery which has been consecrated by the habit of ages. His lines are often abrupt, sometimes a little uncouth, but never

[1] In the New York Independent.

deficient in masculine strength. With no pretension to the finish and smoothness which give grace to the poems of Tennyson, they present frequent surprises of dainty melody, and charm as much by the sweetness of their flow as by the grandeur of their thought."

In October and November, 1868, he gave a course of lectures in the Meionaon. His subjects were, Art, Poetry and Criticism, Historical Notes of American Life and Letters, Hospitality and How to Make Homes Attractive, Greatness, Leasts and Mosts. He was greeted with large and enthusiastic audiences. Among his hearers were Fields, Phillips, Lowell, Pierce, Wasson, Hunt, and many professional and literary people. In January, 1869, he gave in Chickering Hall a course of ten readings from his favorite authors. The attendance was limited to one hundred. He read from the whole range of English poetry, interspersed with conversation and criticism. One of the readings was wholly from Milton; and he also occasionally introduced specimens from the poetry of other countries. This year he read a paper before the Woman's Club, devoted to personal recollections, and with many biographical extracts from his diaries. He spoke in the Sunday-evening lecture-course of the Free Religious Association, and in May gave an address at its annual meeting. In April and May, 1870, he gave fourteen lectures in the philosophical courses in Harvard University. These lectures were given three in each week, but were attended by only a very small number of persons, as they were outside the usual studies of the University. They were based on lectures given in previous years, with such additional observations as seemed pertinent to the subjects. The general title was The Natural History of the Intellect. In the first lecture, given April 26, he said he should follow no system, and that his lectures would be only the dotting of a little curve of personal experience. He would give merely the results of observation, and his course would not be the laying bare of new truths necessarily. He would attempt to give a few anecdotes of the intellect, a mere jotting down of observed facts, a farmer's almanac of mental moods. The strict analysis of the intellect he would leave to others, for the reason that system-makers are but gnats attempting to grasp the universe. He said that metaphysics must alternate with life, and to be truthful must come from a live mind in a practical life. The outsiders have done the most for philosophy, he said, not those who have been analyzers by profession. He quoted this sentence from Augustine, as expressing the spirit of his lectures: "Let others wrangle; I will wonder." The second lecture was devoted to the general subject of the mind, the third to instinct, the fourth to perception, and the fifth to memory. Then followed a discussion of the value of imagination, in two lectures. After that, inspiration became the topic, the essay on that subject in *Letters and Social Aims* being given. It was also continued through two lectures, branching out into a defense of genius. In the tenth lecture, common sense and genius were contrasted. In the remaining lectures, the laws of the mind were dealt with. An attempt seems to have been made in these lectures to give a somewhat more systematic presentation of his theories than he had done before. They contained nothing new, and which he had not before said in his books; but he dwelt somewhat more distinctly on the main features of his philosophy.

In 1870 *Society and Solitude* was published. Many of its essays had long before been given to the public as lectures; that on Art was printed in *The Dial*, and the one on Farming was delivered in Concord in 1858. That on Books was given as a lecture in England in 1848, those on Society and Solitude and Old Age appeared in the first volumes of *The Atlantic Monthly*, while the one on Civilization was a portion of the Washington address of 1862. Higginson saw in these essays a greater variety and a more distinct organic life than in the earlier ones, while they are no less finished and scarcely less concentrated. "It is not enough to say that such papers as these constitute the high-water mark of American literature; it is not too much to say that they are unequalled in the literature of the age. Name, if you can, the Englishman or the Frenchman, who, on themes like these, must not own himself second to Emerson."

In April and May, 1871, he spent six weeks in California with a party of intimate friends; and he delivered a few lectures while there. In August he gave an address at a meeting of the Massachusetts Historical Society on the one hundredth anniversary of the birth of Walter Scott. It was eloquent with thought, and indicated a discriminating and hearty appreciation of Scott's genius. In April he gave six lectures and readings in Mechanics' Hall, at three o'clock Monday afternoons. His first lecture was on literature; and he read from Mrs. Helen Hunt Jackson, Ben Jonson, David Lewis, Henry Thoreau, and one or two others. In one of his lectures he spoke of Byron, who was called the most skillful poet of his time in the use of the English language. In the last one he spoke of the effects of culture on the soul, and its influence in the formation of ideas about life and destiny. The Boston *Journal* gave the following account of the impression made by these lectures: —

"The same consummate magnetism lingers around and upon every phrase; there is the same thrilling earnestness of antithesis, the same delight and brooding over poetry and excellence of expression, as of old. There is no other man in America who can, by the mere force of what he says, enthrall and dominate an audience. Breathless attention is given, although now and then his voice falls away so that those seated farthest off have to strain every nerve to catch the words. The grand condensation, the unfaltering and almost cynical brevity of expression, are at first startling and vexatious; but presently one yields to the charm, and finds his mind in the proper assenting mood. The loving tenderness with which Emerson lingers over a fine and thoroughly expressive phrase is beyond description. It thrills the whole audience; arrests universal attention. The sacredness of the printed page is interpreted in a new and universal light. There is the same passionate adoration displayed over a fine line from a sonnet, or lavished upon one of Thoreau's quaint conceits, which Ingres bestowed upon a specimen of pure drawing. The innate and inexhaustible love of beauty, softening and permeating every utterance, infusing its delicate glow and its delicious harmony into each idea, and investing abstractions with the charms of real and vivid beings, triumphs over age and diffidence, gives to the austere and unworldly philosopher the bloom and enthusiasm of the lover and the poet."

In 1864 he contributed a preface to an American edition of the *Gulistân*, or *Rose Garden*, of Saadi.[1] He had greatly admired this poet, and his account is full of praise. It brings out very clearly the Oriental side of Emerson's mind, and shows his acquaintance with Eastern literature. "When once the works of these poets, he says, are made accessible, they must draw the curiosity of good readers. It is provincial to ignore them. The monotones we accuse, he goes on to say, accuse our own. We pass into a new landscape, new costume, new religion, new manners and customs, under which humanity nestles very comfortably at Shiraz and Mecca, with good appetite, and with moral and intellectual results that correspond point for point with ours at New York and London."

To Professor Goodwin's edition of *Plutarch's Morals*, published in 1870, he wrote a preface. He gave a very interesting account of the literary history of Plutarch since the Middle Ages and the restoration of Greek literature. Some of the lesser works attributed to Plutarch he believes unworthy of him, being either the notes of his pupils, or matter accidentally added to his writings. Having spoken of the claim that Plutarch was a Christian in his teaching, he says, "His thoughts are excellent, if only he had a right to say them." In the company of the world's heroes Plutarch will "sit as the bestower of the crown of noble knighthood, and laureate of the ancient world." He says, at the end of his essay, —

"It is a service to our Republic to publish a book that can force ambitious young men, before they mount the platform of the county conventions, to read the 'Apothegms of Great Commanders.' If we could keep the secret and communicate it only to a few chosen aspirants, we might confide, that, by this noble infiltration, they would easily carry the victory over all competitors.

[1] Printed in The Atlantic Monthly for July, 1864.

But as it was the desire of these old patriots to fill, with their majestic spirit, all Sparta and Rome, and not a few leaders only, we hasten to offer them to the American public."

In January, 1872, being in Washington, he was invited to visit Howard University, which he did. While there he was called on to speak to the students. In an entirely extemporaneous manner he expressed his great regard for books as a means of education, said that each mind has a specialty of its own which must guide the person in selecting his profession, and, apologizing for not being prepared to speak, suggested that a topic would help him to say something to the purpose. His opinions of books being asked for, he spoke of Gibbon, Boswell's Johnson, Shakspere, Burke, and Goethe, with high praise of each. Concerning the selection of a profession, he said, —

"I am of the opinion that every mind that comes into the world has its own specialty; it is different from every other mind; that each of you brings into the world a certain bias, a disposition to attempt something of its own, — something *your* own, — an aim a little different from that of your companions; and that every young man and woman is a failure so long as each does not find what is his or her own bias; that just so long as you are influenced by those around you, so long as you are doing those things you see others do well instead of doing that thing which you can do well, you are so far wrong, so far failing of your own right mark. . . . I conceive that success is in finding what it is that you yourself really want, and pursuing it; freeing yourself from all importunities of your friends to do something which they like, and insisting upon that thing which you like and can do. . . .

"The multitude of professions is endless, and in a right state of society the objects and aims will be much more numerous. For instance, in the German universities now, instead of having five or six or ten professorships, they have sixty or one hundred, — the division of the sciences, the division of the parts of great classes of knowledge, requiring so many instructors. Well, I think that with the progress of society, the divisions of employments will not be sixty or one hundred, but thousands; and finally, if one should say it, as many as there are men, as many as there are women, that the aims will be as many as there are individual souls. Therefore I wish that each young person should learn that secret, that he only can tell himself what it is that he is to do. It is revealed to him in the progress of his mind, always becoming revealed more distinctly. what that object is. He did not know it when he was a child; he did not know it when he was a boy; but, as his mind expands, all is slowly revealed to him; revealed to him by every effort he makes in this direction or against it. For, when he is laboring against his proper calling, he finds himself met with obstacles that increase as he goes. When he is following his proper mission, the leading of his inward guide, he is assisted by every step which he takes. The purpose for which he is made is always becoming more clear to him. I believe that for every active mind, in its own direction, there is a thought waking every morning, a new thought; that every day brings new instruction and facility; that even in the dreams of the night we are helped forward. There is a great difference in our activity of mind. Sometimes we have heavy periods, when we don't think for days or weeks or months; then, periods of activity. I think these depend very much upon ourselves, upon our good behavior. If we use our opportunities, opportunities are multiplied. If we neglect them, if we give up to idle pleasures and amusements, they are withdrawn. The idle person ceases to have thoughts. The active person is always assisted. There are a great many mysterious facts in our history, which the mind, attentive to itself, will always discover, and the admonitions that come thence."

The interest manifested in his conversational address to this company of colored students was one of many indications that the prophet was at last accepted by his countrymen. Yet his own modesty forbade his assuming any honors to himself; and he said to these students, "I am not in the habit of speaking with classes of young persons very much. And I myself, I ought to say, am a solitary man, living in the country, and seeing few people. Now and then I go to Boston or elsewhere and read a paper to a class, but seldom speak in any other manner." Had he been less modest, less retiring and reticent, he would have made a greater outward impression upon his country; but his real power and influence have been more subtly felt and more deeply exerted, because he has sought no applause and desired no praise. He has persistently refused to believe that his influence has been great upon American thought, modestly shrinking from the praises of his co-workers, and saying that his success was owing to the time in which he has lived.

The experiences of these ten years, including the period of the great Rebellion and the work of reconstruction of the Republic, made Emerson more than ever the prophet of good and the inspirer of hope. Age brought with it an even warmer glow of interest in his fellow-men; and the new life of the Republic brought to him an enlarged perception of the organic life of the race in its relations to morals and religion. He came to see a new value in a united religious life for the people, though abating no jot of his soul-trust. As much as ever he rejected religion as a piece of history, as a repetition of what had been said of old time; but he realized more than before how it is that great deeds can be accomplished by the common faith and intuitions of a people. He came more and more to live in an atmosphere of calm and abiding faith, to believe with an even more pronounced conviction that all things work together for good.

XIII.

THE VOICE AT EVE.

EARLY in the morning of July 24, 1872, Emerson discovered that his house was on fire. The roof and the upper rooms were much burned; but every thing was speedily removed by his neighbors, including his library and manuscripts. The family found refuge in the "Old Manse."

Oct. 15 he attended a complimentary dinner in New York in honor of James Anthony Froude, and made a brief address. He said that Froude "has shown at least two eminent faculties in his histories, — the faculty of seeing wholes, and the faculty of seeing and saying particulars. The one makes history valuable; the other makes it readable, interesting." He also said that "the language, the style of his books, draws very much of its excellence from the habit of giving the very language of the times." During this month he set out for Europe with his daughter. He went to Egypt, and, returning, spent several weeks in Paris. In England he was cordially received by his friends. He spent a month in London, then visited Oxford, and made trips into Wales and Scotland. At Oxford he was invited to deliver a course of lectures, at the suggestion of Max Müller, but did not do so. He spoke at Thomas Hughes's Workingmen's College in London. He made a visit to Lord Amberley, and he found new delight in his friendship for Carlyle. His old friends were not forgotten, and his visit was made by them a festival. "I know no American, indeed there can be no other," wrote one of his admirers at this time, "who has in England a company of such friends and disciples as those who gather about Mr. Emerson; no one for whom so many rare men and women have a reverence so affectionate; no one who holds to the best section of English students, and of her most religious and cultivated minds, a relation so delightful to both. The incomparable charm of his manner and of his conversation remains what it always was, and marked always by the same sweetness, the same delicacy, mingled with the same penetration and force."[1] This interest was shown in the organization in England, in 1869, of an association devoted to the publication and diffusion of the works of Carlyle and Emerson. Its kindred objects were the diffusion of education, relief of pauperism, elevation of woman, securing of international peace, the broadening of the national church to include all thinkers, and the diffusion of art and culture.

During his absence his house was rebuilt in exactly the old form. On his return, in May, 1873, he was received with music and a procession by his neighbors, who most cordially welcomed him home. This reception was as surprising to him as it was gratifying. The fine new Free-Library building in Concord, built by William Munroe, a citizen of the town, was dedicated Oct. 1; and Emerson delivered the address. He gave an interesting account of the value and uses of books and libraries.

"I think it not easy, he said, to exaggerate the utility of the beneficence which takes this form. If you consider what has befallen you when reading a poem, or a history, or a tragedy, or a novel even, that deeply interested you, — how you forgot the time of day, the persons sitting in the room, and the engagements for the evening, — you will easily admit the wonderful property of books to make all towns equal; that Concord Library makes Concord as good as Rome, Paris, or London, for the hour, — has the best of each of those cities in itself. Robinson Crusoe, could he have had a shelf of our books, could almost have done without his man Friday, or even the arriving ship.

"The chairman of Mr. Munroe's trustees has told you how old is the foundation of our village library; and we think we can trace in our modest records a correspondent effect of culture amidst our citizens. A deep religious sentiment is in all times an inspirer of the intellect, and that was not wanting here. The town was set-

[1] George W. Smally, in The New York Tribune.

tled by a pious company of nonconformists from England; and the printed books of their pastor and leader, Rev. Peter Bulkeley, testify the ardent sentiment which they shared. The religious bias of our founders had its usual effect, — to secure an education to read their Bible and hymn-book; and thence the step was easy for active minds to an acquaintance with history and with poetry. Peter Bulkeley sent his son John to the first class that graduated in Harvard College, in 1642, and two sons to later classes. Major Simon Willard's son Samuel graduated at Harvard in 1659, and was for six years, from 1701 to 1707, vice-president of the college; and his son Joseph was president of the college from 1781 to 1804; and Concord counted fourteen graduates of Harvard in its first century, and its representation there increased with its gross population."

After speaking of Thoreau and Hawthorne, and their interest in books, he passes on to say, —

"Literature is the record of the best thoughts. Every attainment and discipline which increases a man's acquaintance with the invisible world, lifts his being. Every thing that gives him a new perception of beauty, multiplies his pure enjoyments. A river of thought is always running out of the invisible world into the mind of man. Shall not they who received the largest streams spread abroad the healing waters?

"Homer and Plato and Pindar and Shakspere serve many more than have heard their names. Thought is the most volatile of all things. It can not be contained in any cup, though you shut the lid never so tight. Once brought into the world, it runs over the vessel which received it into all minds that love it. The very language we speak thinks for us by the subtle distinctions which already are marked for us by its words, and every one of them is the contribution of the wit of one and another sagacious man in all the centuries of time. Consider that it is our own state of mind at any time that makes our estimate of life and the world. If you sprain your foot, you will presently come to think that Nature has sprained hers. Every thing begins to look so slow and inaccessible. And when you sprain your mind, by gloomy reflections on your failures and vexations, you come to have a bad opinion of life. Think how indigent Nature must appear to the blind, the deaf, and the idiot. Now, if you can kindle the imagination by a new thought, by heroic histories, by uplifting poetry, instantly you expand, — are cheered, inspired, and become wise, and even prophetic. Music works this miracle for those who have a good ear; what omniscience has music! so absolutely impersonal, and yet every sufferer feels his secret sorrow reached. Yet to a scholar the book is as good or better. There is no hour of vexation which, on a little reflection, will not find diversion and relief in the library. His companions are few; at the moment he has none; but, year by year, these silent friends supply their place. Many times the reading of a book has made the fortune of the man, — has decided his way of life. It makes friends. 'Tis the tie between men to have been delighted with the same book. Every one of us is always in search of his friend; and when, unexpectedly, he finds a stranger enjoying the rare poet or thinker who is dear to his own solitude, it is like finding a brother.

"In books I have the history or the energy of the past. Angels they are to us of entertainment, sympathy, and provocation. With them many of us spend the most of our life, — these silent guides, these tractable prophets, historians, and singers, whose embalmed life is the highest feat of art; who now cast their moonlight illumination over solitude, weariness, and fallen fortunes. You say 'tis a languid pleasure. Yes; but its tractableness, coming and going like a dog at your bidding, compensate the quietness, and contrast with the slowness of fortune, and the inaccessibleness of persons. You meet with a man of science, a good thinker or good wit; but you do not know how to draw out of him that which he knows. But the book is a sure friend, always ready at your first leisure, opens to the very page you desire, and shuts at your first fatigue, as possibly your professor might not.

"It is a tie between men to have read the same book; and it is a disadvantage not to have read the book your mates have read, or not to have read it at the same time, so that it may take the place in your culture it does in theirs, and you shall understand their allusions to it, and not give it more or less emphasis than they do. Yet the strong character does not need this sameness of culture. The imagination knows its own food in every pasture; and if it has not had the *Arabian Nights*, Prince Lee Boo, or Homer, or Scott, has drawn equal delight and terror from haunts and passages which you will hear of with envy.

"In saying these things for books, I do not for a moment forget that they are secondary, mere means, and only used in the off-hours, only in the pause, and, as it were, the sleep, or passive state, of the mind. The intellect reserves all its rights. Instantly, when the mind itself wakes, all books, all past acts are forgotten, huddled aside as impertinent in the august presence of the creator. Their costliest benefit is that they set us free from ourselves; for they wake the imagination and the sentiment, and in their inspirations we dispense with books. Let me add, then, read proudly, — put the duty of being read invariably on the author. If he is not read, whose fault is it? I am quite ready to be charmed, but I shall not make believe I am charmed."

He read a poem in Faneuil Hall Dec. 16, on the centennial anniversary of the destruction of tea in Boston Harbor, which has since been published in his *Select Poems*. On the last day of the year he read this poem again, this time before the Radical Club, at Mrs. Sargent's. At this meeting a reception was given him; Whittier, Longfellow, Hedge, Phillips, Wilson, Henry James, and many others being present. Charles Bradlaugh was also a guest of the club, and in a feeling manner expressed his debt to Emerson, by saying, "I ascribe to Mr. Emerson's essay on Self-Reliance my first step in the career I have adopted. Twenty-six years ago, when too poor to buy a book, I copied parts of that famous lecture." In writing to an English journal, he described Emerson's manner as "so gentle that he seemed only reading to one person, and yet his voice was so distinct that it filled the room in its lowest tones." [1]

In 1874 Emerson was put in nomination by the independent party among the students of Glasgow University, for the office of Lord-Rector. The other candidates were Disraeli and Forster. The usual exciting canvass preceded the election. Emerson received five hundred votes against seven hundred for Disraeli, who was elected. To the committee of the Independent Club, who wrote asking permission to put him in nomination, he sent the following letter: —

"CONCORD, MASS., March 18, 1874.

"GENTLEMEN, — I received a few days since your letter of the 17th of February, inviting me to allow my name to be proposed as one of the candidates for the Lord-rectorship of the University of Glasgow. I confess to a surprise that reached almost to incredulity, which the careful reading of your letter changed into a respect and gratitude to the kind and noble feeling with which you, and the young gentlemen whom you represent, have honored me. Dr. Stirling's letter, which came to me with yours, added its confirmation and the friendliest details to your own.

"At first I thought the proposition so novel, and so unlikely to be sustained by the whole body of the matriculated students, that I must not think of it as other than a kindest compliment of a few friends, and very precious to me as such, but only to be respectfully declined. On thinking it over, I find it is for you, and not for me, to judge of the probabilities of the election; and that you, and not I, must decide whether these are such as to justify you in actually proposing my name to the electors. If you persist, you are at lib-

[1] Sketches and Reminiscences of the Radical Club, p. 293.

erty to propose my name; and, if elected, I shall certainly endeavor to meet your wishes, and those of the university, as to the time and duties which the office shall require. With this letter I shall send to Boston my affirmative reply by the ocean telegraph, as requested by Dr. Stirling.

"Yours with very kind regards,

"R. W. EMERSON."

There could have been no greater evidence of the esteem in which he is held in England than this nomination and the very large vote he received. No other foreigner, probably, had ever received the nomination; and the contest showed a thorough appreciation of his genius on the part of his friends among the students. After the contest was over, he wrote the following letter to the honorary president of the Independent Club: —

"CONCORD, 5th January, 1875.

"MY DEAR DR. STIRLING, — I can not forgive myself for my tardiness in telling you how deeply I have felt your interest and care in my behalf at Glasgow. Yet I was and am deeply sensible of your heroic generosity in the care of my interest in the late election. I could never, from the first to the last act in the affair, bring myself to believe that the brave nomination of the independents would succeed, and could hardly trust the truth of the telegrams, which at last brought me so dignified a result as five hundred votes in our behalf. I count that vote as quite the fairest laurel that has ever fallen on me; and I can not but feel deeply grateful to my young friends in the university, and to yourself, who have been their counselor and my too partial advocate. Of course such an approach to success gave me lively thoughts of what could have been attempted and at least approached in meeting and dealing with the university, if my friends had succeeded; but I hope the stimulus they have given me will not be wholly lost. Probably I have never seen one of these five hundred young men; and thus they show us that our recorded thoughts give the means of reaching those who think with us in other countries, and make closer alliances sometimes than life-long neighborhood. To be sure, the truth is hackneyed, but it never came to me in so palpable a form. It is easy to me to gather from your letters, and from those of Mr. Herkless, and from the printed papers, how generously you have espoused and aided my champions; and it only adds one more to the many deep debts which I owe to you. I never lose the hope that you will come to us at no distant day, and be our king in philosophy.

"With affectionate regards,

"R. WALDO EMERSON."

"MR. J. HUTCHINSON STIRLING, LL.D."

In 1874 he published a collection of his favorite poems, under the title of *Parnassus.* It was the result of his habit, pursued for many years, of copying into his commonplace book any poem which specially pleased him. Many of these favorites had been read to illustrate his lectures on the English poets. The book has no worthless selections, almost every thing it contains bearing the stamp of genius and worth. Yet Emerson's personality is seen in its many intellectual and serious poems, and in the small number of its purely religious selections. With two or three exceptions he copies none of those devotional poems which have attracted devout souls. He makes three selections from Jones Very, but gives none of the exquisite religious pieces of that little-known poet. He gives no one of the poems in which is embodied the religious spirit of transcendentalism, as it has been expressed by Samuel Longfellow, Samuel Johnson, and others. His poetical sympathies are shown in the fact that one-third of the selections are from the seventeenth century. Shakspere is drawn on more largely than any other, no less than eighty-eight selections being made from him. The names of George Herbert, Herrick, Ben Jonson, and Milton frequently appear. Wordsworth appears forty-three times, and stands next to Shakspere; while Burns, Byron, Scott, Tennyson, and Chaucer make up the list of favorites. Many little-known pieces are included, and some whose merit is other than poetical. W. E. Channing, Thoreau, and Sanborn are drawn upon as often as Longfellow, Holmes, or Lowell. Many pieces seem to be included for their historic or personal interest, and some because they describe persons, scenes, or human passions. Burns, Bret Harte, and Holmes are the favorites among humorous poets. Shakspere and Byron furnish nearly all the selections under the head of "Poetry of Terror;" while Shakspere and other Elizabethan poets give him, with a few exceptions, those in the section of "Oracles and Counsels." There is a fine collection of songs, marked by their intellectual and moral qualities, and as being of the highest poetic merit. The section of moral and religious poems is nearly one-half of it taken from the Elizabethan poets, showing how strong is Emerson's affinity for the thought of that period. Even here Shakspere retains the priority, but Wordsworth only falls behind him by one selection. The large number of heroic, narrative, and ballad poems given, as well as those containing personal portraits, show the depth of Emerson's human interest. This selection of poems is eminently that of a poet of keen intellectual tastes. It is not popular in character, omitting many public favorites, and introducing very much which can never be acceptable to the general reader. The preface is full of interest for its comments on many of the poems and poets appearing in these selections.

The hundredth anniversary of the Concord fight was observed on the 19th of April, 1875. On that day the "Minute Man" of young French was unveiled. This fine piece of work was erected on the west shore of the Concord River, at the place where the militia stood when they

"Fired the shot heard round the world."

The first monument was erected where the British soldiers stood. In the brief address which Emerson gave on this occasion he tells the story of the Concord farmer who first suggested the new monument. His whole address was in these words: —

"Ebenezer Hubbard, a farmer who inherited the land in the village in which troops committed depredations, and who had a deep interest in the history of the raid, erected many years ago a flag-staff on his land, and never neglected to hoist the stars and stripes on the 19th of April and the 4th of July. It grieved him deeply that yonder monument, erected by the town in 1836, should be built on the ground on which the enemy stood, instead of that which the Americans occupied in the Concord fight; and he bequeathed in his will a sum of money to the town of Concord, on condition that a monument should be built on the identical spot occupied by our minute-men and militia on that day; and another sum of money, on the condition that the town should build a foot-bridge across the river, where the old bridge stood in 1775. The town accepted the legacy, built the bridge, and employed

Daniel French to prepare a statue to be erected on the specified spot. Meanwhile Congress, at Washington, gave to the town bronze cannons, to furnish the artist with materials to complete his work. His statue is before you; it was approved by the town, and to-day it speaks for itself. The sculptor has rightly conceived the proper emblems of the patriot farmer, who at the morning alarm left the plow to grasp his gun. He has built no dome over his work, believing that the blue sky makes the best background. The statue is the first serious work of our young townsman, who is now in Italy to pursue his profession.

"We had many enemies and many friends in England, but our one benefactor was King George the Third. The time had arrived for the political severance of America, that it might play its part in the history of this globe; and the way of Divine Providence to do it was to give an insane king to England. In the resistance of the colonies he alone was immovable on the question of force. England was so dear to us, that the colonies could only be absolutely united by violence from England; and only one man could compel resort to violence. The king became insane; parliament wavered; all the ministers wavered; Lord North wavered; but the king had the insanity of one idea. He was immovable; he insisted on the impossible; so the army was sent. America was instantly united, and the nation born. On the 19th of April, eight hundred soldiers, with hostile intent, were sent hither from Boston. Nature itself put on a new face on that day. You see the nude fields of this morning; but on the same day of the year 1775 a rare forwardness of spring is recorded. It appears the patriotism of the people was so hot that it melted the snow, and the rye waved on the 19th of April.

"In all noble actions we say 'tis only the first step that costs. Who would carry out the rule of right must take his life in his hand. We have no need to magnify the facts. Only three of our men were killed at this bridge, and a few others were wounded; but here the British army was first fronted and driven back; and if only three men, or only one man was slain, it was the first victory. The thunderbolt falls on an inch of ground, but the light of it fills the horizon. The British instantly retreated. We had no electric telegraph; but the news of this triumph over the king's troops sped through the country to New York, to Philadelphia, to Kentucky, to the Carolinas, with speed unknown before, and ripened the colonies to inevitable decision.

"This sharp beginning of real war was followed sixty days later by the battle of Bunker Hill, then by Gen. Washington's arrival in Cambridge, and his redoubts on Dorchester Heights. In one year and twelve days from the death of Isaac Davis and Abner Hosmer, one hundred and twenty vessels, loaded with Gen. Howe and his army, eight thousand men, and all their effects, sailed out of Boston Harbor, never to return. 'Tis a proud and tender story. I challenge any lover of Massachusetts to read the sixteenth chapter of Bancroft's history without tears of joy."

His *Letters and Social Aims* was published in 1875. It contains the essay on The Comic, which appeared in *The Dial*, and a paper on Persian Poetry, from *The Atlantic Monthly*. Its first essay is a long and carefully elaborated presentation of his theory of poetry, and is his only piece of writing since *Nature* which did not assume the lecture-form. His theory that the poet is the true interpreter of nature and life is presented, while the doctrine of identity again becomes the basis of his thought. Nature and mind exactly correspond with each other, so that nature is a perfect symbol of spirit; and the poet, through his imagination and intuition, acts as the interpreter of this correspondence, — this is the point of view of the essay. The essays in this volume are simpler in style and thought than some of his earlier ones, because he is dealing with the affairs of daily life. In a few of them, however, he reaches the highest mark of his power as a writer. This is the case in the address on the Progress of Culture, and it is also true of the essay on Immortality. Nearly all the other essays had been given as lectures in Boston, between 1860 and 1870. This volume was received with a more general approval and with more of praise by the critics than any of his previous books. A few of them, however, persisted in misjudging as much as ever, as in the case of *The Athenæum*, which said, —

> "In his latest production Mr. Emerson is as crabbed as entertaining, and as 'cock-sure' as when he first startled the Phi Beta Kappa Society with his parodoxes on the relations of man to the universe. One advantage, however, he still possesses over most of the *pseudo*-philosophers at whose head he stands. He is slow in utterance and patient in labor. His method of work is that of great thinkers. Gradually he absorbs and assimilates whatever science or history can furnish, and slowly and reflectively he gives us the result of his thoughts. So patiently does he brood over his eggs, that if they are sometimes addled the fault is scarcely his. Already, however, his influence is on the wane. He wants that last and most useful gift of genius, the power to keep young in soul, and to advance with advancing years." [1]

[1] Athenæum, Jan. 15, 1876. Perhaps the worst instance of misrepresentation was shown in the Catholic World for April, 1878, where Emer-

A collection of his *Select Poems* appeared in 1876, containing the best of the poems in the two previous volumes. It also embraced two or three hitherto unpublished. From this time on his lectures became less frequent, but for that reason all the more notable to those who had listened to him for many years. He read one of the best of his moral and political essays to a brilliant audience in the Old South Church, during the year 1872. It was The Fortune of the Republic, and was immediately put into a volume. The same year he spoke in the same place on The Superlative. In 1879 he gave a lecture on Memory before the Concord School of Philosophy, a lecture in Cambridge on Eloquence, and one before the Harvard Divinity School on The Preacher. In 1880 he gave his hundredth lecture before the Concord Lyceum, on New-England Life and Letters; while before the School of Philosophy his subject was Natural Aristocracy. In the autumn he read an essay before the members of the Divinity School, and early in 1881 he gave a paper on Carlyle before the Massachusetts Historical Society.

During these years there has been a constantly increasing interest in Emerson's books, and a deeper appreciation of his influence. This is shown by the eagerness there has been to hear him, by the discussion of his religious attitude, and by the testimonies to his influence from those affected by his thought. Alger has called him an acute observer and a fearless thinker; while, "by his audacious and sensitive genius, he is a contemporary of the primal minds of all ages."[1] It is this fearless vigor and depth of his thought which has

son is said to borrow all his good things from Montaigne, and to be a mere imitator of Swedenborg. We are told "it is about time to expose this wily old philosopher who has been throwing rhetorical dust into the eyes of several generations." Another instance of petty criticism is to be found in Hain Friswell's Modern Men of Letters, where he says, "there is a certain amount of honest work in Emerson's books, but there is also a good deal of gilt gingerbread and flash jewelry." He is said to corrupt the youth of our time, and that he has done his best to fill them with "an unutterable longing," "with a wide, windy, and dispersed ambition," and with "a curious pantheistic reverence for something — what it is, it is not known."

[1] Christian Examiner, May, 1868.

attracted to him some of the acutest minds among his contemporaries. At a meeting of the Radical Club, in 1873, Tyndall said, "The first time I ever knew Waldo Emerson was when, years ago, I picked up on a stall a copy of his *Nature*. I read it with such delight, and I have never ceased to read it; and if any one can be said to have given the impulse to my mind, it is Emerson. Whatever I have done, the world owes to him."[1] Equally ardent has been Carlyle's praise of his friend. He early said, "I hear but one voice, and that comes from Concord." Later he said that Emerson was "the cleanest mind now living," and that he had not his equal on earth for perception. In 1866 Carlyle said, "Now and then a letter comes from him, and amid all the smoke and mist of this world it is always as a window flung open to the azure. During all this last weary work of mine, his words have been nearly the only ones about the thing done to which I have inwardly responded."[2] Another Englishman, a worker in the fields of humanitarian reform, George Jacob Holyoake, visited him in 1880, and has written out his impressions in these words: —

"Though tall, Mr. Emerson is still erect, and has the bright eye and calm grace of manner we knew when he was in England long years ago. In European eyes, his position among men of letters in America is as that of Carlyle among English writers; with the added quality, as I think, of greater braveness of thought and clearness of sympathy. The impression among many to whom I spoke in America, I found to be, that, while Carlyle inspires you to do something not clearly defined, when you have read Emerson you know what you have to do. However, Mr. Emerson would admit nothing that would challenge the completer merits of his illustrious friend at Chelsea. He showed me the later and earlier portraits of Carlyle, which he most cherished; made affectionate inquiries concerning him personally, and as to whether I knew of any thing that had proceeded from his pen which he had not in his library.

"Friends had told me that age seemed now a little to impair Mr. Emerson's memory, but I found his recollection of England accurate and full of detail. A fine portrait of him, which Mr. Wendell Phillips presented to me, has been generally thought by those who have not seen Emerson to be a portrait of Mr. Gladstone,

[1] Reminiscences of the Radical Club, p. 300.
[2] Harper's Monthly, May, 1881, p. 899.

whom he certainly very much resembles now. Englishmen told me with pride, that in the dark days of the war, when American audiences were indignant at England, Emerson would put, in his lectures, some generous passage concerning this country, and, raising himself erect, pronounce it in a defiant tone, as though he threw the words at his audience. More than any other writer, Emerson gives me the impression of one who sees facts alive and knows their ways, and who writes nothing that is mean or poor."[1]

While such men as Bradlaugh, Holyoake, and Tyndall have been attracted to Emerson by his sturdy advocacy of self-reliance, or because of his eloquent interpretations of nature, others have been drawn to him because of the spirituality of his thought, and for his hopeful outlook upon life. If Bradlaugh has found in his essays stimulus to his radicalism, even more legitimately have they influenced the sermons of Stopford Brooke and Heber Newton. An English writer, who has accepted and defends Emerson's religious stand-point,[2] has this word to say of his influence, —

"There is, perhaps, no writer of the nineteenth century who will better repay a careful and prolonged perusal than Emerson. He enjoys the rare distinction of having ascended to the highest point to which the human mind can climb, — to the point where, as he says of Plato, the poles of thought are on a line with the axis on which the frame of things revolves. . . . He stations himself at the point where the ascending lines of Law pass into Unity. Once attain to that position, and every sentence becomes luminous. The connection of ideas becomes apparent; the illustrations are seen to be pertinent and exact; and the subject to be laid open on all sides by direct and penetrating insight. We can then turn to him, with the same delight, for the philosophical expression of the deep laws of human life, as we do to Shakspere for their dramatic representation. For he is one of the profoundest of thinkers, and has that universality, serenity, and cosmopolitan breadth of comprehension, that place him among the great of all ages. He has swallowed all his predecessors, and converted them into nutriment for himself. He is as subtle and delicate, too, as he is broad and massive, and possesses a practical wisdom and keenness of observation that hold his feet fast to the solid earth when his head is striking the stars. His scientific accuracy and freedom of speculation mark him out as one of the representative men of the nineteenth century."

[1] Co-operative News of Manchester.
[2] The Religion of the Future, John Beattie Crozier, p. 107.

Herman Grimm has borne testimony to Emerson's literary power, in his *New Essays*. When he first saw one of Emerson's books he was greatly attracted to it, as he found that some of its sentences were full of new and vigorous thought. He found there a sense of joy and beauty such as is given by the greatest books. In reading him, he felt as if he had met the simplest and most genuine person, and as if he were listening to that person's conversation. He found himself made captive by thoughts which it seemed as if he were learning for the first time. "He has his faults and his doubtful virtues, and is very likely capricious and capable of flattery. Yet when I again read his sentences, the enchanting breezes of hope and spiritual joy filled my soul anew. The old worn-out machinery of the world was re-created, and I felt as if I had never breathed so pure an atmosphere. I recently heard an American, who had been present at some of Emerson's lectures, say that nothing was more captivating than to listen to this man. I believe it. Nothing will surpass the voice of a man who speaks from the depths of his soul what he considers true." In a note to the translator of his *Life of Goethe*, Grimm has also said, "I can indeed say that no author, with whose writings I have lately become acquainted, has had such an influence upon me as Emerson. The manner of writing of this man, whom I hold to be the greatest of all living authors, has revealed to me a new way of expressing thought." If a new way of expressing thought, even more truly has he given a new way of believing and living. This has been hinted at by Professor C. C. Everett, when he says, —

"We think of no writer who is so typically American as he. His Yankee shrewdness is carried into the most profound of mystical utterances. His mind is always sane. Never unbalanced, never running to extremes, he keeps on his even course. If he unites with his practical insight the intuitions of the eastern seer, to Yankee common sense the transcendentalism of Germany, to the homely wisdom of every-day life the inspiration of genius, these opposing lines never conflict with one another. If he is mystical, he is never misty. The reason is, that he is so much at home in regions that to many seem far off and dim, that, with no change in modes of thought and expression, he can describe them as they are. He can utter the loftiest truth as soon as the humblest. This sanity with which the highest themes are approached by him, has done much to make them seem real and practical to many who would otherwise have regarded them as belonging to the life of dreams."

Emerson has never quite recovered from the nervous shock received at the burning of his house. Yet his health has been almost uniformly good, though suffering sadly from the loss of his memory. The recent years have been quietly spent in the midst of his friends, and in the preparation of his remaining manuscripts for future publication. Gossip has been busy with his name, making him much feebler than he ever has been, and attributing to him a change in his religious convictions. He is yet vigorous, however, and retains something of that youthful look which has always characterized him. His family and his neighbors know nothing whatever of any change in his religious ideas.

He has truly obeyed the voice at eve obeyed at prime, and swerved not from his trust in the soul, his confidence in the progress of man, or his reliance on those spiritual truths which have been the joy of all great souls. His friends have drawn closer to him as the years have gone on, and a greater number with each year have come to see in him a friend to be trusted and a teacher to be followed. Those who once criticised him find new faith in him as a poet, thinker, and critic. What once seemed faults are forgotten in an admiring recognition of his genius. The voice at eve is the voice of a pure and lofty soul, that will be heard more and more gladly through the coming years, as the music of his rich thought floats down the ages that are to follow.

XIV.

THE MAN AND THE LIFE.

EMERSON is eminently domestic in his tastes, loving plain, simple things, and has lived in the most quiet, modest manner possible. His essay on Domestic Life indicates the high esteem in which he holds the home, the regard he has for children, and the culture he would have grow out of the home-life. The home, he thinks, should be for plain living and high thinking; and the house should in its economy bear witness that human culture is the end to which it is built and garnished. Alcott has given the following account of his domestic tastes and habits: —

> "All men love the country who love mankind with a wholesome love, and have poetry and company in them. Our essayist makes good this preference. If city bred, he has been for the best part of his life a villager and countryman. Only a traveler at times professionally, he prefers home-keeping; is a student of the landscape, of mankind, of rugged strength wherever found; liking plain persons, plain ways, plain clothes; prefers earnest people; shuns egotists, publicity; likes solitude, and knows its uses. Courting society as a spectacle not less than as a pleasure, he carries off the spoils. Delighting in the broadest views of men and things, he seeks all accessible displays of both for draping his thoughts and works." [1]

He has been most fortunate in all his domestic relations; [2] while the surroundings of his life have been such as he could desire, and they have been helpful to the life he has sought to live. His house has been well adapted to a scholar's wants, both as to its location and

[1] In his little book on Emerson, partly reprinted in Concord Days.

[2] Emerson has had four children, two sons and two daughters. One son died early, and the other is a much-respected physician in Concord. The older daughter is unmarried, and is the main-stay of the home. The other is married.

construction. About the house is a little farm; and he owns a wood-lot on the west shore of Walden Pond, where Thoreau's hut once stood. His home has been described in these words: —

"A roomy barn stands near the house, and behind lies a little farm of nearly a dozen acres. The whole external appearance of the place suggests old-fashioned comfort and hospitality. Within the house the flavor of antiquity is still more noticeable. Old pictures look down from the walls; quaint blue-and-white china holds the simple dinner; old furniture brings to mind the generations of the past. Just at the right, as you enter, is Mr. Emerson's library, a large, square room, plainly furnished, but made pleasant by pictures and sunshine. The homely shelves which line the walls are well filled with books. There is a lack of showy covers or rich bindings, and each volume seems to have soberly grown old in constant service. Mr. Emerson's study is a quiet room up stairs, and there each day he is steadily at work, despite advancing years." [1]

When Frederika Bremer called one day at his house, she did not find him at home. Going into his library, she thus describes it: [2] —

"I went for a moment into Emerson's study, — a large room, in which every thing was simple, orderly, unstudied, comfortable. No refined feeling of beauty has converted the room into a temple, in which stand the forms of the heroes of science and literature. Ornament is banished from the sanctuary of the stoic philosopher; the furniture is comfortable, but of a grave character, merely as implements of usefulness; one large picture only is in the room, but this hangs there with a commanding power; it is a large oil-painting, a copy of Michael Angelo's glorious Parcæ, the goddess of fate."

She says there stood a large table in the center of the room, at which Emerson wrote. On it were a number of papers, but all in perfect order. Some years later M. D. Conway called on Emerson, and describes his visit, giving us a further glimpse of his study.[3]

"My note of introduction was presented, and my welcome was cordial. Emerson was, apparently, yet young; he was tall, slender, of light complexion; his step was elastic, his manner easy and sim-

[1] Literary World, 1877.
[2] The Homes of the New World, vol. ii. p. 562.
[3] Fraser's Magazine, August, 1864.

ple; and his voice at once relieved me of the trembling with which I stood before him, — the first great man I had ever seen. He proposed to take me on a walk; and whilst he was preparing, I had the opportunity of looking about the library. Over the mantel hung an excellent copy of Michael Angelo's Parcæ; on it there were two statuettes of Goethe, of whom also there were engraved copies on the walls. Afterwards Emerson showed me eight or ten portraits of Goethe which he had collected. The next in favor was Dante, of whom he had all the known likenesses, including various photographs of the mask of Dante, made at Ravenna. Besides portraits of Shakspere, Montaigne, and Swedenborg, I remember nothing else on the walls of the library. The book-shelves were well filled with select works; amongst which I was only struck with the many curious Oriental productions, some in Sanscrit. He had, too, many editions in Greek and English, of Plato, which had been carefully read and marked. The furniture of the room was antique and simple. There were, on one side of the room, four considerable shelves, completely occupied by his MSS.; of which there were enough, one might suppose, to have furnished a hundred volumes instead of the seven which he has given to the world, though under perpetual pressure for more from the publishers and the public."

Emerson's house is of the old New-England sort, large, and hospitable in its very construction. A long hall divides it through the middle. By the side of the entry stands a table, over which is a picture of Diana. His book-shelves are very plain, and reach to the ceiling. A fireplace fills one end of the study, and has high brass andirons; while on the antique mantel over it may now be found, among other articles, a small idol from the Nile. On the other end is a bronze lamp of antique pattern, such as is often pictured to represent the light of science. Back of this room is the large parlor, in which visitors are received, and where many a conversational party has been held.

The gate always remains open. The path from the house to the road is lined with tall chestnut-trees. Back of the house is a garden of half an acre, where both Emerson and his wife are wont to labor. She is passionately fond of flowers, and grows them in profusion. Great numbers of roses are in bloom here in June, while there is a bed of hollyhocks of many varieties. A small brook runs across his land, and pours into the river.

Emerson has a pronounced and an emphatic face, not at all remarkable at the first glance, but striking for its reserved power of expression. His head is high and well-formed, his nose very large, his chin strong, his eye gentle and searching. He is of a slender figure, more than medium height, head small, and shoulders remarkably sloping. "His manner, though dignified, is very retiring and singularly refined and gentlemanly. His face has a thoughtful and somewhat pre-occupied expression, with keen eyes and aquiline nose. His countenance lights up with a rare appreciation of humor, of which he has the keenest sense; but his chief characteristics are beneficence and courtesy, which never fail, whether addressing the humblest pauper or the most distinguished scholar."[1] In manner he is reticent, in general conversation he is not brilliant, and in ordinary intercourse with men he does not appear as a genius. Yet there is a reserved personality, that is commanding, powerful, and charming. It is a personality that carries immense force, that molds and sways others, less by a dazzling brilliancy and the tremendousness of intellect, than by the persuasive might of a pure, unadulterated, and perfectly loyal nature, which never swerves, which goes steadily on to the goal it seeks.

Hawthorne and Miss Bremer used in their diaries almost the same expression about Emerson, — an expression showing the luminous and attracting power of his nature. In speaking of those who called on her in Boston, Miss Bremer says, "Emerson came also, with a sunbeam in his countenance." This was in December, 1850. In April, 1843, Hawthorne made this record in his journal: "Mr. Emerson came, with a sunbeam in his face; and we had as good a talk as I ever remember to have had with him." Curtis has likewise spoken of the "smile that breaks over his face like day over the sky;" and once said, that at Emerson's house it seemed always morning. This sunbeam in his face must be an attractive one to fascinate three such people,

[1] Poets' Homes.

causing them to notice it as a striking characteristic. Miss Bremer, however, could not understand him; and she persisted in thinking him not just right, in consequence of his religious opinions; but she was strongly attracted to him, charmed by his personality, and fascinated by his nobility of character. After being four days in his home, she writes, "I enjoyed the contemplation of him, in his demeanor, his expression, his mode of talking, and his every-day life, as I enjoy the calm flow of a river bearing along, and between flowery shores, large and small vessels, — as I love to see the eagle circling in the clouds, resting upon them and its pinions. In this calm elevation Emerson allows nothing to reach him, neither great nor small, neither prosperity nor adversity." Again she says, "Pantheistic as Emerson is in his philosophy, in the moral view in which he regards the world and life he is in a high degree pure, noble, and severe, demanding as much from himself as he demands from others. His words are severe, his judgments often keen and merciless, but his demeanor is alike noble and pleasing, and his voice beautiful. One may quarrel with Emerson's thoughts, with his judgment, but not with himself. That which struck me most, as distinguishing him from most other human beings, is *nobility*. He is a born gentleman." As the result of her visit to him, she exclaims, "Lovable he is as one sees him in his home and amid his domestic relations."

"Every thing about a man like Emerson is important, says John Burroughs.[1] I find his phrenology and physiognomy more than ordinarily typical and suggestive. Look at his picture there, — large, strong features on a small face and head, — no blank spaces; all given up to expression; a high, predaceous nose, a sinewy brow, a massive, benevolent chin. In most men there is more face than feature; but here is vast deal more feature than face, and a corresponding alertness and emphasis of character. Indeed, the man is made after this fashion. He is all type; his expression is transcendent. His mind has the hand's pronounced anatomy, its cords and sinews and multiform articulations and processes, its opposing and co-ordinating power. If his brain is

[1] Birds and Poets, p. 190.

small, its texture is fine, and its convolutions deep. There have been broader and more catholic natures, but few so towering and audacious in expression, and so rich in characteristic traits. Every scrap and shred of him is important and related. Like the strongly aromatic herbs and simples, — sage, mint, wintergreen, sassafras, — the least part carries the flavor of the whole. Is there one indifferent or equivocal or unsympathizing drop of blood in him? Where he is at all he is entirely, — nothing extemporaneous; his most casual word seems to have laid in pickle for a long time, and is saturated through and through with the Emersonian brine. Indeed, so pungent and penetrating is this quality, that his quotations seem more than half his own."

If the range of his mind is narrow, it is with that narrowness characteristic of all supremely ethical minds. Lowell well remarks that "the artistic range of Emerson is narrow; and so is that of Æschylus, so is that of Dante, so is that of Montaigne, so is that of Schiller, so is that of nearly every one but Shakspere; but there is a gauge of height no less than of breadth; of individuality as well as of comprehensiveness; and, above all, there is the standard of genetic power, the test of the masculine as distinguished from the receptive natures."[1] His is the concentrated mind of the original thinker, and no truly original mind can see in all directions with equal clearness. Yet he is broad in his sympathies, world-wide in his love of truth and in his faith in man. His is a masculine, an inquiring nature. He is a mental pioneer; and he has great power to grasp new leadings of thought, to comprehend the results of modern research in their application to the spiritual nature. This is characteristically shown in his sacred regard for the body, in his giving to its laws ethical sanctions, and in his looking upon all sickness as a sin. He fore-reaches the future in these, as in so many other opinions, and becomes a prophet of that higher faith the world is yet to attain. It has been said, that the thing he most hates is sickness, while disease he regards as a sin. He has himself said he was never confined to a bed for a single day. To him virtue is health; and he quotes Dr. Johnson's saying, that every man is a rascal when he is sick.

[1] My Study Windows, essay on Thoreau.

He believes the outward complaint origi inward complaint, and sees that if we obedient to the laws of the soul and of would be no sickness or disease. His vie ject, as on so many others, have been n Miss Bremer interpreted them by suppo strong and healthy himself to understand weaknesses and sufferings; for he even d ing, as a weakness unworthy of higher singularity of character leads one to su has never been ill." His philosophy led suffering, and to distrust feeling, as it led his successors to despise the body, and to of it. He believed the pure and holy s control the material form it has put forth its sensual dwelling-place, that it may alw and healthy; so he despised suffering a sickness as a sign of the soul's discord wi believed that human suffering arises from to laws that may and ought to be obeyed. the sickness will cease, and the weakness

In the same way, he has regarded mer sign of weakness. He has carefully su himself and distrusted it in others. Vi been his belief in intuition and ecstasy, p been to accept theories which culminat enthusiasm and feeling, yet he has hims spised emotion and undue excitement of nature. Accepting a philosophy which methods of logic and cool argumentation, the slow and toilsome processes of the yet he has himself been remarkably criti ing in his judgments. He has, conseq fallen into those excesses of opinion and have characterized some of the believers Whatever the follies of the transcenden wild excesses of feeling, of judgment, a none of these appear in the sayings and d son. Maintaining a philosophy which h any other given rise to wild extravagan self teaching as truth doctrines that are saturated with the elements of religious fanaticism, yet he has always spoken in a calm, rational, self-poised spirit. What was feeling in others and excess of emotion, giving rise to strange outbursts of imaginative power, has been in him a dispassionate rational process of calm inquiry after the truth. The emotional excesses of Margaret Fuller, her regarding feeling as a signal of great truths revealed to the soul, he distrusted and even held in contempt. She suspected his coldness and critical temper of mind, and he was more than annoyed by her fervent heat of thought and excess of feeling. His poetic temperament brought him into sympathy with a philosophy which the strongly intellectual bent of his nature would otherwise have led him to reject. Hence he has accepted in a dispassionate spirit philosophic opinions, the nature of which in most minds is to excite to feeling and enthusiasm. This fact has had a marked influence on his career, and is shown forth in that calm, self-poised spirit all his words and acts indicate.

Hospitality is another of Emerson's characteristics. His house has been open to friendship and generous entertainment, and made free to those desirous of sharing in its hospitality. He receives with cordiality all who bring to him any generous word or earnest purpose, and in a spirit that is simple, unaffected, and generous. Yet he never obtrudes himself, does not regard his own personal preferences as of interest to others. There is no egotism in his nature, no self-intrusion. He has been wanting in personal ambitions, in endeavors to bring himself before the public. The common and the great, the wise and the ignorant, have alike come to his door, and been welcomed with equal generosity; whoever had a pure, brave, or true thought to give, has been received with delight.

As Sanborn well suggests,[1] he has a genius for friendship. His intimate relations with Alcott, Parker, Hedge, Bartol, Margaret Fuller, Lowell, W. E. Channing, Thoreau, Sanborn, Miss Peabody, Henry James, Carlyle, and

[1] Literary World, May, 1880.

several others, show the attracting power of his personality. To some of these he has been a friend in the largest sense possible, a confidant in difficulties, a helper in times of need. They bear most ardent testimony to the strength of his sympathies and the largeness of his generosity. His fine devotion to his brothers, and his faithful service to many other members of his family, show the largeness of his heart and the loyalty of his nature. He has written much of the sacred joys of friendship, but he has written nothing equal to his own exemplification of its qualities. In this, as in all things else, he has been what he preached; preaching only what he found to be real in his own rich and many-sided experience of the highest things which life can give.

Of a retiring and diffident nature, he has kept aloof from a public life. Yet all the more strongly has he therefore been drawn to the circle of friends with whom he has been in sympathy. Among these persons was the friend of his youth, Sarah Bradford, who became the wife of the Rev. Samuel Ripley. In her old age she went to live in Concord, and was wont to pass each Sunday evening at Emerson's house. With other friends such as this one, long trusted and admired, he was accustomed for many years to spend that evening in conversation on subjects dear to them all. Perhaps he valued no friend more than Mrs. Ripley, and none ever influenced him so long and deeply. After her death, in July, 1867, he said of her, —

"At a time when perhaps no other woman read Greek, she acquired the language with ease, and read Plato, — adding soon the advantage of German commentators. After her marriage, when her husband, the well-known clergyman of Waltham, received boys in his house to be fitted for college, she assumed the advanced instruction in Greek and Latin, and did not fail to turn it to account by extending her studies in the literature of both languages. . . . She became one of the best Greek scholars in the country, and continued, in her latest years, the habit of reading Homer, the tragedians, and Plato. But her studies took a wide range in mathematics, in natural philosophy, in psychology, in theology, as well as in ancient and modern literature. She had always a keen ear open to whatever new facts astronomy, chemistry, or the theories of light or heat had to furnish. Any knowledge, all knowledge, was welcome.

Her stores increased day by day. She was absolutely without pedantry. Nobody ever heard of her learning until a necessity came for its use, and then nothing could be more simple than her solution of the problem proposed to her. The most intellectual gladly conversed with one whose knowledge, however rich and varied, was always with her only the means of new acquaintance. . . . She was not only the most amiable, but the tenderest of women, wholly sincere, thoughtful for others. . . . She was absolutely without appetite for luxury or display or praise or influence, with entire indifference to trifles."

Emerson has taken a keen interest in all which concerned the culture and advancement of his townsmen. He was long a zealous friend of the Concord Lyceum, devoting to it much of his time and thought. When its fiftieth anniversary was celebrated, E. R. Hoar bore testimony as follows to Emerson's influence throughout the town: —

"It was the felicity of the Lyceum, as it was the good fortune of the town, that Mr. Emerson came to live among us. He has delivered before the Concord Lyceum in the last fifty years ninety-eight lectures. Distant be the day when this community shall be free to give full expression to its gratitude to him, and to the love and honor which his townsmen bear to him! But our ceremony would be incomplete if I did not ask you to pause for a moment, and to think what the simple statement of those ninety-eight lectures means. What a wealth of intellectual treasure has been spread out before this people! What keenness of analysis, what treasures of wit and wisdom, what lofty and inspiring thought, what results of a noble life, are contained in those manuscript pages which he has read to us! The presence of Mr. Emerson in Concord has been the education of the town. It has given it its principal distinction in our generation."

He has for many years been a member of the Social Circle, a Concord club organized in 1782, growing out of the revolutionary committee of safety. Societies of a wider character have honored themselves by making him a member. He is connected with the Massachusetts Historical Society and various other American institutions. The French Academy has made him a member of its section of Moral and Political Sciences. He has belonged to several clubs succeeding that organized by the transcendentalists. In 1849 the Transcendental Club was succeeded by the Town and Country Club, mainly organized by the efforts of Alcott. Emerson gave it its name; and he read before it the first essay to which it listened, on Books and Reading. This was on May 2, 1849. Among its members were Garrison, Parker, W. H. Channing, W. E. Channing, Alcott, Phillips, Hedge, Howe, King, Lowell, Weiss, Whipple, Higginson, Very, Pillsbury, and Thoreau. Subsequently he frequently attended the meetings of the contributors to *The Atlantic Monthly*, where his apt and pointed words were listened to gladly. He was not there or elsewhere a frequent talker, being always reticent, and not easy to come into free intercourse with other minds; but when he did speak, it was out of a full and exact mind. He has been an occasional attendant at the Radical Club and other similar gatherings. Strongly inclined to shun society and publicity, he has not for many years taken an active part in the social and literary efforts of this kind.

Emerson is characterized for modesty and simplicity, for guilelessness of character, and for a remarkable loyalty of nature. He has a loyal love for truth, and is eager in the search for it. Fame has not affected, nor has criticism hurt him. Whatever the praise or blame, he has kept steadily on his way, in the same child-like, sincere, and trustful manner. His life has been above reproach; and he has been constantly devoted to human good, steadily loyal to his own ideals. Withdrawn from the strifes and the passions of a public career, living the quiet, peaceful life of the scholar, he has yet been faithful to the great human interests of his time. His life has been as moral, as ethically true, as his teaching has been; he has practiced his own precepts, exemplified his own doctrines. "Beyond almost all literary men on record, Higginson says, his life has been worthy of his words."

He is a Puritan, with all that is harsh, repulsive, and uncomfortable in Puritanism removed; but quite as loyal to moral purposes, as uncompromising in his devotion to the right and the true, as unconcerned for the beauty and the culture and the ease that are not moral. As earnest a lover of culture as Goethe, he yet has none of Goethe's culture for its own sake. As severe a critic as Carlyle, he has none of Carlyle's despair, He has been kind, tender, and sympathetic in his criticisms, though earnest in his condemnation of evil. As a moral teacher, none can refuse to admire him more than Goethe or Carlyle, for the humanness of his manner, method, and aim. By his neighbors, those who have known him longest and most intimately, he is regarded with reverence and devotion. They see in him what constantly reminds them of the saint. He has been called a sage, but he has more than wisdom; he has that loftiness and wholeness of character, that loyalty and self-forgetfulness, that simplicity and wideness of sympathy, and especially that high sense of human faithfulness to the Divine, which characterizes the saintly life.

XV.

LITERARY METHODS.

IT has been Emerson's habit to spend the forenoon in his study, with constant regularity. He has not waited for moods, but caught them as they came, and used their results in each day's work. He has been a diligent though a slow and painstaking worker. It has been his wont to jot down his thoughts at all hours and places. The suggestions which result from his readings, conversations, and meditations are transferred to the note-book he carries with him. In his walks many a gem of thought is thus preserved; and his mind is always alert, quick to see, his powers of observation being perpetually awake. The results of his thinking are thus stored up, to be made use of when required. The story is told, that his wife suddenly wakened in the night, before she knew his habits, and heard him moving about the room. She anxiously inquired if he were ill. "Only an idea," was his reply, and proceeded to jot it down. Curtis humorously says, the villagers "relate that he has a huge manuscript book, in which he incessantly records the ends of thoughts, bits of observation and experience, the facts of all kinds, — a kind of intellectual and scientific scrap-bag, into which all shreds and remnants of conversation and reminiscences of wayside reveries are incontinently thrust."[1]

After his note-books are filled, he transcribes their contents to a larger commonplace book. He then writes at the bottom, or in the margin, the subject of each paragraph. When he desires to write an essay, he turns to his note-books, transcribes all his paragraphs

[1] Homes of American Authors

on that subject, drawing a perpendicular line through whatever he has thus copied. These separate jottings, perhaps written years apart, and in widely different circumstances and moods, are brought together, arranged in such order as is possible, and are welded together by such matter as is suggested at the time. Alcott relates going once to his study, to find him with many sheets of manuscript scattered about on the floor, which he was anxiously endeavoring to arrange in something like a systematic treatment of the subject in hand at the time. The essay thus prepared is read before an audience to test its quality and construction. Its parts are frequently re-arranged. Perhaps in its construction portions of previously used lectures are made to do new service. Should the lecture come at last to be put into one of his books, it is pruned of all but the telling sentences. His lectures which are rapidly composed, for special occasions, have a continuity and flow of thought quite different from the essays in his books. The address on Lincoln, written in one evening, shows this. The published essays are often the results of many lectures, the most pregnant sentences and paragraphs alone being retained. His apples are sorted over and over again, until only the very rarest, the most perfect, are left. It does not matter that those thrown away are very good, and help to make clear the possibilities of the orchard; they are unmercifully cast aside. His essays are, consequently, very slowly elaborated, wrought out through days and months, and even years, of patient thought.

A curious evidence of this method of constructing his essays may be found, by the attentive reader, in the repetition of the same phrases in different essays; showing a lapse of memory sometimes permits him to draw out the same sentences and ideas more than once. Some of his favorite expressions, such as, "Hitch your wagon to a star," are several times repeated. In *Society and Solitude* he twice quotes, in different essays, Wellington's saying, that "uniforms are often masks;" as he does Mrs. Hutchinson's remark, "that the best and highest courages are beams of the Almighty." One of the most striking instances of repetition is to be found in the essays on Farming and Perpetual Forces. The analogies from the convertibility of forces run almost precisely parallel in these essays, showing the same materials were used in their composition. The paragraph on p. 128 of the essay on Farming, beginning, "Who are the farmer's servants?" is almost *verbatim* repeated in the other essay, in the paragraph beginning at the bottom of the first page.[1] In Perpetual Forces, the paragraphs at the bottom of p. 272 and at the top of p. 273 contain the same matter with the paragraph in the essay on Farming beginning at the bottom of p. 129, but arranged in a quite different order. By comparing these with each other, it will be seen how he re-works the materials of his commonplace books. In this way he preserves the best materials of the freshest hours of thought, to be slowly recast and put into form in the quiet of his study. Every mood is thus chronicled, but the results produced from his meditations depend on persistent labor.

"Is it imaginable, Alcott asks, that he conceives his piece as a whole, and then sits down to execute his task at a heat? Is not this imaginable rather, and the key to the construction of his works? Living for composition as few authors can, and holding company, studies, sleep, exercise, affairs, subservient to thoughts, his products are gathered as they ripen, stored in his commonplaces; their contents transcribed at intervals, and classified. It is the order of ideas, of imagination observed in the arrangement, not of logical sequence. You may begin at the last paragraph and read backwards. Each period is self-poised; there may be a chasm of years between the opening passage and the last written, and there is endless time in the composition. These good things have been talked and slept over, meditated standing and sitting, read and polished in the utterance; and so accepted they pass into print."[2]

His essays are all carefully revised again and again, corrected, wrought over, portions dropped, and new matter added. He is unsparing in his corrections, strik-

[1] North American Review, September, 1877, p. 271.
[2] Concord Days, Essay on Emerson.

ing out sentence after sentence; and paragraphs disappear from time to time. His manuscript is everywhere crowded with erasures and corrections; scarcely a page appears that is not covered with these evidences of his diligent revision. An illustration of his corrections may be found in the essay on Plato, in *Representative Men*, which began, when read as a lecture, in this wise: —

> "The work of Plato is that writing, which, in the history of civilization, is entitled to Omar's account of the Koran, when he said, 'Burn the libraries; for, if they contain any thing good, it is contained in this book!' These sentences contain the culture of nations; these are the corner-stone of schools; these are the fountain-head of literatures. Nothing but God can give invention. Every thing else, one would say, the study of Plato would give. A discipline it is in logic, arithmetic, taste, symmetry, poetry, language, rhetoric, ontology, morals, or practical wisdom. There never was such range of speculation. Buonaparte was nicknamed *centmille*. Plato, by his breadth, deserves the name, and much more. Out of him came all things that are still written and debated among men of thought."

Comparing this with the essay as printed, a very clear idea is obtained of his patient habit of close and diligent correction, polishing, making stronger his statements, lopping off all superfluous words and sentences, and refining from all that does not appear to be perfectly relevant and appropriate. The second paragraph of this essay originally stood in his manuscript, in its opening sentences, as follows: —

> "Plato is philosophy, and philosophy Plato. Plato is the glory and the shame of mankind. Vain are the laurels of Rome; vain the pride of England in her Newton, Milton, and Shakspere; whilst neither Saxon nor Roman have availed to add any idea to the catagories of Plato. What a posterity is his! No wife, no children had he; and the thinkers of all civilized nations are his children, and are tinged with his mind."

In the essay on the Uses of Great Men, the paragraph on p. 15 ended with the word "shape," near the bottom of the printed page. A new paragraph began there in the manuscript, which has been omitted. It shows his meaning more clearly than any thing retained, and illustrates his habit of merciless pruning. These sentences, it may be conjectured, were omitted because liable to the charge of extravagance or from fear of their misinterpretation, and because in substance repeated on p. 17. He is speaking of the possibility of interpreting every thing in nature.

> "The possibility of interpretation lies in the identity of the observer with the observed. The genius that has done what the world desired, say, to find his way between ozote and oxygen, to detect the new rock superposition, to find the law of the curves, can do it, because he has just come out of nature, or from being a part of that thing. He knows the way of ozote, because he is ozote. Man is a piece of the universe made alive."

In the essay on Shakspere a portion of the paragraph ending at the top of p. 211 has been omitted. Though a most striking and eloquent passage, it is not difficult to guess why it was dropped. Was it from his desire to keep within the strict limits of truth, and not to appear extravagant in his praise?

> "There is nothing in literature comparable to Shakspere's expression, for strength and for delivery. Men have existed who affirmed that they heard the language of celestial angels talked with them; but that, when they returned into the natural world, though they preserved the memory of these conversations, they found it impossible to transmute the things that had been said into human thoughts and words. But Shakspere is like one who had been rapt into some purer state of sensation and existence, had learned the secret of a finer diction, and, when he returned to this world, retained the fine organ which had been opened above."

His printed essays show many changes after their first delivery as lectures. The essay on Courage, in *Society and Solitude*, contains some matter on the same subject, used in a lecture delivered in Tremont Temple, Boston, in November, 1859. Yet the whole structure of it has been changed; and all the local matter, applicable to the stormy time of John Brown's imprisonment and death, is omitted. The essay on Farming, in the same volume, was given as an address before the Middlesex County Fair, at Concord, in 1858. The opening and closing portions of the address are omitted, and about two pages of new matter added at the end of the essay.

The changes indicated by these examples remind us that almost every thing Emerson has written was prepared for the lecture-platform. Even *English Traits*, apparently an exception, is not entirely so; for he gave several lectures on that subject before his book was published. He has always been mindful of his audience, though no man could accept its dictation less. He has not usually taken the best methods to bring a popular audience to his ways of thinking, but he has never forgotten the faces before him. Some hint of the lecture is in all his essays, though the numberless corrections remove many more traces of it. The literary form he has adopted has been determined by the fact of his being for a half-century a great peripatetic preacher, who has treasured every means his genius could use for the moral instruction and reformation of his countrymen. He has not been primarily a bookmaker, as Carlyle has been, but an unsettled preacher, or a university lecturer on morals without occupying a professor's chair. The books have been an afterthought, lectures printed after the exigencies of the platform demanded new topics.

This method of composition has led to a wonderful power of condensation, and to a marvelous compactness of expression. His concentrated sentences are doubtless wrought out, one by one, in his lonely walks, or in the quiet of his study, and worked over in his mind until the words perfectly fit the thought. His words are thus packed and crammed with thought. Such a method has filled his pages with quotable sentences and proverbial expressions, that jam all we know about a subject into a dozen words. In no other writer are there so many sentences which complete the subject, and which will stand, unsupported and alone, as vindications of the author's thought. An essay packed full of such sentences is hard reading; for each reader must join sentence to sentence, and supply the connections himself. His essays are remarkable for their quick, sharp, intense sentences, found everywhere through his writings. There is an abruptness about his method, that partly comes of his habits of composition, and partly from his manner of exhausting an idea in a few intensely condensed expressions, and then passing immediately to the next subject which occurs. From the center of one idea he passes, without pause, to the very core of the next; and no attempt is made to show their relations. This is a marked characteristic of his writings. John Burroughs says,[1] he "is an essence, a condensation; more so, perhaps, than any other man who has appeared in literature. Nowhere else is there such a preponderance of pure statement, of the very attar of thought over the bulkier, circumstantial, qualifying, or secondary elements." In this way the water is all boiled out, and the condensed meat alone left behind. While few intellectual stomachs can digest such food without dilution, the condensation insures long preservation, and use on all times and occasions, even when bulkier food is not desirable. As a result, "a pinch of him is equivalent to a page or two of Johnson; and he is pitched many degrees higher as an essayist than even Bacon." His books have a wonderful amount of the testing power of all such writings, capacity to stimulate thought, to quicken motives, and to rouse fresh purposes. Every page, each paragraph, suggests so many trains of wholesome and ennobling thought, that it is almost impossible to sit down and read one of his essays through without pause. To obtain the full strength of these writings, they should lie close at hand day and night, to be caught up at every interval, and a few lines carefully conned, to serve as the seed-corn of the day's impulses and of the night's meditations. It does not matter which book one opens, or to which page; all is good, every one has an answering word of life fit to solve one's destiny. Many moods of the human mind find an answering response, while fact and experience may be found set down here in their proper place in relation to the health and sanity of life. Con-

[1] Birds and Poets, p. 186.

cerning this universality of wisdom in these pages. Burroughs thus discourses: —

"I know of no other writing that yields the reader so many strongly stamped medallion-like sayings and distinctions. There is a perpetual refining and recoining of the current wisdom of life and conversation. It is the old gold or silver or copper, but how bright and new it looks in his pages. Emerson loves facts, things, objects, as the workman his tools. He makes every thing serve. The stress of expression is so great that he bends the most obdurate element to his purpose; as the bird, under her keen necessity, weaves the most contrary and diverse materials into her nest. He has a wonderful hardiness and push. Where else in literature is there a mind, moving in so rare a medium, that gives one such a sense of tangible resistance and force? He is a man who occupies every inch of his rightful territory; he is there in proper person to the farthest bound."

His pages are full of apothegms, ready to be quoted on all occasions; and few writers have so many that are so good. Rich and suggestive antitheses appear everywhere, resulting from his faith in nature as the outward expression of spirit. For the same reason the metaphor and simile everywhere abound. These figures of speech are usually true to nature, the result of his close study of her every mood and expression. His style is intensely individual, because it is not imitative, but caught from his own meditations and observations. He deals with the real world without and within, directly, face to face; not primarily with the world pictured in literature. He writes down his own thoughts; and he illustrates his ideas from the pines, meadows, violets, and robins about his own house. He is always original, and many times, as E. P. Whipple has suggested,[1] even more, — "aboriginal," going back to the very first conditions of essential nature. There is "a flavor of the wild strawberry, a fragrance of the wild rose," in his pages, a true picturing of the nature of things. The conventionalities have departed from this spot of earth; and here is a soul that dauntlessly judges of what is, never for one moment hesitating to report what he finds to exist. He has a keen and ready wit, that is never

[1] Notice of his Complete Works, in The Independent.

used for its own sake, but only to flash a clearer light upon some truth he would illustrate. He delights in surprises, in sharp-drawn analogies, and in quick successions of opposite statements. By these methods he pours a flood of light upon many subjects, and perpetually arouses and quickens the mind of his reader. Whoever would read his essays understandingly must be completely awake in all his faculties. Emerson's imagination is brilliant and far-traveled. It illustrates, but seldom confounds or puzzles. He gathers truth by the intuitive method, by absorption, and by the keenness of his insight into every moral and spiritual problem.

His essays are in many ways open to criticism, and some of the critics have made free with them. His illustrations are returned to again and again, as that from the convertibility of forces. Certain types of character and thought he constantly praises, and forces upon the reader's attention. His lack of system, his disregard of the logical order of thought, do not need to be pointed out. His apparent love of contradictions and surprises has puzzled some of the critics, and they have written as if he ought to be a Macaulay or an Irving. He frequently coins new forms of words, or uses words with new meanings. He violates rhetoric, and grammar as well, in some of his sentences, and loves extravagant metaphors, as well as extravagant statements of facts. Concerning such defects as these much could be said, — for much has been said, — as well as on many other topics of interest to those whose business it is to point out an author's faults. The genuine reader of Emerson will not long find any of these defects standing in his way, or allow them to hinder his admiration. What can be said on the subject of these literary defects has been strongly presented by an English writer.[1]

"As regards form, this critic says Emerson is the most unsystematic of writers. The concentration of his style resembles that of a classic, but he everywhere sacrifices unity to richness of detail. . . . He delights in proverbs and quotations, which are in general marvelously apt; but his accuracy is often at fault, and in his

[1] Professor Nichols, in the North British Review for 1867.

tendency to exaggeration he is an American of the Americans. He loves a contradiction for its own sake, and always prefers a surprise to an argument. His epigrams are a series of electric shocks; and though no one is more prevailingly sincere, it is sometimes hard to say whether or not he is wholly in earnest; for a vein of soft irony, his only manifestation of humor, seems to underlie many of his most *prononcé* passages."

"Emerson's most elaborate criticisms are mainly composed of the same mosaic work, and, in the long-run, we get tired of these perpetual jerks. His style, all armed with points and antitheses, lacks that repose which even our modern impatience of rotundity still desiderates. His allusions are sometimes far fetched, and his general naturalness does not save him from occasional affectations and displays of pedantry. In coining words, as, 'Adamhood,' 'fore-looking,' 'spicier,' 'specular,' 'plumule,' 'uncontinented,' 'metope,' 'intimater,' 'antipode,' 'partialist,' he is far from felicitous. Minute critics will find that this disdain of rule extends to a contempt of some of the rules of grammar, as in his employment of such a form as 'shined,' and his continual use of 'shall' for 'will.' More serious defects are his misapplication of terms, as when he speaks of 'the strong *self-complacent* Luther, and the want of taste, dignity, or moderation in such expressions as the following: 'Truth is such a fly-away, such an untransportable and *unbarrelable* a commodity, that it is as *bad* to *catch* as light.' 'The beauty that shimmers in the yellow afternoon of October, who could ever *clutch* it?' 'It seems as if Deity dressed each soul, which he sent into nature, in certain virtues and powers not communicable, and wrote *not transferable*, and *good for this trip only*, on these garments of the soul.' All those are more or less objectionable as violences done to good sense or decorum. They are emphatically 'smart,' and unworthy of the author who is the keenest to perceive and the foremost to censure the flippancy of his countrymen."

Parker complained that there is a want of organic completeness and orderly distribution in Emerson's essays; but, if he had possessed this capacity, much of the present charm and abandon of his composition would be gone. The logical order is certainly wanting; but Parker thought the subtle psychological method, by which the wholeness and the relations of truth are discerned, was also wanting. On the other hand, Alcott has said, in his conversations about Emerson, that there is a very fine subtle thread running through each of his essays, and they are not accidentally put together. This may be said in favor of his method, that it is his own, adapted to his genius; and that his most powerful and convincing essays are those with the least apparent method. The essays on Courage and Inspiration are orderly enough; but they lack the subtle, majestic power of those on Worship and Sovereignty of Ethics, which may be complained of as utterly lacking in logical arrangement. "His style is one of the rarest beauty," as Parker recognized; because it is perfectly adapted to his mental processes, and to the ends he has sought to accomplish. It is simple, without imitation, unique and robust. It is manly, pure, direct, and thoroughly natural. There is no mistiness about his writings, very seldom more than an apparent obscurity; for he has a remarkable power of saying precisely the thing he means. One of his severest critics can not help recognizing that "he is original, natural, attractive, and direct, limpid in phrase, and pure in fancy."[1] He is even more remarkable for the intense moral power with which his essays are surcharged; for the clear, deep intuitions of interior truths they contain; and for their bold, master's grasp of the fact, that beauty, truth, and goodness are glimpses only of the same shining reality. Each of his books, as Alcott suggests, is filled with vigorous thoughts and a sprightly wit. "They abound in strong sense, happy humor, keen criticisms, subtile insights, noble morals, clothed in a chaste and manly diction, fresh with the breath of health and progress."

[1] Ibid

XVI.

LITERARY JUDGMENTS.

WHILE Emerson has been a zealous believer in the inward method of knowing, he has also been a great lover of books. If he has prized intuition as man's highest possession, he has prized literature as its chief means of expression. Books, he tells us, "proceed out of the silent living mind to be heard again by the living mind." His recognition of both these means of receiving and communicating truth has been expressed in these words: —

> "Always the oracular soul is the source of thought, but always the occasion is administered by the low mediation of circumstances. Nature mixes facts with thoughts, to yield a poem. In the spirit in which they are written is the date of their duration, and never in the magnitude of the facts. Every thing lasts in proportion to its beauty. In proportion as it was not polluted by any willfulness of the writer, but flowed from his mind after the divine order of cause and effect, it was not his, but Nature's, and shared the sublimity of sea and sky."[1]

He maintains that knowledge originates with "the oracular soul;" it is an intuition; and all writing is by the grace of God. The knowing soul is the one which sees into the spiritual nature of things, the one that is in harmony with the universe. To such a soul light is given by virtue of this harmony. Hence all true writing is a revelation, a direct gift from God to the intuitive soul. The greatest of all writings are therefore those which express the highest intuitions, which contain direct perceptions of spiritual realities, and reveal the immediate laws of the moral nature. As the intuitive nature relies much on the imagination, Emerson

[1] The Dial, October, 1840; Thoughts on Modern Literature.

values highly all purely imaginative works. Next to direct intuition he values that power of the imagination which flashes light upon so many realities, giving to the poet his penetrating insight into the world without and within. In his own writings he has made a large and a noble use of this gift, especially in his poems. They are constantly beautified and made stronger by his wise and healthful use of the imagination. His pictures of Nature are penetrated with the effects of this power. He sees face to face; but, more than that, he reads the inmost meaning of nature with this richly endowed imagination of his. And next he prizes any book of facts which gives just expression to the realities of nature. He wishes Nature to speak, he believes in facts, and prizes all books which tell us what any genuine observer has seen. "The highest class of books, he says, are those which express the moral element; the next, works of the imagination; and the next, works of science, — all deal in realities, — what ought to be, what is, and what appears." And he finds that all books are ultimately measured by their depth of thought. So he sees in literature one of the best illustrations of the laws by which the world is governed, in that there is no luck in its final judgments, which proceed as if fated to measure out due rewards to those who write. He distrusts all repetition of other men's judgments and all theorizing, but would have us prize the truth which blooms afresh in each individual mind. If all minds were purely and truly intuitional, reading nature and life with open eyes, there would be no need of books; for each soul would then know all things; but as only a few persons are thus intuitional, books have a value of the greatest importance. They store up the intuitions of the past, bringing down to us only the words of the most rarely gifted minds; and by their aid our own minds are awakened to a knowing of the truth for ourselves. In the following paragraphs he brings out the comparative value of intuition and books, in accordance with his theory of knowledge: —

"All just criticism will not only behold in literature the action of necessary laws, but must also oversee literature itself. The erect mind disparages all books. What are books? it saith; they can have no permanent value. How obviously initial they are to their authors. The books of the nations, the universal books, are long ago forgotten by those who wrote them; and one day we shall forget this primer learning. Literature is made up of a few ideas and a few fables. It is a heap of nouns and verbs enclosing an intuition or two. We must learn to judge books by absolute standards.

"When we are aroused to a life in ourselves, these traditional splendors of letters grow very pale and cold. Men seem to forget that all literature is ephemeral, and unwillingly entertain the supposition of its utter disappearance. They deem not only letters in general, but the best books in particular, parts of a pre-established harmony, fatal, unalterable, and do not go behind Virgil and Dante, much less behind Moses, Ezekiel, and St. John. But no man can be a good critic of any book, who does not read in it a wisdom which transcends the wisdom of any book, and treats the whole extant product of the human intellect as only one age revisable and reversible by him.

"In our fidelity to the higher truth, we need not disown our debt in our actual state of culture, in the twilights of experience, to these rude helpers. They keep alive the memory and the hope of a better day. When we flout all particular books as initial merely, we truly express the privilege of spiritual nature; but alas! not the fact and fortune of this low Massachusetts and Boston, of these humble Junes and Decembers of mortal life. Our souls are not self-fed, but do eat and drink of chemical water and wheat. Let us not forget the genial miraculous force we have known to proceed from a book. We go musing into the vault of day and night; no constellation shines, no muse descends, the stars are white points, the roses brick-colored dust, the frogs pipe, mice peep, and wagons creak along the road. We return to the house and take up Plutarch or Augustine, and read a few sentences or pages, and lo! the air swims with life; the front of heaven is full of fiery shapes; secrets of magnanimity and grandeur invite us on every hand; life is made up of them. Such is our debt to a book. Observe, moreover, that we ought to credit literature with much more than the bare word it gives us." [1]

In another essay,[2] in accordance with this last thought, he says the great man must be a great reader, and possess great assimilating power. He must depend upon others, because intuition is not constant; while we must try our own intuitions by those of other minds

[1] The Dial, October, 1840; Thoughts on Modern Literature.
[2] Quotation and Originality, in Letters and Social Aims.

In his address to the students of Howard University, he expressed even more emphatically his appreciation of the value of books.

"Whenever I have to do with young men and women, he said, I always wish to know what their books are; I wish to defend them from bad; I wish to introduce them to good; I wish to speak of the immense benefit which a good mind derives from reading, probably much more to a good mind from reading than from conversation. It is of first importance, of course, to select a friend; for a young man should find a friend a little older than himself, or whose mind is a little older than his own, in order to wake up his genius. That service is performed oftener for us by books. I think, if a very active mind, if a young man of ability, should give you his honest experience, you would find that he owed more impulse to books than to living minds. The great masters of thought, the Platos, — not only those that we call sacred writers, but those that we call profane, — have acted on the mind with more energy than any companions. I think that every remarkable person whom you meet will testify to something like that, that the fast-opening mind has found more inspiration in his book than in his friend. We take the book under great advantages. We read it when we are alone. We read it with an attention not distracted. And, perhaps, we find there our own thought, a little better, a little maturer, than it is in ourselves."

Great as is his praise of books, he says "the divine never quotes, but is, and creates." Genius he regards, after all acknowledgments of the value of books, as surer of its own faintest presentiments than of all history. His theory of knowing, as well as his standard of judgment in literature, is in these words defining originality: "It is being, being one's self, and reporting accurately what we see and are." When we are true to ourselves, in being true to Nature and the Over-soul, our thought becomes an accurate reporter and measurer of all things; and this direct perception of truth is an intuition, a gift of the grace of God. Those who have had this intuitive power most truly have written the great moral, religious, and personal books of the world, which Emerson prizes above all others. He specially values the bibles of the race, the writers of the great religious books, and such authors as Epictetus, Saadi, Thomas à Kempis, Pascal, and Boehme. These books, he says, are to be read on the bended knee; and they are life to all who diligently peruse them. They come home to our hearts, because they contain the secrets which all nature, experience, and intuition teach us. "I read them," he says, "on lichens and bark; I watch them on waves on the beach; they fly in birds, they creep in worms; I detect them in laughter and eye-sparkles of men and women. These are scriptures which the missionary might well carry over prairie, desert, and ocean, to Siberia, Japan, and Timbuctoo. Yet he will find that the spirit which is in them journeys faster than he, and greets him on his arrival, — was there already long before him. The missionary must be carried by it, and find it there, or he goes in vain."

This sense of spiritual reality, the feeling of the infinite, which is the source of all religions and literatures, he finds to be a marked peculiarity of modern literature, and increasingly so. It is shown in one of its characteristic traits, in the modern tendency to accept all books of all ages and times, thus recognizing the universal workings of the Over-soul The curious study into every phase of human history is an outcome of it, and it leads to a bold and systematic criticism of the past. Along with this tendency, which is largely skeptical, goes a subjectiveness which restores the organic unity of the universe to the conceptions of men. It "leads us to nature, and to the invisible awful facts, to moral abstractions, which are not less nature than is a river or a coal-mine; nay, they are far more nature, but its essence and soul." This feeling of the Infinite grows deeper and stronger, pervades all literature, gives form to moral purposes, makes men bold to fight old evils. It is producing a great literature of its own. Concerning this tendency, Emerson wrote these words in *The Dial:* —

"Of the perception, now fast becoming a conscious fact, — that there is One Mind, and that all powers and privileges which lie in any, lie in all; that I, as a man, may claim and appropriate whatever of true and fair or good or strong has anywhere been exhibited; that Moses, Confucius, Montaigne, and Leibnitz are not so much individuals as they are parts of man and parts of me, and my intelligence proves them my own, — literature is far the best expression. All over the modern world the educated and susceptible have betrayed their discontent with the limits of municipal life, and with the poverty of our dogmas of religion and philosophy. They betray this impatience by fleeing for resource to a conversation with nature. A wild striving to express a more inward and infinite sense characterizes the works of every art. The music of Beethoven is said by those who understand it, to labor with vaster conceptions and aspirations than music has attempted before. This feeling of the Infinite has deeply colored the poetry of the period. This new love of the vast, always native in Germany, was imported into France by De Staël, appeared in England in Coleridge, Wordsworth, Byron, Shelley, Felicia Hemans, and finds a most congenial climate in the American mind."

This sense of the real and spiritual, of the Infinite and Eternal, will continue to increase. As it does so, genius "will write in a higher spirit, and a wider knowledge, and with a greater practical aim, than ever yet guided the pen of poet. It will write the annals of a changed world, describe the new heroic life of man, and bind all into a joyful reverence for the circumambient whole." By this power of spiritual truth are all books to be judged. All that have it Emerson loves, all that do not have it he finds to be worthless. This power he regards as a pioneer, a discoverer; and it continually overturns past judgments. He early complained that we take it for granted a great deal is known and for ever settled, and to be read out of books.[1] "But in truth all is now to be begun; and every new mind ought to take the attitude of Columbus, launch out from the gaping loiterers on the shore, and sail west for a new world." A larger share of the books written are worthless; "a few thoughts are all we glean from the best inspection of the paper pile, all the rest is combination and confectionery." He thinks the stock-writers outnumber the thinking men; the larger share of our authors are merely men of talent, who have some feat to perform with words. "Talent amuses; wisdom instructs. Talent shows what another

[1] The Senses and the Soul, in The Dial for January, 1842.

man can do; genius acquaints me with the spacious circuits of the common nature. The one is carpentry; the other is growth." Our senses are yet too strong for us, usurp our attention from the ideal world; so that we lead lives of routine, instead of those of constant moral inspiration. In books Emerson finds the record of the great inspirations of the past, but they are to be used only as aids to new ones of our own. The moment any book, even the greatest, takes the place to us of insight and inward seeing of the truth, that moment it becomes an injury. Rightly used, books serve us a great purpose as educators, guides, and inspirers. They show us the way other men have gone, help us towards the truth we ourselves wish to reach; but they are the helps, not the source or the end, of culture. Books can not take the place of the soul, and when we have nothing more we are but poorly furnished. To sit in silence with God, in the temple of a free mind, or to wander with him along any of the ways of Nature, is worth all the books in the world. Whatever the world of books may contain, we are to set sail, with our own thoughts, for that land of divine truth which ever awaits those who have the seeing eye and the hearing ear.

Emerson seems not to have been affected very largely by any one writer in the formation of his literary style. The names of Carlyle, Goethe, Coleridge, and Landor have been mentioned as among his masters; but the marks of the literary influence of either in his books are but slight. To all of them he may be indebted, but only to a very limited extent has he been affected by either. He has not been an imitator; has said what he had to say in the manner best suiting his own purpose in saying it. He has fully accepted the theory of Carlyle and Fichte, that the writer is the true interpreter of the divine idea of the world. With the spirit and purpose of those who represent this thought, he has been largely in sympathy; but he has carried out this idea in his own manner.

It has been suggested that he was influenced by Landor in his literary style. He was early an ardent reader and a hearty admirer of Landor; and, as he has himself described that writer, there may be seen to be some superficial resemblances. In 1841[1] he said of Landor, "We do not recollect an example of more complete independence in literary history. He has no clanship, no friendships, that warp him." He then pronounced the *Imaginary Conversations* original in form and matter, and said that Landor's books are full of free and sustained thought, keen and precise understanding, industrious observation in every department of life, an experience to which nothing has occurred in vain, and honor for every just and generous sentiment. "His acquaintance with the English tongue is unsurpassed." He is pronounced a master of condensation and suppression. Almost alone among the authors of that time did Emerson find in Landor a perception of the moral power of character. "Whosoever writes, he said, for the love of truth and beauty, and not with ulterior ends, belongs to the sacred class of inspirers; and among these, few of the present age have a better claim to be numbered than Landor." Yet he found some things in Landor he could not approve, much less imitate. He describes him as "a sharp dogmatic man with a great deal of knowledge, a great deal of worth, and a great deal of pride, with a profound contempt for all that he does not understand, a master of all elegant learning, and capable of the utmost delicacy of sentiment, and yet prone to indulge in a sort of coarse imagery and language." He speaks of Landor as having a coarsely defiant nature, as one who, "before a well-dressed company, plunges his fingers in a cesspool, as if to expose the whiteness of his hands and the jewels of his rings." Before his first journey to Europe, Emerson had read the *Imaginary Conversations* with diligence and profit,

[1] In the Dial for October.

his copy showing evidence of constant perusal; yet he said in *The Dial* that Landor had written no good book. In his life of Landor, Forster says, —

"When the American writer Emerson had made the book his companion for more than twenty years, he publicly expressed to the writer his gratitude for having given him a resource that had never failed him in solitude. He had but to recur to its rich and ample page, whereon he was always sure to find free and sustained thought, a keen and precise understanding, an afluent and ready memory familiar with all chosen books, an industrious observation in every department of life, an experience to which it might seem that nothing had occurred in vain, honor for every just and generous sentiment, and a scourge like that of Furies for every oppressor, whether public or private, to feel how dignified was that perpetual censor in his curule chair, and to wish to thank so great a benefactor."[1]

Goethe was a great favorite with the members of the Transcendental Club, and Emerson shared in that admiration. In a conversation, in more recent years, he pronounced Goethe the leading mind of the present century. When Grimm writes of Goethe, he acknowledges his debt to Emerson for the point of view from whence to correctly judge him.[2] A writer[3] of some discrimination has said that the mantle of Goethe has fallen on Emerson. Without doubt Emerson has been affected by the commanding genius and personality of Goethe; but the great German was too realistic, too little a Puritan, to fully receive Emerson's sympathy. His criticisms show the wide space between them. He accuses[4] Goethe of differing from all great minds in "the total want of frankness." "No man was permitted to call Goethe brother. He hid himself, and worked always to astonish; which is an egotism, and therefore little." He characterizes Goethe "as the poet of the actual, not of the ideal; the poet of limitation, not of possibility; of this world, and not of religion and hope; in short, the poet of prose, and not of poetry." He says Goethe's moral perception was not proportionate to his other powers, and so he left the world as he

[1] Walter Savage Landor: a biography, by John Forster, p. 363.
[2] Life and Times of Goethe, preface to American translation.
[3] The Rev. Dr Osgood.
[4] In the Dial.

found it. The German was so great he can not forgive him for not being greater, and thus becoming the one sublime revealer of divine wisdom, redeeming us from idolatries and their legendary luster. Charmed as he is by Goethe's genius, he yet constantly bemoans that incapacity which kept him from the central facts, and from becoming the great poet of the ideal. He can not endure Goethe's realistic mode of thought, and this is the source of all his criticisms. So he says, —

> "If we try Goethe by the ordinary canons of criticism, we should say that his thinking is of great altitude, and all level, — not a succession of summits, but a high Asiatic table-land. He has an eye constant to the fact of life, and that never pauses in its advance. But the great felicities, the miracles of poetry, he has never. It is all design with him, just thought and instructed expression, analogies, allusion, illustration, which knowledge and correct thinking supply; but of Shakspere and the transcendent muse, no syllable. He is the king of all scholars; let him have the praise of the love of truth. We think, when we contemplate the stupendous glory of the world, that it were life enough for one man merely to lift his hands and cry with St. Augustine, 'Wrangle who pleases, I will wonder.' Well, this he did. Here was a man, who, in the feeling that the thing itself was so admirable as to leave all comment behind, went up and down from object to object, lifting the veil from every one, and did no more. His are the bright and terrible eyes, which meet the modern student in every sacred chapel of thought, in every public enclosure."

Emerson does not think it a mere accident, a case of color-blindness, that Goethe had not a moral perception proportionate to his other powers. It was "a cardinal fact of health or disease; since, lacking this, he failed in the high sense to be a creator, and with divine endowments drops by irreversible decree into the common history of genius. He was content to fall into the track of vulgar poets, and spend on common aims his splendid endowments, and has declined the office proffered to now and then a man in many centuries in the power of his genius, — of a redeemer of the human mind. He has written better than other poets, only as his talent was subtler; but the ambition of creation he refused. Life for him is prettier, easier, wiser, decenter, has a gem or two more on its robe; but its old eternal burden is not relieved; no drop of healthier blood flows yet in its veins. Let him pass. Humanity must wait for its physician still at the side of the road, and confess, as this man goes out, that they have served it better, who assured it, out of the innocent hope in their hearts, that a physician will come, than this majestic artist, with all the treasuries of wit, of science, and of power to command."

In his extemporaneous address to the students of Howard University, he said of Goethe: —

"Since Shakspere, there has been no mind of equal compass to his. There is the wise man. He has the largest range of thought, the most catholic mind; a person who has spoken in every science, and has added to the scientific lore of other students, and who represents better than any other individual the progressive mind of the present age. He is the oracle of all the leading students in every nation at this time." He said *Faust* is the book by which Goethe is best known. "It is one of the most disagreeable books that I can read. While I consider Shakspere's *Hamlet* a great and noble work, Goethe's *Faust* is to me a very painful work. And yet that stands with society generally as his leading work. It represents the modern mind, and that is what he aimed at; but it does not represent the Eternal Mind." The maxims and rules of life written for Schiller's *Horen* "are now gathered into a book that I think is one of the most important we possess."

An intimate friendship and sympathy with Carlyle has probably drawn him closer to that writer than to any other. Here, as before, however, the charge of imitation is utterly unmeaning and beside the mark. Such a charge might have had a general meaning in the early days of Emerson's career; but he has proven himself too much a master, too much inclined to do his own thinking, to redeem such a statement now from being entirely valueless. He has found the chief characteristic of Carlyle in his broad humanity and in the altitude of his thought.

"He has the dignity of a man of letters who knows what belongs to him, and never deviates from his sphere; a continuer of the great line of scholars, and sustains their office in the highest credit and honor. If the good Heaven have any word to impart to this unworthy generation, here is one scribe qualified and clothed for its occasion. One excellence he has in an age of mammon and criticism, that he never suffers the eye of his wonder to close. Let who will be the dupe of trifles; he can not keep his eyes off from the gracious Infinite which embosoms us. As a literary artist he has great merits, beginning with the main one, that he never wrote a dull line." [1]

Emerson has also been an ardent admirer of Wordsworth, early read his poems with the keenest interest, imbibed his ideas of nature and the soul, and has drunk deep at the fountain of his thought. As in the case of Carlyle, he has accepted Wordsworth's philosophy, and made many of its ideas vital elements in his own. In the pages of *The Dial* he says of Wordsworth, "More than any poet his success has been not his own, but that of the idea he shared with his coevals, and which he has rarely succeeded in expressing. *The Excursion* awakened in every lover of nature the right feeling. We saw stars shine, we felt the awe of mountains, we heard the rustle of the wind in the grass, and knew again the ineffable secret of solitude. It was a great joy. It was nearer to nature than any thing we had before." Yet it was not a great poem; and, excepting a few strains, it was dull. "It was the human soul in these last ages striving for a just publication of itself. Add to this, however, the great praise of Wordsworth, that more than any other contemporary bard he is pervaded with a reverence of somewhat higher than conscious thought. There is in him that property common to all great poets, a wisdom of humanity, which is superior to any talents they exert." Again, he says Wordsworth "has the merit of just moral perception, but not that of deft poetic execution." [2] Milton would "curl his lip at such slipshod newspaper style," and many of his poems might all be improvised.

"Yet Wordsworth, though satisfied if he can suggest to a sympathetic mind his own mood, and though setting a private and exaggerated value on his compositions, though confounding his

[1] The Dial.
[2] Europe and European Books, in The Dial for April, 1843.

accidental with the universal consciousness, and taking the public to task for not admiring his poetry, — is really a master of the English language; and his poems evince a power of diction that is no more rivaled by his contemporaries, than is his poetic insight. But the capital merit of Wordsworth is, that he has done more for the sanity of this generation than any other writer. Early in life, at a crisis in his private affairs, he made his election between wealth and a position in the world, and the inward promptings of his heavenly genius; he took his part; he accepted the call to be a poet, and sat down, far from cities, with coarse clothing and plain fare, to obey the heavenly vision. The choice he had made in his will, manifested itself in every line to be real."

To Landor Emerson is slightly indebted for his style, sharp, compacted, energetic, — for so much of it as is not fully and characteristically his own. Yet he has none of Landor's coarseness, none of his drowsiness, and none of his dullness of tone. Carlyle has an impetus and an incessant storm of power, sweeping, imperious, awful, that Emerson has not. The style of Carlyle is that of a great body of cavalry rushing impetuous across an open field to crush down an enemy, or that of an incessant roar of reverberating thunder across the heavens. On the other hand, Emerson's may be compared to quick flash after flash of lightning, to constant sharp electric discharges. Carlyle may be regarded as somewhat his inspirer in the field of ethics, in hatred of every modern sin, in the application of the ethical test to every fact of life and nature, and of his faith in the infinite. To Goethe he owes a debt for his appreciation of æsthetic power, and for his ingrafting the sense of beauty on the Puritan austerity. Appreciation of poetic form he may be also in debt for to the German, as well as for his eager sympathy with nature, and his quick, susceptible sympathy with all the forms of human existence. In thus being tutored of literary masters, in many ways greatly unlike each other, he has gathered a wider range of power than he would otherwise have possessed, and he has chosen from each what was most excellent. He has not the poetic power of Goethe, or Carlyle's stormy inspiration; but there is a poise and a mental balance about his writings not to be found in either of the others. Their excesses he lacks, is more of a Puritan, more of a prophet. He has not Goethe's excessive appreciation of life and beauty, and sensitiveness to their presence; but he has a moral power, a self-mastery, a sublime ethical expression, Goethe could not possibly have attained. He has not Carlyle's inspiring power; he does not sweep up the heart of the reader into invisible realms of truth, so that he forgets earth and time; but he walks the solid earth, mindful ever of its commonest duties; yet with his head in the high heavens, communing with celestial wonders. He surpasses all the others in his power to read the common daily life of men, and the facts of this material world, in the language of the celestial regions, finding but one fact and one law through all worlds. So fine a judge of literary qualities as Lowell[1] finds that Emerson has improved on his masters.

"Both Carlyle and Emerson were disciples of Goethe, but Emerson in a far truer sense; and while the one, from his bias towards the eccentric, has degenerated more and more into mannerism, the other has clarified steadily towards perfection of style, exquisite fineness of material, unobtrusive lowness of tone and simplicity of fashion, the most high-bred garb of expression. Whatever may be said of his thought, nothing can be finer than the delicious limpidness of his phrase. If it was ever questionable whether democracy could develop a gentleman, the problem has been affirmatively solved at last. Carlyle, in his cynicism and admiration of force in and for itself, has become at last positively inhuman; Emerson, reverencing strength, seeking the highest outcome of the individual, has found that society and politics are also main elements in the attainment of the desired end, and has drawn steadily manward and worldward."

In Goethe the sense of beauty was supreme, in Carlyle the love of strength has been predominant; but in Emerson all powers and faculties have been held in reverence only as aids to character. His writings have been conceived and executed, only as helps to human life and aids to moral excellence. In this light every page of his must be regarded. He looks on

[1] Essay on Thoreau, in My Study Windows.

events, he reads nature, he judges books, as helps to human development. To him a book is great and precious, only in proportion to its ethical, inspiring, and human power, its capacity to touch and mold man to finer issues of conduct and feeling.

Emerson judges of books by the measure of their spiritual qualities. He does not possess a critical or a purely literary judgment, and this standard he does not apply to the authors he admires. He loves a book because of its affinity to his own mind; for its imaginative, intuitional, and transcendental qualities. He often judges of books very much as we would expect Bunyan, Fox, or Woolman to judge of them, by certain religious affinities to his own mind. Yet he has been almost always correct in his judgments, finding the best books in all literatures, and admiring them for their most genuine qualities. He has had a better, a more correct, taste for books of the past, however, than for those of his own day. While seldom erring about an old book, his generous appreciation, his earnest sympathy, has led him sometimes to find in contemporary books merits they do not really contain. This is shown in his extravagant praise, in *English Traits*, of that very dull writer Wilkinson, in whose mind, he says, is "a long Atlantic roll not known except in deepest waters." This praise grew entirely out of his sympathy with the ideas Wilkinson attempted to present. When Landor praised that friend he loved so well, Emerson was "pestered" by it, and exclaimed, "But who is Southey?"[1] He has called Herbert Spencer a stock-writer, does not like

[1] The professional critics, however, are not always an improvement on Emerson; as witness this from Swinburne's Study of Shakspere, p. 159: "'A democracy such as yours in America is my abhorrence,' wrote Landor once to an impudent and foul-mouthed Yankee philosophaster who had intruded himself on that great man's privacy in order to have the privilege of informing the readers of a pitiful pamphlet on England that Landor had 'pestered him with Southey;' an impertinence, I may add, which Mr. Landor at once rebuked with the sharpest contempt, and chastised with the haughtiest courtesy."

Charles Kingsley, but has a great admiration for Reade's *Christie Johnstone.* He highly appreciates the writings of Ruskin, regards Lowell's *Biglow Papers* as his best work, and calls Bacon's *Essays* "a little bible of earthly wisdom." These opinions are quite sufficient to show that Emerson does not value a book for its literary merits, but for its attitude toward nature, or for its religious and philosophical conceptions. He tests books by his poetical and moral sensibility, rather than by the ordinary canons of criticism. He loves the idealists, and will not think the best of any others. Indeed, an admixture of mysticism suits him well; while the author who can read every material fact as a law of the spiritual world is sure of his praise. Yet he is not merely a mystic himself, — far from it, — for he thinks "the restraining grace of common sense is the mark of all valid minds.'[1] He finds in the imagination a real guide to the secrets of life, and he prizes no writer from whom this gift is absent; but he would have sense and reason accompany even the imagination.

His literary judgments are full of interest as interpreting his own mind and character, as showing his steady faith in the ideal element in literature. He is quick to detect the least swerving from the spiritual basis of thought, and without a moment's hesitation rejects the least utilitarianism of purpose. The fame of Wordsworth he regards as a leading fact in modern literature. He sees in Byron a perverted will; while he thinks Shelley is never a poet, lacking in the original fire of the bard.

He early discerned the genius of Tennyson, and in 1843 wrote of "the elegance, the wit, and subtlety of this writer, his fancy, his power of language, his metrical skill, his independence on any living masters, his peculiar topics, his taste for the costly and gorgeous."[2] He "wants rude truth, however; he is too fine;" but "it is long since we have had as good a lyrist; it will be long before we have his superior." Speaking of the

[1] Letters and Social Aims. [2] The Dial for April.

delicacies and splendors of Tennyson's style, he says, "The best songs in English poetry are by that heavy, hard, pedantic poet, Ben Jonson. Jonson is rude, and only on rare occasions gay. Tennyson is always fine, but Jonson's beauty is more grateful than Tennyson's. It is the natural, manly grace of a robust workman."

He says that Scott, more than any other modern writer, "has inspired his readers with affection to his own personality;"[1] that, in the number and variety of his characters, he approaches Shakspere. All his characters are portrayed with equal skill; and there is remarkable strength and success in every figure of his crowded company.

Outside of the world's religious teachers he places Shakspere as the one unparalleled mind, and says that of works depending purely upon their intrinsic excellence, his are first.[2]

> "No nation has produced any thing like his equal. There is no quality in the human mind, there is no class of topics, there is no region of thought, in which he has not soared or descended, and none in which he has not said the commanding word. All men are impressed, in proportion to their own advancement in thought, by the genius of Shakspere; and the greatest mind values him the most. It is wonderful that it has taken ages to esteem him. We find with wonder that he was not appreciated in his own time; that you can hardly find any contemporary who did him any justice. Still, his fame and the influence of his genius have risen with the progress of time. As there has been opportunity to compare him with other poets and writers, his superiority has been felt, and never so much as at this day. In reading Shakspere you will find yourself armed for the law, the divinity, and for commerce with men."

One of his earliest biographical lectures was on Milton, of whom he wrote with discrimination, and with strong admiration of his prose.[3] He calls *Comus* "the loftiest song in the praise of chastity that is in any language." Of Milton's genius he said, —

[1] Address before the Massachusetts Historical Society on the centennial anniversary of Scott's birthday, Aug. 15, 1871, printed in the Transactions of the society for that year.

[2] Address at Howard University.

[3] Printed in the North American Review for July, 1838, and reprinted in Essays from the North American Review, 1879.

"It is the prerogative of this great man to stand at this hour foremost of all men in literary history, and so (shall we not say?) of all men, in the power to *inspire*. Virtue goes out of him into others. Leaving out of view the pretensions of our contemporaries (always an incalculable influence), we think no man can be named whose mind still acts on the cultivated intellect of England and America with an energy comparable to that of Milton. As a poet, Shakspere undoubtedly transcends and far surpasses him in his popularity with foreign nations; but Shakspere is a voice merely; who and what he was that sang, that sings, we know not. Milton stands erect, commanding, still visible as a man among men, and reads the laws of the moral sentiment to the new-born race. There is something pleasing in the affection with which we can regard a man who died a hundred and sixty years ago in the other hemisphere, who, in respect to personal relations, is to us as the wind, yet by an influence purely personal makes us jealous for his fame as for that of a near friend. He is identified in the mind with all select and holy images, with the supreme interests of the human race. If hereby we attain any more precision, we proceed to say that we think no man in these later ages, and few men ever, possessed so great a conception of the manly character. Better than any other he has discharged the office of every great man, namely, to raise the idea of man in the minds of his contemporaries and of posterity, — to draw after nature a life of man, exhibiting such a composition of grace, of strength, and of virtue, as poet had not described nor hero lived. Human nature in these ages is indebted to him for its best portrait. Many philosophers in England, France, and Germany have formally dedicated their study to this problem; and we think it impossible to recall one in those countries who communicates the same vibration of hope, of self-reverence, of piety, of delight in beauty, which the name of Milton awakens. The idea of a purer existence than any he saw around him, to be realized in the life and conversation of men, inspired every act and every writing of John Milton."

He has spoken of Burns with enthusiasm, and with a fine appreciation of the genuine merits of this poet of common life. He regards Burns as the poet of the middle class, and of that great progressive, modern movement, which, "not in governments, so much as in education and in social order, has changed the face of the world."

"Not Latimer, not Luther, struck more telling blows against false theology than did this brave singer. The Confession of Augsberg, the Declaration of Independence, the French Rights of Man, and the Marseillaise, are not more weighty documents, in the history of freedom, than the songs of Burns. His satire has lost none of its edge. His musical arrows yet sing through the air. He is so substantially a reformer, that I find his great plain sense in close chain with the greatest masters, — Rabelais, Shakspere in comedy, Cervantes, Butler, and Burns.

"Yet how true a poet he is! And the poet, too, of poor men, of gray hodden, and the guernsey coat, and the blouse. He has given voice to all the experiences of common life; he has endeared the farmhouse and cottage, patches and poverty, beans and barley; ale, the poor man's wine; hardship, the fear of debt, the dear society of weans and wife, of brothers and sisters, proud of each other, knowing so few, and finding amends for want and obscurity in books and thought. And as he was thus the poet of the poor, anxious, cheerful, working humanity, he had the language of low life. He grew up in a rural district, speaking a *patois* unintelligible to all but natives; and he has made that lowland Scotch a Doric dialect of fame. It is the only example in history of a language made classic by the genius of a single man. He had that secret of genius to draw from the bottom of society the strength of its speech, and astonish the ears of the polite with these artless words, better than art, and filtered of all offense by his beauty."[1]

No man could have dealt more generously with his co-workers in the fields of American literature than Emerson has done. His own ideals have been high; but he has been very tender of genius, very generous with merit, and kindly sympathetic with all who have followed the same paths with himself. This generosity has sometimes blinded him to the real merits of those who claimed his attention, but it has also helped him to do much for American literature. As Lessing raised his voice against imitation of the French, and called for a genuine German literature, founded on national sentiment, so has Emerson protested against foreign models and in favor of an American literature. His influence has been as healthful and powerful as was Lessing's, creating in this way, as Lessing did, a national literature. If Emerson's influence has not sufficed to create a literature as great as that which followed the example set by Lessing, it may be said that not nearly so many years have elapsed since it began to be felt. If not so

[1] Address at the Burns Festival in Boston, Jan. 25, 1859, on Burns's one hundredth birthday.

great in its effects, the influence has been of the same nature, and founded on the same ideas about the importance of original and independent writing.

His sympathy with genius may be seen in the case of Thoreau, who has been valued by him at his full height, and praised with unstinted appreciation. Not only in the address immediately following Thoreau's death, but elsewhere, he has expressed his love of that rare spirit. In his address at the dedication of the Concord Free Library he protested that Thoreau had not yet been highly enough appreciated by the public. He then said, —

"Henry Thoreau we all remember as a man of genius, and of marked character, known to our farmers as the most skillful of surveyors, and indeed better acquainted with their forests and meadows than themselves, but more widely known as the writer of some of the best books which have been written in this country, and which, I am persuaded, have not yet gathered half their fame. He, too, was an excellent reader. No man could have rejoiced more than he in the event of this day."

In 1852 Theodore Parker dedicated his *Ten Sermons of Religion* to Emerson, "with admiration for his genius, and with kindly affection for what in him is far nobler than genius." On receipt of the book, Emerson wrote the author this appreciative letter: —

"I read the largest part of it with good heed. I find in it all the traits which are making your discourses material to the history of Massachusetts, — the realism, the power of local and homely illustration, the courage and vigor of treatment, and the masterly sarcasm, — now naked, now veiled, — and I think with a marked growth in power and coacervation — shall I say? — of statement. To be sure, I am in this moment thinking of speeches out of this book as well as those in it. Well, you may give the times to come the means of knowing how the lamp was fed, which they are to thank you that they find burning. And though I see you are too good-natured by half in your praise of your contemporaries, you will neither deceive us nor posterity, nor — forgive me — yourself, any more in this graceful air of laying on others your own untransferable laurels.

"We shall all thank the right soldier, whom God gave strength and will to fight for him the battle of the day." [1]

[1] Weiss's Life of Parker, vol. ii. p. 45.

When Parker's society paid tribute to his memory after his death, Emerson gave an address full of love and sympathy for his heroic friend. "It is plain to me, he said, that he has achieved an historic immortality here; that he has so woven himself in these few years into the history of Boston, that he can never be left out of your annals." "His commanding merit as a reformer is this, that he insisted beyond all men in pulpits, — I can not think of one rival, — that the essence of Christianity is its practical morals." In this opinion Emerson entirely sympathized with him; and he must have been drawn to Parker on this very account, and charmed with his perfect loyalty to manhood and right.

Emerson's generous appreciation of Walt Whitman has been the cause of much comment; and it is understood he has somewhat retreated from his first ardent praise, and been mortified that that praise should have been made public. In 1855 he wrote Whitman the following letter: —

> "I am not blind to the worth of the wonderful gift of *Leaves of Grass*. I find it the most extraordinary piece of wit and wisdom that America has yet contributed. I am very happy in reading it, as great power makes us happy. It meets the demand I am always making of what seemed the sterile and stingy nature, as if too much handiwork, or too much lymph in the temperament, were making our Western wits fat and mean.
>
> "I give you joy of your free and brave thought. I have great joy in it. I find incomparable things said incomparably well, as they must be. I find the courage of treatment which so delights us, and which large perception only can inspire.
>
> "I greet you at the beginning of a great career, which yet must have had a long foreground somewhere, for such a start. I rubbed my eyes a little, to see if this sunbeam were no illusion; but the solid sense of the book is a sober certainty. It has the best merits, namely, of fortifying and encouraging.
>
> "I did not know until I last night saw the book advertised in a newspaper that I could trust the name as real and available for a post-office. I wish to see my benefactor, and have felt much like striking my tasks and visiting New York to pay you my respects."

On receipt of this letter Whitman put these words on the cover of his *Leaves of Grass:* "I greet you at the beginning of a great career." This use of a private letter, and parading of his own praise, together with Whitman's excessive sensuousness of expression, undoubtedly abated Emerson's admiration. He has said that Whitman's first poems were much better than the later. The truth of this opinion may be doubted, however; for there is none of that coarse sensuality in the later poems which characterized the earlier, and there is an immense gain in depth of spiritual power. Some of these more recent poems have a remarkable power, and are unsurpassed in the intensity and sweep of their expression. But he is very unequal, and has printed in his books a great amount of rubbish. There is much in Whitman which Emerson must admire, and much which must be repugnant to his correct and puritanic taste, as well as to his exacting moral perceptions. Though there is not a line in Whitman which is necessarily immoral, there is a quite unnecessary plainness of speech, and an open fleshliness, that have made him repugnant to many. Doubtless Emerson's praise was sincere, but the new poetry was not of that kind with which he finds himself in fullest sympathy.

In the first volume of *The Dial*, Emerson introduced to the public the poetry of William Ellery Channing, with words of sympathetic praise.[1] Channing had not yet printed any thing, Emerson's numerous selections from his manuscripts being the first to appear. He said of these poems, —

> "Our first feeling on reading them was a lively joy. So, then, the Muse is neither dead nor dumb, but has found a voice in these cold Cisatlantic states. Here is poetry which asks no aid of magnitude or number, of blood or crime, but finds theater enough in the first field or brookside, breadth and depth enough in the flow of its own thought. Here is self-repose, which to our mind is stabler than the Pyramids; here is self-respect, which leads a man to date from his heart more proudly than from Rome. Here is love which sees through surface, and adores the gentle nature and not costume. Here is religion, which is not of the church of England, nor of the church of Boston. Here is the good, wise heart, which sees that the end of culture is strength and cheerfulness. In an age, too, which tends with so strong an inclination to

[1] New Poetry, in the second number.

the philosophical muse, here is poetry more intellectual than any American verses we have yet seen, distinguished from all competition by two merits, — the fineness of perception; and the poet's trust in his own genius to that degree, that there is an absence of all conventional imagery, and a bold use of that which the moment's mood had made sacred to him, quite careless that it might be sacred to no other, and might even be slightly ludicrous to the first reader."

His name also served to bring before the public Channing's *Wanderer*, a poem mainly characterized by its appreciation of nature and by its biographic accounts of Emerson and Thoreau. In the preface to that poem he says, "there is new matter and new spirit in this writing." "These poems are genuinely original, with a simplicity of plan which allows the writer to leave out all the prose of artificial transitions." "His poems have to me and others an exceptional value for this reason, — we have not been considered in their composition, but either defied or forgotten, and therefore consult them securely as photographs."

XVII.

POETRY.

THEODORE PARKER once said that Emerson is a poet lacking the accomplishment of verse. His poems lack in that smooth, polished, well-trimmed, and proportioned flow of words which characterizes so much of the poetry of the present time. As a poet he is simple, natural, and original; but giving less heed to form than to substance, caring more for the inward beauty than for the clothing of his muse. He has been too original, too true and just to his own genius, to copy from any of the poetical models in fashion during the century. They are too diffuse, gorgeous, and strained, too much concerned for outward beauty and mere melody of form, to please him; and the real place he occupies is with Milton, Herbert, Marvell, and the Elizabethan poets. His love for those poets shows his natural affiliation with them; there he has found his models; and his stoic economy of words, purity of style, and simplicity of thought, all remind us of those noble singers. His moral tone, so lofty, so pure, recalls their puritanic sympathies. He is thoroughly a moral poet; never loves beauty merely for its own sake. He has the quiet and earnest manner of all great moral poets, the steady sense of the value of life, and the constant regard to its well-ordering, which the word-flourish, and lively color, and dilletanteism, of much of the present poetry make impossible.

He is an introspective poet, with great power of giving expression to some of the moods and tendencies of the human mind. He deals with the riddles of being in a lofty spirit. The dark problems of life which concern every soul, and the solution of which forms the eras of human thought, he brings into his poems with rare power, and with a skill few possess. He thus becomes a true interpreter of human motives. His muse turns wholly inward in some of his poems; and the great outward world, at other times so dear, is quite forgotten. He treats of mental experiences, moral purposes, spiritual aspirations, in a happy manner. Yet he speaks rather through the imagination than the heart, is an intellectual more than a sentimental poet. Emotion and passion do not enter largely into his poetry. He has feeling, and great depth of it; but it is not directly expressed. There is much of the Puritan about him, an austere distrust of emotion. He is usually calm, reposeful, earnest with faith, and without the rushes and surges of emotion or the ecstasies of passion.

"His feeling has the quality of depth and earnestness, sometimes hinting at a certain Hebrew solemnity rather than of ardent sympathy. He is not apt to take his readers into friendly counsel; rarely does he draw them near his heart; but rather speaks to them in his grand, austere tones from some lofty height of isolation. Not a trace of effeminacy, of the weak indulgence of even the purest passion, ever impairs the conscious serenity of his spirit. His inspiration flows from the intellect, or rather from the supreme poetic faculty, to a far greater degree than from the affections. Still, he is not without frequent touches of the tenderest pathos."[1]

Emerson has a theory of poetry, and in accordance with it most of his poems have been written. It is, that mind is central, the source of an infinite unity; that the outward world is symbolical of the spirit expressed through it, and that every fact in nature carries the whole sense of nature. He sees a deep and subtle relation between the physical universe and the soul of man. The world is a symbol, an expression to the senses, of spirit; and every outward fact must be interpreted in terms of the inward life. This idea powerfully appeals to his imagination, sets his mind aglow with analogies, and stimulates to the subtlest spiritual interpretations of nature. It gives a mystic character to his poetry, and makes many of his poems seem as obscure at first

[1] Article by E. P. Whipple in The Independent for 1867.

as they are found to be deep with the profoundest meaning when the analogy is penetrated, and they are comprehended. No poet beholds spirit so universally present as he does, or finds God so truly an indwelling life in all things. No poetry is more thoroughly religious, though it has none of the conventional forms of religion. God and the soul speak to him everywhere; every bush is ablaze with the glory of God. Nature is the word of God, the living epistle of truth, the ever-open book wherein we may read the wondrous law of the Over-soul. In him this analogy between nature and spirit "has assumed a new shape, and given birth to a fresh variety of spiritual creation."

"The religious sense with which prophets and holy men have consecrated certain spots by the presence of Deity is carried by him into the universal domain of Nature. To his mystic vision every mountain is a Sinai, every tree of the wood is a burning bush, every breeze is vocal with the still, small voice. In the growth of plants, the flow of streams, the flight of birds, he recognizes the mysterious power which gives vitality to the soul, if it be not indeed, according to his Oriental fancy, the outward projection of the soul itself."[1]

He applies the same ideas in the interpretation of art, a subject on which he has not written so wisely or with so much inspiration as he has concerning poetry. The essence of beauty, he says, is in the mind. In nature it results from the presence of the universal spirit, the unity of all things, and the striving of every natural thing to realize itself in higher forms. It is "a certain cosmical quality or power to suggest relation to the whole world," and always betrays the presence of "somewhat immeasurable and divine."[2] Art is complementary to nature, and must strictly follow its laws.[3] Here, as in poetry, moral power is always present, and must dominate the work. Art must follow the necessary; and hence true art, as well as true poetry, is unconscious in its origin. The artist does not create so much as report. The soul works through him, he is its

[1] Ibid.
[2] Conduct of Life, pp. 267, 268.
[3] Society and Solitude, essay on Art.

unconscious instrument. "The artist does not feel himself to be the parent of his work, and is as much surprised at the effect as we." Carlyle has made much of this idea, maintaining that all great performances of whatever kind are not consciously done, that they are not creations, but reportings of what we have seen in the realms of spirit. That is, all highest truth is an intuition, and comes from a source above the understanding.

To Emerson poetry is the only verity, contains the only reality. The birth of a poet is the principal human event, for he stands among partial men for the complete man. "He is the healthy, the wise, the fundamental, the manly man, seer of the secret; against all appearances he sees and reports the truth, namely, that the soul generates matter." Each poetic mind perceives the world in a way that is its own, thus puts forth out of its own being a world after its own nature. As a manifestation of the Over-soul, — from which the outward world proceeds, as a lessened expression of itself, — does each individual soul reign supreme over matter. Nature, however, is responsive to the spirit it expresses; and as it is the same spirit everywhere manifest, all the manifold phases of nature answer to each other, like to like. It is this identity of manifestation which gives to poetry its imaginative power.

The poet is the world's speaker, giving expression to the meanings of things; for he reads and interprets the spiritual truth which the outward fact means. "He stands one step nearer to things, and sees the flowing or metamorphosis; perceives that thought is multiform; that within the form of every creature is a force impelling it to ascend into a higher form; and, following with his eyes the life, uses the forms which express that life, and so his speech flows with the flowing of nature. All the facts of the animal economy — sex, nutriment, gestation, birth, growth — are symbols of the passage of the world into the soul of man, to suffer there a change, and re-appear a new and higher fact." So the chief value of whatever new fact is brought forth by the poet, is, that it shall enhance "the great and constant fact of Life." This sublime vision of a higher life comes only "to the pure and simple soul in a clean and chaste body." To some it comes so as to lead to heroic deeds and living, to others in power to sing ravishing songs of love and truth; but "words and deeds are quite indifferent modes of the divine energy." The poetic power does not reside in meters, but in the "meter-making argument," in "a thought so passionate and alive, that it has an architecture of its own, and adorns nature with a new thing. The thought and the form are equal in the order of time, but in the order of genesis the thought is prior to the form." Emerson is somewhat indifferent to the studied forms of poetry, caring more for the thought than the meter. This he justifies in Merlin, where he says, —

"Great is the art,
Great be the manners, of the bard.
He shall not his brain encumber
With the coil of rhythm and number;
But leaving rule and pale forethought,
He shall aye climb
For his rhyme,
And mount to paradise
By the stairway of surprise."

As the first condition of poetic power, the poet must believe in his poetry; and all the great poets have been enamored of their sweet thoughts. They know that the "correspondence of things to thoughts is far deeper than they can penetrate, — defying adequate expression; that it is elemental, or in the core of things." It being so much more than can be fully expressed, it is an absolute condition of true poetry, that the poet shall have no theories of what the Infinite ought to reveal to him; but he must exactly report whatever he learns. The poet is a revealer, repeating to men what the Over-soul gives him to know; "for poetry was all written before time was; and whenever we are so finely organized that we can penetrate into that region where the air is music, we hear those primal warblings, and attempt to write them down." The greater the veracity and faithfulness of the poet, the more he keeps out his own fancies, and speaks the living word nature reveals, the more truly is he a poet. Too often the poets can "only hint the matter, or allude to it, being unable to fuse and mold their words and images to fluid obedience." In order to reach the most perfect receptivity, the poet's "cheerfulness should be the gift of the sunlight; the air should suffice for his inspiration, and he should be tipsy with water." If he wishes to fill his brain with fashion and covetousness, and to stimulate his jaded senses with wine and coffee, he will find "no radiance of wisdom in the lonely waste of the pine-woods." As poetry consists in finding the attachments of things to the Infinite, and their consequent relations to each other, so the poet finds truth everywhere; and could he but read the secrets of the simplest thing, he could disclose all truth. He is to read nature with "a sensibility so keen that the scent of an elder-blow, or the timber-yard and corporation works of a nest of pismires, is event enough for him, — all emblems and personal appeals to him." Reading not simply the external beauty, but the spiritual significance, the poet sees "the factory-village and railway fall within the great order not less than the beehive, or the spider's geometrical web." The poet must also be a builder and affirmer, building the world anew, and after a more perfect fashion. "The poet says nothing but what helps somebody," lifts the veil from the hard and cold formalities of life; "gives men glimpses of the laws of the universe; shows them the circumstance as illusion; shows that nature is only a language to express the laws, which are grand and beautiful; and lets them, by his songs, into some of the realities."

A higher office of the poet still is the power of creation, by which he shapes the imperfect towards the perfect. Here we find "that there is a mental power and creation more excellent than any thing which is commonly called philosophy and literature," and that the high poets, as Homer, Milton, and Shakspere "do not fully content us." They do not offer us heavenly bread, and the true poetry is to be found in Zoroaster and Plato, St. John and Menu, "with their moral burdens." Real poetry should bring us back to nature, and make life more harmonious. In gaining this result "it is not style or rhymes, or a new image more or less, that imports, but sanity; that life should not be mean; that life should be an image in every part beautiful; that the old forgotten splendors of the universe should glow again for us, — that we should lose our wit, but gain our reason. And when life is true to the poles of nature, the streams of truth will roll through us in song." It is the inspiring and spiritually-minded poets Emerson loves, those who speak out of the depths of a great faith, and who paint the moral vision of a harmonious world. The bard, he says in Loss and Gain, must yield himself entirely to virtue;

"Must throw away his pen and paint,
Kneel with worshipers.
Then, perchance, a sunny ray
From the heaven of fire,
His lost tools may overpay,
And better his desire."

The real poets have been those capable of "marrying nature and mind, undoing the old divorce in which poetry has been famished and false, and nature been suspected and pagan." When the life that is to be lived after the perfect order of nature, "shall be organized and appear on earth, the Iliad will be reckoned a poor ballad-grinding; for sooner or later that which is now life shall be poetry, and every fair and manly trait shall add a richer strain to the song." Emerson thinks that Swedenborg and Wordsworth have been the agents of this reform, by which poetry is to be regarded for its moral and natural interpretations of the world and of life. He sees, however, the artificial position of these men, that they have not arrived at the full reality, though on the right road; for he regards it as "boyish in Swedenborg to cumber himself with the dead scurf of Hebrew antiquity, as if the divine creative energy had fainted in his own century." The poet should

"not seek to weave,
In weak, unhappy times,
Efficacious rhymes."

He is not to mingle in the base purposes of the world.

"God, who gave to him the lyre,
Of all mortals the desire,
For all breathing men's behoof,
Straitly charged him, Sit aloof."

Yet he is to love the race of men, nor immure himself in a den; for the people must hear him, and find inspiration in his words. He must meditate long and much, that his themes may be great and his inspiration sure. The chords of his harp

"should ring as blows the breeze,
Free, peremptory, clear.
No jingling serenader's art,
Nor tinkle of piano-strings,
Can make the wild blood start
In its mystic springs.
The kingly bard
Must smite the chords rudely and hard,
As with hammer or with mace;
That they may render back
Artful thunder, which conveys
Secrets of the solar track,
Sparks of the supersolar blaze."

In this same poem of Merlin he tells us what it is that makes the song of the true poet so masterful, when he says that his

"blows are strokes of fate
Chiming with the forest tone,
When boughs buffet boughs in the wood;
Chiming with the gasp and moan
Of the ice-imprisoned flood;
With the pulse of manly hearts;
With the voice of orators;
With the din of city arts;
With the cannonade of wars;
With the marches of the brave;
And prayers of might from martyr's cave."

The sympathies of the poet, too, must be as wide as the experiences of men, so that he can enter into appreciation of all their hopes and motives. This sympathy he has expressed in an allegorical poem, such as he often delights in writing: —

"There are beggars in Iran and Araby:
Said was hungrier than all.
Men said he was a fly,
That came to every festival;
Also he came to the mosque
In trail of camel and caravan,
Out from Mecca or Ispahan;
Northward he went to the snowy hills;
At court he sat in grave divan.
His music was the south wind's sigh,
His lamp the maiden's downcast eye;
And ever the spell of beauty came,
And turned the drowsy world to flame.
By lake and stream and gleaming hall,
And modest copse, and the forest tall,
Where'er he went, the magic guide
Kept its place by the poet's side.
Tell me the world is a talisman;
To read it must be the art of man.
Said melted the days in cups like pearl;
Served high and low, the lord and the churl;
Loved harebells nodding on a rock,
A cabin hung with curling smoke,
And huts and tents, nor loved the less
Stately lords in palaces,
Fenced by form and ceremony." [1]

The most popular of Emerson's poems are those devoted to nature and its manifestations. Some of these have a richness of expression, a wealth of meaning, a simplicity of style, and a depth of insight, seldom surpassed. They seem to be almost perfect, so exquisitely true are they, and so grandly fine are their interpretations. They indicate the most intimate acquaintance with nature in all her moods, a close and a sympathetic study of her objects and creatures. Their power consists, not simply in their picturing for us, in the most

[1] These lines have not appeared as from Emerson's pen, but are printed in Channing's Thoreau, p. 161.

faithful manner, the phenomena of the outward world, but much more in that overflowing faith which reads in them the moral and spiritual truths of a Cosmos. He says that "Nature is the representative of the universal mind," and this idea penetrates and absorbs all his poetry. Yet it never stifles and oppresses us with its religiousness; because, in the dogmatic and ordinary sense, it never is religious. It rises to a height far above all formal religion, — to a calm, serene, and majestic faith in the Life that throbs in matchless wonder and ceaseless beauty all around, touching all things with its glory. The poet gives the true meaning of nature, only when he becomes its servant, and lets it sing through him the song of unceasing creation. The true poet finds his verse brought to him by the muse; and it is great and true when it sings through him, even against his will, rising far over his judgment into the unseen and awful heights where his weary feet can not follow. Yet Emerson is not merely a mystic, he does not deal in rhapsody, nor does he picture nature only from his imagination. He has studied nature in a careful manner, not, it is true, as a man of science, but as a poet. He has watched the various phases of nature, even in their details. His picture of "the forest seer," in Wood-notes, so often falsely regarded as a portrait of Thoreau, is an exact account of his own habits and experiences. Few poets have grasped nature as a whole so completely, or caught so clearly, and expressed so finely, that total effect it produces on the mind of man. In one of the most suggestive of his poems, Each and All, he has succeeded in stating the spiritual effect which nature produces, and the relations of objects to each other in the total impression. In that poem he suggests the failure of science to understand nature as it is, when it sees only the dissected detail. Tyndall has admirably stated the same fact in these deeply important words: —

"The ultimate problem of physics is to reduce matter by analysis to its lowest conditions of divisibility, and force to its simplest manifestations, and then by synthesis to construct from these elements the world as it stands. We are still a long way from the final solution of this problem; and when the solution comes, *it will be one more of spiritual insight* than of actual observation."[1]

Emerson has been an observer, a patient student; and he has described Nature with rare accuracy. Her humble forms he knows, and can make them the implements of his poetic skill. His poetry is inspired by the objects and scenes within sight of his own house.

"In his delineations of Nature, even in her slightest hints of color and texture, of form and order, there is a marvelous accuracy of expression, showing a singularly acute and truthful eye, no less than a radiant imagination. In the grand procession of the seasons, no delicate phase escapes his notice. The wonderful processes of seedtime and harvest are watched with the severity of scientific research. He loves the secret haunts of Nature, and is never weary of spying into her mysteries. His acquaintance with her ways has been gained by face-to-face intercourse. He meets her disclosures with the love of an ancient, familiar friend."[2]

The very health of spring is in May-Day. It is fragrant with the budding May. Equally perfect to nature are The Rhodora, The Humble-bee, The Titmouse, The Snow-storm, Wood-notes, and some others. The characteristics of these poems are shown in one of the shortest, Rhodora. There is an exquisite delight in nature itself, a quiet and yet an intense rejoicing in its sights, sounds, colors, and forms; a delicate sympathy with it. The flower,

"Spreading its leafless blooms in a damp nook,"

is an object of keen interest. It is an interest, not merely worldly or inquisitive, but spiritual, and longing to know the secrets of things; that finds the solemn song of nature chanted beside a stagnant pool, in the fresh flower of the woods, which, budding anew into life, reads here afresh the perpetual marvel of the world. One may turn through the pages of many poets before finding again any lines so simple, apparently so trite in their theme, yet possessing so steady a

[1] Fragments of Science, p. 100, An Address to Students.
[2] Whipple.

faith, and a sympathy with nature so intimate and noble, as these that close this little poem: —

"Rhodora! if the sages ask thee why
This charm is wasted on the earth and sky,
Tell them, dear, that if eyes were made for seeing,
Then Beauty is its own excuse for being:
Why thou wert there, O rival of the rose!
I never thought to ask, I never knew;
But, in my simple ignorance, suppose
The self-same Power that brought me there brought you."

The Humble-bee is a gem, true in its descriptions and rich in its suggestions. Some of the lines are fine bits of word-painting, as these: —

"Burly, dozing humble-bee,"
"Thou animated torrid zone,"
"Zigzag steerer, desert cheerer,"
"Insect lover of the sun,"
"Rover of the underwoods."

And this ideal picture of the "epicurean of June" is delightful in its familiarity with the scenes the humble-bee loves, and in its delicate sense of the healthfulness of nature: —

"Aught unsavory or unclean
Hath my insect never seen;
But violets and bilberry bells,
Maple-sap and daffodils,
Grass with green flag half-mast high,
Succory to match the sky,
Columbine with horn of honey,
Scented fern and agrimony,
Clover, catchfly, adder's-tongue,
And brier-roses, dwelt among;
All beside was unknown waste,
All was picture as he passed."

That faithful description of the Snow-storm, printed long ago in *The Dial*, has already become a classic in our language. The lover of true poetry knows it well. In the Wood-notes of the same period is a sketch of the poet's work, showing why Emerson is attracted, as a poet, to nature. The knowledge which the poet

"prizes best
Seems fantastic to the rest:
Pondering shadows, colors, clouds,
Grass-buds, and caterpillar-shrouds,
Boughs on which the wild bees settle,
Tints that spot the violet's petal,
Why Nature loves the number five,
And why the star-form she repeats;
Lover of all things alive,
Wonderer at all he meets,
Wonderer chiefly at himself, —
Who can tell him what he is?"

One of the most perfect of his poems in form, as it is magnetic in effect and correct in description, is the Sea-shore. It admirably shows his capacity of blending correct description and pure coloring with lofty spiritual suggestion. What finer account of the sea, and its relations to man, than that contained in these lines?

"Behold the sea,
The opaline, the plentiful and strong,
Yet beautiful as is the rose in June,
Fresh as the trickling rainbow of July;
Sea full of food, the nourisher of kinds,
Purger of earth, and medicine of men;
Creating a sweet climate by my breath,
Washing out harms and griefs from memory,
And, in my mathematic ebb and flow,
Giving a hint of that which changes not."

The uses of the sea are pictured in this stanza: —

"I with my hammer pounding evermore
The rocky coast, smite Andes into dust,
Strewing my bed, and, in another age,
Rebuild a continent of better men.
Then I unbar the doors; my paths lead out
The exodus of nations; I disperse
Men to all shores that front the hoary main."

The effect of the sea on the imagination of man is set forth in these lines: —

"Leave me to deal
With credulous and imaginative man;
For, though he scoop my water in his palm,

A few rods off he deems it gems and clouds.
Planting strange fruits and sunshine on the shore,
I make some coast alluring, some lone isle,
To distant men, who must go there, or die."

It is this love of all living things, however common or unclean, and this wonder and awe at the mystery and the life all things express, that largely characterize the poetry of Emerson, and give to it much of its subtle power. It is rough and uncouth in appearance and sound, as most poetry is not; but the more it is studied, the more it attracts, and the plainer becomes its harmony, which is more penetrating in its effect than any surface form. It is the poetry of thought, and not of rhythm or color; of an attracting and winning power in nature to sooth and harmonize and make true the soul of man. This is shown in the Wood-notes: —

"Whoso walketh in solitude,
And inhabiteth the wood,
Choosing light, wave, rock, and bird,
Before the money-loving herd,
Into that forester shall pass,
From these companions, power and grace;
Clean shall he be, without, within,
From the old adhering sin."

The mysticism of his thought is more delightful in his poetry than in his prose, and is suggestive of the flowing and receding of all visible forms before the power of the spirit, which alone is alive and stable. Nature chants to him ever a mystic song,

"To the open ear it sings
Sweet the genesis of things,
Of tendency through endless ages,
Of star-dust, and star-pilgrimages,
Of rounded worlds, of space and time,
Of the old flood's subsiding slime,
Of chemic matter, force and form,
Of poles and powers, cold, wet, and warm;
The rushing metamorphosis,
Dissolving all that fixture is,
Melts things that be to things that seem,
And solid nature to a dream."

The attraction of man to nature, and sympathy with it, which comes out through all these poems, the subjects of which are natural objects, is an attraction and sympathy growing out of their oneness of origin. This affinity is full of alluring interest. In many others it finds expression as the power of love to win the heart and hold it pure. The higher the forms of being, the stronger the bonds and fascinations of this love. This harmony and unity is the return of nature and man to the Infinite Love, from whence they came. To return into this harmony is the secret aim and the source of the longing and attraction of all things, which impels them out of the present, "poor and bare," towards the full melody and perfectness of the future.

"The sense of the world is short, —
Long and various the report, —
To love and be beloved."

There is nothing denied to this subtle affinity and attraction.

"The solid, solid universe
Is pervious to love,"

and it

"reconciles
By mystic wiles
The evil and the good."

It is the affinity of man to all things, which is the height of love; and it is a power essential to the poet. The real poet must "give all to love," must love every thing that is, must feel all attractions, and come into secret sympathy with all things. The soul that would know the celestial love, and pierce the deeps of things, must rise into the highest regions, above every passion and low desire,

"Into vision where all form
In one only form dissolves;"

and it is only

"There the holy essence rolls
One through separated souls."

His philosophical poems, though least appreciated, because not understood, are perhaps his best. They are full of power, often entering into the profoundest questions with a wisdom and clearness of vision seldom found. The Sphinx deals with some of the questions discussed in his best essays, and gives a solution even better stated than any he has furnished in prose. The riddle of existence lies in the possibility of man's endless growth, so that ever new heights will open before him, and in his own kinship to every other existence. The Infinite dwells in man as in all things else; the key to one existence being furnished, all being can be known. But man must not seek in time and its forms the answer; he must rise to harmony with the things of the spirit; for he is a "clothed eternity," and in love must find the Infinite which fades not away. In one of his essays he has also interpreted the myth of the Sphinx, and it will throw much light on the poem. All these myths he believes embody some great idea, as Proteus symbolizes the doctrine of identity.

"As near and proper to us is also that old fable of the Sphinx, who was said to sit in the road-side and put riddles to every passenger. If the man could not answer, she swallowed him alive. If he could solve the riddle, the Sphinx was slain. What is our life but an endless flight of winged facts or events? In splendid variety these changes come, all putting questions to the human spirit. Those men who can not answer by a superior wisdom these facts or questions of time, serve them. Facts encumber them, tyrannize over them, and make the men of routine the men of *sense*, in whom a literal obedience to facts has extinguished every spark of that light by which man is truly man. But if the man is true to his better instincts or sentiments, and refuses the dominion of facts, as one that comes of a higher race, remains fast by the soul and sees the principle, then the facts fall aptly and supple into their places; they know their master, and the meanest of them glorifies him." [1]

One of the most striking of these poems is Brahma, which sums up the "Yoga" doctrine of the ancient Hindoos in a few perfect words. The very name given the little poem indicates that it was suggested by his

[1] Essays, first series, p. 29.

studies among these Oriental thinkers. It teaches that subtle ever-present Spirit is the absolute life in all things. The soul can not be slain, nothing can destroy it; for it is one with the Over-soul. To the Infinite, moreover, all forms are alike; and all which men see and know, as human creatures, is phenomenal. The spirit abides alone; in that is life. If we seek its truth and its harmony, turning our backs on the heaven that promises only happiness, we shall find the "abode" of the Infinite. In this poem it is the infinite, absolute, unchanging Deity who speaks; and He is alike the cause of good and evil, light and darkness, faith and doubt. It may be better understood by a quotation or two from the *Bhagavad Gita*. "He who believes that spirit can kill, and he who thinks that it can be killed, both are wrong in judgment. It neither kills, nor is killed. It is not born, nor dies at any time." The soul is "unborn, changeless, eternal both as to future and past time; it is not slain when the body is killed." The last lines of Emerson's poem find their counterpart in the words of the Deity in the *Bhagavad Gita*, who says, "Abandoning all religious duties, seek me as thy refuge." In this book the Infinite Spirit, Brahma, says, "They who serve other gods with a firm belief, in doing so, involuntarily worship me. I am he who partaketh of all worship, and I am their reward. I am the soul which standeth in the bodies of all beings." It also teaches that the souls of men "proceed unbewildered to that imperishable place which is not illumined by the sun or moon, to that primeval Spirit whence the spirit of life for ever flows." Of the same philosophical character are The Visit, Uriel, The World-Soul, and some others. Each summarizes in a few lyrical lines one of his great thoughts; and for those who penetrate the idea which is sung, it is given an added grace and beauty in this poetic form. Of a less philosophical character, but even more profound and suggestive, are a number of such poems as Each and All, The Problem, Letters, and Days. These are among the most inspiring of meditative poems. They are as rigidly simple as they are wondrously suggestive and thought-provoking. Each and All teaches one of the most needed of all lessons we can learn, and in lines of exquisite beauty. Hedge truly characterizes The Problem as "wholly unique, and transcending all contemporary verse in grandeur of style." Such a poem as Letters is but a mere hint; and yet, hint as it is, the depths and heights of religious devotion are all suggested in its half-dozen lines. One of its beauties is, this rigid economy of suggestion; and another, the absolute trust hinted at, but sufficiently disclosed.

Emerson's poetry is personal, touched always with his own emotions, and made living with the spontaneous sympathies of his own ideas. His poetry is to a large extent biographical, far more so than his prose, and throws much light on his personal experiences and motives. The key to many of his poems can be found only in his life, and in his intercourse with his intimate friends. Whoever would understand him, must know his poetry thoroughly; for there alone has he expressed the fullness of his nature, and the innermost of his own mind and heart. His poetry is individual, human, alive; hence it is stimulating in its influence on other poets. In spite of his want of poetic art; though his verses often halt, while the conclusion flags; and though the metrical propriety is recklessly violated, — yet "this defect is closely connected with the characteristic merit of the poet, and springs from the same root, — his utter spontaneity. And this spontaneity is perhaps but a mode of that sincerity which may be noted in his prose. More than those of any of his contemporaries, his poems for the most part are inspirations. They are not made, but given; they come of themselves. They are not meditated, but burst from the soul with an irrepressible necessity of utterance, — sometimes with a rush which defies the shaping intellect."[1] This lyrical power was also noticed by Frederika Bremer, when she says the other American poets speak to society, but Emerson

[1] F. H. Hedge, in Literary World for May 22, 1880.

always merely to the individual.[1] She said of his poems, "They are all to me as a breeze from the life of the New World, in a certain illimitable vastness of life, in expectation, in demand, in faith, in hope, — a something which makes me draw a deeper breath, and, as it were, in a larger, freer world." This inspiring power — so fresh, original, and individual — has been noticed by another critic, himself a poet of no mean ability. Howells says that Emerson, "perhaps more than any other modern poet, gives the notion of inspiration; so that one doubts, in reading him, how much to praise or blame. The most exquisite effects seem not to have been invited, but to have sought production from his unconsciousness; graces alike of thought and of touch seem the unsolicited gifts of the gods." As Howells suggests, however, "it is probable that no utterance is more considered than this poet's, and that no one is more immediately responsible than he" for what he writes. Hedge can not be correct in the supposition that his poems are purely spontaneous, written at fever heat, dashed off in a moment, and without revision. We must suppose them to be wrought out carefully, undergoing the most exacting revision, but retaining all the power of spontaneity and inspiration. His exquisite poem, The Test, in which the muse is supposed to be speaking, correctly represents his own methods.

> "I hung my verses in the wind,
> Time and tide their faults may find.
> All were winnowed through and through,
> Five lines lasted sound and true."

Thoroughly winnowed are all his poems, as are his essays; but in the same way they are inspirations, gathered in the hours of richest thought. For the same reasons they are full of quotable sentences, strong, apt, wise, and exquisitely expressed. His felicity of expression is remarkable, and his painting of nature and human motives perfect. Especially

[1] Homes of the New World, p. 41.

must his poetry be valued for its vigorous moral tone, its pure sense of human relations, and its invincible faith in moral consequences. He is one of the great moral poets, standing, indeed, in the front rank of those who have dealt with human duties. He sees clearly the moral and spiritual relations of men, to each other, to nature, and to God; and the great spiritual laws, typified in nature, by which all human motives and conduct are surrounded.

Steadily has he followed the great ideas and motives which have been the inspiration of his life. His poetry has not descended from its pure heights, or forgotten the truths it had to speak. In his Terminus, which Howells says "has a wonderful didactic charm, and must be valued as one of the noblest introspective poems in the language," he has, in a tender manner, spoken of the old age that has come upon him, and the need to

> "Economize the failing river,"

though he would

> "Not the less revere the Giver."

He has been faithful, he will be faithful still, and fulfill, true to himself, the duties which come with old age. In a perfect line he has sung this faith and trust. It is a worthy last word of a poet so true, faithful, and pure as he.

> "As the bird trims her to the gale,
> I trim myself to the storm of time,
> I man the rudder, reef, and sail,
> *Obey the voice at eve obeyed at prime:*
> 'Lowly faithful, banish fear,
> Right onward drive unharmed;
> The port, well worth the cruise, is near,
> And every wave is charmed.'"

XVIII.

AS A LECTURER.

IN this country Emerson was among those who first made popular the lecture as a means of general culture. He helped make it a moral and intellectual power, a means of quickening influence on life and thought. He may also be said to have founded the Lyceum; for he shaped its character, and made it an efficient instrument of popular instruction. It was in existence when he began to lecture, as a means of diffusing scientific knowledge; but he gave it a literary, moral, and reformatory character, and shaped its destiny.

The first Lyceum was founded by Josiah Holbrook, in 1826. Holbrook was born at Derby, Conn., in 1788, and graduated at Yale. He heard Silliman's lectures, and became deeply interested in chemistry, mineralogy, and geology. In 1824 he opened an agricultural school on his farm in Derby, in which he gave much attention to scientific subjects; but it was continued only a little more than a year. In October, 1826, he published a paper in the *American Journal of Education* on Associations of Adults for the Purpose of Mutual Education. Delivering a course of lectures on scientific subjects in Millbury, Mass., soon after, he induced about forty persons to unite in organizing such a society. At his request it was called the Millbury Lyceum. This was the first organization of the kind in the country. Holbrook had in view the establishment of such societies throughout the country, and a union of them under some general organization. A convention was held in Boston, Nov. 7, 1828, to promote the interests of the Lyceums, and to further their wide-spread organization. Among those who took part in this meeting were Webster, Everett, Dr. Lowell, and George B. Emerson. The American Lyceum, to represent the local societies, was organized at this time probably. Holbrook's idea was mainly scientific; and the Lyceum was to be a means of disseminating scientific knowledge through classes, lectures, and the collection and exchange of scientific specimens. The lectures were on scientific and hygienic subjects exclusively. In 1830 Holbrook began the publication of a series of scientific tracts, and in 1832 he started a journal called *The Family Lyceum.* At this time there were seventy-eight Lyceums in Massachusetts, with a state and county organizations. In 1834 he went to Pennsylvania, and devoted several years in that state to lecturing and the organization of Lyceums. One of his projects at this time was a Universal Lyceum, which should unite the national organizations. He also projected a number of lyceum villages. In 1837, at Berea, O., such a village was actually begun, but soon expired. Holbrook's project was an admirable one, and he devoted himself to it with great zeal.

When Emerson returned from Europe in 1833, he at once took advantage of the interest in this mode of popular instruction, created by Holbrook. Gradually his influence, working with many others, served to mold the Lyceum into a means of general culture; and its special purpose was forgotten in the more general aim.[1] He drew to hear him the eager enthusiasm of that day in Boston, and he inspired his hearers with a genuine desire for culture. His influence and manner during these earlier years have been better described by Margaret Fuller than by any other.[2] In reviewing one of his earlier volumes of essays for *The Tribune*, she said, —

"The audience that waited for years upon the lectures was never large; but it was select, and it was constant. . . . The charm of the

[1] A very few of the Lyceums are yet in existence. The Essex Institute at Salem carried out Holbrook's idea, and is a worthy testimonial of his purpose. Emerson has given no less than forty lectures before it.

[2] Life Without and Within, p. 194.

elocution was great. His general manner was that of the reader, occasionally rising into direct address or invocation in passages where tenderness or majesty demanded more energy. . . . The tone of the voice was a grave body-tone, full and sweet rather than sonorous, yet flexible, and haunted by many modulations, as even instruments of wood and brass seem to become after they have been long played on with skill and taste; how much more so the human voice! In the more expressive passages it uttered notes of silvery clearness, winning, yet still more commanding. The words uttered in these tones floated awhile above us, then took root in the memory like winged seed.

"In the union of an even rustic plainness with lyric inspirations, religious dignity with philosophical calmness, keen sagacity in details with boldness of view, we saw what brought to mind the early poets and legislators of Greece, — men who taught their fellows to plow, and avoid moral evil, sing hymns to the gods, and watch the metamorphoses of nature. Here in civic Boston was such a man, — one who could see man in his original grandeur and his original childishness, rooted in simple nature, raising to the heavens the brow and eyes of a poet. . . .

"Such was the attitude in which the speaker appeared to that portion of the audience who have remained permanently attached to him. They value his words as the signets of reality; receive his influence as a help and incentive to a nobler discipline than the age, in its general aspect, appears to require; and do not fear to anticipate the verdict of posterity in claiming for him the honors of greatness, and, in some respects, of a master."

His manner in his earlier years has also been well described by another[1] of his hearers and admirers: —

"The modulation of his voice in delivering his sentences was wonderfully effective, and I used to think he was one of the best readers I ever heard. Commencing on a key, he would continue on the same up to the last word or two, and then drop into a deep musical tone which was very impressive. Occasionally at the end of a sentence he would suddenly stop, for what seemed a long time, and, with his eyes uplifted upon his audience, looking like one inspired. Every one in the audience seemed to stop breathing, as if afraid to mar the solemn impression produced. Then another sentence would be commenced on another key; and, rising higher and higher, his voice would again drop to lower tones, like the solemn peals of an organ."

On the lecture-platform Emerson seems to be unconscious of his audience, is not disturbed by interruptions of any kind, by hisses, or by the departure of disap-

[1] In a series of letters published in The Gazette of Stapleton, N.Y.

pointed listeners. He usually reads his lectures, though he is not always confined to his manuscript; while he often misplaces his sheets, and stumbles over the chirography. He usually begins in a slow and spiritless manner, in a low tone; and he is not fluent of speech, or passionate in manner. As he proceeds, he becomes earnest and magnetic; while the thrilling intensity of his voice deeply affects and rivets the attention of his audience. He is full of mannerisms in expression and in bodily attitude, seldom makes a gesture, and has little variation of voice. He secures the interest of his hearers by the simple grandeur of his thought, the inspiration of his moral genius, the conviction and manliness which his words express, and by the silvery enchantment of his voice. The glow of his face, the mobile expressiveness of his features, the charm of his smile, add to the interest created by his thought. It is the quality of his ideas, however, which attracts his hearers. His thought often rises to the heights of the purest eloquence. Such passages are sure to command the closest attention. It is the glowing faith and the moral intensity of the seer which gives them their power.

As a lecturer, Emerson makes a large use of surprise, giving a meaning to his words not observed in reading them. He flashes wit into sentences which seem to be sober enough when read in his books. The essayist needs to be interpreted by the lecturer; for his voice and manner become a fine commentary on his written thought, giving to it new and unexpected meanings, and a rich suggestiveness not otherwise to be had. He often gives a wholly unexpected turn to his thought, which surprises and delights the listener, fastening an idea for ever in the memory. Or he suddenly, as if it were a new thought, flashed suddenly upon his mind, after apparently having exhausted a subject, adds in a lower tone some sentence which comes as a revelation, and opens new meanings to the listener. He adds a constantly fresh interest to his topics by such methods as these, which are peculiar to himself. They are so spontaneously used, with such an air of utter unconsciousness, that they never appear otherwise than as the marks of a genuine simplicity and sincerity.

The deep and lasting impression he has made upon his hearers can best be conveyed in their own words. "It is a peculiar pleasure, said Frederika Bremer, to hear that deep, sonorous voice uttering words which give the impression of jewels and real pearls as they fall from his lips."[1] All his admirers have, in the same way, been enthusiasts concerning the inspiring power of his thought and the magnetic impulse of his voice. This power to engage the sympathies, to arrest the attention, to mold purposes, to quicken with great aspirations, has been well described by Lowell: —

"I have heard some great speakers, and some accomplished orators, but never any that so moved and persuaded men as he. There is a kind of undertone in that rich baritone of his that sweeps our minds from their foothold into deep waters with a drift we can not and would not resist. And how artfully (for Emerson is a long-studied artist in these things) does the deliberate utterance, that seems waiting for the first word, seem to admit us partners in the labor of thought, and make us feel as if the glance of humor were a sudden suggestion; as if the perfect phrase lying written there on the desk were as unexpected to him as to us!"[2]

One of his townsmen,[3] long familiar with him as a lecturer, says, "the secret of his profound influence on the minds of his hearers and the literature of the time lies in his creative and inspiring genius, combined as it is with a rectitude and simplicity of the moral sense which makes his criticism as decisive as it is searching." The same writer also says, —

"Except the tones of his voice (nor are these greatly varied), he has few of the graces of an orator. He is neither fluent, nor excellent in action. It is the quality of what he says, not its volume, or its manner of expression, which fascinates or is remembered. His style is admirable. The purity of his English, the salt of his wit, the simple grandeur of his periods, are agreeable accidents of his oratory; but they are only accidents. Its substance is the moral rectitude which it expresses, the immediate flight which it

[1] Homes of the New World, vol. i. p. 254.
[2] My Study Windows, first printed in The Nation.
[3] F. B. Sanborn, in The Boston Commonwealth of Dec. 10, 1864.

makes to the listener's spirit, like an unseen arrow cleaving the white of the target."

His peculiarities on the platform have been well described by another of his admirers, who writes of him at the very zenith of his power as a lecturer: —

"The slight depression at the corners of the mouth, with a touch of sternness; the one arm extended from his side farther and farther as he becomes more animated by his theme; the two or three fingers of the other hand pressed to his palm as if holding tightly some reservation, — all these, and other undefinable characteristics that are photographed on the mind of one who has attentively listened to Emerson, are admirably reproduced in the picture of one of his friends and admirers. But there are some traits which are but faintly, if at all, suggested in the picture referred to, that have been developed in the years that intervened, or which perhaps could not have been even hinted on canvas. In his more recent life, Emerson's American hearers have recognized a less literary style and tone, and a stronger desire to have his views adopted. His paradoxes are stated with more determination. He oftener turns aside from the constructive and affirmative method natural to him to strike some false or sordid standard raised on his path; and one now sometimes sees his lip quiver, his eyes flash, and even a certain wrath expressed in the dilation of his nostril." [1]

Moses Coit Tyler has written with enthusiasm of Emerson as a teacher of eloquence, and claims that both with his voice and his pen his influence has been very great in this direction. He has done a great service in teaching us how to speak English, and how to write strongly and to the point.

"In his own unique way, Tyler says, he is really a marvelous speaker. Let him the fit audience find, though few, and he will illustrate what it is to speak golden words in that natural style of perfect sincerity, tenderness, and thoughtfulness by which every syllable is conducted straight home to the faculty it was meant for. For the enunciation of his own sentences we call him simply a perfect speaker. The manner fits the matter as if cut out for it from eternity. We would not alter it in one particular. Even those qualities which some call faults in his speaking, seem to us merits, — the hesitation, the awkwardness, the peculiar prim

[1] M. D. Conway, in Fraser's Magazine for May, 1869. The picture mentioned was painted while Mr. Emerson was in England in 1848, by David Scott. Some years ago it was sent over to this country for sale. It was bought in Concord, and presented to the Public Library, in the reading-room of which it now hangs.

intonation; they endear him to us all the more, as tokens of the absorption and homespun simplicity of the speaker."[1]

Emerson's inspiring qualities have already been mentioned, and they have been a marked characteristic of his most impressive lectures. In his *Concord Days*, Alcott has admirably described his attitude as that of one repeating words which descend to him from a higher atmosphere.

"See our Ion standing there, his audience, his manuscript, before him, himself also an auditor, as he reads, of the Genius sitting behind him, and to whom he defers, eagerly catching the words, — the words, — as if the accents were first reaching his ears, too, and entrancing alike oracle and auditor. We admire the stately sense, the splendor of diction, and are charmed as we listen. Even his hesitancy between the delivery of his periods, his perilous passages from paragraph to paragraph of manuscript, we have almost learned to like."

This characteristic of extemporaneousness has been a marked one, even in the delivery of his addresses which were read word for word. His seeming attempt to catch fit words to express his thought has given a singular charm to his manner. In his earlier years he tried speaking without a manuscript; but he found he could not do it well, and afterwards attempted it but seldom. His most casual addresses have usually been carefully prepared. That on Lincoln, apparently written with the greatest care, so just and discriminating is it, was prepared between ten o'clock and one of the night before its delivery. He has been too exacting of himself to go before an audience with any other than his best thought, carefully wrought into the best form he could give it. He once read a poem before the Phi Beta Kappa Society on Washington, and suddenly sat down in the midst of it. A friend afterwards inquired the cause, and was told the poem was not what he thought it was. As he read, he became dissatisfied with it, and could not go on. It has been this demand for perfection of expression which has made him so rigidly exacting with his essays, and caused him to

[1] Mr. Emerson as a Teacher of Eloquence, in the Independent.

write them over again and again. Not only has he been patient in his literary elaboration, but he has been mindful of the character of his audiences, and has sought to give each that which it could best assimilate. Though anxious to reach the needs of those to whom he spoke, he has been even more desirous of giving his hearers only that which was worth their attention. He has insisted he could afford to give his hearers only the very best of which he was capable, and that he ought to give them as much as possible in each lecture. This has been another reason for his habit of rigid condensation.

Emerson has always continued a preacher. He has never lectured to amuse, or to interest, or for money alone. Nor has he lectured simply to instruct, but to improve, inspire, and reform. His aim has always been that of the preacher, differing only in manner of treatment and in range of matter. He has been a preacher of religion, not of any outward form of it, but especially of religion as expressed in the garb of the purest morality. A preacher without a pulpit, he surely has been; but all the more influence has he wielded, because perfectly free to obey his own conscience and to speak what has seemed to him the truth. His preaching has consequently been direct, unsparing in its denunciations of evil, and pungent with a strong sense of the follies of modern society. His subjects have nearly always had the strongest moral bearing, and his treatment of them expresses the purpose to purify and elevate the standards of conduct. His marked influence as a lecturer, the secret of his power over so many minds, is to be found in the ethical and prophetic nature of his utterances. He has been more than a lecturer, preacher, or critic; he has been an inspirer, a seer, a moral illuminator.

He has never been a popular lecturer, but he has steadily gained the increasing interest of the cultured and intelligent. Lowell says he "always draws," and it is from this class. "A lecturer now for something like a third of a century, one of the pioneers of the lecturing system, the charm of his voice, his manner, and his matter has never lost its power over his earlier hearers, and continually winds new ones in its enchanting meshes." Alcott says that "such is the charm of his manner, that wherever he appears, the cultivated class will delight in his utterances." It is the cultivated who will best appreciate his lectures, those who have read and thought much. Many amusing anecdotes have been told of the people who have gone to hear him, drawn thither by his reputation. A well-known literary lady once watched with great amusement one of these persons. It was a lady from the fashionable circles, who supposed it to be quite proper and desirable to hear Emerson, the famous lecturer. Her face was a study, as she listened with surprise, then with blank amazement, and as she finally gave up all attempt to comprehend the lecture. Emerson recognizes the fact. that many people do not enjoy his lectures. Some years ago, when invited to Ann Arbor, he inquired, "Are there any people there who have thoughts?"

In conversation Emerson is somewhat reticent, not always expressing himself with freedom and fullness. He hesitates for words, and seems to find it difficult to secure the precise expression he desires. He speaks on the lecture-platform much as he converses. Those who have ascribed to him an artificial and studied manner as a lecturer, are probably not aware of how perfectly natural to the man are all his movements and words. Indeed, his oddity of expression is not, as has so often been said, cultivated, but the natural manner of the man. He talks as he writes. In his conversation there is the same antithesis and abrupt transition to be found as in his books. He does not think continuously; he does not in conversation follow a subject through, but hesitates, skips intervening ideas, is unable, apparently, to hold his mind to all the links of thought. It is not natural to him to do so. He does not think logically, but intuitively, sees and seizes at a glance, in bold generalizations, but is unable to follow and arrange the intervening steps from premise to conclusion His conversational powers, however, have been great; and his conversation is rapt, fascinating, and attractive. In describing a visit to Emerson,[1] as a young man, Conway has given an account of it. Emerson took him to Walden Pond, where they rowed, bathed, and talked.

"Having bathed, we sat down on the shore; and then Walden and her beautiful woods began to utter their pæans through his lips. Emerson's conversation was different from that of any person I have ever met with, and unequalled by that of any one, unless it be that of Thomas Carlyle. Of course there is no comparison of the two possible, but the contrasts between them are very striking and significant. In speaking of that which he conceives to be ignorant error, Mr. Carlyle is vehement; and when he suspects an admixture of falsehood and hypocrisy, his tone is that of rage; and although his indignation is noble and the utterances always thrilling, yet when one recurs to the little man or thing at which they are often leveled, it seems to be like the bombardment of a sparrow's nest with shot and shell. On such Emerson merely darts a spare beam of his wit, beneath which a lie is sure to shrivel; but if he breaks any one on his wheel, it must be some one who has been admitted at the banquet of the gods, and violated their laws. Every one who has witnessed the imperial dignity, or felt the weight of authentic knowledge, which characterize Mr. Carlyle's conversation, to such an extent that even his light utterances seem to stand out like the pillars of Hercules, must also have felt the earth tremble before the thunders and lightnings of his wrath; but with Emerson, though the same falsehood is fatally smitten, it is by the invisible, inaudible sun-stroke, which has left the sky as bright and blue as before. For the rest, and when abstract truths and principles are discussed, whilst Carlyle astonishes us by the range of his sifted knowledge, he does not convey an equal impression of having originally thought out the various problems in other departments than those which are plainly his own; but there is scarcely a realm of science or art in which Emerson could not be to some extent the instructor of the Academies. Agassiz, as I have heard him say, prefers his conversation on scientific questions to that of any other. I remember him on that day at Walden as Bunyan's Pilgrim might have remembered the Interpreter. The growths around, the arrow-head, and the orchis, were intimations of that mystic unity in nature, which is the fountain of poetry to him; either of these, or of many others of the remarkably rich fauna of that region, excited emotions much more solemn than the æsthetic in him. He fully felt that if we only knew how to look around, we would not have need to look above."

[1] Fraser's Magazine for August, 1874.

He is one of the best of listeners, whoever may be speaking, seeming to drink in all that is said, and giving the approval of his gracious smile to whatever attracts his attention. He is even more ready to listen than to speak. What he says is to the point, clearly stated, and in a serious, earnest tone; but his conversation is not brilliant in those ways which gave to Margaret Fuller's marvelous conversational powers a place of their own. It is not his to fascinate and attract by the ceaseless monologue of a versatile talker; for he would make conversation an act of friendship, and finds its charm broken by the presence of more than two. Yet he always speaks wisely, and with a charm and interest all his own. He does not talk easily or much, and needs the stimulus of a sympathetic and vigorous mind to draw out his best treasures of thought. In the midst of a company of bright minds he is not exuberant, never bubbles over; but what he says is marked by a keen wit and a full wisdom, rich, appropriate, and remarkable. His conversation, when his mind is stimulated by a great theme and a sympathetic friend, is inspiring even beyond his lectures; and then he pours forth his thought in the purest strain of noble words. In this way, his influence over his friends has been very great; and to many a mind his conversation has been an inspiration. "I enjoyed Emerson's conversation, says Miss Bremer, which flowed as calmly and easily as a deep and placid river. It was animating to me, both when I agreed, and when I dissented; there is always a something important in what he says; and he listens well, and comprehends and replies well also." Animating and rich and suggestive his conversation surely has been, and the source, doubtless, of much of his subtle influence over those minds which have come nearest to his own.

What an influence his lectures have been! Great teachers have in all ages gathered crowds of students about them. Great preachers have held sway over the lives of admiring multitudes. In our own time some of the best thinkers and writers have consented to address the people on their favorite themes. Reformers have devoted their lives to the spoken advocacy of some great reform. Popular oratory has developed the professional lecturer, who amuses and interests. Political eloquence has ever had its great names, its fascinating orators and debaters. The place of Emerson, however, is unique. He has not been a clergyman, professor, popular lecturer, or a statesman. He has not been a Socrates, Abelard, Savonarola, Whitefield, Webster, or a Phillips. He has not spoken, either from the vantage-ground of a pulpit, professor's chair, or senate chamber; yet how great has been his influence, how magnetic his power, how commanding his position, and how likely to be enduring! No pulpit has cramped him, no professor's chair has narrowed his thought, no party has stultified his influence. He has been a teacher of the people, an inspirer of students, a friend of every great cause. There are few other examples of a man giving his life to teaching his countrymen the highest lessons of religion, culture, and morals, untrammeled by party, sect, or place. He has created a new vocation, opened a new road for the moralist and preacher, hinted at new possibilities of reform, suggested that oratory can be used for a larger purpose. His career as a lecturer may be regarded as one of the most remarkable chapters in literary history, and his devotion to this self-chosen and self-created vocation has been as singular as it has been inspiring. It is as yet impossible rightly to estimate the importance of his influence, or to see how subtle and intrinsic has been the effect of his lectures. The future of religion, morals, and literature in the Republic, alone can rightly decide how important his word, and how penetrating his thought! What he has already accomplished, however, is guaranty of what will follow.

XIX.

PLACE AMONG THINKERS.

EMERSON belongs in the succession of the Idealists. That company he loves wherever its members are found, whether among Buddhists or Christian mystics, whether Transcendentalist or Sufi, whether Saadi, Boehme, Fichte, or Carlyle. These are the writers he studies, these the men he quotes, these the thinkers who come nearest his own thought. He is in the succession of minds who have followed in the wake of Plato, who is regarded by him as the world's greatest thinker. More directly still, Emerson is in that succession of thinkers represented by Plotinus, Eckhart, and Schelling, who have interpreted idealism in the form of mysticism.

The person who lays a stress on the worth of ideas, who regards the mind as existing before the body, and as giving form to it, is an idealist. Idealism looks upon the world of ideas or of mind as original and causative; it beholds the world of matter as proceeding from mind and as shaped by it. Spirit creates, it says; mind is primal. Matter is but a garment of spirit, the material world is phenomenal. As a true idealist, Emerson said, "Mind is the only reality, of which men and all other natures are better or worse reflectors."[1] "Our soul," says Bartol, Emerson's friend and an enthusiastic believer in idealism, "is older than our organism. It precedes its clothing. It is the cause, not the consequence." Idealism says there is a Universal Spirit, of which nature and man are alike manifestations, — a Spirit which is not only the original, but the immanent and sustaining cause of all things. Man is a spark from the Universal Spirit, a torch lighted at

[1] Lecture on Transcendentalism, Miscellanies, p. 323.

this altar, and manifests in miniature all the characteristics of his original. Nature proceeds from the same source, and embodies on a lower plane the thoughts of God; its laws are his ideas. All that nature contains was first in God as types, ideas, thoughts; and its sole purpose is to serve as an outward expression of these. Idealism asserts the unity and perfect correspondence of thought and being or of ideas and things, that the material world is the image or symbol of the ideal or spiritual world. Emerson states this doctrine in saying that "every sensible object subsists not for itself, nor finally to a material end, but as a picture-language to tell another story, of beings and duties."

Strictly speaking, Emerson is not a philosopher. Several philosophic problems have deeply interested him, and he has found for them a solution. His writings constantly touch upon these problems, while these solutions of them are the occasion for many of his best essays and poems. Yet he does not see life and its questions from the purely philosophic outlook, and he is not a reasoner or a dialectician. He trusts to intuition more than to reason, is in sympathy with the moral and theosophic rather than with the metaphysical writers. He prefers Boehme, Schelling, and Coleridge to Descartes, Kant, and Hegel. He is more a seer than a thinker, less a philosopher than a poet. With speculative philosophy, in the strict sense of the word, he has had nothing to do, has probably never made himself familiar with it, and has had little interest in its methods. Its great teachers, with the exception of Plato, he has not studied.

"His intellect is intuitive, says Whipple, contemplative, but not reflective. It contains no considerable portion of the element which is essential to the philosopher. His ideas proceed from the light of genius and from wise observation of Nature; they come in flashes of inspiration and ecstasy; his pure gold is found in places near the surface, not brought out laboriously from the depths of the mine in the bowels of the earth. He has no taste for the apparently arid abstractions of philosophy. His mind is not organized for the comprehension of its sharp distinctions. Its acute reasonings present no charm to his fancy, and its lucid deductions are to him as destitute of fruit as an empty nest of boxes. In the sphere of pure reflection he has shown neither originality nor depth. He has thrown no light on the great topics of speculation. He has never fairly grappled with the metaphysical problems which have called forth the noblest efforts of the mind in every age, and which, not yet reduced to positive science, have not ceased to enlist the clearest and strongest intellects in the work of their solution. On all questions of this kind the writings of Emerson are wholly unsatisfactory. He looks at them only in the light of the imagination. He frequently offers brave hints, pregnant suggestions, cheering encouragements, but no exposition of abstract truth has ever fallen from his keen pen."[1]

With a few qualifications this opinion may be accepted as substantially correct. Emerson belongs to that class of literary geniuses, such as Rousseau, Herder, Lessing, and Coleridge, who are the intellectual awakeners and stimulators of their age; not the thinkers of a generation, but its inspirers. They are moved by feeling, imagination, and intuition; but they open the way to new possibilities of life, action, and thought. Each of these men has produced a great impression on the succeeding generations, which is not at all to be measured by his clearness of thought or by the permanent character of his writings. These men have been the re-constructors of the modern world, the re-builders of life, art, literature, and religion. Emerson belongs to that company of illuminated souls who have done for the modern world what the sages, prophets, and seers did for the ancient world. The revival of Greek literature, science, philosophy, the French Revolution, Voltaire, destroyed the world of the Middle Ages, and left men amidst the ruins in doubt and darkness. From amid the ruins thus produced, these men have been the creators of the modern world, in which man, nature, and progress are the words which represent its leading characteristics.

Emerson is an idealist of the intuitional school; but as he has not been a system-builder, so he has ranged widely for the materials of his thought, finds everywhere aids to the elaboration of his ideas. Emile

[1] The Independent, 1867.

Montégut says he has the traits of the modern sage, — absence of the dogmatic spirit, and a tendency to criticism of principles. The sage follows his own nature, trusts to spontaneity.

"Emerson belongs to this class of philosophers, says Montégut. He has all the qualities of the sage, — originality, spontaneity, sagacious observation, delicate analysis, criticism, absence of dogmatism. He collects all the materials of a philosophy, without reducing it to a system; he thinks a little at random, and often meditates without finding definite limits at which this meditation ceases. His books are very remarkable, not only for the philosophy which they contain, but also for the criticism of our times. He is full of justice towards the doctrines and the society he criticises; he finds that the conservatives have legitimate principles; he thinks that the transcendentalists are probably right; he does not look with scorn upon our socialistic doctrines. He searches for his authorities through the entire history of philosophy; and thus, after having listened to all the modern doctrines with complaisance and patience, he breaks silence to give us maxims that might have issued now from the school of the Portico, and now from the gardens of the Academy. . . . All the names of ancient and modern philosophers are cited together, as if they expressed the same opinion... Skeptics and mystics, rationalists and pantheists, are side by side. Schelling, Oken, Spinoza, Plato, Kant, Swedenborg, Coleridge, meet on the same page. In this country of democracy, all thinkers seem brothers; distance effaces the differences, and blends them all into the same light. Emerson sees the works of our philosophers marked simply with the seal of truth and human genius, and not bearing the stamp of the *genius loci*."[1]

It is this remarkable capacity for drinking from many fountains, culling his sweets from every variety of flower, which justifies Noah Porter in calling him "the wide-minded Emerson."[2] It is this same characteristic which has led to his being called a philosopher, poet, seer, critic, moral diagnoser, literary creator, by different persons. He has been compared with Carlyle, Goethe, Herder, Rousseau, Spinoza, Marcus Aurelius; and yet how different is he from each and all! He writes now like a Puritan moralist, or a Montaigne, or an Epictetus; but anon how like he is to Schelling,

[1] An American Thinker and Poet, Revue des Deux Mondes, Aug. 1, 1847.

[2] Books and Reading, p. 70.

Boehme, or Plotinus! On one page he is a grim believer in fate and nature; the next shows how strong his faith in divine grace, that we are nothing but by the will of God; and only a page or two beyond, he asserts the absolute spontaneity of the mystic; before the essay ends, he is a sober moralist teaching the plainest lessons of duty. That he seizes something of truth from all these many and antagonistic sources is not the most striking characteristic of his mind, but that he blends them into a united and consistent whole. He does this by the aid of insight, not by reason. He does not cull at random the ingredients of his essays; intuition discovers relations and a unity where reason halts and the dialectical method sees only antagonism.

Though Emerson has ranged somewhat widely for the materials of his thought, yet his philosophic affinity has been with a special and a very limited school of thinkers. His manner of thinking was early and very deeply affected by Plato. That great thinker believed in a supersensible world, where all things are in the form of ideas. The material world is but a crude image or reflection of this spiritual world. Man once dwelt in the supersensible world, but his desires brought him into the world of sense. His reason is even yet a direct organ of knowledge of the supersensible, and by its aid he can know its truths with absolute certainty. Mind precedes the body; while the soul is an active, creative principle. Plato dwells much on the powers and eternity of the soul, and from him Emerson learned his own soul-faith. From him, also, Emerson caught his optimism, his trust in the good, and his conviction that evil is but a shadow. Plato strongly insists on the necessity of a moral interpretation of the universe, and he makes perfect truth and perfect virtue to be synonymous. Vice is ignorance, he says, and goodness is a true source of knowledge. In his "new readings" of Plato, in *Representative Men*, in enumerating the several doctrines taught by him, Emerson gives clear indication whence many of his own leading ideas came. He mentions the law of contraries; man as a microcosm, or that each thing reflects all other things; compensation; "the laws below are sisters of the laws above;" "the coincidence of science and virtue;" the supersensible is under the domain of law; "the self-evolving power of spirit;" the scale of the mind, or that life ranges in stages one above the other, each reflecting the one above it; and that man has come up from the lower orders of life in the self-evolving ascent of spirit. All these theories have a prominent place in Emerson's essays, and they may be said to form the substantial basis and framework of his speculations. He probably comes nearer to accepting the whole of Plato's philosophy than that of any other thinker.

As has been the case with nearly every great teacher, Plato has been a fruitful fountain of speculation to later thinkers; and various schools have branched off from him. His most affirmative and his religious ideas gave rise to a school which has had its representatives in every age since his time. Its greatest name in the ancient world was Plotinus, who was also early and earnestly studied by Emerson. In the middle of the third century after Christ, Plotinus took up Plato's theory of the co-eternity of the soul with its ideas, and of the sameness of their substance and origin, and interpreted it as teaching the identity of nature and soul, things and reason. Many of the followers of Plato regarded nature and reason as being distinct; but Plotinus identified them, and taught they were only forms of the same eternal Absolute. Plotinus and the school he formed, known as the Neo-Platonists, were doubtless affected by Pythagoras, Philo, the philosophy of Persia, and perhaps even that of India; but they regarded themselves as legitimate interpreters of the great master. While Plato taught that there were many distinct ideas, that of the Good being the highest, Plotinus elevated the Good or the One above the world of ideas. He regarded the material universe and the universe of ideas as alike emanations from the One. From the One emanates the world of ideas, from ideas the soul, while from the soul emanates the sensible world. This theory re-appears frequently in modern times, as the successive spheres of Swedenborg, the *potences* of Schelling, and it is a favorite teaching of Emerson's. Plotinus taught that man puts forth the world out of himself, because of his lust for the sensible; yet as man subdues the senses he returns back towards God. The chief means to this return is intuition, or ecstasy, by which man rises above the sensible world into a direct knowing and seeing of the supersensible and its truth. Around Plotinus, and his predecessor, Ammonius Saccas, there grew up a distinct school of thought, teaching the philosophic doctrine of the identity of subject and object, mind and matter, and making intuition the method of knowing. One of his disciples was Porphyry, who distinctly taught that matter emanates from the supersensible or from the soul. Amelius departed so far from Plotinus as to teach the unity of all souls in the world-soul, a favorite doctrine of Emerson's. A Christian teacher, Synesius, at the middle of the fifth century made this philosophy the basis of his Christianity. Contemporary with him was Proclus, its last great pagan representative. Not long after, it appeared in a remarkable defense of Christianity by an anonymous writer, known as the Pseudo-Dionysius, or Areopagite. In Emerson's essay on Intellect, there is to be found a striking proof of his great indebtedness to the Platonic school. Its leading ideas are those of the Neo-Platonists, as that the intellect is impersonal, that we are nothing of ourselves, that all thinking is a pious reception of truth from above, that one person knows as much as another, that silence is necessary for the incoming of God's grace, that entire self-reliance belongs to the intellect as a representative of the Over-soul. The basis of this teaching is that of the unity of all souls in the world-soul, the dependence of man for real knowledge upon intuition, and that intuition is a positive source of truth concerning the supersensible world. After eloquently defending these ideas, he points to this company of Greek thinkers for confirmation of their truthfulness; and he pays a glowing tribute to the value of their teaching. That he should in this lecture, in which he presents his own theory of knowing, devote its closing passage to an eloquent defense of the whole school of Platonic thinkers, affords remarkable confirmation of their influence over his thinking. His words are these:[1] —

> "I can not recite, even thus rudely, laws of the intellect, without remembering that lofty and sequestered class of men who have been its prophets and oracles, the high-priesthood of the pure reason, the *Trismegisti*, the expounders of the principles of thought from age to age. When, at long intervals, we turn over their abstruse pages, wonderful seems the calm and grand air of these few, these great spiritual lords, who have walked in the world, — these of the old religion, — dwelling in a worship which makes the sanctities of Christianity look *parvenues* and popular; for 'persuasion is in soul, but necessity is in intellect.' This band of grandees, Hermes, Heraclitus, Empedocles, Plato, Plotinus, Olympiodorus, Proclus, Synesius, and the rest, have somewhat so vast in their logic, so primary in their thinking, that it seems antecedent to all the ordinary distinctions of rhetoric and literature, and to be at once poetry and music and dancing and astronomy and mathematics. The truth and grandeur of their thought is proved by its scope and applicability, for it commands the entire schedule and inventory of things for its illustration."

After Proclus, Neo-Platonism passed over to Christianity, and it became the basis of Augustine's theology. At the end of the fifth century it was taught by Boethius, and at the middle of the ninth it was taken up by John Scotus Erigena. Its ideas frequently appeared down to the time of the Schoolmen, when they affected Albertus Magnus, Duns Scotus, and Thomas Aquinas. At this period they re-appeared in Eckhart in a new and distinct form, and have finally been adopted by a remarkable school of modern thinkers. Eckhart taught at the beginning of the fourteenth century, held high offices in the church, was a famous preacher, but was brought before the Inquisition and had twenty-eight of his doctrines condemned. He based his theology on Neo-Platonism, especially on the teachings of the Pseudo-Dionysius, and was influenced by Augustine, Albertus Magnus, and Thomas Aquinas.

[1] Essays, first series, p. 313.

Though Emerson has not studied Eckhart, many of his favorite ideas will be found presented by that thinker. With Eckhart, perhaps even before with Erigena, the Neo-Platonic doctrine of *emanation* was abandoned for that of *immanence;* and God is regarded as the indwelling life of the world. "The essence of all creatures, he says, is eternally a divine life in Deity." Out of God nothing can exist, the outward world is a symbol of his innermost essence, and evil is but a privation of the fullness of his nature. The soul pre-existed in God, shared in his nature, was not then individual, but free and unconditioned, and as immanent in him shared in the process of creation. The soul is an efflux from God; but as no longer fully sharing in his nature, it has become corrupt. In time it will return into the undeveloped Deity and be at one with him. Death to the individual self, surrender to God, is the condition of this return. Those who have attentively read Emerson will recognize the meaning of Eckhart, when he says there is something in the soul which is above the soul, a divine spark, an uncreated light. This is the unity of all souls in the Over-soul; and it is absolute and free from all names and forms, higher than knowledge, higher than love, and is satisfied only with the super-essential essence. In this perfect union of the soul with God, all that is creaturely, all that is individual, ceases to exist. Knowing, according to Eckhart, is a supernatural vision, the action of God in the soul. With Proclus, he holds that faith is a direct communion with God, and the means of all knowledge. As true knowing is an act of divine grace, God communicating himself to the soul, man must not search or reason or use any power of his own. He must remain quiet, passive, unemployed of outward things, that God may find him a fit receptacle for truth. To the man who has utterly abandoned self, Eckhart says, God communicates all his nature, essence, and life. In the very spirit and manner of Emerson he says the inner voice is the voice of God. To those who would find aid in some outward exercise of religion, he exclaims, "Why abide not in your own selves, and take hold on your own possession? Ye have all truth essentially within you!" He says the righteous man is in substance and in nature without distinction what God is, and that in the moments of intuition the soul is raised above individuality, and ceases to know its separateness from God.

The teachings of Eckhart spread widely throughout Germany. Similar theories were taught by many others, giving origin to a large school of mystics, and finally led to the Reformation. From the stand-point of intuition, of an inner revelation, they criticised the church, and regarded Christianity as a spiritual life separate from its doctrines and ritual. One of their favorite teachings was, that man is a microcosm. As all things are of the same nature and origin, as God dwells in all his fullness in the soul, the soul becomes an epitome of the universe. The doctrine of immanence was expanded by the theory of development through contraries, so that light and darkness, good and evil, clashing with each other, produce creation. All these ideas were taken up by Jacob Boehme, at the beginning of the seventeenth century, woven into a theory of correspondences, and given the form of a nature-philosophy. Hegel says he read much, especially the mystic, theosophic, and alchemistic writings, and in part, at least, Paracelsus, who taught the idea of man as a microcosm, and who first developed the theory that existence is a series of antitheses. William Law, the greatest of Boehme's English disciples, says that "whatsoever the great Hermes delivered in oracles, or Pythagoras spoke by authority, or Socrates debated, or Aristotle affirmed, whatever divine Plato prophesied, or Plotinus proved, — this, and all this, or a far higher and profounder philosophy, is contained in Boehme's writings." He regards the universe as a universal revelation of God, matter as dormant mind, and mind as self-conscious matter; and the inmost of man's nature is in the deepest sense one with the highest in God. He finds in man the measure of all things; so that when he would study nature, the best means to it are to be found in the soul. He sees in nature the same divine life, the same glory and manifestation of God, there is in the soul. As they so exactly correspond, it is enough to look into the soul, if we would know what nature is. He also teaches, that, as God dwells in the soul and the soul in God, passivity is the means to the perfection of this union, and that even now Paradise may be realized by the soul.[1] Boehme's truly noble disciple, William Law, says that "life in an angel and life in a vegetable has but one and the same form, one and the same ground in the whole scale of beings; and the reason is, because nature is nothing else but God's own outward manifestation of what he inwardly is and can do." He says the intuitive knowing of truth "depends upon thy right submission and obedience to the speaking of God in thy soul. Stop, then, all self-activity, listen not to the suggestions of thy own reason, run not in thy own will; but be retired, silent, passive, and humbly attentive to this light within thee."[2] With these general ideas of Boehme's system Emerson thoroughly agrees, but not at all with his more special doctrines. Holbeach justly says that in reading Emerson we might sometimes fancy we had Eckhart before us; and that "the identity of thought and language with the old-world Germans will strike every reader at once."[3]

In this philosophic development we come next to Schelling. In the second or third period of his thinking, he came under the influence of Boehme; and he was also affected by the Neo-Platonists, Eckhart, and some of the other mystics. It is not probable that Emerson was to any more than a limited extent directly affected by Schelling, but it is certain that much of what he has taught is to be found in the writings of this philosopher. Schelling teaches that nature and mind, subject and object, are one and identical in the Absolute, and that this identity is known by intellectual intuition. This is a fundamental conception

[1] Vaughan's Hours with the Mystics.
[2] Quoted in Overton's William Law, Nonjuror and Mystic.
[3] Contemporary Review, February, 1877.

of Emerson's philosophy, and in much else they exactly agree. The theory that man is a living synthesis or microcosm of the universe became the leading idea in Schelling's nature-philosophy, and it has touched modern thought on many sides. He took up, also, the theory of contraries, and regarded nature and spirit as the two great poles of the Absolute. This idea led him, and many others, to make constant use of the magnet as a symbol. Mind and matter, soul and nature, are related as the two poles of the magnet; they are merely the positive and negative manifestations of the Absolute. The idea of Plotinus, that there have been successive emanations, beginning with the One, each lower producing one still lower, was not literally revived by Schelling as it was by Swedenborg; but he held that there are successive grades of phenomenal existence, which he called potences. From the clod up to God there is a continuous ascension of life, and the lower is continually reaching forward that it may realize the higher.

In Schelling's theory of knowledge, a main doctrine is, "that our ideas so completely correspond with things, there is nothing in them which is not in our ideas." "There not only exists outside of us, he says, a world of things independent of us, but our representations agree with them in such a manner that there is nothing else in the things beyond what they present to us. The necessity which prevails in our objective representations is explained by saying that the things are unalterably determined; and by this determination of the things, our ideas are also indirectly determined. By this first and most original conviction, the first problem of philosophy is determined, namely, to explain how representations can absolutely agree with objects existing altogether independently of them." This he finds in the "absolute identity of being and seeming," or subject and object. On this point, he says, —

"How at once the objective world conforms itself to ideas in us, and ideas in us conform themselves to the objective world, it is impossible to conceive, unless there exists between the two worlds — the ideal and the real — a pre-established harmony. But this pre-established harmony itself is not conceivable, unless the activity, whereby the objective world is produced, is originally identical with that which displays itself in volition, and *vice versa*."

As in the case of his predecessors, Schelling not only adopts the theory of identity, but with them also he makes intuition the means of perceiving this identity. "There dwells in us all, he says, a secret, wonderful faculty, by virtue of which we can withdraw from the mutations of time into our innermost disrobed selves, and there behold the eternal under the form of immutability; such vision is our innermost and peculiar experience, on which alone depends all that we know and believe of a supersensible world." These leading ideas of Schelling and his predecessors were accepted by Coleridge, especially the conception of reason as one, that the human is identical with the divine reason. Coleridge was a diligent reader of Schelling, but even more so of Tauler, Boehme, Law, and Fox. With these men he regarded all truth as a direct revelation to the soul. This revelation takes place through reason, which is an intuitive, supernatural factor in man, not personal to us, but the manifestation in consciousness of the universal reason. Reason is therefore a common factor in the human and the divine, by which they are essentially united and made one.

From Plotinus to Coleridge, there has been a continuous succession of thinkers, through Proclus, Eckhart, Boehme, and Schelling, who have maintained a peculiar philosophic doctrine, that of identity and intuition. Other thinkers have held both these theories, but not in the same religious, theosophic spirit which has marked this succession of speculators. These men have held to them in the spirit of mysticism; and though there have been other mystics, it has had here a peculiarity of its own. Emerson is the latest representative of this school of thought. Its philosophic spirit, its doctrines, its religious peculiarities, its moral qualities, may all be found in him. With no one of these men does he fully agree; and he has freely selected, rejected, and combined their teachings in a manner quite his own. The dark background of Being, of which Boehme and Schelling speculated, their peculiar theory of the trinity, which Hegel took from Eckhart as the basis of his philosophy, and many other speculations of these thinkers, Emerson has rejected. As a whole, his philosophy would be pronounced very different from that of any of his predecessors; and yet there can be no doubt he had these men for teachers, and that in a few leading, simple ideas he thoroughly agrees with them. In Plato and Plotinus the foundation of his speculations was laid; and with the aid of Boehme, Coleridge, Carlyle, the German and the English idealists, the edifice of his thought has been erected. The materials thus given have been used in a manner quite his own, with an originality marked and distinct. To them have been added, not only the results of his own vigorous thinking, but many of the commonly accepted theories of the idealists of his time. The theory of intuition was one that filled the German literature which Carlyle and others began to introduce at about the time Emerson was preparing for the pulpit. To that theory was added what naturally followed, the conception of genius as the true oracle of heaven. Goethe and his contemporaries made this a cardinal truth, as well as the notion of absolute individual liberty, another offshoot from the doctrine of intuition. Intimate love of nature, and communion with its divine life, was an extraordinary characteristic, both of Goethe and Wordsworth; and it came from the pantheistic mysticism of Schelling and Coleridge. While the earlier mystics taught Emerson the doctrine of self-renunciation and dependence on God, all the later Germans he read taught individuality and self-reliance. He combined the two ideas and made them one.

To the English Platonists of the Elizabethan era,

Emerson is also largely indebted. In his *English Traits* he has named these men, — More, Hooker, Bacon, Sidney, Lord Brooke, Herbert, Browne, Donne, Spenser, Chapman, Milton, Crashaw, Norris, Cudworth, Berkeley, Jeremy Taylor, — and says, "such richness of genius had not existed more than once before." Though he has not been to any great extent a student of Kant, Fichte, and Hegel, yet he has been largely in sympathy with the general tendencies of thought represented by Lessing, Herder, and Goethe. Traces of their influence frequently appear on his pages. When Herder proclaims the superiority of nature to the results of history, and of intuition over reason, he has the fullest sympathy of Emerson. These Germans made instinctive, intuitive man the ideal man; and they held that all the faculties must work together, as a whole, in securing truth. "Every thing that man undertakes to produce, said Goethe, whether by action, word, or in whatsoever way, ought to spring from the union of all his faculties. All that is isolated is condemnable." They taught the immanence of nature in the human, the doctrines of identity and intuition, as undoubted truths. They saw God in nature, and regarded it, with Goethe, as his living garment. The genius they looked upon as the messenger of truth, the real means of human progress. Herder said that "true morality is religion under whatever form it may show itself," and he rejected all theological discussion as useless. Kant said they are always in the service of God whose actions are moral, and that it is absolutely impossible to serve God otherwise.[1] Carlyle took up this thought, making the Moral Sense the center of man's life, and the link which connects him with God. He refused any attempt to explain mind, but looked to nature as its representative and symbol. He saw life and law everywhere present, and said all things make on us an identical impression when rightly seen. This is true because of the absolute unity of things, because there is but One Mind. He made self-renunciation his first moral doctrine, and action ac-

[1] Hillebrand's German Thought.

cording to God's laws the second. He saw in man the epitome of nature; and he strenuously maintained the theory of the unity of the mind, that all its powers must work in common. He saw in the believing man the true worker, and he measured the intellect by the moral life.[1] The universe is to him "but one vast symbol of God," while "through every star, through every grass-blade, and most through every living soul, the glory of a present God beams." All religions, he asserts, are but symbols and outward expressions of infinite truths within. "The one end, essence, and use of all religion, past, present, and to come, is this only; to keep the moral conscience, or inner light, of ours alive and shining." Hence, historic religions lost their old value to him, as they did to Lessing; and this spirit was communicated to Emerson. Indeed, with this whole movement, represented by all the great Germans from Lessing to Novalis, and by Coleridge, Wordsworth, and Carlyle in England, Emerson has been in sympathy. Those ideas which became to them the universal truths lying at the basis of all thinking, he has accepted in the same spirit.

His readings of the Oriental mystics, especially those of Persia and India, have had their effect on Emerson's writings. He has found there a wide affinity with his own speculations, and a presentation of all his leading ideas. The intensity with which these ideas are there presented, the imaginative power of these writings, and the absoluteness of the soul-trust which they indicate, has attracted and deeply interested him.

The teachings of his predecessors Emerson has accepted rather as the basis for a social and moral reformation of life than as a philosophy. The philosophy has been incidental, merely a ground-work of faith and conviction, not a speculative system. He has presented a theosophy rather than a philosophy in his writings, a spiritual rather than an intellectual theory of the universe. For this reason, doubtless, his real place in the stream of philosophic speculation has so often been mistaken. Yet that place is a clearly defined one; and a

[1] Crozier's Religion of the Future.

comparison of his theories with those of the men already named, will show how intimate his relations with them. He has given expression to his philosophic attitude by saying it was his desire to put away all discussions and disputes for a discovery of moral laws. In a conversation with Brownson, he once said, "I find myself in the midst of a truth which I do not understand. I do not find that any one understands it. I only wish to make a clean transcript of my own mind." That is, he saw no hope of arriving at the truth, by any methods of reasoning, but would take instead that transcript of truth given to the mind by intuition. His attitude towards all dialectical and scientific methods he well expressed when he said, "A person seeking truth is like a man going out in a dark night with a lantern in search of something." So poor does he find the lantern of the understanding in comparison with the sun of intuition! It is idle, useless, to seek truth, to go in search for it; as it is a revelation, an act of God's grace in the soul. The outward world, helpful as it is, can teach us nothing but through its affinity to what is given in us by the Infinite Reason; all the methods of understanding and induction are like a lantern in a dark night. Even in his study of nature, and in his use of the conclusions of science, he constantly indicates his affinity of thought to Boehme and Schelling. In his pages will not be found the science of either as science; but their method of looking at nature, their acceptance of it as an expression of the divine, and their theory of its exact correspondence to the moral and spiritual world, will be found everywhere through his writings.

Emerson is not only an idealist, but a mystic. Individual as his mysticism may be in many of its features, he is only to be understood when placed in the company of the great mystics of all ages, and his teachings compared with theirs. That he is something more than a mystic does not make this statement any the less true. He is not a skeptic or a rationalist, in the philosophic sense; and he has no real affinity with either of these schools of thought. His mysticism has broken away from all sectarian and historic limits, and accepted the ground of universal religion. It has planted itself deeply and strongly on an ethical basis, has rejected mere feeling, and has displayed great practical wisdom. As a result, his mysticism is more in sympathy with the tendencies of modern life than that of any of his predecessors. Yet the tendencies and sympathies of his mind are clearly shown by his interest in the occult, and in the significance he attaches to dreams.[1] As a genuine mystic, he dwells on the prophetic powers of the soul; and though he repudiates modern spiritualism, he maintains with continued emphasis his faith in the mind's supersensuous functions.

NOTE. — Essential aid to the comprehension of Emerson's writings will be found in Vaughan's Hours with the Mystics and Hunt's Essay on Pantheism. Though neither of these authors fully understands or appreciates his subject, yet each furnishes valuable aid to the general student of the history of opinions. The careful reader of these books will not longer doubt where Emerson belongs as a thinker. Ullmann's Reformers before the Reformation furnishes valuable aid to an understanding of the German mystics; while Professor Lasson, in Ueberweg's History of Philosophy, presents an able summary of the speculations of Eckhart and his successors. Overton's William Law, Nonjuror and Mystic, has some good chapters on mysticism, and a fair account of Boehme. Tulloch's work on The Cambridge Platonists, being the second volume of his Rational Theology and Christian Philosophy in England in the Seventeenth Century, will give a few hints of Emerson's debt to the Elizabethan thinkers. Hillebrand's Lectures on German Thought indicate to how large an extent many of Emerson's ideas were common property among the German writers of the time of Lessing and Goethe. Crozier's Religion of the Future gives the best statement yet made of Emerson's relations to Carlyle. Eucken's Fundamental Concepts of Modern Philosophic Thought traces the origin and development and present value of several of those ideas Emerson has made fundamental in his philosophy. Among other works consulted in the writing of this chapter, are the essays of Martineau and Shairp, Thompson's lectures on Plato, and the histories of philosophy by Bowen, Lewes, Maurice, Schwegler, Morell, Ueberweg, and Chalybäus.

[1] See essay on Demonology in North American Review for March, 1877.

XX.

UNIVERSAL SPIRIT.

ECKHART says that God "has the substance of all creatures in himself," that "he is a Being who has all being in himself," and that "all things are in God and all things are God." This is the fundamental postulate alike of transcendentalism and mysticism. Emerson accepts it by saying there is in all things a unity so supreme that the ultimate fact we reach, "on every topic, is the resolution of all into the ever-blessed One."[1] "Under all this running sea of circumstance, whose waters ebb and flow with perfect balance, lies the aboriginal abyss of real Being. Essence, or God, is not a relation, or a part, but the whole. Being is the vast affirmative, excluding negation, self-balanced, and swallowing up all relations, parts, and times within itself."[2]

This is his fundamental proposition, the existence of Being, or God, as the *substans*, life, or essence of all things. He makes Being an absolute unity, outside of which nothing whatever exists. God is All in all. All things proceed from this center, and can never depart from their relations to it. All things are manifestations or revelations of God; all help to show forth his nature. "God is the all-fair," he says. He is more than that; "Truth, goodness, and beauty are but different faces of the same All."[3] "God is, and all things are but shadows of him."[4]

God is the life in all things, not only, but in each thing he is present with all his attributes; "so that all the laws of nature may be read in each fact." "The

[1] Essays, first series, p. 61.
[2] Ibid., p. 108.
[3] Miscellanies, p. 22.
[4] Essays, first series, p. 281.

true doctrine of omnipresence is, that God re-appears with all his parts in every moss and cobweb. The value of the universe contrives to throw itself into every point."[1] When we try to define God, however, we can not; he is beyond all definition, because he includes all definitions. "Of that ineffable essence which we call Spirit, says Emerson, he that thinks most will say least."[2]

> "We can foresee God in the coarse, and, as it were, distant phenomena of matter; but when we try to define and describe himself, both language and thought desert us, and we are as helpless as fools and savages. That essence refuses to be recorded in propositions; but when man has worshiped him intellectually, the noblest ministry of nature is to stand as the apparition of God. It is the organ through which the universal spirit speaks to the individual, and strives to lead back the individual to it."[3]

In Wood-notes he has written these words concerning the pervasive and immanent character of the Universal Spirit: —

> "Thou meetest him by centuries,
> And lo! he passes like the breeze;
> Thou seek'st in globe and galaxy,
> He hides in pure transparency;
> Thou askest in fountains and in fires,
> He is the essence that inquires.
> He is the axis of the star;
> He is the sparkle of the spar;
> He is the heart of every creature;
> He is the meaning of each feature;
> And his mind is the sky,
> Than all it holds more deep, more high."

Emerson teaches that God is the substance of the universe, the material out of which all things are formed, and the life which animates all which exists. Not only the substance of the universe, so that all things whatsoever partake of his nature and being, but also the fountain in man, that we call the soul. He says with Fichte, "that all existence in time has its root in a higher existence above time; that, strictly speaking, there is but

[1] Ibid., p. 91. [2] Miscellanies, p. 59. [3] Ibid., p. 60.

one life, one animating power, one living reason; and that the greatest of errors, and the true ground of all error, is the delusion of the individual that he can exist, live, think, and act of himself. The first of thought and being, the starting-point and substance, at once the subject and object of speculation, is the one, true, and absolutely self-existent Being, — the God whom all hearts seek. And that each individual moment of man's life on earth is contained within the development of the one original divine life; that whatever meets the view, and seems beyond that one life, is not beyond it, but within it; that to see things truly, means to see them only in and through the one original life; that the light and life of religion, light and life of God, is the only true light and life, the only science and the only virtue,"[1] — all this is as true to Emerson as to Fichte.

Though Spirit refuses to be recorded in propositions, yet it is not merely as a universal essence that we are to regard it. "Self-existence is the attribute of the Supreme Cause,"[2] and by that Emerson means much the same that other idealists express by the word *personality*. Upon those who are unnecessarily afraid of defining God, he urges a disregard of a seeming consistency with their own words, and that they permit the soul to speak out its own deep sentiments of affection and trust. "In your metaphysics you have denied personality to the Deity; yet when the devout motions of the soul come, yield to them heart and life, though they should clothe God with shape and color."[3] The theory is nothing, but it is every thing to yield the soul supremely to the love of God. We are to accept God as he appears in that moment of our union with him, nothing questioning, nothing doubting. As he appears then a person, a spirit communing with spirit, so we are to accept him.

To limit Emerson's idea of the Infinite Spirit to what he has said directly about God, would be to do him great injustice. His idea of God is presupposed in his idea

[1] Flint's Philosophy of History, vol. i. p. 414.
[2] Essays, first series, p. 61. [3] Ibid., p 50.

of the soul, and must be studied in conjunction with it. The conception he entertains of the soul necessitates belief in God as a supreme intelligent Existence. A thinking soul can not hold communion with an unthinking essence. A self-reliant soul can not be merged in an ocean of being, and it can find its power only in perfect harmony with a self-reliant personality like its own. Emerson's attitude is not that of the theologian and philosopher, but that of the poet, the seer, and the worshiper. God is so near to his soul, and so dear to his thought, he is so absorbed in the joy of that blessed union, he forgets to ask any questions. Strangers study each other critically; but friends, bound heart to heart, forget all matters of clothing and complexion. He assumes God to exist, stops not to define, but pushes on to a realization of those relations in which man stands to him. He looks at every subject, studies every object, in the light of its relations to God; but to name God wherever he sees him would be an endless task. This constant naming of an inexhaustible idea and reality would only serve to lower it; but in refusing to name it, he all the more surely expresses its protean nature and its constant presence. His absorbing belief in the reality of God, and his acceptance of that belief as vitally necessary to the health of the mind, he has earnestly expressed in one of his more recent essays. His faith in the self-sufficingness of the laws of God, and his refusal to accept them as limited by any historical forms, are as stoutly as ever asserted in the same words.

"Unlovely, he says, nay, frightful, is the solitude of the soul which is without God in the world. To wander all day in the sunlight among the tribes of animals, unrelated to any thing better; to behold the horse, cow, and bird, and to foresee an equal and speedy end to him and them, — no; the bird, as it hurried by with its bold and perfect flight, would disclaim his sympathy, and declare him an outcast. To see men pursuing in faith their varied action, warmhearted, providing for their children, loving their friends, performing their promises, — what are they to this chill, houseless, fatherless, aimless Cain, the man who hears only the sound of his own footsteps in God's resplendent creation? To him, it is no creation; to him, these fair creatures are hapless specters; he knows not what to make of it; to him, heaven and earth have lost their beauty How gloomy is the day, and upon yonder shining pond, what melancholy light! I can not keep the sun in heaven, if you take away the purpose that animates him. The ball, indeed, is there; but his power to cheer, to illuminate the heart as well as the atmosphere, is gone for ever. It is a lamp-wick for meanest uses. The words, *great*, *venerable*, have lost their meaning; every thought loses all its depth, and has become mere surface.

"But religion has an object. It does not grow thin or robust with the health of the votary. The object of adoration remains for ever unhurt and identical. We are in transition from the worship of the fathers which enshrined the law in a private and personal history to a worship which recognizes the true eternity of the law, its presence to you and me, its equal energy in what is called brute-nature as in what is called sacred history. The next age will behold God in the ethical laws, — as mankind begins to see them in this age, self-equal, self-executing, instantaneous, and self-affirmed, needing no voucher, no prophet, and no miracle besides their own irresistibility, — and will regard natural history, private fortunes, and politics, not for themselves, as we have done, but as illustrations of those laws, of that beatitude and love. Nature is too thin a screen: the glory of the One breaks in everywhere."[1]

He accepts the truth there is in both theism and pantheism, recognizing alike the absolute unity and the endless diversity of the manifestation. The pantheism of the theologians and philosophers, however, never had an existence as an historical faith; and he has been too earnest a believer to accept any thing so shadowy and unreal. He has avoided alike the anthropomorphism of the theistic faiths; and the failure to recognize a transcendent unity, which has been the defect of the pantheistic theories. Theodore Parker long ago clearly defined Emerson's position, showing him not to have been at any time a pantheist, as that word is used by theologians.

"He has an absolute confidence in God. He has been foolishly accused of pantheism, which sinks God in nature; but no man is further from it. He never sinks God in man; he does not stop with the law, in matter or morals, but goes to the Law-giver; yet probably it would not be so easy for him to give his definition of God, as it would be for most graduates at Andover or Cambridge. With his confidence in God he looks things fairly in the face, and never dodges, never fears. Toil, sorrow, pain, these are things

[1] The Unitarian Review, January, 1880; essay on The Preacher.

which it is impious to fear. Boldly he faces every fact, never retreating behind an institution or a great man. In God his trust is complete; with the severest scrutiny he joins the highest reverence."[1]

Emerson ignores those sharp distinctions and definitions which would have saved him from the charge of pantheism. He really holds to "the sublime creed, that the world is not the product of manifold power, but of one will, of one mind; and that one mind is everywhere active, in each ray of the star, in each wavelet of the pool; and whatever opposes that will is everywhere balked and baffled, because things are made so, and not otherwise."[2] He will always doubtless be open to the charge of pantheism, because, though he maintains so persistently that the world is the product of one will and one mind, yet he so emphasizes the unity of nature and man with God as to seem to blot out all distinctions. He sometimes says that man becomes God in his moments of ecstatic intuition. Such phraseology is undoubtedly pantheistic; but it is poetical, not to be read literally. When it is read in the light of his clear judgment and sound common sense, and of his clear intellectual perceptions, it will be found susceptible of another interpretation. He is a theist of the school of Goethe, Carlyle, F. W. Newman, and Theodore Parker; a mystic who accepts devoutly the theism of intuition, and who finds God a living reality within his own soul.

If a pantheist is one who asserts the absolute unity of matter and mind, then Emerson is a pantheist. He rejects that sharp distinction between matter and mind, good and evil, which has sometimes been accepted as the characteristic of theism. Should this definition be maintained, Emerson could not by any possibility be called a theist. He holds to the doctrine of the one substance as strongly as Spinoza did. Does he also assert that there is but one thinker, one self-acting agent? If he does, then is he a pantheist. He certainly would seem to do so, for what else does he mean by his doc-

[1] Massachusetts Quarterly Review. [2] Miscellanies, p. 120

trine of the Over-soul? He regards the mind of man as a part of the Infinite Mind, but he asserts for man moral freedom. He also strongly declares that each mind is different from every other mind,[1] and he teaches the individuality of the soul in a very positive manner. In thus maintaining the freedom and uniqueness of the individual soul, he makes himself a theist.

[1] Essays, first series, pp. 40, 69.

XXI.

NATURE.

THE law of contraries, as expressed by Plato and his successors, was revived by Eckhart and Boehme; and it became an important element in the nature-philosophy of Schelling and Goethe. With Boehme,

"These contraries are his trade-winds, whereby he voyages to and fro, and traverses with such facility the whole system of things. He teaches that the Divine unity, in its manifestation, or self-realization, parts into two principles, variously called light and darkness, joy and sorrow, fire and light, wrath and love, good and evil. Without what is termed the darkness and the fire, there would be no love and light. Evil is necessary to manifest good. Not that every thing is created by God for evil. In every thing is both good and evil; the predominance decides its use and destiny."[1]

This idea occupied a prominent place in the speculations of Kant, Schelling, Goethe, and in all the German thought of their day.

"The scientific investigation of nature showed a particular bias during this period to the adoption of a duality of forces as dominant there. In mechanics, Kant had given a theory of the antithesis of attraction and repulsion; in chemistry, the phenomena of electricity, abstractly conceived as positive and negative, were assimilated to magnetism; in physiology, there was the antagonism of irritability and sensibility, etc. As against these dualities, Schelling passed forward to the unity of all opposites, of all dualities, not the abstract unity, but to the concrete ideality, the harmonious concert and co-operation of the whole heterogeneous variety. The world is the actuose unity of a positive and negative principle, and those two opposing forces, in conflict or coalition, lead to the idea of a world-organizing, world-systematizing principle, the soul of the universe."[2]

[1] Vaughan's Hours with the Mystics, vol. ii. p. 109.
[2] Schwegler's History of Philosophy, p. 290.

Schelling saw in mind and matter, simply the polar opposites of the Absolute, the Absolute being truly seen only at the indifference point of the two poles. The magnet became with him, as with Goethe and many others, the symbol of this unity of nature and soul in the Universal Spirit. In mind and matter, subject and object, is the same substance, the same life, the same identical power; but one is positive, the other negative. All things manifest this tendency; each thing has its positive and its negative manifestation. This is a universal law, the first law expressed by the Universal Spirit in its creative development.

This theory occupies an important place in Emerson's philosophy. Mind is also with him the positive, matter the negative, expression of the Universal Spirit, or the Absolute Substance; and this polarity is essential to its manifestation. He sees in mind and matter, subject and object, not unlike things, but the polar expressions of the same absolute reality. As an essential thing in itself nature has no existence, but it is the negative expression of Universal Mind. "Every thing in nature, says Emerson, is bipolar, or has a positive and negative pole. There is a male and female, a spirit and a fact, a north and a south. Spirit is the positive, the event is the negative. Will is the north, action the south, pole."[1] "Whilst the world is thus dual, he says, so is every one of its parts. The entire system of things gets represented in every particle. There is somewhat that resembles the ebb and flow of the sea, day and night, man and woman, in a single needle of the pine, in a kernel of corn, in each individual of every animal tribe."[2] This polarity appears as motion and rest,[3] so that nature is one stuff with two ends; or as nature and thought in perpetual tilt and balance.[4] In man it is expressed as a double consciousness, as a private and public nature whose interests are not the same.[5]

[1] Essays, second series, p. 98. [2] Essays, first series, pp. 86, 87.
[3] Essays, second series, pp. 175, 176. [4] Conduct of Life, p. 36.
[5] Ibid., p. 40.

As nature and thought are the magnetic poles of the Universal Mind, as both inhere in and are nothing apart from that Central Life they manifest, it follows they exactly correspond to each other. They reflect and interpret each the other. They are identical in nature, identical in their laws, identical in the impression they make, simply because each is the Universal Spirit in its positive or negative form. It is the same magnetism, but different only in appearing at the opposite ends of the magnet. This view of mind and matter leads to the doctrine of identity, which in one form or another is a cardinal one with all the idealists and mystics. Even so orthodox a mystic as William Law says, "Body and Spirit are not two separate, independent things, but are necessary to each other, and are only the inward and outward conditions of one and the same being."[1] The doctrine of identity Emerson expresses in these words: "A perfect parallelism exists between nature and the laws of thought."[2] This relation between matter and mind, he says, is not a fancied one, but stands in the will of God;[3] so that "the laws of the moral nature answer to those of matter as face to face in a glass."[4] "Intellect and morals appear only the material forces on a higher plane. The laws of material nature run up into the invisible world of the mind," and in those laws we find a key to the facts of human consciousness.[5] Identity of nature and man, matter and mind, object and subject, gives the basis and the means of knowledge. "Things are so strictly related, that from one object the parts and properties of any other may be predicted."[6] Man and nature are so much alike, that man can know nature by what it is in himself. "Man carries the world in his head, the whole astronomy and chemistry suspended in a thought. Because the history of nature is charactered in his brain, therefore is he the prophet and discoverer of her secrets."[7] Man

[1] Spirit of Love.
[2] Letters and Social Aims, p. 7.
[3] Ibid., pp. 8, 9.
[4] Nature, pp. 30, 31.
[5] Perpetual Forces, p. 273.
[6] Essays, second series, p. 177.
[7] Ibid., p. 178.

can understand the objective world, only because he is of like nature with it. The maxim of Plotinus, Boehme, and Schelling, that "like can be known only by like," is fully accepted by Emerson.

"The possibility of interpretation, he says, lies in the identity of the observer with the observed. Each material thing has its celestial side; has its translation, through humanity, into the spiritual and necessary sphere, where it plays a part as indestructible as any other." Man "is not representative, but participant. Like can only be known by like. The reason why he knows about them is, that he is of them; he has just come out of nature, or from being a part of that thing. Animated chlorine knows of chlorine, and incarnate zinc, of zinc. Their quality makes his career; and he can variously publish their virtues, because they compose him. Man, made of the dust of the world, does not forget his origin; and all that is yet inanimate will one day speak and reason."[1]

The material world Emerson regards as precipitated mind, while Nature is a symbol of the Absolute. Matter is undeveloped mind. He says "that which once existed in intellect as pure law, has now taken body as Nature. It existed in the mind in solution; now, it has been precipitated; and the bright sediment is the world."[2] In *Nature* Emerson seems to have been affected by the theory of Plotinus, who says creation resulted from a fall on the part of pure souls, whose sense-desires they put forth as nature. If he was at all affected by that theory, however, it was only temporarily. He has regarded matter as the first scale, or sphere, of being. From it life rises in successive forms of development, through mind, to complete union with the Universal Spirit. How nature came to exist he seems not to have attempted to solve. He appears to entertain the opinion of many idealists, that self-manifestation is a necessity of the Absolute. The process of the return of matter, the lowest form of that manifestation, back into its original, he explains by the theory of continuous self-development. "Every natural fact, he says, is an emanation. Not the cause, but an ever novel effect, nature descends always from above. It is un-

[1] Representative Men, p. 17. [2] Miscellanies, p. 180.

broken obedience. The beauty of these fair objects is imparted into them from a metaphysical and eternal spring. In all animal and vegetable forms, the physiologist concedes that no chemistry, no mechanics, can account for the facts; but a mysterious principle of life must be assumed, which not only inhabits the organ, but makes the organ."[1] Nature is alive with God, fluid and volatile with his presence. As God sees nature, it is "a transparent law, not a mass of facts,"[2] — a method by which laws are revealed to the soul and expressed by it. Nature is a revelation to man of that Universal Soul in which he belongs, of which he is a part; and it serves also to reveal to him the laws of his own nature. "The genesis and maturation of a planet, its poise and orbit. the bended tree recovering itself from the strong wind, the vital resources of every animal and vegetable, are demonstrations of the self-sufficing, and therefore self-relying, soul."[3] Nature was once thought, and towards thought it always tends. "The world is mind precipitated, and the volatile essence is for ever escaping again into the state of free thought. Hence the virtue and pungency of the influence on the mind, of natural objects, whether inorganic or organized. Man imprisoned, man crystallized, man vegetative, speaks to man impersonated."[4] "Man is fallen; nature is erect, and serves as a differential thermometer, detecting the presence or absence of the divine sentiment in man."[5]

Nature is growing, ever proceeding towards spirit. "We can point nowhere to any thing final, but tendency appears on all hands; planet, system, constellation, total nature is growing like a field of maize in July, is becoming somewhat else, is in rapid metamorphosis. The embryo does not more strive to be man than yonder burr of light we call a nebula tends to be a ring, a comet, a globe, and a parent of new suns."[6] The inherent, quickening life of Nature, *natura naturans*, is drawing all things towards their perfect realization of

[1] Miscellanies, p. 191.
[2] Essays, first series, p. 274.
[3] Ibid., p. 62.
[4] Essays, second series, p. 190.
[5] Ibid., p. 174.
[6] Miscellanies, p. 194.

themselves in spirit. This process of evolution Emerson thus describes: —

"It publishes itself in creatures, reaching from particles to spicula, through transformation on transformation to the highest symmetries, arriving at consummate results without a shock or a leap. A little heat, that is, a little motion, is all that differences the bald, dazzling white, and deadly cold poles of the earth from the prolific tropical climates. All changes pass without violence, by reason of the two cardinal conditions of boundless space and boundless time. . . . How far off is the trilobite, how far the quadruped! how inconceivably remote is man! All duly arrive, and then race after race of men. It is a long way from granite to oyster; farther yet to Plato, and the preaching of the immortality of the soul. Yet all must come, as surely as the first atom has two sides."[1]

Nature is in a constant process of development, growing more and more perfect. Its rocks are becoming vegetable; its vegetables, animal; its animals, man. Man has come up through every form of life below him, yet retains his sympathies with every form, and reproduces in his own development every phase of life below him. In his essay on Circles, and elsewhere, Emerson illustrates the perpetual law of development through the law of contraries, or through the mutual conflicts of the various forces of the world. He finds there are no fixtures in nature, that permanence is but a word of degrees, and that every ultimate fact is but the first of a new series. In the essay on the Sovereignty of Ethics, he shows how the Universal Spirit works throughout nature to secure what is right. In securing the right a final victory in every struggle, progress is secured. His theory is outlined in these paragraphs: —

"'Tis in the stomach of plants that development begins, and ends in the circles of the universe. 'Tis a long scale from the gorilla to the gentleman, — from the gorilla to Plato, Newton, Shakspere, — to the sanctities of religion, the refinements of legislation, the summits of science, art, and poetry. The beginnings are slow and infirm, but 'tis an always accelerated march. The geologic world is chronicled by the growing ripeness of the strata from lower to higher, as it becomes the abode of more highly organized plants and animals. The civil history of men might be traced by the successive meliorations as marked in higher moral generalizations, —

[1] Essays, second series, p. 174.

virtue meaning physical courage, then chastity and temperance, then justice and love; bargains of kings with peoples of certain rights to certain classes, then of rights to masses; then at last came the day when, as the historians rightly tell, the heroes of the world were electrified by the proclamation that all men are born free and equal.

"Every truth leads in another. The bud extrudes the old leaf, and every truth brings that which will supplant it. . . . In the pre-adamite, Nature bred valor only; by and by she gets on to man, and adds tenderness, and thus raises virtue piecemeal.

"When we trace from the beginning, that ferocity has uses, only so are the conditions of the then world met; and these monsters are the scavengers, executioners, diggers, pioneers, and fertilizers, destroying what is more destructive than they, and making better life possible. We see the steady aim of Benefit in view from the first. Melioration is the law. The cruelest foe is a masked benefactor. The wars, which make history so dreary, have served the cause of truth and virtue. There is always an instinctive sense of right, an obscure idea, which animates either party, and which in long periods vindicates itself at last. Thus a sublime confidence is fed at the bottom of the heart, that, in spite of appearances, in spite of malignity and blind self-interest, living for the moment, an eternal, beneficent necessity is always bringing things right; and, though we should fold our arms, — which we can not do; for our duty requires us to be the very hands of this guiding sentiment, and work in the present moment, — the evils we suffer will at last end themselves through the incessant opposition of Nature to every thing hurtful."

In speaking of the correlation of forces, and other laws of nature, he even more explicitly states the method of this development.

"These attempts of latest science are a slow showing of particulars of the broad and older assertion of philosophers, that each new fact was only a variety under the same old law, which Newton expressed when he said, 'The world was made at one cast.' It is only a particular instance of unity that Buffon and the physiologists taught, when they showed that Nature, in the creation of all her animal forms, from the lowest and oldest fossil up to mammals and man, has worked on one plan, from which she has never swerved. As this unity exists in the organization of insect, beast, bird, still ascending to man, and from the lowest types of man to the highest, so it does not less declare itself in the spirit or intelligence of the brute. In ignorant ages it was common to vaunt the human superiority by underrating the instinct of other animals. Better discernment finds that the only difference is of less and more. Experiment shows the dog to reason as the hunter does; and all the animals show the same good sense in their humble walk that man, who is their enemy or friend, does; and if it be in smaller measure, yet it is not damaged, as his is often, by freak and folly. St. Pierre says of animals, that a moral sentiment seems to have determined their physical organizations. This unity of design in the creation — this unity of thought — is the key to all science. There is a kind of latent omniscience, not only in every man, but in every particle; that convertibility which we see in plants, whereby the same bud becomes a leaf, bract, sepal, flower, seed, as the need is, so that repairs are made, and when one part is wounded the deficiency is supplied by another. This self-help and self-creation proceed from the same power which works in the feeblest and meanest structures, by the same design in a lobster, or in a worm, as a wise man would if imprisoned in that low form. It is the effort of God, the Supreme Intellect, in the extremest boundary of his universe; and long before Newton, a broader philosophy asserted the perfect agreement between matter and mind, and affirmed that there is nothing on earth which is not in the heavens in a heavenly form, and nothing in the heavens which is not on earth in an earthly form; their expression of that mystery in which all poetry and all language is founded, that we are able to find symbols of our sentiments and thoughts in the objects of nature; that the whole of nature agrees with the whole of thought."[1]

This is Schelling's idea, that the Absolute is to be completely perceived in nature.[2] In nature he saw a life-power constantly at work, in a universal process of self-evolution. In the rock and the pure soul is the same life and the same life-development. This life-power continuously rises from its lowest level in matter, through successive grades or stages or scales of being, to self-consciousness in man. In matter there is to be found only spirit dormant, the possibility of self-development. All higher forms manifest in nature have come from matter by this life-process; and man is only matter brought back through successive potences or scales of being to reason, to freedom, and self-conscious realization of the Infinite Spirit. As we rise in the scale of being, we come to a constantly increasing energy, to greater internal power and capacity for self-guidance, and to a higher form of freedom. Matter is subject, man as a pure soul is free. This highest

[1] Newspaper report of lecture on Natural Religion, delivered in Horticultural Hall, Boston, before the Free Religious Association, April 4, 1869.

[2] Schwegler's History of Philosophy.

potence shares in the life of God no more than the tree does, as Eckhart says, only as it realizes itself and its union with the Universal Spirit. In this whole conception of nature and life Emerson shares in the theories of his predecessors, especially as they have been expressed by Schelling. The following brief summary of Schelling's philosophy might almost answer as an epitome of Emerson's: —

"Universal unity must be the principle of all interpretation of nature. The first principle of a philosophical theory of nature is, to look for polarity and dualism everywhere. On the other hand, all consideration of nature must end in recognition of the absolute unity of the whole, a unity, however, which is to be discerned in nature only on one of its sides. Nature is, as it were, the instrument by which absolute unity eternally makes real all that has been pre-formed in the absolute mind. The absolute, then, is completely to be perceived in nature; although the world of externality produces only in series, only successively and in infinite gradation, what is at once and eternally in the world of truth."[1]

Emerson regards the laws working throughout nature as the methods of that life-process by which the Universal Spirit, as actualized in matter, returns into full realization of itself again in spirit. The laws of matter are really the laws of spirit. They are the thoughts of God, the pulse-beats of his being. They are the methods of the incoming of the Absolute to nature and man, whereby these finite manifestations of the Universal Spirit are being drawn up to complete development in harmony with God. Emerson sees law in morals, in thought, in every act of communion with God, as much as in matter, invariable everywhere, and always of the same nature. Because the Over-soul is the life in all things, and an absolute unity in all things, law reigns everywhere with its invariable methods. He believes that the inflexible law of matter runs up into the subtile kingdom of will and of thought; that, if our planet never loses its way through space,

"a secreter gravitation, a secreter projection, rule not less tyrannically in human history, and keep the balance of power from age

[1] Schwegler's History of Philosophy, p. 292.

to age unbroken. For, though the new element of freedom and an individual has been admitted, yet the primordial atoms are prefigured and pre-determined to moral issues, are in search of justice, and ultimate right is done. Religion or worship is the attitude of those who see this unity, intimacy, and sincerity; who see that, against all appearances, the nature of things works for truth and right for ever.

"'Tis a short sight to limit our faith in laws to those of gravity, of chemistry, of botany, and so forth. Those laws do not stop where our eyes lose them, but push the same geometry and chemistry up into the invisible plane of social and rational life, so that, look where we will, in a boy's game, or in the strifes of races, a perfect re-action, a perpetual judgment keeps watch and ward. And this appears in a class of facts which concerns all men, within and above their creeds. . . . The curve of the flight of the moth is pre-ordained; and all things go by number, rule, and weight. . . . But, in the human mind, this tie of fate is made alive. The law is the basis of the human mind. In us it is inspiration; out there in Nature we see its fatal strength." [1]

Emerson finds that there is no chance and no anarchy in the universe.[2] Even man is hooped on every side by necessity, the necessity of acting according to the eternal laws.[3] Not even in a single case can one fantastical will prevail over the law of things, or in any manner derange the order of nature.[4] Law demands as complete an obedience in morals as in matter; for it is the "same fact existing as sentiment and as will in the mind, which works in Nature as irresistible law, exerting influence over nations, intelligent beings, or down in the kingdoms of brute or of chemical atoms." [5] Piety and skepticism, he thinks, unite in declaring that nothing is of us or our works; that all is of God.[6]

All things are under the method and the law of the Infinite Spirit. A higher law than that of our will regulates events; for God exists, and there is for us nothing but a believing love in him. Whatever we may do, we can not overturn a single law; and the only result of neglecting any law is that we are crippled by it. There is a soul at the center of nature, and over the

[1] Conduct of Life, pp. 190–192.
[2] Ibid., p. 287.
[3] Ibid., pp. 16, 17.
[4] Ibid., p. 41.
[5] Sovereignty of Ethics, p. 406.
[6] Essays, second series, p. 71.

will of every man, so that none of us can wrong the universe. It has so infused its strong enchantment into nature, that we prosper when we accept its advice; and when we struggle to wound its creatures, our hands are glued to our sides, or they beat our own breasts. The whole course of things goes to teach us faith. We need only obey."[1] Every good which comes to us is by obedience to the law of God, an obedience which we shall freely elect to accept, when we know what it is; and in it we shall find all our freedom. "The last lesson of life, the choral song which rises from all elements and all angels, is a voluntary obedience, a necessitated freedom."[2]

He illustrates moral and spiritual obedience by reference to the laws of nature. Water drowns us; but, if we obey its conditions, we can float our ship on it through all seas. There is no porter, he says, like gravitation. There are laws of force, however; and we can not tamper with or warp them. "The man must bend to the law, never the law to him." All the forces of nature, when man obeys their conditions, become his servants. Then "no force but is his force. He does not possess them; he is a pipe through which their currents flow. If a straw be held still in the direction of the ocean-current, the sea will pour through it as through Gibraltar. If he should measure strength with them, if he should fight the sea and the whirlwind with his ship, he would snap his spars, tear his sails, and swamp his bark; but by cunningly dividing the force, tapping the tempest for a little side-wind, he uses the monsters, and they carry him where he would go."[3] Until the other day steam was a devil to be dreaded; but we have learned its law, become obedient to it, and now it is one of our best servants. Emerson finds that right drainage destroys typhus, that every other pest is not less in the chain of cause and effect, and may be fought off.[4] As we make all material forces our servants and helpers by

[1] Essays, first series, p. 124. [2] Conduct of Life, p. 209
[3] Perpetual Forces, North American Review, September, 1877, p. 274.
[4] Conduct of Life, pp. 27, 28.

accepting their conditions and obeying their laws, so "we arrive at virtue by taking its direction instead of imposing ours."

"The forces are infinite. Every one has the might of all; for the secret of the world is that its energies are *solidaires*; that they work together on a system of mutual aid, all for each and each for all; that the strain made on one point bears on every arch and foundation of the structure. But if you wish to avail yourself of their might, and in like manner if you wish the force of the intellect and the force of the will, you must take their divine direction, not they yours. Obedience alone gives the right to command. It is like the village operator who taps the telegraph-wire and surprises the secrets of empires as they pass to the capital. So this child of the dust throws himself by obedience into the circuit of the heavenly wisdom, and shares the secret of God."[1]

From his doctrine of universal law grows Emerson's first moral principle, that of self-renunciation. We are to renounce all that is individual, personal, and selfish, and to follow the universal ends of nature. "We can not bandy words with nature; and if we measure our individual forces against hers, we may easily feel as if we were the sport of an insuperable destiny."[2] "We can not bring the heavenly powers to us; but, if we will only choose our jobs in directions in which they travel, they will undertake them with the greatest pleasure. It is a peremptory rule with them, that they never go out of their road."[3] But if we take their way, all is strength and peace for us. By renouncing our own will and accepting theirs, we gain all the might of their power, and all wisdom comes in upon us. "We need only obey. There is guidance for each of us, and by lowly listening we shall hear the right word."[4] "There is a principle which is the basis of things, which all speech aims to say, and all action to evolve, a simple, quiet, undescribed, undescribable presence, dwelling very peacefully in us, our rightful lord; we are not to do, but to let do; not to work, but to be worked upon; and to this homage there is a consent of all thoughtful and just men in all ages and conditions."[5] How im-

[1] Perpetual Forces, p. 279.
[2] Essays, second series, p. 188.
[3] Society and Solitude, p. 26.
[4] Essays, first series, p. 124.
[5] Conduct of Life, p. 185.

perative he makes this condition of self-renunciation and obedience to God may be seen when he says that the true artist "must disindividualize himself, and be a man of no party and no manner and no age, but one through whom the soul of all men circulates, as the common air through the lungs. He must work in the spirit in which we conceive a prophet to speak, or an angel of the Lord to act; that is, he is not to speak his own words, or do his own works, or think his own thoughts; but he is to be an organ through which the universal mind acts."[1] Not only is this the manner of action for the artist, but for all men in all vocations. It is the method by which wisdom is to be obtained, and that by which character is to be possessed. Emerson would say as strongly as Epictetus does, that we are to be absolutely resigned to the will of God. We are to have no other thought, no other wish, than to become perfectly obedient to God, accepting his laws, doing his will, becoming the organs through which he acts. By renouncing all that is individual and particular, by obedience to the law of God, the Over-soul becomes our guide, and we are drawn into the methods of the universal mind. Then all truth opens before us, and we are led in the way of peace.

Nature is a perfect symbol of the spiritual; a picture, to the senses and the understanding, of the heavenly laws. It is an object-lesson in the truths of the soul, and it presents objectively all the realities of the Infinite. It is, especially, a lesson in moral truths, a method of discipline to the soul. It leads us to freedom through obedience, and to know that we can come to the highest self-realization only as we become the organs of the Universal Spirit.

Emerson has been as constant an observer of nature as Tyndall or Darwin, but his method of interpretation has been that of Schelling and Wordsworth. The value of investigation he fully realizes, and he makes no mistakes in his own use of scientific facts. To one who

[1] Society and Solitude, p. 43.

spoke to him of the help received from his pages, he gave this statement of his own method: —

"The fields and forests, the life of plants and animals, and the teeming industries of men, on every hand, are open to the vision of us all. These have been my teachers. You are free to gather from the original sources as well as I. What is needed by students is the habit of original investigation, and the courage to write down personal thoughts and observations."

He has seen in the study of nature a corrective to the speculations of the mind, and his interest in this study has grown largely out of his regarding the laws of nature as really laws of the spiritual world. Elizabeth P. Peabody reports that in one of his lectures in Boston, in 1860, he said, "If you wish to understand intellectual philosophy, do not turn inward by introversion, but study natural science. Every time you discover a law of things you discover a principle of mind." Thus has he found a corrective against the fancies of too great subjectivity, and a test for the speculative conclusions of the intuitive method. He has made a faithful application of both corrective and test in working out his own theories.

He has caught up with quick avidity the ripest conclusions of modern science, and made them take their place in the world he interprets. He knows the value of scientific facts, and where they belong. "Emerson has a scientific method, said his friend Agassiz, of the severest kind, and can not be carried away by any theories." Another great scientific teacher, Tyndall, as the result of his careful and frequent reading of Emerson's books, pronounces this striking judgment: —

"In him we have a poet and a profoundly religious man, who is really and entirely undaunted by the discoveries of science, past, present, and prospective. In his case, poetry, with the joy of a bacchanal, takes her graver brother science by the hand, and cheers him with immortal laughter. By Emerson scientific conceptions are continually transmuted into the finer forms and warmer lines of an ideal world."

XXII.

MIND, AND THE OVER-SOUL.

MIND is the positive manifestation of the Universal Spirit. Because positive, it is the source and center of things. Emerson thinks we can not define it, that we know not what it is but as we see and realize it in ourselves. In man it appears as intellect, but it is susceptible of no divisions.[1] It is the same power, the same faculty, when it acts as will, reason, or affections, and in every manifestation acts as a single force. This view of mind is shared in by the school of thinkers to which he belongs, and has been made prominent in the writings of Carlyle. The mind is both that which sees and that which is seen. It is hid from our cunning definitions, as from our comprehension, through its perfect transparency, and is too near for us to realize its nature. All the terms of mind, he says, are derived from those of matter; and all the laws of matter can be applied to thought by evident analogy. This is true, because mind and matter are one in the Universal Spirit, corresponding precisely with each other. Every law of nature, he said in his lectures on the Natural History of the Intellect, is a law of mind; and these laws are to be discovered by the solar microscope of analogy. To gravity or centrality in matter corresponds truth in the mind. Polarity is the next most universal law of nature, and to this corresponds sex in mind. So he would understand the mind, not by any *a priori* process, but through the study of nature and the observation of their constant correspondence in methods and laws.

A brief synopsis of this course of lectures will give a clearer understanding of his theory of mind, though it

[1] Essays, first series, p. 295.

must necessarily be very imperfect. In watching the stream of thought, he said in the third lecture, we come upon something in man that knows more than he does. This is *instinct*, a shapeless giant, unfinished at the two extremities, the source of all our knowing. Above this first crude power is *perception*, the intellect applied to the facts of life and individualizing them. It sees things in relations, discerns their unity. An acute perception is the source of genius, so that a mere hint leads us into the truth. All depends on the angle of our vision as to what we see in the world, for mind makes the world to be whatever it is. The next faculty is *memory*, which deals in second-hand thoughts, but is the bitumen matrix in which the other faculties work. Its characteristics are tenacity, choice, rapidity, and logic. Then follows *imagination*, which reveals the constant relations between matter and mind. God does not talk to us in prose, but by use of symbols, correspondences, and hints; and imagination takes hold of these, and reveals how nature is the key to spirit. A new figure of speech is of immense value to mankind, and the productions and changes of nature give rise to the nouns of language. A good image, drawn from any simple fact in nature, never rests there, but flies round the globe to find constantly new applications to life. Hence all physical facts are words for spiritual facts. We are always asking how many mental laws can be applied to matter, how many diameters can be drawn clear through from mind to matter; for the laws of matter are but adopted metaphysics. It is, therefore, the poet who can read the mind, because he applies imagination in the comprehension of those analogies which relate it to matter. Analysis hinders this process; but intuition, with the aid of imagination, reads the secret. The imagination transubstantiates every-day bread into everlasting symbols. After imagination follows *inspiration*, the knowing of truth. He made *genius* his next topic, and said its characteristic is a neglect of yesterday in reliance on the inspiration of to-day. It breaks all rules, and tramples on the laws of the race with its strong sandals. It looks after causes, and it mortgages the one whom it possesses to his ideas. He defined genius and common sense as being of the same family, and said that an ounce of mother-wit is worth a pound of clergy.

Turning from the faculties of the mind to its laws, he said that physical laws may be applied to mental phenomena, not only qualitatively but quantitatively. In proportion to the clearness with which the law of identity is perceived, is the depth of the mind. The first law of mind, then, is *identity;* and it is quite indifferent whether we say "all is matter" or "all is spirit." The second law is that of *degree*, constant ascent from egg to full growth. It is the scale in the mind, by which we rank thoughts and put the sensual as lower than the moral. The third law is that of *detachment*, the power to make subjects objects, to separate sensations from each other, to regard thoughts as apart from our own mind. It separates the mind from what it observes, and it is a measure of intellectual power. Another law is *pace*, the measure of the mind's rapidity. It makes degrees of intellect, for rapidity of movement in thoughts determines the capacity of the mind. Life is age-long to him who uses the telegraph in thought. The law of *bias* is, like the universal polarity of matter, a bent of the mind in a certain direction; so that each soul is unique, has a special capacity. It is a Divine whisper to each soul; but the voice is still after it is given, and we may obey it or not. God makes but one of each kind, and a bias in some one direction is the first mark of a master. In the last lecture he spoke of *veracity* as the primary rule of the intellect. He said there is too much negation in the world, and that the highest minds are affirmative. The bulwark of morality is found in not accepting degrading, negative views; nor was any thing ever gained by acknowledging the omnipotence of limitations.

As matter is the negative manifestation of the Universal Spirit, and has all its life and its development through the direct immanence of the Absolute, so is mind an expression of the Universal Spirit in its positive power. Man is the Universal Spirit present in a material organism. He is of the Divine, he lives in the Divine; every power he manifests is that of the Divine Life. Emerson does not regard the human soul as a separate individuality, totally cut off from other beings, but as a manifestation of the Universal Being. He says, "the soul in man is not an organ, but animates and exercises all the organs; is not a function, like the power of memory, of calculation, of comparison, but uses these as hands and feet; is not a faculty, but a light; is not the intellect or the will, but the master of the intellect and the will; is the background of our being, in which they lie, — an immensity not possessed, and that can not be possessed. From within or from behind, a light shines through us upon things, and makes us aware that we are nothing, that the light is all."[1] This "background of our being" was understood by Eckhart, who wrote of it as a "simple ground" in the soul, where man is in perfect union with God. It is the soul as it was before separated from God in a life of desire and individual self-seeking. Eckhart says, —

> "There is something in the soul which is above the soul, divine, simple, an absolute Nothing. . . . I have called it a Power, sometimes an Uncreated Light, sometimes a Divine Spark. It is absolute, and free from all names and forms, as God is free and absolute in himself. It is higher than knowledge, higher than love, higher than grace; for in all these there is distinction. . . . This Light is satisfied only with the super-essential essence. It is bound on entering into the simple ground, the still waste, wherein is no distinction, neither Father, Son, nor Holy Ghost, — into the unity where no man dwelleth. There is it satisfied in the light, there it is one; there is it in itself, as this Ground is a simple stillness in itself, immovable."

This is the doctrine of the Over-soul, as conceived in the fourteenth century by the father of German thought. It is the conception of spirit as one, that there is a state in the soul wherein it is in perfect union with the world of souls. This idea of the ground in the soul Tauler still further developed. He calls it the center of the soul, that depth where God always

[1] Essays, first series, p. 246.

dwells. To him it is the moral sentiment, that eternal sense of the right which abides unchanged in the soul of man. This center of man's nature is so grounded in God that the spirit is sunk and dissolved in the inmost of the Divine nature. Through this ground "God pours himself out into our spirit, as the sun rays forth its natural light into the air, and fills it with sunshine, so that no eye can tell the difference between the sunshine and the air. If the union of the sun and air can not be distinguished, how far less this divine union of the created and uncreated Spirit! Our spirit is received and swallowed up in the abyss which is its source." This Ground, Spark, or Light, is a depth in the soul where the divine and the human are one, and wherein the soul is not conscious of distinction from God.

After this idea had been carried some steps farther on in its development, we find Schelling declaring that there is but one Reason, the human and the divine being identical. From him this thought was taken up by Coleridge, who passed it on to Emerson. Coleridge believed in a supersensuous, impersonal light in man, which he calls reason; and he identifies it with the Universal Reason.

"He speaks of Reason as an immediate beholding of supersensible things, as the eye which sees things transcending sense. He identifies Reason in the human mind with Universal Reason; calls it impersonal; indeed, regards it as a ray of the Divinity in man. In one place he makes it one with the light which lighteth every man; and in another he says that Reason is the presence of the Holy Spirit in the finite understanding, at once the light and the universal eye. It can not be rightly called a faculty, he says, much less a personal property of any human mind. We can not be said to possess Reason, but rather to partake of it; for there is but one Reason, which is shared by all intelligent beings, and is in itself the Universal or Supreme Reason. He in whom Reason dwells can as little appropriate it as his own possession, as he can claim ownership in the breathing air, or take in the cope of heaven." [1]

Emerson writes of the Universal Mind, or the Oversoul, as Coleridge writes of the Universal Reason. It is one and universal, and is a light which possesses and

[1] Shairp's Studies in Poetry and Philosophy, p. 168.

guides man. To this idea Emerson adds the conception of God as the soul of the world, as the Universal Mind pervading all things, and regards the human mind as an integral part of the Absolute Mind. So he says there is "one mind common to all individual men," while "every man is an inlet to the same and to all of the same."[1] This common mind in all men is the Over-soul. Each person is an inlet out of this great ocean, and it pours the same waters into all. We are filled with this flood, and are nothing but dry and dusty banks without it. To Emerson, as to Tauler and Coleridge, the Over-soul is within us a moral law; so that we learn what is right and true, not by experience, but because there is in us the fountain of all wisdom and authority. Man can know the truth, because God is a light within him revealing all things. The suggestions given him by Schelling and Coleridge he has developed into a consistent theory of knowledge and of the relations of man to God. Sometimes almost in the very phrases of Coleridge he announces his central doctrine of the "Over-soul:"—

"Our first experiences, he says, in moral as in intellectual nature, force us to discriminate a universal mind, identical in all men. Certain biases, talents, executive skills, are special to each individual; but the high, contemplative, all-commanding vision, the sense of Right and Wrong, is alike in all. Its attributes are self-existence, eternity, intuition, and command. It is the mind of the mind; we belong to it, not it to us. It is in all men, and constitutes them men. In bad men it is dormant, as health is in men entranced or drunken; but, however inoperative, it exists underneath whatever vices and errors. The extreme simplicity of this intuition embarrasses every attempt at analysis. We can only mark, one by one, the perfections which it combines in every act. It admits of no appeal, looks to no superior essence. It is the reason of things.

"The antagonist nature is the individual, formed into a finite body of exact dimensions, with appetites which take from everybody else what they appropriate to themselves, and would enlist the entire spiritual faculty of the individual, if it were possible, in catering for them. On the perpetual conflict between the dictate of this universal mind and the wishes and interests of the individual, the moral discipline of life is built. The one craves a private

[1] Essays, first series, p. 3.

benefit, which the other requires him to renounce out of respect to the absolute good. Every hour puts the individual in a position where his wishes aim at something which the sentiment of duty forbids him to seek. He that speaks the truth executes no private function of an individual will, but the world utters a sound by his lips. He who doth a just action seeth therein nothing of his own; but an inconceivable nobleness attaches to it, because it is a dictate of the general mind. We have no idea of power so simple and so entire as this. It is the basis of thought, it is the basis of being. Compare all that we call ourselves, all our private and personal venture in the world, with this deep of moral nature in which we lie, and our private good becomes an impertinence, and we take part with hasty shame against ourselves."[1]

Above the individual man, then, is this Over-soul, "within which every man's particular being is contained and made one with all others." It is a "Unity," "the eternal One;" and "man is the façade of this temple wherein all wisdom and all good abide."[2] Each individual man is an incarnation of this universal man, and in him are all its properties expressed. There is but one Reason, which is the mind of the world; and every man is an inlet to all of it.[3] The Over-soul descends into man; and he is a pensioner on its bounty, helpless without it. On this side of our natures Emerson sees no separation of man from God; but as this is true only on one side, he does not regard man as a mere manifestation of God. "As there is no screen or ceiling, he says, between our heads and the infinite heavens, so is there no bar or wall in the soul where man, the effect, ceases, and God, the cause, begins. The walls are taken away. We lie open on one side to the deeps of spiritual nature, to the attributes of God."[4] This unity of man and God he finds to be so intimate, that he says to us, —

"Draw, if thou canst, the mystic line,
Severing rightly his from thine,
Which is human, which divine."[5]

When man is perfectly obedient to the workings of the Over-soul, and becomes just at heart, "then in so far

1 Essay on Character, in the North American Review for April, 1866.
2 Essays, first series, pp. 244-246.
3 Society and Solitude, p. 45.
4 Essays, first series, pp. 244, 247.
5 Conduct of Life, p. 173.

is he God; the safety of God, the immortality of God, the majesty of God, do enter into that man with justice" and obedience.[1] "Ineffable is the union of man and God in every act of the soul. The simplest person, who in his integrity worships God, becomes God; yet for ever and ever the influx of this better and universal self is new and unsearchable."[2] In such words as these Emerson is thoroughly a mystic. Eckhart has the same meaning, when he says, "God and I are one in knowing, God's essence is his knowing, and God's knowing makes me to know him. Therefore is his knowing my knowing. The eye whereby I see God is the same eye whereby he seeth me; mine eye and the eye of God are one eye, one vision, one knowledge, and one love."

The idea of Eckhart and Emerson, as it is of Boehme, Schelling, Coleridge, and all others who accept the conclusions of mysticism, is that of the absolute oneness of the Universal Spirit, that there is but one essential being and life, that this life is present in all things, that man has his life in the Universal Spirit, that all his thinking is its expression through him.[3] Eckhart says the soul is in God, and God in her; and what she doeth she doeth in God, and God doeth in her. Tauler tells us that "the spirit becomes the very truth which it apprehends. God is apprehended by God. We become one with the same light with which we see, and which is both the medium and object of our vision." He says again, "God is a Spirit; and our created spirit must be united to and lost in the uncreated, even as it existed in God before creation. Every moment in which the soul re-enters into God a complete restoration takes place. This is when the

[1] Miscellanies, p. 178. [2] Essays, first series, p. 265.

[3] Fichte, in his Characteristics of the Present Age, says the individual is but a "single ray of the *one* universal and necessary Thought." "There is but One Life, he says, but *one* animating power, one Living Reason, which is the only possible independent and self-sustaining Existence and Life, of which all that seems to us to exist and live is but a modification, definition, variety, and form." He again says that "it is only by and to mere earthly and finite perception, that this one and homogeneous Life of Reason is broken up and divided into separate individual persons."

inmost of the spirit is sunk and dissolved in the inmost of the divine nature, and is thus new-made and transformed. God thus pours himself out into our spirit, as the sun rays forth its material light, and fills the air with sunshine, so that no eye can tell the difference between the sunshine and the air." In the godly man "God lives, forms, ordains, and works." Then hath "the created spirit lost itself in the Spirit of God; yea, is drowned in the bottomless sea of Godhead."

Emerson not only sees God immanent in nature, so that its life and laws are actual expressions of his being and nature, but he is immanent in man, so that all his thoughts and his very life are God's thoughts and life. Man is an inlet from the ocean of Being, a spark from off the Infinite Altar, a needle that conducts the Magnetic Power of the universe. The Soul of the world pours its truth into him, and he is what it makes him to become. The Over-soul is that Infinite Life, in which all souls find their common origin and continued existence. It is the banyan-tree of Eternity, which sends down a multitude of shoots to grow as separate trees, but above are all united in one common life. So the Over-soul sends down into Nature its growing branches of truth, and these take root as human beings; but above they are united in the Universal Spirit. They have a life of their own, but they are nothing unless constantly sustained by that Life from which they proceed. In writing of the doctrine of compensation, Emerson says men who can not accept it do not see "that *He*, that *It*, is there, next and within; the thought of the thought; the affair of affairs; that he is existence, and take him from them, and they would not be." [1] There is, then, but one Soul, the Soul that is over and within all things.

All souls stand in like relations to the Over-soul, receive from it their life, have in them its nature, and so have like endowments and capacities. This leads Emerson to the conclusion that "the differences

[1] The Sovereignty of Ethics, p. 409; North American Review, April, 1866.

between men in natural endowment are insignificant in comparison with their common wealth." He goes so far as to say that everybody knows as much as the *savant*, because all stand in like relations to the Over-soul. This is the idea which lies at the foundation of his interpretation of history, that "there is one mind common to all individual men." As nature is a revelation of God in the unconscious, so is history a revelation of God in the conscious domain of freedom. The whole of history is necessary to realize the whole of the Soul, as each man expresses but a part of it. Yet we can best understand history by our own life, and each individual reads all history in his own person. This is true, because history is a revelation of the Over-soul, its expression in time; and each person has the key to it in himself, for he has his life also in the Over-soul. History is a repetition on a large scale of what each person experiences and knows. "Of the Universal Mind each individual man is one more incarnation. All its properties consist in him. Each new fact in his private experience flashes a light on what great bodies of men have done, and the crises of his life refer to national crises." [1]

[1] Essays, first series, p. 4.

XXIII.

INTUITION.

AS like can only be known by like, as man knows God only because he is of the nature of God, it follows that all knowing is a direct perception or an intuition. All the mystics, from Plotinus to Emerson, find in man a supersensuous factor, or faculty, through which we know the things of God and the spiritual world. Schelling calls it an intellectual intuition, and Coleridge knows it as reason; but it necessarily follows as a consequence of the primary ideas of mysticism. Eckhart said, "I have a power in my soul which enables me to perceive God." "I know something higher than science, says Schelling, a beholding of that which is in God." "The mortal eye, he says, closes only in the highest science when it is no longer the man who sees, but the Eternal Beholding which has now become seeing in him." How fully Schelling anticipated Emerson's theory of intuition may be seen from this statement of his teachings on the subject, —

"Schelling asserts that there is a capacity of knowledge above or behind consciousness, and higher than the understanding, and that this knowledge is competent to human reason, because this Reason itself is identical with the Absolute. In this act of knowledge, which he calls the *intellectual intuition*, as distinguished from the intuitions of sense, there exists no distinction of subject and object, no contrast of knowledge with existence; all difference is lost in mere indifference, all plurality in simple unity. The Absolute is identical with the reason which apprehends it. Because man is himself a manifestation of the Absolute, he can know the source and essence of his being only by falling back behind the limits and conditions of his phenomenal existence, and knowing himself as he really is, — God. All things are God; in him we live and move and have our being. Of course, the act is ineffable, it is the vision and the faculty divine. He who is incapable of it is incompetent for philosophy. This is what Cousin means by his doctrine of the impersonality of reason. That by which I apprehend the truth, he says, is not *my* reason, nor *your* reason, but Reason itself, as such, or in abstract; also, the truth itself, thus known, is not my truth or your truth, but truth as such, or the Absolute, identical with the faculty which apprehends it."[1]

Emerson accepts in full the doctrine of intuition, as it had been elaborated by the thinkers who preceded him. All the truth we know, he says, comes to us as an instinct; and we are to trust the instinct, though we can render no reason for what it teaches.[2] All our true thinking is a pious reception of the truth we have done nothing to create. "We do not determine what we think. We only open our senses, clear away, as we can, all obstruction from the fact, and suffer the intellect to see. We have little control over our thoughts. We are the prisoners of ideas. They catch us up for moments into their heaven, and so fully engage us, that we take no thought for the morrow, gaze like children, without an effort to make them our own. By and by we fall out of that rapture, bethink us where we have been, what we have seen, and repeat, as truly as we can, what we have beheld. As far as we can recall these ecstasies, we carry away in the ineffaceable memory the result; and all men and all the ages confirm it. It is called Truth. But the moment we cease to report, and attempt to correct and contrive, it is not truth."[3]

In words such as these Emerson indicates his theory of the mind and of knowledge. He maintains that all knowledge is a revelation, an intuition direct to the receiving soul. The source and essence of genius, of virtue, and of life, he says, is that which we call spontaneity or instinct. "We denote this primary wisdom as Intuition, whilst all later teachings are tuitions. In that deep force, the last fact behind which analysis can not go, all things find their common origin."[4] Thus all knowing is a direct, simple perception. We know

[1] Bowen's Modern Philosophy; p. 342.
[2] Essays, first series, pp. 297-299.
[3] Ibid., p. 298
[4] Ibid., p. 56.

things because they are of like nature with ourselves, because one life flows through them and through us. In true knowing, there is no effort on our part, except to open the way for the truth to shine in. The process of knowing we can not explain; all philosophy is here at fault. That we have this faculty of intuition is all we know, and we should not seek to explain it. Through it God speaks all things to us, and makes it impossible that we should listen to any other voice.[1]

Emerson lays the greatest possible stress on this theory of spontaneity and intuition. He appears sometimes to take away all self-direction and all need of human search for truth.

"God enters, he says, by a private door into every individual. Long prior to the age of reflection is the thinking of the mind. Out of darkness it came insensibly into the marvelous light of today. In the period of infancy it accepted and disposed of all impressions from the surrounding creation after its own way. Whatever any mind doth or saith is after a law; and this native law remains over it after it has come to reflection or conscious thought. In the most worn, pedantic, introverted self-tormentor's life, the greatest part is incalculable by him, and must be, until he can take himself up by his own ears. What am I? What has my will done to make me what I am? Nothing. I have been floated into this thought, this hour, this connection of events, by secret currents of might and mind; and my ingenuity and wilfulness have not thwarted, have not aided to an appreciable degree."[2]

He says man is a stream whose source is hidden, for our being is descending into us from we know not whence.[3] It is this influx of being from above which brings us truth. The perceiving and revealing soul knows the truth when it is presented, and can not be deceived by any fancies of the individual self.[4] There must be faithfulness to the truth, however, and obedience to its commands. "We must not tamper with the organic motion of the soul. 'Tis certain that thought has its own proper motion; and the hints which flash from it, the words overheard at unawares by the free mind, are trustworthy and fertile when obeyed, and not per-

[1] Ibid., p. 57.
[2] Ibid., p. 297.
[3] Ibid., p. 244.
[4] Ibid., p. 254.

verted to low and selfish account."[1] Again he says, "The one condition coupled with the gift of truth is its use. That man shall be learned who reduceth his learning to practice."[2] The condition is, "If we live truly, we shall see truly."[3] Character is an exact expression of how much truth we have. "Exactly parallel is the whole rule of intellectual duty to the rule of moral duty;"[4] and the intellect sinks as the moral nature descends, while it rises with it. "The infallible index of true progress is found in the tone the man takes. If he have not found his home in God, his manners, his forms of speech, the turn of his sentences, the build, shall I say, of all his opinions, will involuntarily confess it."[5] The intuition must find expression in an action; it can not be held as a private good. The intuition "rises in thought, to the end that it may be uttered and acted. The more profound the thought, the more burdensome. Always in proportion to the depth of its sense does it knock importunely at the gates of the soul, to be spoken, to be done."[6] It is by this most rigid law of action and character Emerson saves himself from those evil results which the bold insistance on the method of intuition have worked in some minds. It is dangerous for a weak mind to believe that all its impulses are divine revelations, that every seeming intuition is to be followed, that we are what we are by means of a power outside of ourselves entirely. To such a theory, there must be a rigid balance and checks. These Emerson has supplied in a most faithful manner. No intuition is to be regarded that does not conform to the highest moral conduct, the tendency of which is not to elevate and purify the life. To none but the pure in heart are these intuitions opened, according to Emerson, "for *so to be* is the sole inlet of *so to know*."[7]

Another condition of intuition is silence and medi-

[1] Letters and Social Aims, p. 181.
[2] Miscellanies, p. 213.
[3] Essays, first series, p. 59.
[4] Ibid., p. 303.
[5] Ibid., p. 260.
[6] Society and Solitude, p. 34
[7] Essays, first series, p. 290.

tation. In this Emerson is fully in accord with all the mystics. We must sit alone, if we would receive the truth; let the Over-soul pour into us its flood. He says that if any man would know what the great God speaketh, he must go into his closet and shut the door. "He must greatly listen to himself, withdrawing himself from all the accents of other men's devotion. Even their prayers are hurtful to him, until he have made his own."[1] We must listen only to that Divine Voice which speaks within us, and to do that we must shut out all the rest of the world. Hence, the epochs of our life come "in a silent thought by the wayside as we walk;"[2] for in that silent inward communion the way of life for us is revealed. "Silence, he says, is a solvent that destroys personality, and gives us leave to be great and universal."[3] We forget the individual cares and ambitions, and find strength and peace in the truth.

The Spanish mystic, St. Theresa, says we ought to sit alone and wait for God to come to us, in no wise dictating the method of his coming. Madame Guyon regarded her own silent prayers of intuition as immeasurably better than any the church provided. In the same spirit, Eckhart declared that "he who is at all times alone is worthy of God." All the mystics say that God speaks within, and we must sit alone, that we may listen to his voice, and that he may have free opportunity to communicate his truth.

We test our intuitions by action, character, and silence; and we are to exclude from them all egotism. "This distemper is the scourge of talent." We must put our act or word aloof from us, and "see it bravely for the nothing it is." Emerson cautions us to beware of the man who says he is on the eve of a revelation. Such presumption "is speedily punished, inasmuch as this habit invites men to humor it, and, by treating the patient tenderly, to shut him up in a narrower selfism, and exclude him from the great world of God's cheer-

[1] Ibid., p. 267. [2] Ibid., p. 144. [3] Ibid., p. 311.

ful, fallible men and women."[1] The egotism of knowledge is not only dangerous, but it excludes us from the light. The truth comes to only those who are ready absolutely to obey it, who propose no substitutes or explanations. "The idiot, the Indian, the child, and unschooled farmer's boy, stand nearer to the light by which nature is to be read, than the dissector or the antiquary."[2] The man of science interposes his own explanations, his own conjectures; and, having offered them, he stands by them, thinks them the truth, and forgets nature in their acceptance. He ought, however, to be only a mouthpiece, an interpreter, of nature, having no desire but to say how it is with her. So it is that we are to accept the voice of the Over-soul. We are not to speculate about it, not to interpret it, only to hear and obey. The simple mind, that asks no questions, but yields to its command, is the highest and truest. The conditions of this absolute trust Emerson has stated in these words: —

"I conceive a man as always spoken to from behind, and unable to turn his head and see the speaker. In all the millions who have heard the voice, none ever saw the face. As children in their play run behind each other, and seize one by the ears and make him walk before them, so is the spirit our unseen pilot. That well-known voice speaks in all languages, governs all men; and none ever caught a glimpse of its form. If the man will exactly obey it, it will adopt him, so that he shall not any longer separate it from himself in his thought; he shall seem to be it, he shall be it. If he listen with insatiable ears, richer and greater wisdom is taught him, the sound swells to a ravishing music, he is borne away as with a flood, he becomes careless of his food and of his house, he is the fool of ideas, and leads a heavenly life. But if his eye is set on the things to be done, and not on the truth that is still taught, and for the sake of which the things are to be done, then the voice grows faint, and at last is but a humming in his ears. His health and greatness consist in his being the channel through which heaven flows to earth, in short, in the fulness in which an ecstatical state takes place in him."[3]

The nature of this power he has also described: —

"We distinguish the announcements of the soul, its manifestations of its own nature, by the term *revelation*. These are always

[1] Conduct of Life, p. 115. [2] Essays, first series, p. 36.
[3] Miscellanies, p. 200.

attended by the emotion of the sublime. For this communication is an influx of the Divine mind into our mind. It is an ebb of the individual rivulet before the flowing surges of the sea of life. Every distinct apprehension of this central commandment agitates men with awe and delight. A thrill passes through all men at the reception of new truth, or at the performance of a great action, which comes out of the heart of nature. In these communications, the power to see is not separated from the will to do; but the insight proceeds from obedience, and the obedience proceeds from a joyful perception. Every moment when the individual feels himself invaded by it is memorable. By the necessity of our constitution, a certain enthusiasm attends the individual's consciousness of that divine presence. The character and duration of this enthusiasm varies with the state of the individual, from an ecstasy and trance and prophetic inspiration — which is its rarer appearance — to the faintest glow of virtuous emotion, in which form it warms, like our household fires, all the families and associations of men, and makes society possible. A certain tendency to insanity has always attended the opening of the religious sense in men, as if they had been 'blasted with excess of light.' The trances of Socrates, the 'union' of Plotinus, the vision of Porphyry, the conversion of Paul, the aurora of Boehme, the convulsions of George Fox and his Quakers, the illuminations of Swedenborg, are of this kind. What was in the case of these remarkable persons a ravishment, has, in innumerable instances in common life, been exhibited in less striking manner. Everywhere the history of religion betrays a tendency to enthusiasm. The rapture of the Moravian and Quietist; the opening of the internal sense of the Word, in the language of the New-Jerusalem church; the *revival* of the Calvinistic churches; the *experiences* of the Methodists, — are varying forms of that shudder of awe and delight with which the individual soul always mingles with the universal soul. The nature of these revelations is the same; they are perceptions of the absolute law. They are solutions of the soul's own questions. They do not answer the questions which the understanding asks. The soul answers never by words, but by the thing itself that is inquired after." [1]

Emerson believes in the Inner Light of the Quaker, the Ecstasy of Plotinus, the Divine Illumination of Swedenborg. Truth is not the result of thought, it is not to be attained to by reasoning, least of all is it a product of the senses and understanding; it is a divine light, an inward illumination. He frequently calls this instinct, or intuition, The Moral Sentiment. Through it comes every law of conduct; and it gives us those moral commandments which are eternal, because out of the very

[1] Essays, first series, p. 255.

core of Being. This power "puts us at the heart of Nature, where we belong, in the cabinet of science and of causes, — there where all the wires terminate which hold the world in magnetic unity, — and so converts us into universal beings."[1]

"This wonderful sentiment, which endears itself as it is obeyed, seems to be the fountain of intellect; for no talent gives the impression of sanity, if wanting this; nay, it absorbs every thing into itself. Truth, Power, Goodness, Beauty, are its varied names, — faces of one substance. Before it, what are persons, prophets, or seraphim, but its passing agents, momentary rays of its light?

"The moral sentiment is alone important. There is no labor or sacrifice to which it will not bring a man, and which it will not make easy. Under the action of this sentiment of the Right, his heart and mind expand above himself, and above Nature.

"Devout men, in the endeavor to express their convictions, have used different images to suggest this latent force; as, the light, the seed, the Spirit, the Holy Ghost, the Comforter, the Dæmon, the still small voice, etc., — all indicating its power and its latency. It refuses to appear, it is too small to be seen, too obscure to be spoken of; but, such as it is, it creates a faith which the contradiction of all mankind can not shake, and which the consent of all mankind can not confirm."

"We affirm that in all men is this majestic perception and command; that it is the presence of the Eternal in each perishing man; that it distances and degrades all statements of whatever saints, heroes, poets, as obscure and confused stammerings before its silent revelation. *They* report the truth. *It* is the truth. When I think of Reason, of Truth, of Virtue, I can not conceive of them as lodged in your soul and lodged in my soul, but that you and I and all souls are lodged in that; and I may easily speak of that adorable nature, there where only I behold it, in my dim experiences, in such terms as shall seem to the frivolous, who dare not fathom their consciousness, as profane."

"We pretend not to define the way of its access to the private heart. It passes understanding. The soul of God is poured into the world through the thoughts of men. When the Master of the Universe has ends to fulfill, he impresses his will on the structure of minds."[2]

He insists again and again that is impossible to know the character of this intuitive power, or the manner of its incoming to the mind. With Plotinus, he calls it an ecstasy. He expresses his belief "that nothing great and lasting can be done except by inspiration," which

[1] Character, p. 358. [2] Ibid., pp. 358-360.

finds expression in enthusiasm. Ecstasy is a normal experience of all who live aright. "Poets have signalized their consciousness of rare moments, when they were superior to themselves, — when a light, a freedom, a power, came to them, which lifted them to performances far better than they could reach at other times."[1] All great achievements of whatever kind are accomplished by enthusiasm and abandonment.[2] Life itself is an ecstasy,[3] and, when true to its highest law, is only an abandonment to the will of God. Even in nature there "is no private will, no rebel leaf or limb; but the whole is oppressed by one superincumbent tendency, obeys that redundancy, or excess, of life, which, in conscious beings, we call *ecstasy*."[4] This power of intuition or revelation in man, this power of communion with God, of receiving the Over-soul into our own natures in a new access of truth, is "always a miracle, which no frequency of occurrence or incessant study can ever familiarize, but which must always leave the inquirer stupid with wonder."[5]

"The path is difficult, secret, and beset with terror. The ancients called it *ecstasy* or absence, — a getting out of their bodies to think. All religious history contains traces of the trance of saints, — a beatitude, but without any sign of joy, earnest, solitary, even sad; 'the flight,' Plotinus called it, 'of the alone to the alone;' Μυεσις, the closing of the eyes, — whence our word, *Mystic*. The trances of Socrates, Plotinus, Porphyry, Boehme, Bunyan, Fox, Pascal, Guyon, Swedenborg, will readily come to mind. This beatitude comes in terror, and with shocks to the mind of the receiver."[6]

Some minds are more capable of intuition than others, and become the revealers of new truths. "Rare, extravagant spirits come to us at intervals, who disclose to us new facts in nature. Men of God have, from time to time, walked among men, and made their commission felt in the heart and soul of the commonest hearer."[7] "In all ages, souls out of time, extraordi-

[1] Letters and Social Aims, pp. 243–248.
[2] Essays, first series, p. 292.
[3] Conduct of Life, p. 35.
[4] Miscellanies, p. 195.
[5] Essays, first series, p. 301.
[6] Representative Men, p. 99.
[7] Essays, first series, p. 25.

nary, prophetic, are born, who are rather related to the system of the world than to their particular age and locality. These announce absolute truths."[1] These great men become the leaders and the centers of the world's advancement. "An institution is the lengthened shadow of one man," and "all history resolves itself very easily into the biography of a few stout and earnest persons."[2] "Mankind have, he says, in all ages, attached themselves to a few persons, who, either by the quality of that idea they embodied, or by the largeness of their reception, were entitled to the position of leaders and law-givers. These teach us the qualities of primary nature,—admit us to the constitution of things."[3] Again he says, "A man, a personal ascendency, is the only great phenomenon. When nature has work to be done, she creates a genius to do it. Follow the great man, and you shall see what the world has at heart in these ages. There is no omen like that."[4] In the general introduction he wrote to an English book on *The Hundred Greatest Men*, published in 1879, he very characteristically sets forth his theory of the great man. It is the theory of all the great Germans of the eighteenth century he defends therein. Hamann believed in absolute individual liberty; Lavater proclaimed the autocratic power of genius; while Lessing, Herder, Fichte, Goethe, and all the others, preached this doctrine of the power of the great man. Cousin made it the central thought in his interpretation of history, and Carlyle gave to it his entire approval. The whole of that introduction is in these words:—

"The Spanish historians tell us that it was not any of the wild and unknown animals, or fruit, or even the silver and gold of the new world, but the wild *man*, that concentrated the curiosity of the contemporaries of Columbus. And we all of us remember in the charming account of the prince of the Pelew Islands, brought in the last century into England, that what most of all the splendid shows of London fastened his eye with mystery of joy, was the mirror in which he saw himself. In like manner it is not the monster, it is not the remote and unknown, which can ever powerfully

[1] Conduct of Life, p. 178.
[2] Essays, first series, pp. 53, 54.
[3] Representative Men, p. 25.
[4] Miscellanies, p. 198.

work on the human mind; the way to touch all the springs of wonder in us is to get before our eyes as thought, that which we are feeling and doing. The things that we do we think not. What I am I can not describe any more than I can see my eyes. The moment another describes to me that man I am, pictures to me in words that which I was feeling and doing, I am struck with surprise. I am sensible of a keen delight. I be, and I see my being, at the same time. The soul glances from itself to the picture with lively pleasure. Behold what was in me, out of me! Behold the subjective now objective! Behold the spirit embodied!

"What does every earnest man seek in the deep instinct of society, from his first fellowship — a child with children at play -- up to the heroic cravings of friendship and love, — what but to find himself in another mind; because such is the law of his being that only can he find out his own secret through the instrumentality of another mind. We hail with gladness this new acquisition of ourselves. That man I must follow, for he has a part of me; and I follow him that I may acquire myself.

"The great are our better selves, ourselves with advantages. It is the only platform on which all men can meet. If you deal with a vulgar mind, life is reduced to beggary. He makes me rich, him I call Plutus, who shows me that every man is mine, and every faculty is mine; who does not impoverish me in praising Plato, but contrariwise is adding assets to my inventory.

"An etherlal sea ebbs and flows, surges and washes hither and thither, carrying its whole virtue into every creek and inlet which it bathes. To this sea every human house has a water-front. Every truth is a power. Every idea from the moment of its emergence begins to gather material forces, after a little while makes itself known. It works first on thoughts, then on things; makes feet, and afterwards shoes; first hands, then gloves; makes men, and so the age and its material soon after. The history of the world is nothing but a procession of clothed ideas. As certainly as water falls in rain on the tops of mountains, and runs down into valleys, plains, and pits, so does thought fall first in the best minds, and runs down from class to class, until it reaches the masses, and works revolutions.

"The Universal Man is now coming to be a real being in the individual mind, as once the Devil was. All questions touching human life the daily press now discusses. I will not say that there is no darker side to the picture, or that what is gained in universality is not lost in enthusiasm. We have in the race the sketch of a man which no individual comes up to. I figure to myself the world as a hollow temple, and each several mind as an exponent of some sacred part therein; each a jet of flame affixed to some capital or triglyph or rosette, bringing out its significance to the eye by its shining.

"We delight in heroes, but we can hardly call them a class; for the essence of heroism is that it takes the man out of all class

We call them providential men. They draw multitudes and nations after them, as the nation shares the idea that inspires them. I know the pure examples are few; a few benefactors scattered along history to make the earth sweet. For the most part, the mud of temperament clouds the purity, and we see this sheathed omnipotence in characters we can not otherwise respect. They show their legitimate prerogative in nothing more than their power to misguide us. For the perverted great derange and deject us, and perplex ages with their fame.

"The great men of the past did not slide by any fortune into their high place. They have been selected by the severest of all judges, Time. As the snow melts in April, so has this mountain lost in every generation a new fragment. Every year new particles have dropped into the flood as the mind found them wanting in permanent interest, until only the Titans remain.

"Nothing good, nothing grand has been withheld. The ages of Time, the resources of Being, play into our tutelage. Here the world yields to us its soul. To our insight old sages live again. The old revolutions find correspondence in the experiences of the mind. Wonderful spiritual natures, like princedoms and potentates, stand bending around us. Each one of the century represents a department of life and thought."

Emerson is not a hero-worshiper, — does not make the great man so important as do Carlyle, Cousin, and Herder. With him the great man is one who is able to express more clearly some idea which others also accept. He says every great man is a unique, it is true, but also that every soul is individual and unrepresented. The genius of any kind is but a mouth-piece of the soul, and the soul is open to all. If he has some fortunate power, he has weaknesses to balance it; and in his total power he is no greater than others. Great men are to be accepted, only as showing us what we can become, only because we see in them what is in us. "There is any thing but humiliation in the homage men pay to a great man; it is sympathy, love of the same things, effort to reach them, — the expression of their hope of what they shall become when the obstructions of their malformation and mal-education shall be trained away. Great men shall not impoverish, but enrich, us. Great men, — the age goes on their credit; but all the rest, when their wires are continued, and not cut, can do as signal things, and in new parts of nature."[1] If we trust

[1] Letters and Social Aims, p. 202.

the great man too much, it will be to our hurt. He must never take the place of that Over-soul, which is the guide, and should be the only final trust, of us all. "The man has never lived, Emerson says, that can feed us ever."[1] We must not attach ourselves too closely to any great man, lest his defects cause us to lose faith in the truth. No man must usurp the place of the soul, or stand to us instead of the descending of God's truth into us from above.

"Our exaggeration of all fine characters arises from the fact that we identify each in turn with the soul. But there are no such men as we fable; no Jesus, nor Pericles, nor Cæsar, nor Angelo, nor Washington, such as we have made. We consecrate a great deal of nonsense, because it was allowed by great men. There is none without his foible. I verily believe if an angel should come to chant the chorus of the moral law, he would eat too much gingerbread, or take liberties with private letters, or do some precious atrocity. It is bad enough that our geniuses can not do any thing useful, but it is worse that no man is fit for society who has fine traits. He is admired at a distance, but he can not come near without appearing a cripple. . . . The magnetism which arranges tribes and races in one polarity is alone to be respected; the men are steel-filings. Yet we unjustly select a particle, and say, O steel-filing number one! what heart-drawings I feel to thee! what prodigious virtues are these of thine! how constitutional to thee, and incommunicable! Whilst we speak, the loadstone is withdrawn, down falls our filing in a heap with the rest; and we continue our mummery to the wretched shaving. Let us go for universals; for the magnetism, not for the needles. Human life and its persons are poor empirical pretensions. A personal influence is an *ignis fatuus*."[2]

It is the magnetism of the Spirit which Emerson always preaches. A few of the steel-filings are more completely drawn, for the time being, into its influence than others; and their attracting power is greater, only for this reason. "He who is immersed in what concerns person or place, can not see the problem of existence."[3] So he says, that, however great and welcome may be the claims and virtues of persons, "the instinct of man presses eagerly onward to the impersonal and illimitable."[4] Again, he says, "No historical person begins to

[1] Miscellanies, p. 103.
[2] Essays, second series, pp. 219, 220.
[3] Essays, first series, p. 296.
[4] Ibid., p. 284.

content us," and because "there is no such critic and beggar as this terrible Soul."[1] He believes in the vast and illimitable Soul, and all that persons can do is to give us some hint of its operations. To it we must turn, in it we must put our trust; not in persons, however great. "Before the revelations of the Soul, time, space, and nature shrink away. The soul looketh steadily forwards, creating a world before her, leaving worlds behind her. She has no dates nor rites nor persons nor specialties nor men. The soul knows only the Soul; the web of events is the flowing robe in which she is clothed."[2] The great man is great, only wherein he has been obedient to the voice of the Spirit. All men ought and may be thus obedient. Emerson, consequently, dwells most emphatically on the need of Soul-trust, of accepting that teaching which the Universal Mind gives to every person. "A man should learn to detect and watch that gleam of light which flashes across his mind within, more than the luster of the firmament of bards and sages."[3] He is to trust that power within, because it is the Universal Mind speaking through him, and because he represents somewhat of its nature no other person can express. Each person is to trust himself, because "the power which resides in him is new in nature; and none but he knows what that is which he can do, nor does he know until he has tried."[4]

Emerson's doctrine of self-trust is really that of Soul-trust. It depends on his doctrine of self-renunciation, rejection of all individual desires and purposes, that the Spirit may speak through us. It depends on man's being an inlet of the Over-soul, on his doctrine of immediate intuition and revelation. We are not to trust the individual self, but that Self which unites man in immediate cognition with God. "Nothing is at last sacred but the integrity of your own mind,"[5] because the mind is the descending Spirit. "No law can be sacred to me but that of my nature,"[6] because it is the law of the Over-

[1] Society and Solitude, p. 274.
[2] Essays, first series, p. 249.
[3] Ibid., p. 39.
[4] Ibid., p. 40.
[5] Ibid., p. 44.
[6] Ibid.

soul. "The magnetism which all original action exerts is explained when we inquire the reason of self-trust. Who is the Trustee? What is the aboriginal Self on which a universal reliance may be grounded? The inquiry leads us to that source, at once the essence of genius, of virtue, and of life, which we call Spontaneity, or Instinct."[1] Whoever so lives that this power works freely in him will find that "it is not by any known or accustomed way; he shall not discern the footprints of any other; he shall not see the face of man; he shall not hear any name; the way, the thought, the good, shall be wholly strange and new. It shall exclude example and experience. All persons that ever existed are its forgotten ministers."[2] Emerson asks why it is that we prate of self-reliance; and says it is not because the individual is a confident power in himself, but because he is the agent of that Soul which speaks through him. God will deign to enter and inhabit, only the man who puts off all foreign support, and stands alone.[3] This is the doctrine of self-renunciation in another form. We surrender ourselves absolutely to the will of God, obey his laws, hearken only to his voice, and then we become strong with his strength and wise with his truth. That this is what he means by self-trust, Emerson has himself distinctly stated. "It is, he says, our practical perception of the Deity in man. It has its deep foundations in religion. If you have ever known a good mind among the Quakers, you will have found *that* is the element of their faith." He says that books or men can not "compare with the greatness of that counsel which is open to you in happy solitude. I mean that there is for you the following of an inward leader, — a slow discrimination that there is for each a Best Counsel, which enjoins the fit word and the fit act for every moment."[4] Emerson agrees with the Quakers, and all other mystics who believe in an Inward Light, or guidance. In his doctrine of self-reliance, however, he comes nearer to Swedenborg's idea of self-hood; and he approaches also

[1] Ibid., p. 55.
[2] Ibid., p. 60.
[3] Ibid., p. 78.
[4] Letters and Social Aims, pp. 276, 277.

very closely to Hegel's conception of personality. We reject the individual self, accept the guidance and influx of the Over-soul, and therein we find a higher and truer self. In rejecting the individual for the universal, as Emerson so constantly urges us to do, we are not to overlook that personality which separates us from all other souls.

"Every mind has a new compass, a new north, a new direction of its own, differencing its genius and aim from every other mind, — as every man, with whatever family resemblances, has a new countenance, new manner, new voice, new thoughts, and new character. Whilst he shares with all mankind the gift of reason and the moral sentiment, there is a teaching for him from within, which is leading him in a new path, and, the more it is trusted, separates and signalizes him, while it makes him more important and necessary to society. We call this specialty the *bias* of each individual. And none of us will ever accomplish any thing excellent or commanding except when he listens to this whisper, which is heard by him alone. Swedenborg called it the *proprium*, — not a thought shared with others, but constitutional to the man. A point of education that I can never too much insist upon is this tenet, that every individual man has a bias which he must obey, and that it is only as he feels and obeys this that he rightly develops and attains his legitimate power in the world. It is his magnetic needle, which points always in one direction to his proper path, with more or less variation from any other man's. He is never happy nor strong until he finds it, keeps it; learns to be at home with himself; learns to watch the delicate hints and insights that come to him, and to have the entire assurance of his own mind. And in this self-respect, or hearkening to the privatest oracle, he need never be at a loss. In morals, this is conscience; in intellect, genius; in practice, talent; not to imitate or surpass a particular man in *his* way, but to bring out your own new way; to each his own method, style, wit, eloquence." [1]

[1] Letters and Social Aims, p. 274.

XXIV.

FATE AND FREEDOM.

ETHICS have their foundation in intuition, according to Emerson. With Kant, he does not distinguish between morality and religion, but makes them one and the same, the product of man's natural, universal inspiration. He describes the moral sentiment in the very same words with which he describes the workings of religious intuition. Morality results from the direct presence of God in all things, from his delegating divine power to every atom and man. It is everywhere the same life that is manifest, the life of the great Indwelling God; so that it is the same fact existing in man and atom. "There is no difference of quality, but only of more or less." The immanent presence of God gives to all things the law of his nature, the direction of his thought. This obedience of all things to the attractions of the Indwelling God is law in nature, morality in man. This fatal necessity of obedience to the law of God is the basis of thought, but there it is made alive with moral power. "In us it is inspiration; out there in Nature we see its fatal strength. We call it the moral sentiment."[1] To the objector, he emphasizes this necessity of law and obedience:—

> "Let me show him that the dice are loaded; that the colors are fast, because they are the native colors of the fleece; that the globe is a battery, because every atom is a magnet; and that the police and sincerity of the universe are secured by God's delegating his divinity to every particle; that there is no room for hypocrisy, no margin for choice."[2]

Emerson is not a fatalist, though he uses the word fate so often. He uses the words law, necessity, fate, in

[1] Conduct of Life, p. 192. [2] Ibid., p. 193.

a sense quite other than that usually given them. He means by them the invincible order and unity of the world of spirit, that its methods are perfect and invariable; that justice can never be violated; that the truth is always the same, and always faithful to itself. The moral sentiment speaks to us the law of God, which never changes, which can not be broken. So he says, —

"The lessons of the moral sentiment are, once for all, an emancipation from that anxiety which takes the joy out of all life. It teaches a great peace. It comes itself from the highest place. It is that, which, being in all sound natures, and strongest in the best and most gifted men, we know to be implanted by the Creator of men. It is a commandment at every moment, and in every condition in life, to do the duty of that moment, and to abstain from doing the wrong. And it is so near and inward and constitutional to each, that no commandment can compare with it in authority. All wise men regard it as the voice of the Creator himself."[1]

It is thus he regards the moral sentiment, as the direct voice of God to the soul of man, through intuition. His doctrine of necessity and fate is in entire agreement with it. He recognizes man's relations to nature and the force of the environment, he gives full credit to circumstances, the laws of heredity he fully recognizes. In his essay on Fate, as well as elsewhere, he has written of their influence. All conditions within which the free spirit acts, he knows under the one word, fate. By it he means the limiting, circumscribing conditions of material existence, the limits which nature sets for the action of the soul. In the following paragraphs his meaning may be fully seen: —

"An expense of ends to means is fate, — organization tyrannizing over character. The menagerie, or forms and powers of the spine, is a book of fate; the bill of the bird, the skull of the snake, determines tyrannically its limits. So is the scale of races, of temperaments; so is sex; so is climate; so is the re-action of talents, imprisoning the vital power in certain directions. Every spirit makes its house, but afterwards the house confines the spirit."

"Nature is, what you may do. There is much you may not. We have two things, — the circumstance and the life. Once we

[1] The Preacher, p. 8.

thought positive power was all. Now we learn that negative power, or circumstance, is half. Nature is the tyrannous circumstance; the thick skull; the sheathed snake; the ponderous, rock-like jaw; necessitated activity; violent direction; the conditions of a tool, like the locomotive, strong enough on its track, but which can do nothing but mischief off of it; or skates, which are wings on the ice, but fetters on the ground. The book of Nature is the book of Fate."

"A man's power is hooped in by necessity, which, by many experiments, he touches on every side, until he learns its arc. The limitations refine as the soul purifies, but the ring of necessity is always perched at the top. If we give it the high sense in which the poets use it, even thought itself is not above Fate; that, too, must act according to eternal laws; and all that is willful and fantastic in it is in opposition to its fundamental essence. Last of all, high over thought, in the world of morals, Fate appears as vindicator, leveling the high, lifting the low, requiring justice in man, and always striking soon or late, when justice is not done. What is useful will last; what is hurtful will sink."[1]

In morals and religion fate becomes the polar opposite of spontaneity and the laws or conditions of intuition. So frequent is Emerson's use of the word *fate*, many of his readers are led astray by it, and forget that his primary idea is that of spontaneity, or intuition; while fate is only the term to indicate its limits, that intuition is only for those who obey its laws. Emerson accepts both spontaneity and fate, intuition and law; but he does not attempt to reconcile them by any philosophical explanation: —

"If there be irresistible dictation, he says, this dictation understands itself. If we must accept fate, we are not less compelled to affirm liberty, the significance of the individual, the grandeur of duty, the power of character. This is true, and that other is true. But our geometry can not span these extreme points, and reconcile them. What to do? By obeying each thought frankly, by harping, or, if you will, pounding on each string, we learn at last its power. By the same obedience to other thoughts, we learn theirs; and then comes some reasonable hope of harmonizing them. We are sure, that, though we know not how, necessity does comport with liberty, the individual with the world, my polarity with the spirit of the times."[2]

There is fate everywhere, in matter, mind, and morals, as bound or limitation; but fate also has its lord, its

[1] Conduct of Life, pp. 6, 11, 16, 17. [2] Ibid., p. 2.

limits. In man there is free will, and freedom itself becomes then a necessity. There is always choosing and acting in the soul, and intellect annuls fate. The condition of freedom Emerson puts into these words: "So far as a man thinks, he is free."[1] When a man renounces his own whims and guesses, takes the divine directions, learns and obeys the laws of God, then he conquers, and becomes the master of fate. The first step to the mastering of fate is, that we shall recognize the invariable will of God, the absolute order and unity of the universe. The second is, self-renunciation and obedience, perfect acceptance of that will and those laws. Wherever there are any facts whose law is not known and obeyed, there is fate. On the other hand, freedom is knowledge of the infinite law, and obedience to it. There is organization behind, liberty before, because intellect is constantly discovering the laws of the world, and by obeying masters them. "Liberation of the will from the sheaths and clogs of organization which he has outgrown, is the end and aim of this world."[2] All experience, all thought, leads to this blessed result: —

> "Just as much intellect as you add, so much organic power. He who sees through the design, presides over it, and must will that which must be. Our thought, though it were only an hour old, affirms an oldest necessity, not to be separated from thought, and not to be separated from will. They must always have co-existed. It apprises us of its sovereignty and godhead, which refuse to be severed from it. It is not mine or thine, but the will of all mind. It is poured into the wills of all men, as the soul itself which constitutes them men. I know not whether there be, as is alleged, in the upper region of our atmosphere, a permanent westerly current, which carries with it all atoms which rise to that height; but I see, that, when souls reach a certain clearness of perception, they accept a knowledge and motive above selfishness. A breath of will blows eternally through the universe of souls in the direction of the right and necessary. It is the air which all intellects inhale and exhale, and it is the wind which blows the worlds into order and orbit."[3]

Freedom within bonds, necessitated freedom, is what Emerson teaches. Here especially he recognizes the law of antinomy as developed by Kant and Hegel, by

[1] Ibid., p. 19. [2] Ibid., p. 30. [3] Ibid., p. 22.

which we rise through contrasts and opposition to a higher point of view, to a higher truth, which absorbs, and holds within itself, the two oppositions. Fate and freedom are alike true, though they antagonize each other. They are the same truth seen from opposite directions, and neither phase of this truth can be spared. If, however, an explicit affirmation of free will is desired, Emerson has given it: —

> "Morals implies freedom and will, he says. The will constitutes the man. He has his life in Nature, like a beast; but choice is born in him; here is he that chooses; here is the Declaration of Independence, the July Fourth of zoölogy and astronomy. He chooses, — as the rest of the creation does not. But will, pure and perceiving, is not willfulness. When a man, through stubbornness, insists to do this or that, something absurd or whimsical, only because he will, he is weak; he blows with his lips against the tempest, he dams the incoming ocean with his cane. It were an unspeakable calamity if any one should think he had the right to impose a private will on others. That is the part of a striker, an assassin. All violence, all that is dreary and repels, is not power, but the absence of power. Morals is the direction of the will on universal ends." [1]

The world is a unity, under the direction of perfect order; that is, it obeys invariable law. Man can elect to obey or disobey this order, to keep the laws or to break them. When he keeps them, rising to that point where he understands them as the workings of the perfect methods of God, then he gladly, of his own free will, accepts them, and finds they impose no restraints, that they are one with the highest spirit of free intelligence. When we yield up the attempt to guide ourselves, and accept the guidance of that great Soul in whom we live, then do we for the first time discover what it is to have freedom of will, to have, not the impulse and license of the disorderly soul, but the perfect liberty of those who know and joyously follow the true and the right. To this thought Emerson constantly returns, and urges the vital need of overcoming all private, selfish desires, all individual purposes and motives, all wishes which separate from the great order

[1] Character, p. 356.

of the world and the life of our fellow-men, and of accepting those things alone which are universal. When we have attained the true point of outlook upon life, when we see the order of the world is sacred and necessary, we gladly accept the pain and retribution consequent upon our own disobedience. We rejoice that no hurt can be brought upon God's fair world, though we must suffer. This doctrine of lowly trust and obedience, of having no will but the will of God, Emerson has clearly taught in one of the most striking and beautiful passages in all his writings. It should be remembered, however, that in this trust and submission he finds the very conditions of self-reliance and personal freedom.

"A man should be a guest in his own house, and a guest in his own thought. He is there to speak for truth; but who is he? Some clod the earth has snatched from the ground, and with fire has fashioned to a momentary man. Without the truth he is a clod again. Let him find his superiority in not wishing superiority; find the riches of love which possesses that which it adores; the riches of poverty; the height of lowliness, the immensity of to-day; and, in the passing hour, the age of ages. Wondrous state of man! Never so happy as when he has lost all private interests and regards, and exists only in obedience and love of the Author."

"We perish, and perish gladly, if the law remains. I hope it is conceivable that a man may go to ruin gladly, if he see that thereby no shade falls on that he loves and adores. . . . Cripples and invalids, we doubt not there are bounding fawns in the forest, and lilies with graceful, springing stem; so neither do we doubt or fail to love the eternal law, of which we are such shabby practicers. Truth gathers itself spotless and unhurt after all our surrenders and concealments and partisanship, never hurt by the treachery or ruin of its best defenders."

"Have you said to yourself ever, 'I abdicate all choice, I see it is not for me to interfere. I see that I have been one of the crowd; that I have been a pitiful person, because I have wished to be my own master, and to dress, and order my whole way and system of living. I thought I managed it very well. I see that my neighbors think so. I have heard prayers. I have prayed, even; but I have never until now dreamed that this undertaking the entire management of my own affairs was not commendable. I have never seen, until now, that it dwarfed me. I have not discovered, until this blessed ray flashed just now through my soul, that there dwelt any power in nature that would relieve me of my load. But now I see.'

"What is this intoxicating sentiment that allies this scrap of dust to the whole of Nature, and the whole of Fate, — that makes this doll a dweller in ages, mocker at time, able to span all outward advantages, peer and master of the elements? I am taught by it that what touches any thread in the vast web of being touches me. I am representative of the whole; and the good of the whole, or what I call the right, makes me invulnerable.

"How came this creation so magically woven that nothing can do me mischief but myself, — that an invisible fence surrounds my being, which screens me from all harm that I will to resist? If I will stand upright, the creation can not bend me. But if I violate myself, if I commit a crime, the lightning loiters by the speed of retribution, and every act is not hereafter but instantaneously rewarded according to its quality. Virtue is the adopting of this dictate of the universal mind by the individual will. Character is the habit of this obedience, and religion is the accompanying emotion of reverence which the presence of the universal mind ever excites in the individual."[1]

All good for man consists in his obedience to the laws of God, all evil in his disobedience. Truth and virtue, Emerson says, are an influx from God, in response to our obedience to him. "Vice is the absence or departure of the same."[2] Evil is selfishness, personal preference, the desiring a good apart from others. "Every personal consideration that we allow costs us heavenly state. We sell the thrones of angels for a short and turbulent pleasure."[3] His conception of evil he has exactly stated in these words: —

"Good is positive. Evil is merely privative, not absolute; it is like cold, which is the privation of heat. All evil is so much death, or nonentity. Benevolence is absolute and real. So much benevolence as a man hath, so much life hath he. Whilst a man seeks good ends, he is strong by the whole strength of nature. In so far as he roves from these ends, he bereaves himself of power, or auxiliaries; his being shrinks out of all remote channels, he becomes less and less, a mote, a point, until absolute badness is absolute death."[4]

This conception of evil, as merely a deprivation of life in its fullness, is common to the mystics. Schelling says, that, though evil is necessary, it is nothing real. Eckhart sees in it necessary phases of the return

[1] Sovereignty of Ethics, p. 410.
[2] Essays, first series, p. 108.
[3] Ibid., p. 279.
[4] Miscellanies, p. 120.

of man to God, or a means to the realization of man's perfection. This idea anticipates Emerson's attitude towards this problem, as does Eckhart's assertion that sin is necessary to the development of good in man. He says we should not wish not to have sinned, and this thought Emerson has also more than once expressed.

Emerson says that "for the intellect there is no crime."[1] When we apprehend the laws of the world, we see they can not be broken so far as the laws are concerned, that they act always the same whether we obey them or not; consequently no law, no truth, no principle, is ever violated or ever can be, so far as the law in itself is concerned. It is in us alone the evil is done, the violation is wrought. So perfect does he regard the order of the universe, he can not think of any actual flaw in it, any real discord. But when we do violence to our own natures, forsaking the law of God, then conscience declares we have done wrong, and demands renewed obedience. "Saints are sad, he says, because they behold sin from the point of view of the conscience, and not of the intellect; a confusion of thought. Sin seen from the thought, is a diminution or *less;* seen from the conscience or will, it is a pravity or *bad*. The intellect names it shade, absence of light, and no essence. The conscience must feel it as essence, essential evil. This it is not; it has an objective existence, but no subjective."[2] Again he says, "That pure malignity can exist, is the extreme proposition of unbelief. It is not to be entertained by a rational agent; it is atheism; it is the last profanation. The divine effort is never relaxed; the carrion in the sun will convert itself to grass and flowers; and man, though in brothels, or jails, or on gibbets, is on his way to all that is good and true."[3] Yet he says that "every thing is superficial, and perishes, but love and truth only."[4] "He who loves goodness, harbors angels, reveres reverence, and lives with God. The less, however, we have to do with our sins, the better. No man

[1] Essays, second series, p. 80.
[2] Ibid.
[3] Representative Men, p. 138.
[4] Ibid., p. 139.

can afford to waste his moments in compunctions."[1] We are not to think constantly about our own good, but to look forward towards loyalty to God and the universal good which results from it. Thus he makes all evil to be lack of harmony, good in the making. Sin is disobedience, selfishness, disloyalty. In his first book he taught that life is for discipline, to teach us the lessons of spiritual loyalty. The same idea he has maintained in all his books. We try ourselves against the laws of the world, seek to go forward in ways of our own. We are permitted to do so, only because it is by free choice, by our own seekings and experiments, we at last gladly and willingly accept the liberty which is obedience. These missteps, these experiments, and struggles forward, teach us the way of truth as otherwise we could not learn it. "We are used as brute atoms, until we think; then we use all the rest. Nature turns all malfaisance to good."[2]

Emerson has well taught the fact which all historians of social progress now recognize, that man has developed by experience, by conflict of interests, by survival of those men and interests fittest to carry forward social order. In his essay on War he gave it full recognition, and in that entitled Considerations by the Way he developed it more fully. He says the spawning productivity of nature "is not noxious or needless. You will say, this rabble of nations might be spared. But no, they are all counted and depended on. Fate keeps every thing alive so long as the smallest thread of public necessity holds it on the tree. The coxcomb and bully and thief class are allowed as proletaries, every one of their vices being the excess or acridity of a virtue. The mass are animal, in pupilage, and near chimpanzee. But the units whereof this mass is composed are neuters, every one of which may be grown to a queen-bee." We find the majority of men are unripe, have not yet come to themselves; while in the passing moment the quadruped interest is very prone to prevail.[3] He says "the first lesson of history is the good

[1] Ibid., p. 137. [2] Conduct of Life, p. 221. [3] Ibid.

of evil. Good is a good doctor, but Bad is sometimes a better."[1] His meaning is indicated in numerous historical illustrations, all showing there is a tendency in things to right themselves. "The war or revolution or bankruptcy that shatters a rotten system allows things to take a new and natural order. The sharpest evils are bent into that periodicity which makes the errors of the planets and the fevers and distempers of men self-limiting. Nature is upheld by antagonism. Passions, resistance, danger, are educators. We acquire the strength we have overcome." So he holds that men are indebted to their vices and defects for a best part of their education. Moral deformity he finds to be good passion out of place. When the impulse which creates the evil is wisely directed, directed in conformity with the methods of nature, then it is good. Equally true it is of communities, that an apparent evil may result in good. He says "we can not trace the triumphs of civilization to such benefactors as we wish. The greatest meliorator of the world is selfish, huckstering trade."[2] It is not because trade is selfish that it is the means of good, but because it unites nations in common interests. Commerce can prosper only where there are good laws, and a large measure of justice is secured. For the sake of trade, where no higher ends are regarded, law and good order are established. There is always at work in the affairs of the world, according to Emerson, a power which compels man to be just; so that what is useful and right will last, what is hurtful will sink.[3] In trade, therefore, and everywhere else, it is only the true, just, and right which prospers. And in many other ways Emerson is far from being merely an individualist in his views of human progress. If he would have us sit alone and listen to the Inward Voice, he does not regard that as the only means of human development. To a remarkable degree he recognizes the value of united action, he sees that the race is a *solidarité*, and he entirely

[1] Ibid., p. 222. [2] Society and Solitude, p. 149.
[3] Conduct of Life, p. 17.

rejects the theory that one can be perfect while any other is imperfect. Though so strong a believer in the great man, yet he clearly enough sees that social concert is necessary to human progress. He also recognizes the development which has been secured by the general advance of intelligence. Indeed, Emerson is too broad-minded to see no truth but in one direction. Those who criticise him for his extreme individualism are usually not capable of that breadth of view he has always shown, and do not as clearly perceive as he does, that there is truth in both the individualistic and the socialistic theories of progress.

Emerson is an optimist who never doubts, who thoroughly believes that all things are good at heart. He will not, therefore, believe in any evil which is more than a temporary lack of harmony. He sees God everywhere, and everywhere delegating his law and order to the world. "There is no chance, he says, and no anarchy in the universe. All is system and gradation."[1] It is his large faith in law, as the highest method of freedom, which permits him to believe there is no real evil in the world. He sees a perfect law of compensation at work everywhere, a method of cause and effect so exact, that there can be no good or evil which is not deserved. Every condition has grown out of precedent conditions. Life is to us what we make it. Emerson has outgrown anthropomorphism; he does not believe in a God of arbitrary decrees. The methods of God he regards as perfect in their order, system, and invariableness. All conformity to those methods is good, all disregard of them evil. So he regards every evil men suffer from as evidence that the laws of God are not obeyed. Those laws are self-executing; and the results they produce in us are the exact measures of our obedience to them, and hence of our deserving. God has no favorites, his laws affect all alike. Emerson sees that this perfect order in the universe, self-executing, invariable, a law of compensation, a law also of cause and effect, insures for each

[1] Ibid., p. 287.

one a destiny of his own selecting. God judges no man, nor chooses heaven or hell for any. Men always receive and enjoy precisely that measure of good or evil they deserve, which results from their measure of obedience to the laws of God. "He is great whose eyes are opened to see that the reward of actions can not be escaped, because he is transformed into his action, and taketh its nature, which bears its own fruit, like every other tree."[1]

No evil ever escapes unpunished, according to Emerson. Whatever theory the intellect devises as explaining the problem of evil, he finds the conscience always proclaiming that all evil is to be dreaded and shunned as real. Retribution for evil done he finds to be exacting and instantaneous. In his essay on Compensation, he has given to the world a noble theory of rewards and punishments. He sees God present everywhere, in the fullness of his being, with the whole vigor of his life, and in the entire power of his law. So he says, —

"The true doctrine of omnipresence is, that God appears with all his parts in every moss and cobweb. The value of the universe contrives to throw itself into every point. If the good is there, so is the evil; if the affinity, so is the repulsion; if the force, so the limitation.

"Thus is the universe alive. All things are moral. That soul, which within us is a sentiment, outside of us is a law. We feel its inspiration; out there in history we can see its fatal strength. Justice is not postponed. A perfect equity adjusts its balance in all parts of life. The dice of God are always loaded. . . . Every secret is told, every crime is punished, every virtue rewarded, every wrong redressed, in silence and certainty. What we call retribution is the universal necessity by which the whole appears wherever a part appears. . . . Crime and punishment grow out of one stem. Punishment is a fruit that unsuspected ripens within the flower of the pleasure which concealed it. Cause and effect, means and ends, seed and fruit, can not be severed; for the effect always blooms in the cause, the end pre-exists in the means, the fruit in the seed. . . . Pleasure is taken out of pleasant things, profit out of profitable things, power out of strong things, as soon as we seek to separate them from the whole. We can no more halve things and get the sensual good, by itself, than we can get an inside that shall have no outside, or a light without a shadow.

[1] Ibid., p. 201.

"Life invests itself with inevitable conditions, which the unwise seek to dodge, which one and another brags that he does not know, that they do not touch him, — but the brag is on his lips, the conditions are in his soul. If he escapes them in one part, they attack him in another more vital part. If he has escaped them in form, and in the appearance, it is because he has resisted his life, and fled from himself; and the retribution is so much death."[1]

Here, again, we see the vital significance of what Emerson teaches concerning self-renunciation and obedience. As we renounce all selfish ends, all whims of our own, and seek exactly to obey the laws of the world, are we made strong and whole. As we disobey, retribution follows. Emerson points out how this retribution results from the failure to obey the laws of God. As we exercise the muscles, they grow stronger. If we study, we grow wiser. Strength comes only by exercise, wisdom only by search for it. Muscles not used grow powerless; who does not study remains ignorant. Everywhere it is the same. Love begets love. "The exclusionist in religion does not see that he shuts the door of heaven on himself, in striving to shut out others. Treat men as pawns and ninepins, and you shall suffer as well as they. If you leave out their heart, you shall lose your own."[2] It is not merely that men treat you as you treat them; but all narrowness and exclusiveness make little the soul, dwarf its sympathies, cramp its energies. "All infractions of love and equity in our social relations are speedily punished."[3] They are punished by fear, hatred, and war. The tyrant is constantly in danger of losing his life from the hatred of those he enslaves. The selfish rich man finds many dangers besetting his riches. "The league between virtue and nature, Emerson says, engages all things to assume a hostile front to vice. The beautiful laws and substances of the world persecute and whip the traitor. He finds that things are arranged for truth and benefit, but there is no den in the wide world to hide a rogue. Commit a crime, and

[1] Essays, first series, pp. 91-94. [2] Ibid., p. 99. [3] Ibid

the earth is made of glass." On the other hand, the law holds with equal surety for all right action. "Love, and you shall be loved. All love is mathematically just, as much as the two sides of an algebraic equation. The good man has absolute good, which, like fire, turns every thing to its own nature, so that you can not do him any harm."[1]

From this law of compensation and retribution, as Emerson interprets it, grow two results, — that men are seen as they are, and that all men are capable of receiving from life an equal good. For the moment we may have credit for virtue we do not possess, by those who do not penetrate to moral causes; but we soon appear to all the wise as we are. Foolish are they who think they can cheat God, and that his laws will forget to act. On the contrary, every disobedience of the laws of the world instantly betrays itself; and our nature depreciates, weakens.

"As much virtue as there is, so much appears; as much goodness as there is, so much reverence it commands. All the devils respect virtue. The high, the generous, the self-devoted sect, will always instruct and command mankind. Never was a sincere word utterly lost. Never a magnanimity fell to the ground, but there is some heart to greet and accept it unexpectedly. A man passes for what he is worth. What he is engraves itself on his face, on his form, on his fortunes, in letters of light. Concealment avails him nothing; boasting nothing. There is confession in the glances of our eyes, in our smiles, in salutations, and the grasp of hands. His sin bedaubs him, mars all his good impression. Men know not why they do not trust him, but they do not trust him. His vice glasses his eyes, cuts lines of mean expression in his cheeks, pinches the nose, sets the mark of the beast on the back of the head, and writes O fool! fool! on the forehead of a king.

"If you would not be known to do any thing, never do it. A man may play fool in the drifts of a desert, but every grain of sand shall seem to see. He may be a solitary eater, but he can not keep his foolish counsel. A broken complexion, a swinish look, ungenerous acts, and the want of due knowledge, — all blab.

"On the other hand, the hero fears not, that, if he withhold the avowal of a just and brave act, it will go unwitnessed and unloved. One knows it, — himself, — and is pledged by it to sweetness of peace, and to nobleness of aim, which will prove in the end a better proclamation of it than the relating of the incident. Virtue is

[1] Ibid., pp. 103, 104.

the adherence in action to the nature of things, and the nature of things makes it prevalent. It consists in a perpetual substitution of being for seeming.

"The lesson which these observations convey is, Be, and not seem. Let us acquiesce. Let us take our bloated nothingness out of the path of the divine circuits. Let us unlearn our wisdom of the world. Let us lie low in the Lord's power, and learn that truth alone makes rich and great."[1]

The law of compensation brings men to the same level, so far as the benefits are concerned which nature gives. The genius has his defects and his larger duties and anxieties. The plowman is ignorant in books, but he has his own ability and enjoyment, and his clearer perception of realities. "The walls of rude minds, Emerson says, are scrawled all over with facts, with thoughts."[2] "We are all wise, he adds. The difference between persons is not in wisdom, but in art."[3] Again he says, "The permanent interest of every man is, never to be in a false position, but to have the weight of Nature to back him in all that he does. Riches and poverty are a thick or thin costume, and our life — the life of all of us — identical."[4] We all get out of life much the same results. All experiences teach the same laws of renunciation, obedience, and self-reliance. As we receive only what we pay for, if we have much, we have many burdens with it. Because, however, each soul is of the nature of the Universal Mind, it has free access into all truth. Each man is an inlet to all wisdom when his mind is open to reason, and he "is made a freeman of the whole estate. What Plato has thought, he may think; what a saint has felt, he may feel; what at any time has befallen any man, he can understand." This is the thought of his lines which serve as the motto to the essay on History. As an organ of the Universal Mind, each soul is admitted into every thought and aspiration of the greatest souls.

"I am owner of the sphere,
Of the seven stars and the solar year,
Of Cæsar's hand, and Plato's brain,
Of Lord Christ's heart, and Shakspere's strain."

[1] Essays, first series, pp. 142, 143.
[2] Ibid., p. 300.
[3] Ibid., p. 302.
[4] Conduct of Life, p. 286.

In morals, however, we can not be alike; for obedience receives a reward evil can not possibly find. On virtue there is no tax; "for that is the incoming of God himself, or absolute existence, without any compensation." This incoming of God to the soul is a gift of grace to those who make pure the channels of their being for its reception, but all men are equal so far as every quality is concerned but the moral.

"In the nature of the soul is the compensation for the inequalities of condition. The radical tragedy of nature seems to be the distinction of *more* and *less*. How can *less* not feel the pain; how not feel indignation or malevolence towards *more*? Look at those who have less faculty, and one feels sad, and knows not well what to make of it. He almost shuns their eye; he fears they will upbraid God. What should they do? It seems a great injustice. But see the facts nearly, and these mountainous inequalities vanish. Love reduces them, as the sun melts the iceberg in the sea. The heart and soul of all men being one, this bitterness of *His* and *Mine* ceases. His is mine."

"The compensations of calamity are made apparent to the understanding also, after long intervals of time. A fever, a mutilation, a cruel disappointment, a loss of wealth, a loss of friends, seems at the moment unpaid loss, and unpayable. But the sure years reveal the deep remedial force that underlies all facts."[1]

The identification of morals and religion has not been a peculiarity of Emerson's. The idealists have had this thought before them from the time of Plato, and by the mystics it has been made prominent. In the same way, the unity of being and knowledge has not been new to Emerson. The mystics, who have found their center of thought in the teachings of Plotinus, Eckhart, Boehme, and Schelling, have all said that conduct and knowledge always stand at the same level in each human soul. Many of the idealists have accepted the same conclusion, as it was very clearly taught by Plato. Schelling and Carlyle alike say that intellect and goodness always go together, always are of equal power in the individual. Emerson says "the good man will be the wise man."[2] The moral sentiment to him "seems to

[1] Essays, first series, pp. 110, 113.

[2] Essays, first series, p. 215

be the fountain of intellect," and it is the basis alike of thought and being.[1] "The high intellect, he says, is absolutely at one with moral nature."[2] This idea he has even more explicitly stated in these words: "There is an intimate inter-dependence of intellect and morals. Given the equality of two intellects, — which will form the most reliable judgments, the good, or the bad hearted? So intimate is this alliance of mind and heart, that talent uniformly sinks with character. The bias of errors of principle carries away men into perilous courses as soon as their will does not control their passion or talent."[3]

He believes that the human being is so thoroughly a unit that a defect in any part of it appears in all the others. "I find the unity in human structures, he says, rather virulent and pervasive; that a crudity in the blood will appear in the argument; a hump in the shoulder will appear in the speech and handiwork. If his mind could be seen, the hump would be seen."[4] That is, the body is a picture, a likeness of the soul, and reflects the soul's true nature.

The analogous doctrine of moral affinity also appears in Emerson's pages. He says "society exists by chemical affinity,"[5] and that in any company a rapid self-distribution takes place, into sets and pairs. This idea he presents in the essay on Spiritual Laws, where he says that a man is a selecting principle, gathering his like to him wherever he goes. "Nothing is more deeply punished, he says, than the neglect of the affinities, by which alone society should be formed."[6] This affinity is expressed through the eyes. Souls that are fitted to each other look into each other's eyes and read each other's secrets without words. This idea occasionally appears in the essays, and it is the main thought of the poem on The Visit. Goethe has given expression to the same thought.

[1] Character, p. 358.
[2] Sovereignty of Ethics, p. 405.
[3] Conduct of Life, p. 189.
[4] Ibid., p. 38.
[5] Society and Solitude, p. 13.
[6] Essays, first series, pp. 129, 135.

"The unit of the visit,
The encounter of the wise, —
Say, what other meter is it
Than the meeting of the eyes?
Nature poureth into nature
Through the channels of that feature.
Single look has drained the breast;
Single moment years confessed."

In judging Emerson's moral theories, it should not be forgotten that he is an optimist, who believes there is no evil, that there is nothing in the universe but what is good. He refuses to see the evil, to recognize that burden of pain and misery, which afflicts so many minds. All is good, all is under the perfect domain of Absolute Love, all tends to a blessed destiny; this is Emerson's belief. This faith in the universal good has increased with him as he has grown older, giving to his life a serenity and peace and trust of the deepest and profoundest character. The carrion that rots in the sun, the criminal who breaks every law of man and God, are yet on their way to blessedness. It is easy to misunderstand and misrepresent this optimism; less easy, perhaps, to state it so as not to appear to annul moral distinctions. Whoever will give heed, however, to Emerson's declaration, that every wrong is punished, and that no moral evil can prosper at last, will see that he does not ignore the proper distinctions to be made in regard to conduct. He believes in universal progress, that all things are on their way to perfect harmony with God; he believes that evil and pain and misery are means to this final restoration; but he also believes that the morally pure and holy is, in the end, the only means to the perfect realization of this great consummation. He believes the good is absolute and the evil only phenomenal. The evil is a part of the discipline by which the soul is restored to its union with the Over-soul. This optimism determines all his views of life, as well as his theories of man and the universe and religion. It is to him an unfailing source of confidence in the integrity of man and nature, and it colors his every thought with an aspect of joy and hope.

XXV.

CONCERNING IMMORTALITY.

MYSTICISM delights to dwell upon the complete union with God which is possible to the soul. The mystic goes so far in this direction as to speak of man's absorption in God, of the soul as being lost in Godhead. It is always difficult to decide the precise meaning of such language. It is yet a debated question whether the Buddhist, who is a pure mystic, believes in annihilation or in an utter cessation of that which is merely individual. Only a few European mystics have gone so far as to leave any doubt as to their meaning. Emerson employs their language, and he accepts their view of immortality. What he means when he writes of this subject can only be clearly understood through the aid of the doctrines of mysticism. The mystic repeats constantly the injunction, that we are to abandon self, and become one with God. Tauler says that man must "simply yield himself to God; ask nothing, desire nothing, love and mean only God." "Some will ask, he says, what remains after a man hath thus lost himself in God? I answer, nothing but a fathomless annihilation of himself; an absolute ignoring of all reference to himself personally; of all aim of his own in will and heart, in way, in purpose, or in use. For in this self-loss man sinks so deep, that, if he could, out of pure love and loveliness, sink deeper, yea, and become absolutely nothing, he would do so right gladly." He even goes so far as to say that "when the soul enters into the unmixed light, she, with her created I, sinks so deeply into her own nothingness, that she can not by her own power regain the sense of separate existence as creature." By this he does not mean annihilation, not even extinction of personality; for he adds, "But God upholds her with his uncreated power, and *keeps the soul still herself.*" So far from believing in absorption of the soul into the ocean of Being, is Tauler, that he asserts the "free self-determination of man," and says that God, in being free and uncreated, is "alone equal to the soul as touching freedom." Man becomes nothing, and yet God alone has freedom equal to his! Tauler's "nothing," as in the case of the other mystics, is not annihilation, absorption, or cessation of personality. It is perfect harmony with God, and cessation of all passion, all merely individual desire. Schelling says that man has the immanent ground of his being in the Absolute, is nothing apart from the indwelling God; yet he maintains that man is free and personal. "So little, he says, do immanence in God and freedom contradict each other, that only what is free is, in so far as it is so, in God; while what is devoid of freedom, is, in so far as it is so, of necessity without God." Freedom, therefore, consists in a rejection of what is individual and selfish, for a personal self-determination in harmony with God. This is Emerson's idea, when he dwells so strongly upon what is individual, and rejects it as the soul's greatest enemy. When he bids us renounce all that is individual and particular, he does not ask us to cease to exist or to become absorbed in the Universal Spirit. He also bids us have self-reliance; and he says that each soul is a new and unmeasured power, unlike all other souls. He rejects the individual, local, notional, selfish; he retains the personal, divine, and eternal.

The *Theologia Germanica* sees the soul's freedom in submission to Eternal Goodness. It says this world is an outer court of eternity, that it is a paradise "in which all things are lawful save one tree and the fruit thereof; nothing is contrary to God but self-will, — to will otherwise than as the Eternal Will would have it." That this world is a part of paradise, that the *now* is eternity, is Emerson's own idea. It is the key to his conception of immortality. Schelling had the same thought. "The I, he says, and its essence, undergoes neither con ditions nor restrictions. Its primitive form is that of Being, pure and eternal. We can not say of it, *it was*, or *it will be*, we can only say, *it is*. It exists absolutely. It is then outside of time and beyond it. The form of its intellectual intuition is eternity. Now, since it is eternal, it has no duration, for duration only relates to objects; so that eternity properly consists in having nothing to do with time." The soul is eternal, and in its powers is the promise of immortality. Yet we know of a truth that the soul is immortal, not by words or by any outward assurance, only by depth of soul, only by perfect harmony of purpose with the Over-soul.[1] This thought Emerson has thus expressed: —

"There is nothing capricious in nature. In nature the implanting of a desire indicates that the gratification of that desire is in the constitution of that creature that feels it. If there is a desire to live in a larger sphere, or with more knowledge and power, it is because life and knowledge and power are good for us, and we are the rational depositories of such things. A future state is an illusion for the ever-present state. It isn't length of life, but depth of life; it isn't duration, but a taking of the soul out of time. The spiritual world takes place, the ever-present, that which is always the same. And this is the way we rise in being. I know that the universe can receive no detriment, that there is a remedy for every wrong, and a satisfaction for every soul.

"I have heard that death takes us away from ill things, not from good. I have heard, that, when we pronounce the name of man, we pronounce the belief of immortality. All great natures delight in stability; all great men find eternity affirmed in the very promise of their faculties. Life is not long enough for art, not long enough for friendship. The evidence from intellect is as valid as the evidence from love. The being that can share a thought and feeling so sublime as confidence in truth, is no mushroom; our dissatisfaction with any other solution is the blazing evidence of immortality."[2]

He thinks, that, as soon as thought is exercised, this belief is inevitable. "As soon as virtue glows, this belief confirms itself. It is a kind of summary or completion of man. It can not rest on a legend; it can not be quoted from one to another; it must have the assur-

[1] Essays, first series, pp. 257, 258.

[2] Newspaper report of a lecture delivered before the Parker Fraternity, Dec. 6, 1870.

ance of a man's faculties that they can fill a larger theater, and a larger term than nature here allows him."[1] He finds that this faith rests on a deep trust in the Universal Spirit alone, on the conviction that nothing can depart from its relations to God. In writing of the power and influence of the moral sentiment, how it absorbs and commands every other purpose and desire, he says "it makes no stipulations for earthly felicity; does not ask, in the absoluteness of its trust, even for the assurance of continued life."[2] This is the ground of Emerson's trust, faith in Spirit, supreme confidence in the will of God. As God orders, as in his law and love is best, man is to accept his destiny. When his trust is strong enough, when he sees to the end of this result, he will find that this is absolutely the best. Emerson has faith in the individual soul, but he has greater faith in the Infinite Goodness which surrounds and contains all things. He adopts Goethe's idea, however, that, "in order to manifest ourselves as a powerful living principle in the future, we must be one;" but he does not adopt Goethe's other opinion, as he is sometimes supposed to do, that "such incomprehensible subjects lie too far off, and only disturb our thoughts if made the theme of daily meditation." "An able man, says Goethe, who has something to do here, and must toil and strive day by day to accomplish it, leaves the future world till it comes, and contents himself with being active and useful in this." Emerson expresses a similar opinion in his essay on Immortality, but in a quite different spirit than Goethe's. He would not shun the subject because indifferent to it, or merely because it is incomprehensible, but because he has a higher ground of trust than his own personal future. Immortality is to him not a thing of time or place, but capacity of soul. The true revelation is in the soul, in its ascent to the sublimer heights of being, and not in words that satisfy a low curiosity. When we accept joyfully the tide of being which floats us into the secrets of nature, and live and work with her, "all unawares the advancing soul has built and

[1] Conduct of Life. [2] Character, p. 373.

forged for itself a new condition, and the question and the answer are one."[1] Emerson's idea is that of Hegel. as Rosenkranz has expressed it in these words: "He remarks that immortality is a quality of mind which is already present, and need not first be mediated by death. It is among the most unhappy errors of mankind that they have expected the truth of spirit, the so-called eternal life, as a *beyond*, or something which begins with death. He everywhere says that we are now and here in the midst of the absolute."[2] Man's immortality is involved in the infinity and eternity of all that is real and spiritual. Emerson accordingly assures us that "the ground of hope is in the infinity of the world, which infinity re-appears in every particle." "Every thing is prospective, and man is to live hereafter. That the world is for his education, is the only sane solution of the enigma."[3] Trust in the soul, as an eternal life in God, is what he here expresses. The capacities of the soul affirm the inspirations of affection and of the moral sentiment.[4] In the Threnody, which commemorates the death of his first son, he has expressed his convictions in words of the strongest meaning.

"Wilt thou not ope thy heart to know
What rainbows teach, and sunsets show?
Verdict which accumulates
From lengthening scroll of human fates,
Voice of earth to earth returned,
Prayers of saints that inly burned,—
Saying, What is excellent,
As God lives, is permanent;
Hearts are dust, hearts' loves remain;
Heart's love will meet thee again."

These lines are expressive enough and clear enough in their meaning, it would seem. In the last lines of the poem he returns to the same thought:—

"House and tenant go to ground,
Lost in God, in Godhead found."

[1] Essays, first series, pp. 257–259.
[2] Hegel as the National Philosopher of Germany.
[3] Letters and Social Aims, pp. 298, 299.
[4] Society and Solitude, p. 300.

By losing life we find it, by absolute obedience we gain perfect freedom, by absorption into God we gain true personality. Emerson always recognizes these antinomies of existence, and finds in immortality a losing of self to gain a higher self.

Elsewhere he has expressed himself very strongly, as in the essay on The Method of Nature. There he says we can not describe the natural history of the soul, but we know it is divine. We do not know if the qualities of the bodily frame have been together before; but we do know the qualities of the soul "did not now begin to exist, can not be sick with my sickness, nor buried in my grave; before the world was they were."[1] When it is asked whither we come and where we are bound, he says the answer can be found only in ourselves, in those intuitions which open to us the world of truth. We fancy that with the dust we depart, and are not; but in so far as the truth enters us, we are immortal with its immortality.[2] He sees the significance of this belief; for he says it is not what we believe concerning it, but *the universal impulse to believe* that is the material circumstance, and is the principal fact in the history of the globe.[3] The knowledge, he says, that we traverse the whole scale of being, from the center to the poles of nature, through the power of thought, and have some stake in every possibility, "lends that sublime luster to death, which philosophy and religion have too outwardly and literally striven to express in the popular doctrine of the immortality of the soul. The reality is more excellent than the report. Here is no ruin, no discontinuity, no spent ball."[4] This trust in thought, in mind, is all the promise we have; but we have found in our experience that it is enough to cover the chasm of death with flowers, for our faculties prophesy for themselves an interminable future of action.[5] All these questions we lust to ask about the future, are a confession of sin. No answer in words can reply to a question

[1] Miscellanies, p. 214.
[2] Ibid., p. 279.
[3] Essays, second series, p. 76.
[4] Ibid., p. 189.
[5] Conduct of Life, pp. 208, 209.

of things. It is not an arbitrary decree of God, but in the nature of man, that a veil shuts down on the facts of to-morrow; for the soul will not have us read any other cipher than that of cause and effect. By this veil which curtains events, it instructs the children of men to live in to-day. His attitude is really one of absolute trust in God, with whom he leaves all the result. The life we now live is so wonderful, so anchored in the Divine, we need take no thought of the morrow. The immortal life is ours now; why worry about the future! In a funeral address he once said, —

"There is to my mind something so absolute in the action of a good man, that we do not, in thinking of him, so much as make any question of the future. For the spirit of the universe seems to say, He has done well; is not that saying all?"[1]

His trust in the soul appears in words like these: —

"A man who has read the works of Plato and Plutarch and Seneca and Kant and Shakspere and Wordsworth, would scorn to ask such *school-dame* questions as whether we shall know each other in the world beyond the grave. Men of genius do not fear to die; they are sure that in the other life they will be permitted to finish the work begun in this; it is only mere men of affairs who tremble at the approach of death."[2]

With him the belief in immortality is involved in his faith in the soul, which is so absolute as to make all questions of duration and residence of little moment. No one could ask, Is God immortal? With Emerson's trust in the soul, it would be as idle to ask concerning it the same question. His thought comes out in such passages as this: —

"Our dissatisfaction with the materialist statement, in whatever form it comes, is a blazing evidence of tendency. The soul does not age with the body. On the borders of the grave the wise man looks forward with equal elasticity of mind and hope; and why not after millions of years on the verge of still newer existence? for it is the nature of intelligent beings to be for ever new to life."[3]

[1] At the funeral of George L. Stearns, Medford, April 14, 1867.

[2] This is from a newspaper report of a lecture on the Relation of Intellect to Morals, delivered in Boston, in 1866, in a course of six on The Philosophy of the People.

[3] From a newspaper report of the lecture on Immortality, as given before the Parker Fraternity, Dec. 4, 1870.

The same thought was once expressed by him in a conversation, when he uttered this most suggestive sentence: "There is hope of a world in which we may see things but once, and then pass on to something new."[1] Here is his faith, in the soul as one with the infinite Over-soul, and sharing in all that God is; and in a life of unending search and attainment, of aspiration and fulfillment, that can not be measured by time. Though he himself refrains from every attempt to put into mortal words these immortal things, for they can be declared no more than the roses' bloom and fragrance can be expressed, yet whoever has genuinely entered into the spirit of his words will surely have found these things there. They furnish the very spirit which animates all his most inspired and inspiring essays.

[1] To a friend, after he had delivered the lecture on Immortality in San Francisco.

XXVI.

THE RELIGION OF THE SOUL.

EMERSON'S philosophic conception of intuition determines his attitude towards every religious problem. When he says that all writing comes by the grace of God, and all doing and having,[1] he expresses the central idea embodied in his essays. Religion is, therefore, for him the inward attraction of the soul for the Universal Spirit, alike a motive and a law of life, an impulse towards truth, a temper and a spirit of trust and obedience. It is a motive, and not a creed; an attraction for truth, and not a church. Its attractions and its truths are too vast for absolute statement; it is a life, and not a dogma. He will not, therefore, attempt to define the spiritual laws; he will set no limits to their operation in his own thought. Consequently no religious writer dogmatizes less, or has less of definition. He shuns expression on the great religious problems, God and immortality, not because he in any sense doubts, but because he believes so much, because no definition is adequate to these great thoughts. He must not be judged as a theologian; he has no capacity for logical statement and rigid abstraction.[2] He is a Fox, an à Kempis, or a Fénelon, a spiritual poet, a seer, a prophet. He would lead men to the truth, and not define it for them. He would make the spiritual realities conscious facts to each mind, and not set them to

[1] Essays, second series, p. 71.

[2] Among those who have criticised Emerson's religious views are Dr. Manning, in his Half-Truths and the Truth; Joseph Cook, in several of his published lectures; and James Freeman Clarke, in a lecture delivered in 1865. The last is the only one of these critics who has shown himself acquainted with Emerson's philosophy, or who has done justice to his religious views. One of the best of his sympathetic expounders is Crozier, in his Religion of the Future

words to be chanted on Sunday. He has spoken of the great truths of the moral and spiritual nature, out of the soul's depths, direct to the heart and mind of other men. There has been no attempt to justify these truths; no logic, argument, reasons. He has announced them as the scientist does the laws of nature, declaring they prove themselves true in the experience of each soul, and of all mankind.

He has been a severe critic of the historic forms of religion, but his real attitude toward all that is genuine has been one of affirmation. More than once has he said, —

"Speak the affirmative; emphasize your choice by utter ignoring of all that you reject, seeing that opinions are temporary, but convictions uniform and eternal, — seeing that a sentiment never loses its pathos or its persuasion, but is youthful after a thousand years."[1]

He sees so much truth in which all men can unite, he would have all which divides them forgotten. As it is, in his opinion, the non-essential, the mere outward form, which divides them, he would have all emphasis removed from it. So he pours forth his rich counsel of charity and liberality, in favor of unity and against division. It is not because he lacks in conviction, or because he thinks one statement as good as another, that he takes this position; but because the truth rises sublimely above all sects and parties to assert itself in the hearts of all men.

"Be not betrayed, he urges, into undervaluing the churches which annoy you by their bigoted claims. They, too, were real churches. They answered to their times the same need as your rejection of them does to yours. I agree with them more than I disagree. I agree with their heart and motive; my discontent is with their limitations and surface and language. Their statement is grown as fabulous as Dante's Inferno. Their purpose is as real as Dante's sentiment, and hatred of vice. Always put the best interpretation on a tenet. Why not on Christianity, wholesome, sweet, and poetic? It is the record of a pure and holy soul, humble, absolutely disinterested, a truth-speaker, and bent on serving, teaching, and uplifting men. Christianity taught the capacity, the

[1] The Preacher, p. 14.

element, to love the All-perfect without a stingy bargain for personal happiness. It taught that to love him was happiness, — to love him in other's virtues."[1]

To class Emerson as a champion of any party in religion would be unjust. No man has deeper convictions than he, but he does not hold them as by the charm of any sectarian name. He sees on all sides, respects the truthful in all sects, loves the good in all religions. He is not even a Christian in any party sense whatever, nor by any means a rejecter of Christianity, much less its foe. He sees the good in it, recognizes its great service in the inculcation of a pure, spiritual religion and a noble morality, loves its lofty spirit of truth and devotion; but he is not carried away by it, will not accept its dictation, or be committed to its defense. He is not a system-builder, finds little interest in the problems which divide sects and religions from each other. A theological student from Harvard once went to him with an account of the differences of opinion there among the Unitarian divinity students. "I am not much interested in these discussions, said he; but still, it does seem deplorable that there is such a tendency in some people to creeds which would take man back to the chimpanzee. I have very good grounds for being a Unitarian, and a Trinitarian too. I need not nibble for ever at one loaf, but eat it, and thank God for it, and earn another."[2] In the same spirit, he expressed himself toward the larger question of the relations of systems of thought to each other, when he said, "I see no objection to being called a Platonist, a Christian, or any other affirmative name, — and no good in negation." This attitude towards religion is characteristic of Lessing, Herder, Goethe, and Carlyle. Lessing's *Nathan the Wise* was a great lesson in comparative religions, showing that the essence of all faiths is the same. In the second part of his *Wilhelm Meister*, Goethe goes even farther, when he writes of the three reverences, and recognizes the spirit of worship instead of the history of religion. Even Schleiermacher rejected the

[1] The Preacher, p. 9. [2] Fraser's Magazine, August, 1864.

historic, and found Christianity, not in literary records, but in the attainment of freedom by the soul; and Hegel made this thought the basis of his philosophy of history. Herder went so far as to ask if Christianity would not pass away, as other historic religions have done, and a higher form of faith succeed to it. Though Carlyle praised Christianity as the religion of sorrow and self-renunciation, yet he did it in a spirit which showed how little he cared for the outward forms. He saw in religion, not a church, not an historic faith, but the union of the soul with God through intuition, which is possible to all men, and which annuls and condemns every other worship.

The nearness of God, the sacredness of the divine laws, the over-arching presence of the spiritual world, the sublimity and awful sanctity of those hours when the soul is filled with the divine spirit, the authority of the religious sentiment and the conscience, — these convictions unite Emerson to the world's great religious teachers. These truths he finds to be perfectly natural to man; they find their authority in the relations of man to the Cosmos. He finds in Christianity their truest and most spiritual expression; and hence he loves its teachings, accepts its spirit, rejoices in its moral conquests. When it attempts to make these sentiments synonymous with a person, book, or history, he repudiates its teaching, and rejects its influence as pernicious. He is thoroughly a Christian in his acceptance of those great truths of the spiritual life which have given Christianity its influence in the world; but all that is special, supernatural, authoritative, he rejects. The soul is its own authority, all worlds are one, the same religious sentiments and truths appear under whatever garb of sect. He loves the Christian spirit when genuinely manifested, as a profound conviction and sense of spiritual realities, as a high, commanding enthusiasm for what is right and holy; but all there is in it worthy of notice and respect comes from a universal religious sentiment. It has no power in and of itself, as an historic mode of worship, to charm and inspire the soul of man.

The old enthusiasm of faith, the old consecration to truth, the old profound conviction of the nearness of God and of the sacredness of the inward law of the soul, Emerson would have reproduced. That enthusiasm which makes martyrs, which weds men for ever to great truths, which makes all things else undesirable compared with devotion to the will of God, he believes in, and thinks necessary to the best life. He is himself an enthusiast of this kind, though he carefully suppresses mere feeling as unworthy and misleading, and looks at all things through the intellect. Mere faith, with Jacobi, or feeling, with Schleiermacher, he is not content with; for his intellectual convictions must also be satisfied. He has refused to define or limit the spiritual, and yet he has never made it merely a feeling or an ecstasy. He is a mystic who is calmly intellectual, a thinker who refuses to apply the measuring rod of reason to the soul, a theist who is unable to find limits to the being of God, a Christian who refuses to accept any historic form or name. He refuses to be classified, for the truth appears under all disguises. His is the religion of the soul, whose forms and service and book and messiah are to be found alone in the active, aspiring mind.

The fact that Emerson early withdrew from the church, and that he has gradually abandoned the outward observances of religion, has led many to regard him as a skeptic, or in some way as a disbeliever. It was not from any doubts, however, about spiritual truths, that caused him to abandon religious forms and to reject the historic faith of his time.[1] It was an

[1] The following letter concerning Emerson's religious position was written by his son to a gentleman in Indianapolis, in 1880, and may be regarded as authoritative: —

CONCORD, Feb. 17.

DEAR SIR, — Some weeks ago my father received a letter from you inquiring if a statement made to you by a friend in Boston with regard to him was true. The statement was, that, under the influence of Rev. Joseph Cook, he had changed his religious beliefs, and accepted the doctrines of the Orthodox Congregationalists. My father receives many letters, but now very seldom writes one.

More than once before letters have been received by him from persons in the West asking almost the same question that you ask, one gentleman stating, that at Minneapolis Rev. Joseph Cook had stated in a public lecture that Mr. Emerson and Mr. Alcott had publicly renounced their early religious beliefs, accepted Jesus as their Saviour, the Bible as divine, and joined the Orthodox church. Paragraphs have

excess of faith in spiritual truths which made him a skeptic towards all that is outward and formal. His skepticism is that of the mystic, not that of the materialist or agnostic. He has not rejected the truths of religion, but he has rejected the dogmas and the historic claims of Christianity. In abandoning formal prayer, he did not cease to believe in prayer as communion with God, or in man's need of divine guidance. In fact, he has been intoxicated with the things of the soul; and he has lived in the highest atmosphere of faith and devotion.

Wherever the doctrine of intuition has been fully accepted, trust in the outward matters of religion has died out. If God directly reveals himself to the soul, there is no need of reading bibles, or of attending church, or of accepting sacraments. Fox abolished sacraments and forms, he repudiated the priest and minister; the Light was enough. The Sufis believe that God opens his truth to them in feeling, so they reject all books and religions. One of their poets says, "What is the Kaaba to me? I need God only." They describe themselves, much in the spirit of Emerson, as

> "Owning nor book nor master; and on earth
> Having one sole and simple task, — to make
> Their hearts a stainless mirror for their God."

Jelaleddin Rumi gives expression to this idea in a man-

lately appeared in the newspapers stating essentially the same thing. Therefore, it seems to me fair that persons who have been, perhaps, led out of the old paths by Mr Emerson's teachings, and are now told that he has admitted that he went astray, and has returned to even a stricter fold than that from which he went forth, should know the truth. I therefore asked and received leave from my father to answer your note.

The statement is, in every respect, incorrect. Mr. Emerson is acquainted with Rev. Mr. Cook, who has called upon him, when he has exchanged with the Orthodox clergyman of Concord; and, by invitation of the latter gentleman, Mr. Emerson went on one or two occasions, several years since, to hear Mr. Cook preach in this town. Except on these occasions Mr. Emerson has never had any relations with Mr. Cook. He never reads his lectures. He has not joined any church, nor has he retracted any views expressed in his writings after his withdrawal from the ministry. His last words given to the public on matters of morals and religion may be found in his paper in The North American Review for June, 1878, on the Sovereignty of Ethics, and in his lecture entitled The Preacher, delivered to the divinity students at Harvard University less than a year ago, and now printed in the Unitarian Review for January, 1880.

Mr Emerson's friends and readers can judge for themselves whether these papers confirm the truth of the tale that is going about as to his conversion to Orthodoxy.

Truly yours,

EDWARD WALDO EMERSON

ner quite parallel to that in which Emerson constantly uses it.

> "He needs a guide no longer who hath found
> The way already leading to the Friend.
> Who stands already on heaven's topmost dome
> Needs not to search for ladders. He that lies,
> Folded in favor, on the Sultan's breast,
> Needs not the letter or the messenger."

Hafiz says "the object of all religions is alike. All men seek their beloved, and all the world is love's dwelling; why talk of a mosque or a church?" In the Hindoo *Vemana* is to be found the same thought, in words which might have been taken from almost any of Emerson's essays: "God dwells in all things in his fullness. All worship is one; systems of faith are different, but God is one." Many of the mystics are of this opinion. Boehme holds all means and ordinances valueless but as preparations for receiving the divine operation within, which leads us directly to God. Luther said of a religious thinker of his time, that he was "one of those for whom nothing will do but spirit! spirit! and not a word of scripture or sacrament." Weigel, one of the men from whom Jacob Boehme received his initiation into mysticism, declared the schools of his time utterly barren; and equally barren did he find all religious forms, creeds, and teaching. Weigel bade Boehme "withdraw into himself, and wait, in total passivity, the incoming of the divine word, whose light reveals unto the babe what is hidden from the wise and prudent." Many other mystics and idealists have had the same conception of religion, the same distrust of its outward forms. It led Coleridge to write his *Confessions of an Inquiring Spirit*, in which he deals freely with the Bible. The same spirit of freedom towards the outward matters of religion appears in the writings of Theodore Parker and Frances Power Cobbe, who stand on the same ground as that held in common by Boehme, Fox, and Emerson. In the name of the spirit within, all have freely criticised the outward expressions of religion.

Emerson would have no mediators of any sort whatever between God and the soul. Each person may have within him all the light he needs, all the truth he can acquire; and he never permits any great man or any famous book to usurp the place of that light for a moment. So he says, —

"The relations of the soul to the divine spirit are so pure, that it is profane to seek to interpose helps. It must be that when God speaketh he should communicate, not one thing, but all things; should fill the world with his voice; should scatter forth light, nature, time, souls from the center of the present thought; and new date and new create the whole. Whenever a mind is simple, and receives a divine wisdom, old things pass away, — means, teachers, texts, temples, fall; it lives now, and absorbs past and future into the present hour. All things are made sacred by relation to it, — one as much as another. All things are dissolved to their center by their cause; and, in the universal miracle, petty and particular miracles disappear. If, therefore, a man claims to know and speak of God, and carries you backward to the phraseology of some old moldered nation in another country, in another world, believe him not."[1]

Because his faith in the soul never wavers, he will have naught to do with any thing which assumes to take its place. In the soul there is a constant *Thus saith the Lord;* and this alone is to be obeyed. God speaks within, giving assurance, courage, and peace; and this trust is sublime, all-absorbing, wonderful. It is the one power of the world that has made man whatever he is. Without it he is nothing; with it he can be and do all things.

Men make dogmas of the intuitions they receive, and religion is corrupted in consequence. "All positive rules, ceremonial, ecclesiastical, distinctions of race or of person, are perishable; only those distinctions hold which are, in the nature of things, not matters of positive ordinance."[2] The creeds and the rituals perish because they are not rooted in any actual truth; but in their destruction religion thrives, and grows to nobler results. "God builds his temple in the heart, on the ruins of churches and religions."[3] Yet all attempts to embody

[1] Essays, first series, p. 57. [2] The Preacher, p. 8.
[3] Conduct of Life, p. 178.

religion in creed and ritual affirm the need of spiritual truth and the greatness of the soul's testimony. "The multitude of false churches accredits the true religion."[1] Though false now, all were once true, and testify, in the devotion they inspire, to the worth of that sentiment out of which they grew.

"The sentiment, of course, is the judge and measure of every expression of it, — measures Judaism, Stoicism, Christianity, Buddhism, or whatever philanthropy or politics or saint or seer pretends to speak in its name. The religions we call false, were once true; they also were affirmations of the conscience correcting the evil customs of their times. The populace drag down the gods to their own level, and give them their egotism; whilst in Nature is none at all, God keeping out of sight, and known only as pure law, though resistless. Every nation is degraded by the goblins it worships instead of the Deity. The Dionysia and Saturnalia of Greece and Rome, the human sacrifice of the Druids, the Sradda of Hindoos, the Purgatory, the Indulgences, and the Inquisition of Popery, the vindictive mythology of Calvinism, are examples of this perversion."

On the same theme he further writes: —

"Every particular instruction is speedily embodied in a ritual, is accommodated to humble and gross minds, and corrupted. The moral sentiment is the perpetual critic on these forms; thundering its protest, sometimes in earnest and lofty rebuke, but sometimes also it is the source, in natures less pure, of sneers and flippant jokes of common people, who feel that the forms and dogmas are not true for them, though they do not see where the error lies."[2]

He writes with the most unsparing words of the defects of religion, resulting from these attempts to embody the moral sentiment in historical faiths: —

"I fear, he says, that what is called religion, but is perhaps pew-holding, not obeys, but conceals, the moral sentiment. I put it to this simple test: Is a rich rogue made to feel his roguery among divines or literary men? No? Then 'tis rogue again under the cassock. What sort of respect can these preachers or newspapers inspire by their weekly praises of texts and saints, when we know they would say just the same things if Beelzebub had written the chapter, provided it stood where it does in the public opinion?

"Any thing but unbelief, any thing but losing hold of the moral intuitions, as betrayed in clinging to a form of devotion, or a theological dogma, as if it was the liturgy or the chapel that was

[1] Essays, second series, p. 173. [2] Character, p. 363.

sacred, and not justice and humility, and the loving heart and serving hand." [1]

Because the spirit of religion is ever the same, though its forms change, the old faiths become myths to us; but in our time we are coming more and more to accept the inward sentiment, and to repudiate the historic form.

"The religion of one age is the literary entertainment of the next. We use in our idlest poetry and discourse the words Jove, Neptune, Mercury, as mere colors, and can hardly believe that they had to the lively Greek the anxious meaning, which, in our towns, is given and received in churches when our religious names are used; and we read with surprise the horror of Athens, when, one morning, the statues of Mercury, in the temples, were found broken, and the like consternation was in the city, as if, in Boston, all the orthodox churches should be burned in one night."

"The changes are inevitable; the new age can not see with the eyes of the last. But the change is in what is superficial; the principles are immortal, and the rally on the principle must arrive as people become intellectual. I consider theology to be the rhetoric of morals. The mind of this age has fallen away from theology to morals. I conceive it an advance. I suspect, that, when the theology was most florid and dogmatic, it was the barbarism of the people; and that, in that very time, the best men also fell away from theology, and rested in morals. I think that all the dogmas rest on morals, and that it is only a question of youth or maturity, of more or less fancy in the recipient; that the stern determination to do justly, to speak the truth, to be chaste and humble, was substantially the same, whether under a self-respect, or under a vow made on the knees at the shrine of Madonna." [2]

Emerson's thoroughly undogmatic attitude towards all religious questions is abundantly shown in his criticism of the religious life of the present time. He finds it ungirt, frivolous, lacking in a deep sense of spiritual things, unmindful of the constant presence of the Divine. He has repeatedly declared his sympathy with those former phases of religious thought which absorbed men in the sense of the supernatural. It is the historic forms, the party dogmas, he distrusts, towards which he is a skeptic. His sympathies with the great religious thinkers and seers, and with all those ages which have been moved by deep and profound religious convic-

[1] The Preacher, p. 10. [2] Character, pp. 363, 365.

tions, show how really religious he is. His mind is intoxicated with the sense of God, absorbed in the things of the soul. In the critical, skeptical tendencies of the present he finds a "withering" effect, and that, though the understanding is active, the sentiments sleep. Their effect on the minds of most persons, he has described in these words: —

"I see in them character, but skepticism; a clear enough perception of the inadequacy of the popular religious statement to the wants of the heart and intellect, and explicit declarations of this fact. They have insight and truthfulness; they will not mask their convictions; they hate cant; but more than this I do not readily find. The gracious motions of the soul — piety, adoration — I do not find. Scorn of hypocrisy, pride of personal character, elegance of taste and of manners and pursuit, a boundless ambition of the intellect, willingness to sacrifice personal interests for the integrity of the character, — all these they have; but that religious submission and abandonment which give man a new element and being, and make him sublime, — it is not in churches, it is not in houses. I see movement, I hear aspirations; but I see not how the great God prepares to satisfy the heart in the new order of things."[1]

Again and again has he expressed his sense of the inadequacy of the religious culture of the present time, and pronounced it cold, lifeless, and unworthy. One more example will suffice.

"The religion of seventy years ago was an iron belt to the mind, giving it concentration and force. A rude people were kept respectable by the determination of thought on the eternal world. Now men fall abroad, — want polarity, — suffer in character and intellect. A sleep creeps over the great functions of man. Enthusiasm goes out. In its stead a low prudence seeks to hold society stanch, but its arms are too short; cordage and machinery never supply the place of life.

"I will not go into the metaphysics of that re-action by which wit takes the place of faith in the leading spirits, and an excessive respect for forms out of which the heart has departed becomes most obvious in the least religious minds. To a self-denying, ardent church, delighting in rites and ordinances, has succeeded a cold, intellectual race, who analyze the prayer and psalm of their forefathers; and the more intellectual reject every yoke of authority and custom with a petulance unprecedented. It is a sort of mark of probity and sincerity to declare how little you believe;

[1] The Preacher, p. 4.

while the mass of the community indolently follow the old forms with childish scrupulosity, and we have punctuality for faith, and good taste for character." [1]

When Emerson comes to deal with the central doctrine of Christianity, he rejects it in the name of the soul. He sees no need of a messiah who has a perpetual mediator in his own intuitions. Emerson finds in Jesus a person of wonderful intuitions and great depth of soul, such a person as may appear in any land or time.

"Men appear from time to time, he says, who receive with more purity and fullness these high communications. But it is only as fast as this hearing from another is authorized by its consent with his own, that it is pure and safe to each; and all receiving from abroad must be controlled by this immense reservation.

"It happens now and then, in the ages, that a soul is born which has no weakness of self, — which offers no impediment to the Divine Spirit, — which comes down into Nature as if only for the benefit of souls; and all its thoughts are perceptions of things as they are, without any infirmity of earth. Such souls are as the apparition of gods among men, and simply by their presence pass judgments on them. Men are forced by their own self-respect to give them a certain attention. Evil men shrink, and pay involuntary homage by hiding or apologizing for their action." [2]

He says these "rare, extravagant spirits come to us at intervals, who disclose to us new facts in nature. I see, he says, that men of God have, from time to time, walked among men, and made their commission felt in the heart and soul of the commonest hearer." These rare spirits he recognizes everywhere, in all religions and times. He finds no antiquity in what they say, for their thought belongs as much to us as to them. Their thought is human and universal, for no person or persons have a monopoly in the truth. He says Jesus astonishes sensual people, and they do not see any place for him in the order of history; but "as they come to revere their intuitions and aspire to live holily, their own piety explains every fact, every word." [3] So he regards Jesus as one of these rare spirits, pure and

[1] Sovereignty of Ethics, p. 415. [2] Character, p. 361.
[3] Essays, first series, p. 25.

noble, a sublime teacher, "our best, our dearest saint," but in no way different from many another inspired soul.[1] He could only reveal the Soul, as others have done, and tell us of its glad power; but we may ourselves have the same vision, because we have the same nature, he had. The moment men trust in him they cripple themselves and degrade the soul. The moral sentiment, the gift of intuition, supersedes his teaching, as it does that of every other. Men gain in moral power in so far as they follow this inward leader; they inevitably lose by every effort to substitute for it a man, church, or book. It will not permit of any substitutes. Its inspirations can not be stored up more than the manna of the wilderness.

"It is serenely above all mediation. In all ages, to all men, it saith, *I am;* and he who hears it, feels the impiety of wandering from this revelation to any record or to any rival. The poor Jews of the wilderness cried, 'Let not the Lord speak to us; let Moses speak to us!' But the simple and sincere soul makes the contrary prayer: 'Let no intruder come between thee and me; deal THOU with me; let me know it is thy will, and I ask no more.' The excellence of Jesus, and of every true teacher, is, that he affirms the Divinity in him and in us, — not thrusts himself between it and us. It would instantly indispose us to any person claiming to speak for the Author of nature, the setting forth of any fact or law which we did not find in our consciousness."[2]

Emerson insists that the moral sentiment is quite sufficient as the guide of men, that its word is the only command they can at last obey. All voices of truth utter its words, all religions are its expressions. He sees in the other religions of the world an interest Christianity does not afford, because we study them without any of those limiting associations attaching to a religion which once laid its dogmatic command on us.

[1] In the Horticultural-Hall lecture on Natural Religion, before the Free Religious Association, April 4, 1869, Emerson said, "I have sometimes thought, and indeed I always do think, that the sect of Quakers, in their representatives, appeared to me to have come nearer to the sublime history and genius of Christ than any other of the sects. They have kept the traditions perhaps for a longer time, kept the early purity, did keep it for a longer time; and I think I see this cause, I think I find in the language of that sect, in all the history and all the anecdotes of its leaders and teachers, a certain fidelity to the Scriptural character."

[2] Character, p. 359.

"I am far, he says, from accepting the opinion that the revelations of the moral sentiment are insufficient; as if it furnished a rule only, and not the spirit by which the rule is animated. For I include in these, of course, the history of Jesus, as well as those of every divine soul which in any place or time delivered any grand lesson to humanity; and I find in the eminent experiences in all times a substantial agreement. The sentiment itself teaches unity of source, and disowns every superiority other than of deeper truth. Jesus has immense claims on the gratitude of mankind, and knew how to guard the integrity of his brother's soul from himself also; but in his disciples, admiration of him runs away with their reverence for the human soul, and they hamper us with limitations of person and text. Every exaggeration of these is a violation of the soul's right, and inclines the manly reader to lay down the New Testament, to take up the Pagan philosophers. It is not that the Upanishads or the Maxims of Antoninus are better, but that they do not invade his freedom; because they are only suggestions, whilst the other adds the inadmissible claim of positive authority, — of an external command, where command can not be. This is the secret of the mischievous result, that, in every period of intellectual expansion, the church ceases to draw into its clergy those who best belong there, the largest and freest minds: and that in its most liberal forms, when such minds enter it, they are coldly received, and find themselves out of place. This charm in the Pagan moralists, of suggestion, the charm of poetry, of mere truth (easily eliminated from their historical accidents, which nobody wishes to force on us), the New Testament loses by its connection with a church. Mankind can not long suffer this loss, and the office of this age is to put all these writings on the eternal footing of equality of origin in the instincts of the human mind. It is certain that each inspired master will gain instantly by the separation from the idolatry of ages." [1]

When this doctrine of immediate inspiration is lost, then "the base doctrine of the majority of voices usurps its place, and miracles, prophecy, poetry, the ideal life, the holy life, exist as ancient history merely; they are not in the belief, nor in the aspiration, of society." [2] Jesus was a true prophet, saw God incarnated in all men; but "the idioms of his language and the figures of his rhetoric have usurped the place of his truth, and the churches are not built on his principles, but on his tropes. Christianity became a mythos, as the poetic teachings of Greece and of Egypt, before. He spoke of miracles, for he felt that man's life was a miracle,

[1] Ibid., p. 369.

[2] Miscellanies, p. 123.

and all that man doth; and he knew that his daily miracle shines, as the character ascends. But the word miracle, as pronounced by Christian churches, gives a false impression; it is monster. It is not one with the blowing clover and the falling rain."[1] Thus did Emerson early express his faith in the natural character of religion, and assert that its office is to carry forward what life everywhere reveals, to higher conclusions. It fulfills, but never annuls, the promise of nature and man. This narrow regard for the personal and miraculous passes away as soon as a genuine culture appears, and the Christian traditions lose their hold. "The dogma of the mystic offices of Christ being dropped, and he standing on his genius as a moral teacher, 'tis impossible to maintain the old emphasis of his personality; and it recedes, as all persons must, before the sublimity of the moral laws."[2] The way to preach Jesus to this age, he once said, is to be silent about him. The old ideas, the old persons, will cease to attract us the moment we have an intuition, which will send us forward to new and better conquests for the moral nature. The fealty to person and form will cease; yet the truth will not fade, but grow more bright and sure the deeper our intuition.

"Inspiration will have advance, affirmation, the forward foot, the ascending state; it will be an opener of doors; it will invent its own methods; the new wine will make the bottles new. Spirit is motive and ascending. Only let there be a deep observer, and he will make light of new shop and new circumstance that afflict you; new shop or old cathedral, it is all one to him. He will find the circumstances not altered, as deep a cloud of mystery on the cause, as dazzling a glory on the invincible law."[3]

Emerson finds that the Soul is a terrible critic of all that is personal. "No historical person begins to content us," he says.[4] There are no such men as we fable, no such Jesus. He cares not for the individual, but for the universal.[5] This thought of the little value of persons he applies to Jesus, when he says, —

[1] Ibid., p. 125.
[2] Conduct of Life, p. 182.
[3] The Preacher, p. 13.
[4] Society and Solitude, p. 274
[5] Essays, second series, pp. 219, 220.

"Christianity is rightly dear to the best of mankind; yet was there never a young philosopher whose breeding had fallen into the Christian church, by whom that brave text of Paul's was not specially prized, — 'Then shall also the Son be subject unto Him who put all things under him, that God may be all in all.' Let the claims and virtues of persons be never so great and welcome, the instinct of man presses eagerly onward to the impersonal and illimitable, and gladly arms itself against the dogmatism of bigots with this generous word out of the book itself." [1]

He has written with great enthusiasm of the Bible as being of the highest and truest form of literature. All true writing, he holds, must be by the inspiration of God; and books are to be valued just in proportion to their power to inspire us. As a book of the most inspiring thought, he puts the Bible in the very first rank; yet its value is, that we find what it says true in our own souls. It shows us, therefore, how true the soul is to itself, that it ever gives the same word to those who seek its truth. In an early number of *The Dial* he expressed his sense of the value of the Bible.

"The most original book in the world is the Bible, he there said. This old collection of the ejaculations of love and dread, of the supreme desires and contritions of men proceeding out of the region of the grand and eternal, by whatsoever different mouths spoken, and through a wide extent of times and countries, seems, especially if you add to our canon the kindred sacred writings of the Hindoos, Persians, and Greeks, the alphabet of the nations, — and all posterior writings, either the chronicle of facts under very inferior ideas, or, when it rises to sentiment, the combinations, analogies, or degradations of this. The elevation of this book may be measured by observing how certainly all observation of thought clothes itself in the words and forms of speech of that book. For the human mind is not now sufficiently erect to judge and correct that scripture. Whatever is majestically thought in a great moral element, instantly approaches this old Sanscrit. It is in the nature of things that the highest originality must be moral. The only person who can be entirely independent of this fountain of literature and equal to it, must be a prophet in his own proper person. Shakspere, the first literary genius of the world, the highest in whom the moral is not the predominating element, leans on the Bible; his poetry presupposes it. If we examine this brilliant influence — Shakspere — as it lies in our minds, we shall find it reverent, not only of the letter of this book, but of the whole frame of society which stood in Europe upon it, deeply indebted to the tra-

[1] Newspaper report.

ditional morality, in short, compared with the tone of the Prophets, *secondary*. On the other hand, the Prophets do not imply the existence of Shakspere or Homer, — advert to no books or arts, only to dread ideas and emotions. People imagine that the place which the Bible holds in the world, it owes to miracles. It owes it simply to the fact that it came out of a profounder depth of thought than any other book, and the effect must be precisely proportionate. Gibbon fancied that it was combinations of circumstances that gave Christianity its place in history. But in nature it takes an ounce to balance an ounce."[1]

The great religious books, the scriptures, of the world, he sees are the slow growths of deep religious convictions, which require centuries in their formation. They voice the aspirations of a nation, the desires of a race, the experiences of generations. They are all alike in character, teach the same moral truths, and have their origin in the same manner.

"The Bible itself is like an old Cremona; it has been played upon by the devotion of thousands of years, until every word and particle is public and tunable. And whatever undue reverence may have been for it by the prestige of philonic inspiration, the stronger tendency we are describing is likely to undo. What divines had assumed as the distinctive revelations of Christianity, theologic criticism has matched by exact parallelisms from the Stoics and poets of Greece and Rome. Later, when Confucius and the Indian scriptures were made known, no claim to monopoly of ethical wisdom could be thought of; and the surprising results of the new researches into the history of Egypt have opened to us the deep debt of the churches of Rome and England to the Egyptian hierology."[2]

Averse as Emerson is to the religious forms that have become artificial, and that take the place of the moral sentiment in the affections of men, yet he loves those forms that are natural, and which grow immediately out of the soul's needs. This is seen in such paragraphs as this: —

"Religion is as inexpugnable as the use of lamps, or of wells, or of chimneys. We must have days and temples and teachers. The Sunday is the core of our civilization, dedicated to thought and reverence. It invites to the noblest solitude and the noblest society, to whatever means and aids of spiritual refreshment. Men may well come together to kindle each other to virtuous living."[3]

[1] The Dial, October, 1840. [2] Letters and Social Aims, p. 161.
[3] Character, p. 370.

His respect for Sunday, and his desire that religious culture shall not be neglected, he has expressed in another essay; and with a hint, also, at the character of that culture.

"All civil mankind have agreed in leaving one day for contemplation against six for practice. I hope that day will keep its honor and its use. A wise man advises that we should see to it that we read and speak two or three reasonable words every day, amid the crowd of affairs and the noise of trifles. I should say boldly that we should astonish every day by a beam out of eternity; retire a moment to the grand secret we carry in our bosom, of inspiration from heaven. But certainly on this seventh let us be the children of liberty, of reason, of hope; refresh the sentiment; think as spirits think, who belong to the universe, whilst our feet walk in the streets of a little town, and our hands work in a small knot of affairs. We shall find one result, I am sure,—a certain originality and a certain haughty liberty proceeding out of our retirement and self-communion, which streets can never give, infinitely removed from all vaporing and bravado, and which yet is more than a match for any physical resistance.

"It is true that which they say of our New-England œstrum, which will never let us stand or sit, but drives us like mad through the world. The calmest and most protected life can not save us. We want some intercalated days, to bethink us, and to derive order to our life from the heart. That should be the use of the sabbath,—to check this headlong racing, and put us in possession of ourselves once more, for love or for shame.

"The sabbath changes its forms from age to age, but the substantial benefit endures. We no longer recite the old creeds of Athanasius or Arius, of Calvin or Hopkins. The forms are flexible, but the uses not less real. The old heart remains as ever with its old human duties. The old intellect still lives, to pierce the shows to the core. Truth is simple, and will not be antique; is ever present, and insists on being of this age and of this moment. Here is thought and love, and truth and duty, new as on the first day of Adam and of angels."[1]

Nowhere has Emerson shown his distrust of religious forms so strongly as in what he has written about prayer. He regards it, not as a petition, but as an act of intuition.

"Prayer looks abroad, he tells us, and asks for some foreign addition to come through some foreign virtue, and loses itself in endless mazes of natural and supernatural, and mediatorial and miraculous. Prayer that craves a particular commodity—any

[1] The Preacher, p. 14.

thing less than all good — is vicious. Prayer is the contemplation of the facts of life from the highest point of view. It is the soliloquy of a beholding and jubilant soul. It is the spirit of God pronouncing his works good. But prayer as a means to effect a private end is meanness and theft. It pre-supposes dualism, and not unity in nature and consciousness. As soon as the man is at one with God, he will not beg. He will then see prayer in all action. The prayer of the farmer kneeling in his field to weed it, the prayer of the rower kneeling with the stroke of his oar, are true prayers heard throughout nature."[1]

In his first book he expressed his deep appreciation of the value of prayer.

"In the uttermost meaning of the words thought is devout, and devotion is thought. Deep calls unto deep. . . . Is not prayer also a study of truth, — a sally of the soul into the unfound infinite? No man ever prayed heartily, without learning something."[2]

He once called prayer a plunge into the unfound infinite; and he has made it synonymous with intuition, as well as regarding it as a craving and earnest desire to be willing to accept and obey the laws of God. It is the response of the soul to the attractions of the Over-soul, the joyous acceptance of its guidance. With Madame Guyon he regards "intuition as a continuous word, potent, ineffable, ever uttered without language; the immediate, unchecked operation of resident Deity." With this conception of intuition she could not simply ask God for aid, but she believed that through it direct communion with God was to be obtained. So she lost faith in the formal prayers of the church, but found all things in what she called the prayer of silence, — "that prayer which, unlimited to times and seasons, unhindered by words, is a state rather than an act, a sentiment rather than a request, — a continuous sense of submission, which breathes, moment by moment, from the serene depth of the soul, Thy will be done." Her idea is almost identical with Emerson's, when she describes her prayer of intuition and silence, as one of "rejoicing and possession, wherein the taste of God was so great, so pure,

[1] Essays, first series, p. 67. [2] Miscellanies, pp. 71, 72.

unblended, and uninterrupted, that it drew and absorbed the powers of the soul into a profound communion, without act or discourse." Yet Emerson finds the trusting submission to the laws of God, which recognizes their unity and beauty, to be an act of prayer. It is not the weeding a field which is prayer, but the craving to be at one with God, which the farmer may express even in his daily work. Tauler had precisely Emerson's conception of prayer when he said that "so soon as a man prays for any creature, he prays for his own harm." "He who seeks God, he says again, if he seeks any thing beside God, will not find him; but he who seeks God alone in the truth, will find him, and all that God can give with him." Without words the soul prays as it reaches forward to realize its harmony in God, asking for no temporal good, desiring nothing but that perfect peace which comes of union with the Over-soul.

Emerson closed his Divinity-school address by asserting his faith that there will come a new teacher, who will lead religion forward to greater heights than ever yet attained.

"The Hebrew and Greek scriptures contain immortal sentences, that have been bread of life to millions. But they have no epical integrity; are fragmentary; are not shown in their order to the intellect. I look for the new Teacher, that shall follow so far those shining laws, that he shall see them come full circle; shall see their rounding, complete grace; shall see the world to be the mirror of the soul; shall see the identity of the law of gravitation with purity of heart; and shall show that the Ought, that Duty, is one with Science, with Beauty, and with Joy."[1]

He has again and again repeated this declaration of the imperfection of Christianity, that religion is progressive, and that a more perfect expression of its truths will yet come to men. What this pure religion will be he points out in these words: —

"There will be a new church founded on moral science, at first cold and naked, a babe in the manger again, the algebra and mathematics of ethical law, the church of men to come, without shawms

[1] Ibid., p. 146.

or psaltery or sackbut; but it will have heaven and earth for its beams and rafters; science for symbol and illustration; it will fast enough gather beauty, music, picture, poetry. Was never stoicism so stern and exigent as this shall be. It shall send man home to his central solitude, shame these social supplicating manners, and make him know that much of the time he must have himself to his friend. He shall expect no co-operation, he shall walk with no companion. The nameless Thought, the nameless Power, the super-personal Heart, — he shall repose alone on that." [1]

In other words, he believes religion will cease to be any thing but intuition, communion with God; and morality, or obedience to God's laws. All that is of sect or party, all that is of historic forms, will pass away; and the spiritual and moral sentiment will alone remain. He says the life of the old traditions is not in the historic legend about which they are formed, "but in the moral sentiment and the metaphysical fact which the legends enclosed, — and these survive." This central, surviving core of unchanging truth, will one day so attract some rare, pure genius, that he will teach only what it asserts. This happy day is yet far off. But he says, —

"It is true that Stoicism, always attractive to the intellectual and cultivated, has now no temples, no academy, no commanding Zeno or Antoninus. It accuses us that it has none; that pure ethics is not now formulated and concreted into a *cultus*, a fraternity with assemblings and holy-days, with song and book, with brick and stone. Why have not those who believe in it and love it left all for this, and dedicated themselves to write out its scientific scriptures to become its Vulgate for millions? I answer for one, that the inspirations we catch of this law are not continuous and technical, but joyful sparkles, and are recorded for their beauty, for the delight they give, not for their obligation; and that is their priceless good to men, that they charm and uplift, not that they are imposed.

"It has not yet its first hymn. But that every line and word may be coals of true fire, ages must roll ere these casual wide-falling cinders may be gathered into broad and steady altar-flame." [2]

He sees rich promise of this new faith in the wider humanitarian spirit of our time, and in that desire, everywhere manifest, to look at man simply as man,

[1] Conduct of Life, p. 210. [2] Sovereignty of Ethics, p. 417.

regardless of his sect or nation. And every thing is promised in the new regard for the individual. The new faith will throw each person upon his own resources, so far as the old dogmatic supports are concerned; but it will draw his fellows closer to him in friendship and love. Of this slow process, now going on, by which the new faith is being brought to men, he says, —

"Of course, each poor soul loses all his old stays; no bishop watches him; no confessor reports that he has neglected the confessional; no class-leader admonishes him of absences; no fagot, no penance, no fine, no rebuke. Is not this wrong? is not this dangerous? 'Tis not wrong, but the law of growth. It is not dangerous, any more than the mother's withdrawing her hands from the tottering babe, at his first walk across the nursery-floor; the child fears and cries, but achieves the feat, instantly tries it again, and never wishes to be assisted more. And this infant soul must learn to walk alone. At first he is forlorn, homeless; but this rude stripping him of all support drives him inward, and he finds himself unhurt; he finds himself face to face with the majestic Presence, reads the original of the Ten Commandments, the original of Gospels and Epistles." [1]

The new faith will make all men prophets and apostles of the Spirit. Then America will have a pure religion of its own, for a completed nation will not borrow its faith. Its service will be devotion to man, its bible the inward voice of God, its commandments the laws of nature, its gospel the moral sentiment. It will win and delight men by a loftier spirit of truth and love. It will unite all truth, it will give new motives to life, it will make love the law of human relations. The new faith will rest on what is natural to man. "The first position I make, he says, is that natural religion supplies still all the facts which are disguised under the dogma of popular creeds. The progress of religion is steadily to its identification with morals." [2] Hence he finds that "sensible and conscientious men all over the world are of one religion, — the religion of well-doing and daring, men of sturdy truth, men of integrity and feeling for others. My inference is, he

[1] Character, p. 371. [2] Sovereignty of Ethics, p. 417.

adds, that there is a statement of religion possible which makes all skepticism absurd."[1] In his address at the second annual meeting of the Free Religious Association, he made such a statement of his own belief. It so fully illustrates his religious position it ought to be read in full.

"I think we have disputed long enough. I think we might now relinquish our theologic controversies to communities more idle and ignorant than we. I am glad that a more realistic church is coming to be the tendency of society, and that we are likely one day to forget our obstinate polemics in the ambition to excel each other in good works. I have no wish to proselyte any reluctant mind; nor, I think, have I any curiosity or impulse to intrude on those whose ways of thinking differ from mine. But I am ready to give, as often before, the first simple foundations of my belief, that the Author of nature has not left himself without a witness in any sane mind; that the moral sentiment speaks to every man the law after which the universe was made; that we find parity, identity of design, through nature, and benefit, to be the uniform aim; that there is a force always at work to make the best better, and the worst good. We have had, not long since, presented to us by Max Müller, a valuable paragraph from St. Augustine, not at all extraordinary in itself, but only as coming from that eminent Father in the Church, and at that age in which St. Augustine writes: 'That which is now called the Christian religion existed among the ancients, and never did not exist from the planting of the human race until Christ came in the flesh; at which time the true religion, which already subsisted, began to be called Christianity!' I believe that not only Christianity is as old as the creation, — not only every sentiment and precept of Christianity can be paralleled in other religious writings, — but more, that a man of religious susceptibility, and one at the same time conversant with many men, — say, a much-traveled man, — can find the same idea in numberless conversations. The religious find religion wherever they associate. When I find in people narrow religion, I find also in them narrow reading. Nothing really is so self-publishing, so divulgatory, as thought. It can not be confined or hid. It is easily carried; it takes no room; the knowledge of Europe looks out into Persia and India, and to the very Caffirs. Every proverb, every fine text, every pregnant jest, travels across the line; and you will find it at Cape Town or among the Tartars. We are all believers in natural religion; we all agree that the health and integrity of man is self-respect, self-subsistency, a regard to natural conscience. All education is to accustom him to trust himself, discriminate between his higher and lower thoughts, exert the timid

[1] The Preacher, p. 7.

faculties until they are robust, and thus train him to self-help, until he ceases to be an underling, a tool, and becomes a benefactor. I think wise men wish their religion to be all of this kind, teaching the agent to go alone, not to hang on the world as a pensioner, a permitted person, but an adult, self-searching soul, brave to assist or resist the world; only humble and docile before the source of the wisdom he has discovered within him.

"As it is, every believer holds a different creed; that is, all the churches are churches of one member. All our sects have refined the point of difference between them. The point of difference that still remains between churches, or between classes, is in the addition to the moral code, that is, to natural religion, of something positive and historical. I think that to be the one difference remaining. I object, of course, to the claim of miraculous dispensation, — certainly not to the doctrine of Christianity. This claim impairs, to my mind, the soundness of him who makes it, and indisposes us to his communion. This comes the wrong way; it comes from without, not within. This positive, historical, authoritative scheme is not consistent with our experience or our expectations. It is something not in nature; it is contrary to that law of nature, which all wise men recognize, namely, never to require a larger cause than is necessary to the effect. George Fox, the Quaker, said, that, though he read of Christ and God, he knew them only from a like spirit in his own soul. We want all the aids in our moral training. We can not spare the vision nor the virtue of the saints; but let it be by pure sympathy, not with any personal or official claim. If you are childish, and exhibit your saint as a worker of wonders, a thaumaturgist, I am repelled. That claim takes his teachings out of logic and out of nature, and permits official and arbitrary senses to be grafted on the teachings. It is the praise of our New Testament that its teachings go to the honor and benefit of humanity, — that no better lesson has been taught or incarnated. Let it stand, beautiful and wholesome, with whatever is most like it in the teaching and practice of men; but do not attempt to elevate it out of humanity by saying, 'This was not a man;' for then you confound it with the fables of every popular religion; and my distrust of the story makes me distrust the doctrine as soon as it differs from my own belief. Whoever thinks a story gains by the prodigious, by adding something out of nature, robs it more than he adds. It is no longer an example, a model; no longer a heart-stirring hero, but an exhibition, a wonder, an anomaly, removed out of the range of influence with thoughtful men. I submit, that, in sound frame of mind, we read or remember the religious sayings and oracles of other men, whether Jew or Indian or Greek or Persian, only for friendship, only for joy in the social identity which they open to us; and that these words would have no weight with us if we had not the same conviction already. I find something stingy in the unwilling and disparaging admission of these foreign opinions, — opinions from all parts of the world, — by our churchmen, as if only to enhance, by their dimness, the superior light of Christianity. Meantime, observe, you can not bring me too good a word, too dazzling a hope, too penetrating an insight from the Jews. I hail every one with delight, as showing the riches of my brother, my fellow-soul, who would thus think, and thus greatly feel. Zealots eagerly fasten their eyes on the differences between their creed and yours; but the charm of the study is in finding the agreements, the identities, in all the religions of men.

"I am glad to hear each sect complain that they do not now hold the opinions they are charged with. The earth moves, and the mind opens. I am glad to believe society contains a class of humble souls who enjoy the luxury of a religion that does not degrade; who think it the highest worship to expect of Heaven the most and best; who do not wonder there was a Christ, but that there were not a thousand; who have conceived an infinite hope for mankind; who believe that the history of Jesus is the history of every man, written large." [1]

These words may be taken as a distinct statement of Emerson's religious position. They indicate the positive, the affirmative, nature of his faith, and yet that he will not commit his instinctive trust to the limits of any formula. "I am too young yet by some ages, he says, to compile a code;" [2] and he has expressed the same thought about the making of a creed. Little inclined as he may be to enforce these opinions as a creed, yet they will command attention for their boldness and originality. Though they strip religion of all its rites and forms, yet they make it the commanding concern and interest of mankind. If this faith of the soul may never attract but a few, because most need the aid of history and definite statement, yet it will ever remain a powerful protest against formalism, and an inspiration to a purer worship. Because Emerson's is purely a religion of the spirit, no historic faith will seek to gather sanctions for its teachings, out of his inspirations; no sect will build on his foundation; no school of thinkers will name him as its head. He speaks of the truth, but he would not put himself in

[1] Proceedings at the Second Annual Meeting of the Free Religious Association, held in Tremont Temple, Boston, May 27 and 28, 1869. Reprinted in Freedom and Fellowship in Religion, p. 384.

[2] Essays, second series, p. 84.

its stead. In his teachings and in his life he is a great moral influence, he is an awakener and stimulator of the spiritual in man, while in his intellectual convictions he is a penetrating spirit of truth. He is a lark that heralds the coming day, a sunbeam that dissipates darkness. All the more pervasive, because purely moral and spiritual, will be his influence, reaching all hearts, pervading all forms, entering all sanctuaries, sustaining all right moral considerations, and invigorating every true resolve. Life will seem more sacred, the world holier, truth more sure, man diviner, heaven nearer, whenever we love the truth in that untrammeled spirit he has sought to vindicate. Whatever flaws may be found in his philosophic methods, none will be found in those moral and spiritual truths to which he has devoted his life for half a century. As we look truly at his life, and consider attentively the word he has spoken, we can but say, —

> "So long hast thou been loyal to thyself,
> So long hast thou been loyal to the world,
> So long hast thou been loyal to thy God,
> That howso men may look upon thy faith,
> Thy face looks at them tranquil with its truth."

INDEX.

G.

H.

I.

J.

K.

L.

M.

N.

O.

P.

Q.

R.

S.

T.

U.

V.

W.